LOST ACRE

Also By Andrew Caldecott

Rotherweird
Wyntertide

LOST ACRE

Andrew Caldecott

Illustrated by
Sasha Laika

Jo Fletcher
BOOKS

First published in Great Britain in 2019 by

Jo Fletcher Books
an imprint of
Quercus Editions Ltd
Carmelite House
50 Victoria Embankment
London EC4Y 0DZ

An Hachette UK company

A CIP catalogue record for this book is available
from the British Library

HB ISBN 978 1 78747 376 8
TPB ISBN 978 1 78429 806 7
EBOOK ISBN 978 1 78429 804 3

10 9 8 7 6 5 4 3 2

Typeset by CC Book Production

Printed and bound in Great Britain by Clays Ltd, Elcograf S.p.A.

For my children

PRINCIPAL CHARACTERS

Outsiders

Doktor Heinrich Flasche	A physicist
Jonah Oblong	A modern historian, Master of Form IV
Dr Obern	A plastic surgeon
Varia	A ballerina

The town of Rotherweird

Rhombus Smith	Headmaster
Hengest Strimmer	Head of North Tower Science
Vixen Valourhand	A North Tower scientist
Gregorius Jones	Head of Physical Education, Master of Form VIB
Godfery Fanguin	Former teacher
'Bomber' Fanguin	His wife, a fine cook
Angela Trimble	School Porter
Sidney Snorkel	The Mayor
Cindy Snorkel	The Mayor's wife
Gorhambury	The Town Clerk
Madge Brown	Assistant Head Librarian
Marmion Finch	The Herald

Fennel Finch (née Croyle)	His wife
Percy Finch	Their son
Bert Polk	Co-owner of *The Polk Land & Water Company*
Boris Polk	Co-owner of *The Polk Land & Water Company*
Orelia Roc	Owner of *Baubles & Relics*, an antique shop
Aggs	A general person
Estella Scry	A clairvoyant
Ember Vine	A sculptress
Amber Vine	Ember's daughter
Gurney Thomes	Master of the Apothecaries
Sister Prudence	A Senior Apothecary
Portly Bowes	The Town Crier
Horace Cutts	A butcher
Mr Jeavons	The town archivist
Mr Blossom	Master of the Metalworkers
Mr Norrington	A baker
Denzil Prim	Head Gaoler of Rotherweird Gaol
Bendigo Sly	Snorkel's eavesman
Mors Valett	The town undertaker

Former lead characters, now deceased:

Mrs Deirdre Banter	Orelia's aunt
Hayman Salt	Municipal Head Gardener
Professor Vesey Bolitho	Astronomer and Head of South Tower Science (see Fortemain)
Robert Flask	A modern historian
Sir Veronal Slickstone	A businessman and philanthropist

Rotherweird Countrysiders

Bill Ferdy	Brewer and landlord of *The Journeyman's Gist*
Gwen Ferdy	Bill's daughter
Megan Ferdy	Bill's wife
Ferensen	A nomadic close neighbour of the Ferdys'
Carcasey Jack	A torturer
Gabriel	A woodcarver

Rotherweirders working abroad

Tancred Everthorne	An artist
Pomeny Tighe	An ambitious young woman
Persephone Brown	Madge Brown's sister

Elizabethans

Sir Henry Grassal	Owner of Rotherweird Manor
Sir Robert Oxenbridge	Constable of the Tower of London
Geryon Wynter	A mystic
Calx Bole	Wynter's servant
Hieronymus Seer	See Ferensen
Morval Seer	Hieronymus' sister, a chronicler and artist
Thibo Fortemain	See Professor Bolitho
Estella	See Scry
Nona	See Madge Brown
Tyke	An enigma
Bevis Vibes	An orphan
Benedict Roc	A Master Carver
Hubert Finch	Rotherweird's first Herald

The Clauds (all deceased save Ambrose XIII)

Ambrose I	Priest and poet
Ambrose VII	The Vagrant Vicar, an author
Ambrosia I	A dissolute of the Stuart court
Ambrose XIII	The Unlucky

Creatures of the mixing-point

Strix	An owl-boy
Panjan	A pigeon boy
The Mance	A dog-boy, also known as Cur

Old History

Brother Hilarion	A monk and naturalist
Brother Harfoot	His lay companion
Coram Ferdy	A young boy
Gorius	A *speculator* (scout) in the Roman legion XX *Valeria Victrix* (see Gregorius Jones)
Ferox	A legionary (and weaselman)
Druid hedge-priests	

CONTENTS

Old History   1

PROLOGUE   7
1: *A Town of Sorts*   9

OUT OF TOWN   11
1: *Valourhand Penitent*   13
2: *A Historian in Waiting*   15

IN TOWN   17
1: *The Winter Solstice*   19
2: *First Orders*   26
3: *A Guest of Honour*   31
4: *Decision Time*   38

OUT OF TOWN   41
1: *Winter Cleaning*   43

UNDER TOWN   45
1: *Finch Underground*   47
2: *Of Household Gods*   55
3: *Free Fall*   57
4: *'I return to my own'*   69
5: *Filling a Void*   72

6: *The Foreign Coin* 81

7: *Actions and Reactions* 85

8: *A Visit to the Butcher* 88

IN TOWN 93

1. *Checks and Balances* 95

2: *Advent Windows* 98

3: *A Hollow Christmas* 103

4: *A Warning Ignored* 106

5: *The Manor Reclaimed* 111

6: *True or False?* 117

7: *Servant or Master* 124

8: *Of Transport and Tears* 126

9: *Without Precedent* 129

Old History 133

IN AND OUT OF TOWN 135

1: *Keeping Up Appearances* 137

2: *Wynter's Blade* 139

3: *Last Chance Saloon* 142

4: *Envoi* 144

5: *The Rogue Mechanicals* 149

6: *Filling the Gaps* 153

7: *Manifesto* 160

8: *An Unexpected Synergy* 163

9: *Caveat Emptor* 165

10: *Midnight Ramblers* 169

11: *The Dark Rickshaw* 175

OUT OF TOWN 179

1: *Spring Steps* 181

2: *A Bard in Lost Acre* 193

Old History   203

IN TOWN   207
1: *A Clairvoyant Looks Back*   209
2: *Île Flottante*   214
3: *Payday*   226
4: *None of Your Business*   228

OUT OF TOWN   231
1: *Mr Fluffy*   233
2. *The Cost of Taking the Shilling*   241

OUT OF TOWN   249
1: *Therapy Time*   251

IN TOWN   259
1: *Corps de Ballet*   261
2: *Dressings Up and a Dressing Down*   264
3: *Return of the Natives*   272
4: *Visceral Reactions*   275
5: *Who's Who?*   283
6: *Open Doors*   287
7: *After the Lord Mayor's Show*   309
8: *Fly-by-Night*   314
9: *A Trap to Lay*   323
10: *The Fanguins Have a Dilemma*   325
11: *The Pool of Mixed Intentions*   330
12: *After the Hunt*   333

Old History   337

IN TOWN   339
1: *The Morning After*   341
2: *The Tower Opens*   348

3: Taking Advantage 357

4: The Temptation of Prudence 363

5: Of Webbed Feet 366

Old History 369

OUT OF TOWN 375

1: Habits Die Hard 377

2: Pre-emptive Bids 386

3: The Reluctant Skipper 388

4: Last Things 393

5: The Double Address 396

6: Down into the Dark 401

7: A Loss Found 403

8: A Gathering of Forces 406

9: Oblong Oblivious 410

ENDGAME 413

1: A Sight to Behold 415

2: An Ultimatum 417

3: A Mixing of Opposites 419

4: The Poisoning 421

5: Escape by Water 437

6: The Finishing Line 439

7: Myrmidon 442

8: The Tree of Good and Evil 457

9: Two Journeys: Over Ground and Underground 459

10: Is Ignorance Bliss? 461

11: A Phoenix Rises 466

12: Dead Men's Shoes 468

13: Absolution 470

14: A Final View 473

Acknowledgements 475

ILLUSTRATIONS

Marsh

p. v

Wynter's Arrival

'A new arrival'

p. 33

Orelia Sleeping

'It felt like a holy place . . .'

p. 59

Wynter/Bole

'Servant or Master'

p. 125

Snorkel's Fall

'His limbs danced'

p. 146

Mistletoe

'A visceral death'

p. 157

Carcasey Jack

'I remove the crust.'

p. 177

Strix's Mother
'Consequences'
p. 206

Oblong Meets Persephone Brown
'Oblong and Persephone'
p. 247

White Tile
'The white tile'
p. 308

Strimmer
'The pack had been starved'
p. 332

Scry
'Part transformed'
p. 356

Gabriel's House
'The meadow turned red-orange . . .'
p. 385

The Underground Lake
'Fashioned by nature'
p. 436

Old History

66 million years BC (or so).

Creatures of the deep scramble for land, so toxic is the irradiated dust. Creatures of the land seek water to cleanse their coated hides. It is noon, but the sun hides her face, as she has for months. After the blast and the pulse of radiation, darkness and ice invade: impact winter. The skeletal ribs of giant herbivores protrude through the snow like a ship's graveyard. Everywhere photosynthesis fails.

Alive, just, lungs labouring to expel the clogging soot, she stumbles on, dragging her spent wings behind: the last of her species. It is not the urge for survival which impels her, but the eggs she carries, hope in a shell.

It is sudden as lightning.

Her physical being is sundered, only to reappear in a world transformed – forests basking in sunlight, pure air, the scent of fresh water, green grass underfoot. She ignores the unfamiliar insects scissoring past and hauls her ailing body along the river line.

This is a time without names, but later they will place her in the stars.

Draco.

AD 63. Lost Acre.

Opposition roots in local ritual, not the hearts or minds of individuals: destroy their spirit by destroying their places of worship. These are Rome's standing orders from Africa to Gaul. They even reach the legion *XX Valeria Victrix* in Britannia, the empire's remotest province.

So now auxiliaries set about destroying the stone circle on the crown of the island with mallets, fire and sour wine. Only the central stone is too deep and durable to break.

Downriver, the legionaries face a more frustrating time, for their quarry – an entire community – has taken flight in coracles and vanished without trace into the oak woods which rise from the river.

Gorius, the legion's lead scout, its *speculator*, is tasked to observe, analyse and advise. Outside the wood, he can hear the coarse expletives of the legionaries above the scraping hiss of swords returning to scabbards. He wonders if the unexpected but perfectly sculpted tile at his feet holds the answer.

Beside him, his tribune watches, incredulous, as Gorius' body disintegrates on stepping forward.

Gorius arrives in a wholly unfamiliar place. Its nature tallies with nowhere. Even the grass is different.

Ferox joins him minutes later and snarls at the surrounding press of tribesmen.

'He is mine,' barks a hedge-priest in dark robes, pointing his staff at Ferox. Behind him, tribesmen shout, jabbing their spears skywards, women jeer and silent children glare. Their cheeks and foreheads are smeared with patterns in red and blue. A young man holds aloft a cage. Weasel heads dart in and out of the squared bars.

Opposite stands what must be a rival faction. Their priest is in white, almost a physical twin but for the colour of his robes. He approaches without hostility while his supporters maintain a disciplined calm.

'*Pertines ad me*,' he says to Gorius in Latin. *You belong to me.* 'Be happy. Fate has chosen for you the better path.'

AD 409. The coast of Britannia.

Gorius has travelled far to witness this moment of madness. He looks down on the ships bobbing in the bay as they set their sails, a hotchpotch reflecting the empire's fading power. The occasional galley sits alongside Celtic ships with their flat bottoms and high prows and merchantmen with decks cleared for horses and ballistae. At least the Count of the Saxon Shore still knows how to organise.

It is a brilliant day; the white cliffs dazzle; seabirds dance behind the sterns in the hope of discarded offal.

A local, arms whorled in woad, sidles along the clifftop. Gorius' tanned skin marks him out as one of *them*, a man in the know.

'Are they all leaving?' the local asks.

'All the soldiers, to a man.'

'Why?'

'Their general would kill an emperor to become an emperor. Then another general will set out to kill him. This is a retreat to nowhere.' *Here*, he thinks, *with these natural frontiers, they could have fashioned a new empire from the ashes of the old. Instead, they limp back to a doomed homeland.*

He has had a life of sorts, drifting from camp to camp, playing the retired veteran, but now . . . now only he and Ferox, his tribune, who is still loose in the other place, remain. And five centuries or more must pass before he can fulfil his oath to the hedge-priest and repay his debt for the longest of long lives.

He sits and watches as masts and decks merge to mere blurs and Britannia is left to her own devices.

AD 1017. The Rotherweird Valley.

Gorius sits on a grassy bank where meadows yield to rising beech woods. He tips his head and basks in the midsummer's day sun, which, tiring at last, has a coppery sheen. Only the unusual leaves tumbling down the slope testify to something out of the ordinary – that, and his age. He smiles. Demigod is too strong a word; a masculine dryad, perhaps. Since his brief transformation, his hearing has been enhanced from birdsong to insects – and footsteps, too. He does not turn; the approaching aura is enough.

They called them hedge-priests in the legion: they looked alike, with white hair falling to the shoulders, faces like arid riverbeds, spindly arms and legs coiled with sinews and veins. After such a long absence, he is unsure whether this is his captor or not, but this hedge-priest clearly knows the distant past.

'Did you see your tribune?' he asks.

Still Gorius does not turn, though he drops his head in acknowledgement before returning it to the sun. 'No, I avoid him, but he's a survivor, is Ferox.'

The hedge-priest sits down beside him and looks down the valley towards the settlement. 'They haven't followed you.'

'The Hammer did its work. They're scattered all over the island like soldiers after a victory.'

'It took years to perfect that brew, and I was lucky in my brewer.' The old man's hands are stained purple by hops. 'What now?' he asks.

Gorius adjusts the question and returns it. 'I suppose there'll be a next time after another millennium.'

'There will, but you're safe. You can't play the Green Man twice; not you, not me.'

Pieces fall into place: they are Green Men both. The indelible bond encourages candour.

Gorius voices his concern. 'A rope can lose only so many threads before it snaps. The bond between here and the other place is weakening.'

'It will be worse next time,' replies the hedge-priest, as if presenting fact, not opinion. A hand delves into his robe and emerges with an offering. 'A token of my gratitude,' he says with a smile, which is slightly pinched.

Two long tubes intertwine like the snake on a caduceus before joining in a single mouthpiece. The surface is decorated with fangs, claws and wings: exquisite workmanship in the finest silver. Letters run along the sides, an unfamiliar word: *escharion*.

Gorius, ever the scout, weighs the probabilities and trusts in intuition. The pipes are too perfectly aligned for mere decoration. This is an instrument, one which plays for a purpose, not a token of gratitude, or not just that. It will initiate a new task which, for whatever reason, the hedge-priest is unwilling to specify.

'Such craftsmanship is above my station, but thank you.'

'Another time perhaps,' replies the hedge-priest, the instrument vanishing back into his robes.

Gorius replays the exchange: a token of *my* gratitude, the hedge-priest had said, not *ours*. 'What became of your people?' he asks.

It is the hedge-priest's turn to adjust a question and return it. 'What became of Rome?' he replies, turning back the way he had come.

Gorius gazes across the grassland. The sun is losing intensity, its warmth now lazy, burnished and benign. He loves this valley with her fluctuating moods and colours. He will stay here, keeping fit and playing the fool when necessary.

Far off – and this is intuition only – there will be a final mission, and that superbly wrought instrument, the escharion, will be there.

PROLOGUE

A Town of Sorts

How to distil the heart of a town? How to interpret first impressions, so often the most insightful? As with humankind, physique impresses before spirit: the showy places – here, Market Square dominated by the Town Hall, Parliament Chamber and the giant cowl of Doom's Tocsin; the Golden Mean, the one street which runs straight and true; the flamboyant winding aerial walkway known as Aether's Way.

Then perhaps the conspicuous secrets: the forbidding (in both senses) wall enclosing the Manor and the large sign on the ornate portico of Escutcheon Place: HERALD – NO VISITORS.

Next, the visitor's eye might rest on the popular ports of call: the more alluring shops; *The Journeyman's Gist*, the town's single tavern; Rotherweird School; the Library, and Grove Gardens, the municipal green space. Add to these the cosmetic touches: the colourful costumes, the ubiquitous carvings in wood and stone and the multicoloured bicycle rickshaws whose silent vacuum technology highlights absentees from the wider world: no cars, no hoardings, no street signs, no road markings.

If you look harder, the town's skill-sets emerge as embodied by her twelve Guild Halls, from the Toymakers, with a roof crowded with moving mechanicals, to the Apothecaries, the largest and most austere, hidden away in the poor quarter. There is also the South Tower's conspicuous observatory at the heart of Rotherweird School.

Beneath the physicality and talents, what is the spirit of this place? A portcullis guarding each way in, in the north and the south, open at dawn and closed at sunset, an embodiment of the town's fierce independence and hostility to outsiders. Mobile stalls laden with produce for sale or barter must arrive and leave before these great gates rise and fall, confirming a like suspicion for the valley's countrysiders. Hats are doffed with a jaunty rather than slavish air to Guild Masters, the Mayor, the Headmaster and the Herald: this is a society based on respect rather than deference. Nobody mumbles into handheld machines: here, horror of horrors, people communicate face to face.

Enter a house, any house, to discover another absentee: there are no portraits or photographs of the dead, no diaries or letters or memoirs by or about the deceased. This town has banished history. She lives, by law, in the present.

Houses and streets are lit by gas-lamps fuelled by methane from the marsh. No heads bow over screens, large or small; no antennae or satellite dishes disfigure the roofscape. There is no theatre, for that might encourage satire, irreverence and an eye for history. News is left to the flamboyant Town Crier, an actor-writer who lives in the present and whose doggerel answers to no one. He processes and broadcasts what he sees and hears, colourfully and with a studied neutrality.

But beneath this easy flow swirl deeper counter-currents and eddies, there to be exploited by anyone with the requisite knowledge and a mind to.

OUT OF TOWN

I

Valourhand Penitent

Flash, dark, flash, dark . . . The low dawn sun is filtered by the trees, like an early black and white film. *My shame is being recorded for posterity,* Valourhand mused, reliving every few steps the sweeping breath of the ice-dragon and Hayman Salt's brave stand beside the frozen river. She had put him on the shoreline as her chosen decoy, knowing the dragon would be drawn to Salt as a man who had known the mixing-point. Instead, with bow and acid arrow at the ready, she had been overwhelmed by the sheer magnificence of the beast. The brief moment of opportunity had passed, leaving poor Salt to be *shivered* to pieces. She was guilty of his manslaughter, at best.

She had opted for exile as due penance – death by boredom in the company of idiots in the wider world – only to reconsider on reaching the Ten-Mile Post on the borders of the Rotherweird Valley. The prospect of Hoy's prim streets truly nauseated her.

A vigorous internal debate ensued:

That's why exile is a punishment: you give up familiar comforts for the primitive.

The better punishment would be to go back and fight Wynter to the death.

But that's no punishment; it's what you would have done if Salt had survived.

Valourhand compromised by retracing her steps to the last bend in the road with an open view of the town. She would stay there until the electoral declaration at mid-afternoon on the Winter

Solstice. If nothing untoward occurred, she would leave Rother-weird and never return.

As she waited, two clouds, anvil-shaped, black as slate, mush-roomed into the blue. At three o'clock to the minute, the temperature plummeted, the birds fell silent and the ground shook.

Omens.

Wynter had surely come.

The voice protesting against exile prevailed, but on terms: she would abandon the town, but not the valley. Let adventure find her; she would not seek it out.

2

A Historian in Waiting

In deepening dusk, sitting astride a branch of the great tree by the mixing-point in Lost Acre, Oblong glumly imagined a line of would-be suicides lined up on a bridge parapet, launching into the void one by one as he tried to talk them down. What a failure of advocacy! Pomeny Tighe had swung herself into the mixing-point and disappeared despite his entreaties. Would he *ever* succeed in a challenge which mattered?

Wynter's treatment of Pomeny Tighe had been peculiarly cruel. Centuries earlier, he had secretly configured the stones to reverse time, leaving Tighe to face a slow descent from extreme old age into second childhood, and then tricked her back into the mixing-point at the Winter Solstice with the false promise of a cure. The sphere they had provided for this purpose had disappeared with her in the mixing point. But what had the sphere been designed to do? He had not the faintest idea.

A growl disturbed his reverie and balance, the latter restored by a fortuitous branch behind his back. A white-furred, wolfish animal with smouldering blue eyes was prowling around the tree. Another joined, then three more arrived at an unhurried trot. Their sniffing had an aggressive quality, which set Oblong to wondering: if they were the hounds and he was the quarry, who was their master?

But as if of one mind, they raised their snouts and loped off into the dark.

Relief never lasted in Lost Acre. Minutes later, an avian form swooped past him, head swivelling towards his face, before planing back to the forest below.

It's calling the flock, thought Oblong. *I'll be plucked from my branch like an apple.*

He dropped to the ground. Ankles turning on the frozen earth, he ran to the tile.

An hour later, tramping through the water meadows towards town, arms crossed against the cold and eyes dipped to avoid the freezing sleet, more questions spawned: Who had won the election? Had Wynter made his move? What was lying in wait for Morval Seer?

These conundrums arrived in a mildly self-important wrapping, for was he not Rotherweird's only modern historian? It was down to him to unravel, interpret and record.

IN TOWN

I

The Winter Solstice

Bill Ferdy cleared, washed and shelved an array of glasses in *The Journeyman's Gist* before sweeping the floor; menial tasks which summoned memories of his youth, but for one unique feature: on the fireside blackboard, game scores had been supplanted by as-yet-unresolved electoral bets. *May the result not reflect the final odds*, he prayed:

Snorkel	1/2
Strimmer	1/1
Roc	2/1

Beads of sleet scurried past. Ferdy pitied the infirm and the young, dragged to the Island Field by the *Popular Choice Regulations* to hear the outcome of the election, leaving him, a countrysider, as the lone presence in town.

When beer and conversation flowed, time flew; in their absence it positively crawled. 2.56, 2.57, 2.58 . . .

As the minute hand on the mantelpiece clock finally achieved the vertical and Ferdy's prayer ended with a plea for communal good sense, ill omens struck, one for each chime.

A violent tremor set windows rattling and Ferdy's feet and glasses dancing.

Dust, a swirling orange, billowed down from the higher ground of Market Square.

Slates cracked and shattered from a fusillade of ballot-balls, which bounced off roofs into the cobbled streets. Democracy had spectacularly imploded.

Then came silence.

On the Island Field beyond the South Bridge, the bets on Ferdy's blackboard had been voided by an act of God. *The Thingamajig*, Rotherweird's aerial ballot box, had shattered at the climax of its automated count, her cargo of stone ballot-balls energised by unseen forces seconds before the earthquake.

'Citizens of Rotherweird, we are checking it's safe to return. Thereafter a curfew will be imposed for the public good.'

Estella Scry's amplified voice, backed up by the electricity arcing between the Apothecaries' conductor-sticks, held sway over a crowd in shock. She had catered for electoral success or defeat, but not for a spoiled vote, an apocalyptic storm, earth tremors and whatever transformation lay beneath the pall of dust enveloping the town. But there was no time to reflect. She must *act*.

She passed a list of three names to Gurney Thomes, who read them slowly out loud. 'Sidney Snorkel, Mr Gorhambury and Orelia Roc.'

'Just so. Take them to the prison on suspicion of sabotage.'

Thomes bridled, both at so lowly a task and her peremptory tone. 'I *am* Master of the Apothecaries, Miss Scry.'

'You decide who stays free is the message – or would you rather they were in awe of Hengest Strimmer?'

Touché.

Strimmer overheard, but did not mind. He enjoyed watching inadequate people shift to and fro like leaderless lemmings. With a failed election and his two rivals under arrest, a vacuum remained to be filled. Scry had promised him power and he believed her.

'Roc is missing,' said Thomes.

A senior Apothecary, Sister Prudence, tall, hair in a bun, serene in her severity, stepped forward, not waiting to be asked, and announced, 'Orelia Roc broke the cordon and headed upriver with the PE teacher. He's an imbecile, but she's not, which makes it a surprising decision in the circumstances.'

Thomes could only agree. 'How upriver?' he asked, looking at the ice, which had been transformed by the quake into a scumble of moving crevasses and cliffs.

'They had skates.'

'Check for bodies,' said Scry. 'Give Master Thomes and me a ten-minute start, then let them back to their homes – and keep them there.'

Snorkel belatedly found his voice. 'This is outrageous. I'm a former head of state, a candidate, a public servant – *and* I was winning the vote—'

Sister Prudence raised a stick to his face. 'You're a corrupt little man with no future, but as you enjoy the sensation of power . . .'

Her stick crackled and the former Mayor subsided into a scowling grimace. Beside him, Gorhambury, immaculate in suit and tie, stood pale and immobile. He could not fault his pending incarceration. Ballot boxes should not explode, and as Town Clerk, he was responsible for due electoral process. The Apothecaries had no business meddling, but Rotherweird's constitution had frozen in the headlights of novelty. In his head he hunted through a forest of *Regulations* for precedent without finding any. The town had lurched off-piste, without sign or marker.

The two anvil clouds had separated like exhausted boxers and the snow was easing back to sleet. Even in the gloom, the town's roofscape had subtly changed.

As Thomes led his prisoners over the bridge, Scry said, 'You come with me, Mr Strimmer.'

'The only way to deal with bullies is counter-attack,' Miss Trimble whispered to Boris as they watched, powerless.

'Cometh the hour, cometh the man,' replied Boris mysteriously.

*

Remorse knifed Godfery Fanguin as the captives were led away. *So many failures.* He should have foreseen the ice-dragon and Valourhand's fatal attempt at interception, and he should not have allowed his feud with Snorkel to bring about this disastrous election. Worst of all, he should have kept a firm eye on Orelia.

And he felt excluded. Whatever intelligence had driven Orelia and Jones upriver, they had not shared it with him; nor could he seek solace with other friends, for Valourhand, Finch, Everthorne and Oblong were all inexplicably missing.

Disenchanted with humankind (including himself), he retreated into scientific curiosity. Had Bolitho's sphere moved the observatory to Lost Acre? What had Bole's sphere done to Rotherweird? And what of Wynter?

He turned to his wife. 'Bomber, why don't you head home while I do a recce?'

'There's a curfew.'

'Bugger curfews. Something's afoot up there.'

'And something's afoot down here. Housekeeping isn't bailing you out a second time.'

Fanguin squinted at his wife in puzzled dismay.

'And don't give me that "liberal-in-shock" look,' she continued. 'Snorkel knew he was losing and sabotaged the vote. Gorhambury did nothing to stop him. And your Miss Roc abandoned us in our hour of need. Somebody had to take over.'

Looking around him, Fanguin realised she was not alone in that view.

With the prisoners, Scry and Strimmer gone, the remaining Apothecaries at last moved aside and the town drew in her citizens.

Just beyond the school, Fanguin stopped at the mouth of a narrow alley. 'I won't be long,' he said brusquely to Bomber.

'Don't be,' she replied, equally curt, as Fanguin trotted out of sight.

Orange dust hung in the lingering dampness, but halfway up the alley the domestic gas supply revived. Windows of all shapes and sizes flickered into life. Hands poked through, checking panes for damage, closing shutters, pulling curtains.

There'll be work for the roofers, but otherwise no serious harm, Fanguin concluded.

A failsafe mechanism had kept the streetlamps dark, so accentuating the two green-orange sparks which were dancing towards him from the direction of Market Square. Close to, they resolved into outlandish insects with luminous thoraxes and gauzy wings hooked at the apex. They darted, hovered, then darted again, now a few feet above his head.

Finding their way back to Lost Acre, mused Fanguin as they disappeared down a culvert.

He hurried on to Market Square, where he was greeted by a familiar figure.

'Good evening, Doctor Fanguin.' Scry sounded friendly, if on edge.

Behind her, in the space between Doom's Tocsin and the Town Hall, soared an unfamiliar windowless and doorless tower festooned in carvings.

'It's real,' she added as he examined it. 'Old oak through and through.' She sounded business-like, but nonplussed. 'Whoever built it used block, pulleys and vacuum technology. There's no rock or debris. The old surface has vanished, cobbles and all. But I need help with the vegetation.' On the rim of the hole clumps of spear-shaped grass lay flat. 'Best not with your finger,' she added as Fanguin leaned in.

He swayed backwards as if he had never intended anything else, picked up one of the many sticks brought down by the storm and poked gingerly. Two stems whipped up; cactus-like spikes thrust and retracted.

'See in the middle?' said Fanguin. 'They're trying to flower. Trees and plants throw seed when distressed.'

'And when feeling the urge to colonise,' added Scry as she turned to a nearby Apothecary. 'Show him your catch.' The Apothecary uncapped his hands. The luminous insect changed colour, acquiring veins the hue of the hand which held it. 'It has tiny toes too. Forget the curfew, Doctor Fanguin. Find what you can and report to the Apothecaries in the morning.' Despite the air of command, her fingers pleated the sides of her coat; she was still on edge. 'If you returned to Rotherweird after a long absence, where would you go?'

That at least was a no-brainer. '*The Journeyman's Gist*, where else?' he replied.

She hurried off into the darkness. A man, loitering nearby, followed her: Strimmer, the only candidate still in circulation.

Fanguin's remorse returned. Was Orelia still alive? With the gates closed, he could do nothing for her now, so he hurried home to gather the tools of his trade, head abuzz with puzzles. Who had built the tower, for whom? Why was Scry, a suspected Eleusian, so taken by surprise? He had half an explanation: if she had killed Bole's familiar, as they believed, she must be hostile to Bole, and so hardly privy to his grand stratagem. The web of conspiracy had a complexity which offered a smidgen of hope. They might be scattered, but the enemy was divided.

A note from Bomber awaited him:

Unexpected job, flan in oven. B.

Fanguin turned up the gas-lamp and surveyed their front hall. Exposed threads disfigured the rug's pleasing pattern; two banisters, despite his best attention, hung loose, peppered with nail-holes; and his amateur repainting of the walls had created a displeasing stripy effect: all symptoms of the slow slide from comfort to straitened circumstances.

Doctor Fanguin, Scry had said, two times. *A mistake, or a promise of better times to come?* Conjoined, those two words sounded so very *right.*

He gathered a specimen box, a tube-light, a pair of forceps and a magnifying glass before heading back to the tower and its narrow surrounding ring of Lost Acre's soil.

2

First Orders

The mantelpiece clock, still an inch off-centre, chimed dusk into evening. Bill Ferdy unlocked the great door to find the street empty but for an Apothecary who growled, 'Get back! Haven't you heard? There's a curfew.'

He returned inside, pulled himself a pint, a rare treat for a landlord, and sat in the *Senex*, a tall oak-backed chair next to the fire reserved by tradition for the oldest customer.

Ten minutes later the Apothecary outside repeated his order.

'I've nowhere to get back to,' replied a male voice, all calmness and authority.

After a pause, the Apothecary sounded less assertive. 'Who *are* you?'

'That's tomorrow's tale – but you may consider yourself privileged to be the first to address me.'

The pub's door opened to admit an ascetic-looking middle-aged man, gaunt in body and face. He neither walked nor shuffled but glided in, holding his stick clear of the floor. Under a dark tan cloak, the stranger wore velvet knickerbockers and a thick jersey with no shirt.

'Your tavern is empty and it's twenty-five past six,' he exclaimed. 'When did that last happen?'

'The day of my father's death,' replied Ferdy truthfully.

The man appeared pleased with the answer. 'And I dare say the inn was packed with revelry on the day of your birth?'

'I imagine it was.'

'A witness to birth and death: that's how worthwhile places are. I've endured a long journey – I'll have the same as you, please.'

'Good choice.' Ferdy placed a tankard under the barrel. 'First is always on the house.'

The stranger offered a hand, the fingers tapered, nails well kept. 'The name is Geryon Wynter.'

Ferdy continued to draw the beer. He had been part of the company opposing Sir Veronal Slickstone and had hosted the late-night meeting at *The Journeyman's Gist* after Finch's abduction. He had heard Ferensen's account of the primordial impact that had formed the Rotherweird Valley, Lost Acre and the gateways between them, as well as the delivery of the Elizabethan prodigies into the care of Sir Henry Grassal, who had later been murdered by the young Slickstone. He knew about Wynter's seizure of the Manor, the terrible experiments in the mixing-point and Wynter's execution after Sir Robert Oxenbridge had returned to the valley to rescue those he could. He knew too that Professor Bolitho, or Fortemain, as he had once been, had opposed Wynter; that the Eleusian women had escaped the fate of their male counterparts and some at least had lived on, and that Wynter's resurrection had long been prophesied.

However, Ferdy had been on the fringe in recent months, and Ferensen's disappearance had not helped.

The stranger appeared to read his misgivings. 'You may have heard talk of me, Mr Ferdy, but, rest assured, I have been misunderstood. All I ask is a chance to correct the record.'

Wynter, if it was truly him, spoke easily, assured rather than arrogant. He sat in the *Senex*, eyes fixed on the fire, fingers running from table to glass to cheek as if rediscovering the rich variety in the feel of surfaces. He did not turn when Scry and Strimmer entered.

Connections, sensed Ferdy. Strimmer's default expression of bored disdain had given way to intense interest in the new arrival. Half of him whispered, *Kill the conspiracy now*, but he lacked the where-withal, and in any case, the other half was deeply intrigued. He cast a fly instead.

'We have a visitor to Rotherweird. Meet Mr Geryon Wynter.'

As Wynter stood up and turned to the new arrivals, Scry swayed, her arms clutching at space, her eyes glassy with tears. She tottered towards the newcomer as if to a lovers' reunion.

Wynter took a hand and kissed it. 'Estella,' he said.

'Apple brandies for all,' murmured Strimmer to Ferdy.

'Geryon ... Mr Wynter ... you're untouched, you're ... as you were,' Scry mumbled.

Wynter turned his hand over, palms up. 'My lifeline resumes,' he said.

Scry blinked. Was Wynter aware of her new profession? But how could he know? She dismissed the remark as coincidence.

'And this is?' asked Wynter.

Ferdy delivered the brandies. Scry, after a sip, recovered her composure. 'Hengest Strimmer. He is a scientist with modern talent. You will like him.'

Wynter placed a finger on Strimmer's brow. 'Head of the North Tower, no less.'

Strimmer pushed Wynter's hand away and said angrily, 'How dare you, an outsider, come waltzing in here as if you own the place!'

The older man smiled, as if the insult were a compliment.

'Your sentiment is admirable, Mr Strimmer, and rest assured I share it. Rotherweird is for Rotherweirders. Only one fact is wrong. I lived here long before you – before Estella, before Slickstone.'

The reference to Slickstone reined Strimmer in. Sir Veronal had been peculiarly reticent about his age and Wynter had that same timeless quality. Nonetheless, he judged it important to sound incredulous. 'Really?' he said, eyebrows raised.

'Congratulations are due,' replied Wynter. 'You have fulfilled a prophecy: *He will be mocked at dusk and believed in the morning.* It's carved in Latin on the top pediment of the left column in the portico of Escutcheon Place.'

Strimmer, intrigued but also infuriated, could not restrain himself. 'What do you know of Slickstone's *Recipe Book?*'

'First, it's not his. Second, as you clearly remain sceptical, on the third page you'll find the red circle furthest right and the blue circle furthest left.' Wynter seamlessly changed subjects. 'The curfew must end tomorrow at dawn. I was explaining to the good Mr Ferdy here how we have been sorely misunderstood. We'll summon the town to Market Square at half past ten and make good.'

'Where have you been?' stammered Scry.

'Where I told you I'd be – in Death's dark vale,' replied Wynter, drawing up two chairs to the fire. 'Now, let's talk of ordinary things.'

Half an hour later Oblong burst in. He had with difficulty negotiated admission through the South Gate, where the regular guard had been displaced by an Apothecary.

He had expected *The Journeyman's Gist* to be heaving with customers and post-election analysis. 'My dear Ferdy, what *is* going on?'

Ferdy raised a restraining arm as Oblong spotted Strimmer, his old enemy, sitting by the fire with Estella Scry and an imposing elderly man whom he did not recognise.

'There's a curfew,' hissed Scry.

Strimmer smirked. 'Did you hear that, Oblong? Scram.'

Wynter rose again to his feet. 'It's never wise to exclude a historian from history. I am Mr Geryon Wynter.'

Oblong shook his hand without thinking. 'Where are you from?' he mumbled, also without thinking.

'Death's dark vale,' intervened Strimmer.

Wynter, ignoring him, continued, 'Unfortunately, the law against studying Rotherweird's past allows rumour and charlatans to flourish, but for the moment we must obey it.' He smiled. 'You look in need of a drink.'

'I need to check my rooms,' replied Oblong limply. 'They're rather high up.'

'You do that,' muttered Strimmer.

'Until tomorrow morning then,' added the stranger, 'when the people of Rotherweird will decide their future.'

Oblong left befuddled. Sir Veronal Slickstone had exuded menace, but Geryon Wynter had been charm itself.

Denzil Prim greeted his new charges like long-lost relatives, with arms akimbo and a cordial grin. Having been handsomely paid by the Apothecaries, he had worked hard at the script. 'A red-letter day,' he crowed, 'a Mayor and a Town Clerk. Welcome to Prim Hall. What's the offence, gents? I bet it's somat colourful?'

'Rotting the fabric of state,' barked Thomes.

Impatient to return to the greater game, the one Scry and Strimmer were busy playing, he commandeered a rickshaw and hurried back to the Hall of the Apothecaries.

3

A Guest of Honour

Thomes' humour did not improve when he entered his private rooms to find the table in his library-cum-dining room had been set for five with the Apothecaries' finest: silverware and crystal, silver-gilt candle sconces flying on slender silver stems and decanters inscribed with the Apothecaries' motto: *The world is not thy friend, nor the world's law.*

'Who ordered this?'

'Miss Scry, Master.'

'She does not decide my guests.'

'She said you would approve. She said tonight is the night the Apothecaries rise.'

Thomes looked closer. At least the Master's goblet still marked his place at the head of the table.

'Whom am I asked to approve?'

'Miss Scry, Sister Prudence, Mr Strimmer . . . and one other.'

'What other?'

'Your guest of honour. He's in the Hall, Master, with Miss Scry. He's found all sorts of hidden letters in our carvings. He's extraordinary, Master, a stranger who knows everything about everything.'

'We'll soon see about that,' growled Thomes, stalking from the room.

In the Great Hall he found Sister Prudence perched on a ladder among the carved parables. She was waving a torch behind the Good Samaritan's cloak.

'An unmistakable "s",' she announced before turning to Thomes. 'It's quite extraordinary, Master! That message in the Founder's portrait – *levamus*, which you'll remember Miss Scry translated – it's also recorded in our oldest carvings. Mr Wynter knows where every letter is, he's been right every time.'

An austere figure stepped from the shadows behind the blazing fire.

'Mr Geryon Wynter,' said Scry, 'Master Thomes.'

Thomes ignored Wynter's proffered hand. 'What is the meaning of this?'

Wynter's sibilant voice imposed despite its quietness, respectful, but laced with menace. 'It means this prophecy is as old as your Founder.'

Sister Prudence climbed down the ladder, took Thomes by the arm and showed him the letters. *The man must have an accomplice on the inside*, Thomes decided, not wanting to admit that the letters looked as old as the carvings which held them.

'If you're so damned knowledgeable, Mr—'

'Wynter, Geryon Wynter,' reminded Scry, a warning tone in her voice.

'Tell me why the Apothecaries rise?' continued Thomes aggressively.

Wynter moved to the Great Hall's central doorway. The architrave was decorated with a vine, rooted on the right, with tendrils reaching through the leaves and grapes on the higher stems; true to life. Here the letters lacked any shyness: *This* was carved on one side, *Vine* on the other, with *Me* in the middle.

'I am the true vine, you are the branches, for without me ye can do nothing,' intoned Sister Prudence. 'John, Chapter Five.'

'Then it should be *I*, not *me*,' chipped in Strimmer. 'And "I" would surely look better over the door.'

Wynter's forefinger followed the letters of the three words in a different, unnatural order.

A new arrival

'H ... i ... e ...' muttered Strimmer, but Scry was ahead of him.

'Hiems venit,' Scry cried in tones of near-ecstasy. '*Hiems venit*: Wynter comes!'

Thomes and Sister Prudence exchanged glances. The vine appeared on the Guild's earliest bookplates with the same words interwoven. Both had a vivid memory of the moment when the First Chord, the opening firework of the Vulcan's Dance celebrations, had rearranged its fiery letters high in the sky, from *Fatherly Wonder* to *Herald of Wynter*.

Thomes hesitated. For an impostor, Wynter had uncanny connections with past and present. He watched Strimmer watching Scry. *He's playing a waiting game*, thought Thomes, *and so must I.*

Scry laid the ground for the next scene in Wynter's return. 'I have taken a liberty, Master, confident that you'd approve. I've arranged an evening meal in the library in the Elizabethan style.'

'I know you have,' said Thomes, attempting a graceful smile.

'Ah, a *First* Supper,' added Wynter.

Scry allowed Thomes to lead the way.

The gaslights in the dining room had been extinguished. *An echo of Sir Veronal*, mused Strimmer, and another clue pointing to Wynter being more than the fraud suggested by first reactions. *When the grossly improbable is the only solution, embrace it.* Sister Prudence's dislike of the ostentation on view was palpable: Apothecaries did not indulge in Mammon. But she could hardly challenge the Master in front of his guests.

Thomes sat at the head of the table, waving Scry to his right and Wynter to the left. Strimmer and Sister Prudence took their places opposite each other. Thomes probed Wynter's scientific knowledge, followed by Strimmer, then Sister Prudence. Scry chipped in with supplementary questions.

His command of theory, the sequence of discovery and the current uncertainties from the multiverse to an elusive unified 'theory of everything' reconciling general relativity with quantum-field theory dazzled, the more so for a sprinkling of personal anecdote which leavened the deep science. He gave the impression of having known many of these travellers on the road to truth. Conversation hummed; Thomes and Sister Prudence, initially sceptics, succumbed.

As the plates were cleared, Wynter raised a hand, and this time, everyone paid attention. 'I thank you, Master Thomes. A good supper should engage four of the five senses, as this one has.'

'All five, if you include the tinkle of silver,' added Thomes, intent on maintaining his place in the conversational hierarchy.

'Might I compliment the cook?'

'She's not one of us and not very interesting,' Thomes muttered.

'In the best cooking, the sum of the parts exceeds the whole. That is both arithmetically interesting and worthy of congratulation.'

Minutes later, apron sagging around her waist, Bomber entered. She sensed peculiarities: the stranger had the ascendancy; Scry, a hard woman, in her experience, appeared to be besotted and even Strimmer was looking mildly subservient.

'Mrs Fanguin? I am Geryon Wynter.'

Scry registered a further example of a recurring puzzle: nobody had mentioned the cook's name.

'Eggs and bullock's cheek: your fricassee shows both delicacy and skill. Thank you.'

Bomber, untrained in the receipt of compliments, executed an action unperformed since childhood. She curtsied.

Scry took over. 'Recent events, Mrs Fanguin, require an explanation which only Mr Wynter can give. Please help spread the word: he will address the Parliament Chamber at half past ten tomorrow morning.'

'They'll be there,' added Wynter, no trace of doubt in his voice. 'It is written.'

*

Thomes accommodated Scry's wish to stay the night; she was an honorary member, after all.

As midnight chimed, Scry, near anonymous in an Apothecary's black night robe and white nightcap, tiptoed down the dingy passage which held the guest bedrooms. She knocked and, receiving no answer, lifted the latch and entered. Light from a single candle bathed Wynter's face. He sat facing her, hands resting on his knees, eyes shut, fingers playing his kneecaps. He was awake.

She had never liked Sir Henry Grassal, with his feudal airs and graces. Here was her father figure, her inspiration. She wanted to touch him, to feel this skin which had cheated death.

'You were masterful,' she said.

He rose, went to the open window and inhaled. The breeze ruffled his silver hair.

'You left me with a request,' she added.

'I prefer the word *labour* – the language of legend.' Wynter smiled. 'How did Fortemain die? You would not come to admit failure.'

'A trap.'

Wynter opened the word out, added decoration. 'A mechanical device of fiendish design. Be so good as to describe it.'

'I used sharpened hoops of silver steel, held back by springs and triggered by a pressure plate.'

Wynter laughed. 'A moleman-trap! And dear Fortemain always thought himself *so* superior. To think he could elude me ...'

Scry hesitated. Wynter's last remark rang false. *Fortemain thought himself so superior* ... To Bole, maybe, but surely not to Wynter.

'I actually came to ask about old friends,' she said.

'Calx joined me in death, and you will never see Nona again.'

Scry struggled to contain her triumph: Bole, the foul *Potamus*, had fallen and she, *only* she, would be Wynter's acolyte. 'I'm sorry,' she stammered.

'I know,' he replied.

He knew, he *always* knew.

'Who carved the prophecies in the Hall downstairs? Who—?'

'Mr Bole's life-work – I trust you admired his artistry.'

How? Scry wondered. The Potamus had clumsy hands, crude and fleshy, like the rest of him. But the wretched man was dead and she must rise above envy.

Wynter sat down before continuing, 'About tomorrow in the Chamber: I want a few children of an adventurous age near the aisles, spades by the outside door and a ladder against the portico of Escutcheon Place.'

'*Spades?*'

'And a pick or two.'

Scry did not further question these requests; indeed, she found their oddness reassuring. Wynter had retained his cryptic playfulness. 'Thank you, Mr Wynter.'

'Thank you, Estella.'

Only on the way back did the northeasterly view from the passage window catch her eye. On the town's highest prominence stood a large octagonal building.

The church had vanished.

4

Decision Time

Fanguin suppressed his anxieties by devoting meticulous care to the spreading of Bomber's rich, dark marmalade. In the 'no' corner: he hated the Apothecaries, a secretive puritan clique embedded in the town's fabric; he deeply disliked Strimmer, and Estella Scry was a suspected Eleusian changeling, a Fury in human disguise.

But in the 'yes' corner . . .

'Last night Estella Scry called me *Doctor* Fanguin. Twice. And she asked my opinion.'

'I thought there was a curfew.'

'Don't open it!' Fanguin shrilled as Bomber's hands closed on the specimen box on the sideboard.

'You've not used that in months. Don't tell me you're actually in work.' She peered through the glass. The balled vegetation looked unfamiliar. Beneath it, an equally unknown captive stirred.

'I'm to report to the Apothecaries at nine. Shall I, shan't I?'

'Shall. You're being unusually dainty with that knife, Fanguin.' Bomber put her elbows on the table and awarded him a broadside stare. He knew what that meant: he had missed something obvious. Not a haircut, no new jewellery . . .

'Is my evening ever a worthwhile topic?' she asked frostily.

'You were, ah yes, working.' Fanguin grimaced as a Rotherweird penny dropped. 'Working despite the curfew – don't tell me, cooking for the Apothecaries?'

'And why not? I fashioned an Elizabethan dinner from *The Good*

Housewife's Jewel – a recipe book from 1585, as you were no doubt about to ask.'

'Sorry . . .'

Her need to share her garnered praise overcame her anger. 'I was complimented.'

He frowned. 'Not by that skunk Thomes?'

'By a stranger – only I'm not sure he really was. He talked deep science and seemed to know all there is to know about the town.'

'And the name of your admirer?' he asked.

'Wynter: Mr Geryon Wynter.'

Fanguin choked on his marmalade as an Apothecary passed along the street, attempting to mimic the Crier's gift for rhyme, if not metre:

> *'Sound the trumpet,*
> *Beat the drums,*
> *Ten-thirty in the Chamber*
> *Wynter comes.'*

OUT OF TOWN

I

Winter Cleaning

Staying true to her self-imposed sentence, Valourhand marched on towards Rotherweird Westwood. From the west a slither of angry orange-red caught the walls of a stone house set on gently rising ground. It attracted Valourhand's attention, not for any welcoming features, for it had none, but for the unlit windows and open front door.

She crossed a frozen tributary of the Rother and the unkempt meadow, passing a warped shed stained brown-black by creosote and supported by mushroom-shaped stones. Beside the house a lopsided kennel with a mean space in front had been fenced off with barbed wire. The corpse of a mangy dog lay in the entrance, head half out. Protruding bones pointed to starvation.

The exterior of the house also exuded neglect: rust caked the single water butt; vertical stains from broken gutters disfigured the walls. Beyond the wide-open door, dry mud spattered the stone floor of a small bare entrance hall devoid of boots, coats or hats. A cracked saucer on a low bench held a single candle and matches.

She lit the candle and explored. Each floor had one generous front room, with smaller rooms at the back, including a kitchen-scullery downstairs and a bathroom upstairs. Grime coated every surface. Drapes and covers had been savaged by moths.

Valourhand loathed waste in all its forms. The windows promised a view. The downstairs fireplace had handsome cornerstones. Oak panelling skulked beneath the dirt.

The house had recently been occupied. A cold store held a joint, almost picked clean, as well as eggs, a loaf, butter and a jug of thick yellow soup. Firewood and kindling looked freshly cut. She laid a fire and lit it.

A Rotherweird gold guinea coin gleaming beneath the sitting room's central table snapped Valourhand from her torpor. By law, Rotherweird guineas were collected and re-minted every fifty years, but despite the eighteenth-century date, the patina was fresh and untouched by time. Bole would have gathered money to ease Wynter's progress to power, but what could this remote farmhouse have to offer either of them?

At least she now had a penance worth the name: cleansing these Augean stables.

The following morning, she buried the dog. Wheals along the back spoke of beatings. The creosote shed contained the remains of hens, also left without water or food. A rear room contained a plethora of traps and tiny manacles made for animals, of the owner's personal design, judging by the small furnace and welding equipment. Bizarrely, a high shelf in the same room held a large English dictionary in three volumes.

Days passed as Valourhand scrubbed and polished and burned. She slept downstairs, having no wish to use the bed of a torturer.

UNDER TOWN

I

Finch Underground

Oak on oak squeaked and grumbled as the great tower settled onto the supporting beams. Propelled on runners from sculpted apertures in the rock, they crisscrossed the shaft at the moment of ascent. Pulleys, their task done, festooned the cavern walls. Ropes snagged on projecting rocks; counterweights dotted the ground.

Up above, the circular rim of the opening eyed Finch like a Cyclops peering into a sack. He admired the workmanship and engineering, hydraulics, vacuum-technology, carving, joinery and timing devices all perfectly calibrated to raise the tower into place at the allotted moment.

The soles of his feet reported no aftershock, not that he had expected any: one dramatic strike on the Winter Solstice, the day allotted to Rotherweird's election, would meet Wynter's Messianic expectations. Bole had served his master well.

He inspected the ropes within reach and the rock wall, but the former were too loose and the latter too sheer to climb. In any event, the gap between the tower and the opening looked uninvitingly narrow.

He retrieved his tube-light and peered at his pocket watch. Time had flown: four o'clock had passed already, but above him Market Square was mute. He could hear no celebrations of an election result, but also no clamour of concern. Something must be seriously amiss.

I have to investigate – but where and how?

First decision: explore from underground. If Wynter and Bole were back, he would surely be a prime target for retribution. His ancestors had supplanted Wynter and the killings of Mrs Banter and Veronal Slickstone had demonstrated the Eleusians' relish for vengeance.

Second decision: try to reach the South Tower Observatory in Rotherweird School. The previous evening, on the eve of the election, he had chanced on Valourhand near Salt's house, swathed in warm clothes with a parcel under her arm.

'You're all dressed up, Glamourhand!'

'A night out, so needs must.' She had paused, but Finch knew that self-questioning look: *should she share her intelligence?* For once, she did. 'Oblong dropped into *Baubles & Relics* – he showed us Bolitho's sphere, the one you gave him to place in the mixing-point. We think it shifts the observatory to Lost Acre, so Bolitho can study the comet from there.'

'Why are you telling me this?'

'We've underestimated Calx Bole. Every move is plotted. To have any chance, we must pool the little we know.'

Finch would have passed on his own discoveries about Bole's alter ego, the master carver Benedict Roc, but a raised hand silenced him. Valourhand's current business was apparently too urgent to interrupt.

'Good luck with the expedition then.'

'I'll need it. Whatever you do, don't follow us. I mean it, Finch. You're needed here.'

She had awarded him a cursory hug, as uncharacteristic for her as sharing secrets.

Finch was now east of the Golden Mean and in unfamiliar territory. For several hours, he trudged on, using red wool markers to minimise repetition, but he could find no way south. He consumed his last two sandwiches, then slept.

Waking brought a change of luck. Cold air slapped his cheek and he traced the draught to a narrow shaft above a cramped dead end. Abandoning his backpack, he tied the tube-light to his ankle and clambered up onto a narrow ledge which opened out into a huge cavern. The tube-light made little impression, but directly below he could see a monorail snaking away into the gloom. He recognised it as the track for the moleman's railway. While wide enough to accommodate a man walking with care, the leap down looked precarious.

He prayed to Finches past and jumped. His trailing leg caught an outcrop, but arms honed by years of heaving heavy tomes in the *archivoire* found and gripped the rail. He hauled himself up and peered around. The ledge was now unreachable. For better or worse, he had burned his boats.

The rail's narrowness made walking awkward, but he sustained an even pace until the gradient steepened. When his feet began to slip backwards, he resorted to all fours, hands clasping the edge, tube-light dangling from his neck. A small platform with room to sit down and recuperate came as a relief. He flipped a nearby lever, with no visible consequence.

He looked up, which proved to be a mistake. The rail spun beneath him like a thread of spaghetti in boiling water, making him feel horribly exposed, a tiny firefly engulfed by darkness.

Since the tower's ascent, he had heard only his own breathing and movements; now the growing rumble behind him sounded as dramatic as thunder. His palms registered a *vibrato* in the track: he had inadvertently summoned Bolitho's rail-car. Would it topple him into the void?

Get a grip, he rebuked himself. *It must stop here*. And it did. He clambered on, leaned over and flicked the lever back to re-launch the car up the slope towards the South Tower.

He applauded himself – prematurely. Journey's end had not changed, but a huge purple-yellow sac now hung from the ceiling just yards from the halt. His head brushed the skin, which reformed as he passed like a balloon filled with liquid.

Finch walked back for a closer examination. The sac was pulsing like a lung. Inside, a ghostly embryonic shape, head tucked into its body, began to twitch. Above the sac, a thin circular line marked the rock, clear as ink.

He drew tentative conclusions: Bolitho's observatory had been transported to Lost Acre. The geology of the other place must match Rotherweird's; hence the perfect fit. On that working hypothesis, the egg-like structure had been laid in Lost Acre and made the reverse journey, which was quite a coincidence of placement and timing. And there the puzzles began. Bolitho could have no reason to import a monstrosity from Lost Acre – and why would Bole imperil his master's new kingdom?

Two dots of light danced up the tunnel, resolving into outsize luminous grasshoppers. Ignoring Finch, they settled on the sac, prospecting the surface while generating a high-pitched hum with their hind legs. The pulse within the sac quickened. *Moving into labour*, thought Finch. *I have to warn the town.*

He ran back and climbed the iron rungs to the drain cover. He raised the lid gingerly and peered out, only to be dazzled by dappled noonday sunshine. The observatory had vanished, but Apothecaries were guarding the perimeter, facing outwards. Behind their backs, they held electrical devices, judging by the flashes of static. They would arrest him, or worse, but he could see no alternative. To return, he must destroy the sac, *but how?*

He wrenched a loose iron rung from the wall. Gelatinous liquid was already oozing from the sac onto the tunnel floor, filaments no thicker than fishing line. The attendant insects attacked him with unexpected ferocity. He swatted one away, then crushed a second – just as a claw cut through the membrane. A long leg followed: jointed and toed, with the colour and consistency of a crayfish. It felt for the floor and settled. A crab-like face pressed against what remained of the membrane; stalked eyes fixed on Finch.

Finch ran to the rail-car and boarded as the hatchling emerged. A scything front claw dislodged the car's braking mechanism. The chassis hurtled forward to the screech of a falling pulley, accelerating to breakneck speed in seconds and leaving his pursuer snapping at thin air.

A reckless exuberance seized Finch. He leaned first one way then the other as the wild fairground ride swept away books, duties, estranged wife and disappointing son. Silver hair streaming, face buffeted by the rush of air, he yelled at the dark, *'Yahoo! Yahaa!'* Rotherweird's last Herald would be going to his Maker in style.

Fate, or the laws of physics, decided otherwise.

Once through the cavern and under the Rother, the rail started to climb and the rail-car slowed to a halt within feet of its platform terminus.

Reason returned.

The damaged chassis would surely rush back, seesawing like a pendulum before coming to rest in the darkness below, leaving him to starve or jump. He disembarked seconds before the rail-car slipped back into the gloom.

He felt exhausted. Bookish life had not prepared him for action-packed adventure. He tried to remember his last visit. Was it up and right, or up and left? He walked to the intersection, where cracks from the quake crisscrossed the ceiling. He chose right, walking on tiptoe like a dancer, fearful that pressure of feet or sound might bring the tunnel down.

He reached the line of levers for Bolitho's optical instruments, but the telescopes had been removed. The door beyond opened and a familiar figure brought a schoolboy exchange of greetings.

'Finch!' said Jones.

'Jones!' said Finch.

'Ssssh!' they both said in unison as the ceiling puffed dust.

Dried blood stained Jones' hands and forearms. His expression was grim, his lips pursed, his fists clenching and unclenching. 'A trap killed the moleman – steel spikes through the chest – he had no chance.' His delivery had the clipped bluntness of a military report.

'Where?'

'Close to your cell. Sorry, Finch. It's not your fault – but it's worse. On the other side there's a rock wall. At the Solstice it opened and Orelia went in.'

'Why?' Finch was still struggling to connect this subterranean drama with events above ground.

'Rotherweird has a mixing-point too. Orelia's copy of *Straighten the Rope* was bound in Wynter's skin. They came here to resurrect him.'

That made horrible sense.

'Did Orelia come out?'

'I don't know. But the wall closed again, solid as a . . . rock.' Jones began to mumble. 'The footprints are troubling. Two women and a man go in. A man and a woman come out – only the man coming out has different feet to the man going in, and the woman who escapes has tiny feet.'

'Roc does not have tiny feet.'

'No.'

Finch shook his head. Something did not fit. Why was Jones here? Why had Orelia headed for the greater danger?

Jones, sensing the implicit accusation, looked miserable. He had failed in gallantry, his defining virtue. 'A woman screamed, so we divided forces – I went this way, she went over there.' He pointed to the two routes. 'It was a *terrible* scream,' he added defensively.

Finch shuddered. He had forgotten Morval Seer. 'She must be distraught,' the Herald said.

In Jones' considerable experience, in the presence of sudden death, banality rather than eloquence marked the decent man. Finch's understatement wrenched him back to present priorities.

'I once knew a military man who after a battle liked to say, "*Tend to the living and forget the dead*". He was wrong. Tending to the dead revives the living. Follow me.'

The moleman was lying on the dining table, arms crossed over his chest and clasping a pair of telescopes. His body had been cleaned and combed. Defying *rigor mortis*, the last horrified look of surprise had eased to a gentle smile. Morval Seer stood beside him, hands as stained with grime and blood as Jones's. A large rope encircled the central pillar.

'This is the king-post,' Jones explained. 'Once we topple it, we've only minutes to escape. Fortemain designed it. Perhaps he knew this is how it would end.'

To Finch's amazement, Morval spoke, her words, both meaningless and meaningful, emerging in fits and starts.

'*Life . . . thin air . . . vision melted . . . solemn pageant . . . great globe of a man . . . dissolve . . . a dream.*' Her expression eased. She had said her piece.

'The shock restored her voice,' whispered Jones, 'but the words just tumble out.'

Finch felt the need for a positive response. 'We have a text too, don't we, Jones, for saying now . . .'

He and Jones bowed their heads and uttered Fortemain's self-penned epitaph:

> '*Earth to sky and sky to earth*
> *Matter matters in rebirth,*
> *Sky to earth and earth to sky,*
> *Life's mutations do not die.*'

Morval, having found a modicum of closure, kissed the mole man on the forehead and slung a sack of her belongings over her shoulder.

'Not the tunnels,' said Finch. 'There's a monstrosity from Lost Acre back there and it doesn't like Heralds.'

Morval, walking to the far doorway, summoned Finch with a crooked finger.

Jones coiled the rope around his waist. Feet set as for a tug-of-war, he leaned back and pulled. The king-post stood firm at first, then juddered, then fell. Above their heads, the entire complex of rooms began to creak like a labouring ship in a storm.

Morval hurried them into a shaft with rungs set into one side. Behind them, the sounds of falling earth and sundering timber declared the final entombment of Vesey Bolitho, alias Fortemain, and his inseparable talpid companion, telescopes across their shared torso, in a barrow fit for a king.

They climbed out to find twilight and Venus conspicuous over-head. The surface of the marsh betrayed no sign of the disturbance below.

They crossed themselves.

Jones broke a long silence. 'The town gates are closed.'

'And the marsh is impenetrable,' added Finch.

'Not with Morval to guide us,' replied Jones, 'and with my galumphing footsteps to follow. But we've no key to get in.'

They looked at each other. Morval really needed a dose of familial warmth.

'The Ferdys,' they said in unison.

2

Of Household Gods

They trudged on, stars coming and going in a ragged sky. Morval Seer knew the way and walked with pace and directness. Trees were down. A dead sheep lay in the lee of a hedge. Beside her, Finch caught fragments of nonsense – '*soul's light . . . bescreening night . . . confining prison . . .*' – but she led them unerringly to the Ferdys' house, where the hoped-for welcome did not materialise. Shuttered and plunged in darkness, the house offered only her front door, obligingly unlocked.

The essentials had been left as if for strangers on a short-term let: linen on the beds and enough crockery and cutlery for six people. There were basic provisions, including firewood and a store of root vegetables in a shed behind the house, but anything of value, artistic, material or sentimental, had been removed.

Shortly after their arrival, Morval Seer turned feverish.

'Exhaustion,' suggested Jones.

'Grief,' added Finch.

Wear and tear of every kind was their final common diagnosis. Jones laid and lit a fire as Finch tended the daughter he had never had. Her disconnected word-chains hinted at meaningful origins, but not even Finch, no ordinary speaker himself, could find the key. He took notes by her bedside as she rambled on, delirious.

Jones tracked down medicinal leaves and roots. He had run through these meadows long before this house existed. He knew every stand of trees and every stream, and Man's contribution, for good or ill. He could not fathom his role, but despite his natural humility, he sensed that he mattered in some way, and that like the silver double-pipe with its single mouthpiece, the escharion, he too would be there at the end.

3

Free Fall

Orelia Roc had lost her energy. She had followed Jones through the heaving ice and then across the marsh. She had been felled by Nona's vicious blow. She had been stricken with grief at Everthorne's loss and left in shock by the dark brilliance of Bole's strategy. Pillowing her head against the great subterranean tree, she slept, but it was not a restorative slumber, for images from the past assailed her: Salt's bubble whirling through the wormhole on Midsummer's Eve, Slickstone holding forth in *The Journeyman's Gist*, Everthorne whispering, 'Rugs, rugs and more rugs!' moments before making love to her, the catboy on the roof of her aunt's burning house, spitting the words, 'Where is the book, child?' A cast of ghosts, all dead now.

Please, take me, she mouthed in her coma. *Take me too.*

But Hope, slumbering at the bottom of the box, summoned two images from those still living: Morval Seer, slipping free of her hateful companion in the cage in Lost Acre, and young Tyke's face, beautiful and impassive in the firelight in the changelings' treehouse.

Orelia awoke with her spirits marginally revived. She left Everthorne's body on the platform beneath the mixing-point and she checked the rock wall, but it had returned to its solid, wholly impenetrable state.

Wynter's farewell had had an epitaph ring: '*Let her lie with him for ever.*'

She was immured.

*

Back in the cavern, her nostrils twitched. Mrs Banter liked to smother herself in exotic essences, but this fragrance released images of summer: bees and blossom, bare-armed bathers, meadows ready for harvest. Nature's gift, surely – but from where?

The tree, while rich in leaf out of season, bore no flowers, but a climber twined its way high into the branches.

She squeezed through the narrow space between the trunk and the rock wall – and there it was, rising through a tangle of roots, unmistakably a rose with dark crimson petals. The stems had parted, exposing a dark space at the base of the tree. She tightened the isolarion, the beige linen scarf which Professor Bolitho had left her, around her neck and squeezed through.

She did not so much fall as spiral down between the roots, aghast at how a single tree could sustain such a vast network. Tunnels opened on either side, looking more like inverted branches. They were sentient too, withdrawing or bending to let her pass. Silvery shafts of light permeated the gloom. She felt disembodied, no more than a tiny life force, until the violent jolt of landfall.

She found herself on a circular stone platform in a bowl surrounded by high cliffs: a place of extremes. On her left, one cliff face, sheeted with ice, rose from a frozen lake dotted with ice floes like stepping stones. An effulgent blue liquid seeped from outcrops at varying heights. To the right, lava flowed from fissures in the opposite wall into a fiery lake dotted with islands of pumice. A shiny marble pavement divided these contrasting lakes, a temperate middle way – and her only realistic route out. Vegetation hugged the banks of the path, the lanceolate leaves variegated red-blue, but without flowers as yet.

In each lake stood a mottled-white ovoid sculpture on a plinth about a metre high.

Halfway down the causeway she found a stone bench with its ends raised and smooth like pillows: an invitation to lie, rather than sit.

'It felt like a holy place . . .'

It felt like a holy place.

On lying down, the stone under her back had the yielding quality of soft ground. Gazing into the ribbon of the Milky Way and inhaling air both warm and fresh, her anxieties eased and she fell deeply asleep, and this time it was a restorative slumber.

The dawn light woke her, bringing the marble to dazzling life. She walked on to find a steep staircase in darker stone winding its way up to the crater's rim. The steps, wide enough for two abreast, were vertiginous but safe. Looking down one last time at the opposing lakes, Orelia reflected on other polarities: passion and reason, engagement and aloofness, instinct and judgement. She thought of the personalities of her friends and prayed that Rotherweird could hold its middle way.

Beyond, the rocky ground gave way to the spongy peat of a high heath in ordinary winter weather. She saw two familiar buildings: close by, Bolitho's observatory, and far in the distance, the bell tower of Rotherweird's church. Oblong must have placed his sphere in the mixing-point, and maybe Bole had too somehow.

Everthorne's death had induced in Orelia a devil-may-care atti-tude. If hostile life forms barred her way, so be it. The observatory it had to be.

She changed her mind within a few paces when a scaly snout erupted from a hole in the ground. A bloated, elongated wood-louse with a shark's crescent mouth and teeth nearly removed her ankle, only retreating when she stamped hard on the ground. Similar holes pockmarked the slope like a sieve. A more ambitious lunge from another hole fell short.

Orelia froze. Her neck prickled; she scratched, but the needling sensation persisted, prompting her to unwind the isolarion. A green fleck glowed in the material, then another beside the first. Holding the scarf in front of her, she experimented, step by cautious step. The green specks continued to move and finally she understood: if she kept to the green, nothing attacked. The isolarion was a map and like all Bolitho's bequests, a gift with purpose. She crouched and, probing the ground beneath her feet with her fingers, discovered she was walking on a seam of greenish rock where the creatures could not burrow. Bolitho had placed the observatory where only someone armed with his map could safely go.

The maze-like path coiled and double backed on itself, which made for tortuous work, but her pace improved as she gained confidence. She was not attacked again.

The door to the observatory held fast. 'But I'm an invited guest,' Orelia said out loud, fingering the isolarion. She tapped in search of a mechanism, to no avail, but a glance through the spy-hole provoked a sequence of clicks and the door swung open.

'Eureka!' she shouted.

Once inside, globe-lights on the walls oscillated and flared into life.

The journey from Rotherweird had not disturbed the books, a silver pencil on the work surface beneath the telescope or Bolitho's spectacular untidiness. Sheets of paper were strewn across the floor like confetti from a giant's wedding.

The telescope looked out only at blue sky – maybe that was the point. The dark star, whose dying streamers had been conspicuous even in daytime, was nowhere to be seen.

Beneath the telescope, she found a single piece of paper with a numbered list:

1. Robert Flask?
2. Ambrose Claud(s)?
3. Rootwork.
4. Spring Equinox.
5. Cobbled together.

The first name she found disturbing. Bole had chosen his victims carefully for their knowledge, skills or potential for deception – in

Everthorne's case, all three. In the flurry of events they had overlooked Robert Flask, Oblong's predecessor as the outsider Master of Modern History at Rotherweird School – and the person whose disappearance had coincided with Slickstone's arrival.

The second on the list sounded vaguely familiar. It took her a moment to remember that Fanguin had once bought a book by Ambrose Claud, an eighteenth-century antiquarian, at the Hoy Book Fair. He had never portrayed the book as in any way remarkable, but the plural Clauds was puzzling. More hidden connections?

The third she linked to her recent journey through the roots of the great tree, but any wider significance eluded her.

As to the fourth, the seismic events of recent months had occurred on Midsummer Day and the Winter Solstice, so the Spring Equinox would certainly fit a final curtain call.

The last made no sense, unless to suggest that the other four all interacted.

The isolarion and the eye-recognition device meant these cues had been left for her to find – but would Bolitho have gone to such extreme lengths if he had expected to survive Wynter's return? She recalled the woman's scream beneath the marsh. Morval Seer? She crossed herself and placed the sheet in her trouser pocket.

Orelia continued her search for clues, suspecting Bolitho was testing her. *Only the worthy shall know*. A steel arm with a nib set above a spool of graph paper in a glass case had run a line like a regular heart-beat – until it suddenly fractured into a series of violent loops and stopped. *The dark star's dying moment?* she wondered.

She closed the door, fearing the worst.

As she walked on, the heath gave way to meadowland and the isolarion turned from green to red. In the far distance the river disappeared at the base of a range of hills. She thought she could make out a sluice-like structure, like a mouth with teeth, but she had no wish to investigate. Luck had been ominously generous so far.

Some hours later she recognised the great tree silhouetted against the skyline. There she and Ferensen had faced Ferox-alias-Bole and Sir Veronal Slickstone in the snow. Below the white tile, not far from the river's edge, the grass had been flattened by a circle of shaped stones set in the ground like a pavement. They ran in one direction, but had no grooves and gave no indication of their use.

Enough mysteries for one day. She ran up the slope to the white tile.

They had treated the tiles as bus stops, each serving one route between Lost Acre and Rotherweird, but this time the tile misbehaved, delivering Orelia to a high clearing shadowed by towering yews. Swathes of ferns wore a veneer of frost. A chill mist dampened her face and hair.

She jumped as a bearded countrysider detached himself from a nearby tree trunk. He walked up to her, sank to his haunches and ran his hand across the tile's surface.

'They sicken, or fear sickness to come,' he said. His voice, though mellow, had a distant, matter-of-fact quality and he spoke as if the trees were colleagues and she an interloper. Indeed, he had an arboreal quality himself, his face burnished, trunk solid and tall; even the tow-coloured hair had a spent, autumnal quality. 'Best follow me,' he added.

He moved lightly for his build, with a long stride. Orelia struggled to keep pace. He neither asked why she was here nor who she was, so maybe he knew – or maybe he didn't care.

The path held level until they reached a deep gorge, where a roofed shelter festooned with pulleys and wheels hugged the precipitous slope. The vertical supporting struts were beautifully carved with recognisable insects and birds. Far away a cloud of moisture marked a waterfall. She pointed.

'It feeds the Winterbourne stream,' he said.

'So we're in Rotherweird Westwood,' she murmured, although the landscape was far wilder than she had imagined it would be.

For the first time he turned to look at her. 'Townsfolk never come here, and who can respect what they do not know?'

She ignored the implicit rebuke. 'Did that clearing have a name?'

'Which clearing?'

'Where you found me.' She decided against *where I arrived*, as she could not read him.

'There are several such places.' He knelt and tugged a lever in the decking. A heavy rope coated in pitch snapped up from below. It joined the platform at head height and ran taut across the chasm. He attached a contraption to the rope with hand holds and stirrup-like rests for the feet.

'Don't twist to look at the view,' he warned her. 'Don't lean in or out. Keep the knees together and slightly up. What do you weigh?'

'Average for my height.'

'That's meaningless.' He rummaged in a box of weighted belts.

She indulged an urge to ruffle his deadpan demeanour. 'Naked or dressed?'

'As you are,' he said.

She gave him her weight; he gave her a belt and they shuffled forward to the platform edge.

'Don't be surprised by the acceleration; we need the momentum. The air will sting. And be sure to drop off as soon as we get there.'

She did not take his warnings seriously – as a child she had used a similar device from cliff to beach without a problem – but now the line sagged dramatically as they launched into a break-neck descent. The air slapped her face; her arms shook with the strain. The slower climb up to the receiving platform was in its way worse.

The ordeal was repeated twice more, from woodland over gorge to more woodland. The view opened to the northeast and far, far below on the lower slopes she glimpsed meadows filled with live-stock. She released one hand for a better look – but her remaining arm could not hold her weight and the carrier swung violently.

He twisted, seizing her by the waist as the carriage limped to the finish.

'Bloody fool,' he muttered, as he set off up a steep incline.

'I'm so sorry – thank you—' stammered Orelia.

He did not acknowledge the apology. In silence, he took the path into the deep shadow thrown by the escarpment rim. Welcome handrails appeared at the steepest sections. In failing light they arrived at a planked forecourt illuminated by globe-lights.

'The Witan Hall,' he said.

Columns on either side of a double door had been carved with birds, insects, plants and animals, the motifs complex and intertwined, but without the grotesquery favoured by the Woodworkers' Guild.

'Is this your seat of government?' she asked.

'No, it's our place of refuge. We have dormitories cut into the rock, stocked larders and abundant fresh water. This is the only way in.'

The exterior suggested a modest chamber behind and so it was – but platforms reached by ropes and ladders multiplied to the left and right, leading to narrower doors and more passages. A chimney snaked through the ceiling from a huge fireplace. The twisted flue reminded her of the changelings' treehouse.

A welcome figure strode towards her, arms wide.

'Ferensen!'

'The fire has a most efficient back-burner,' he said. 'Wash off the toil and a little of the grief, then we can talk.'

Oralia gladly accepted the offer. Megan Ferdy appeared and led her to a rudimentary shower cubicle smelling of resin. Simple woollen dresses and shawls hung from pegs. She abandoned her outer clothes: time to renew.

Refreshed in mind and body, she returned to the Hall to find Ferensen installed by the fire.

'My possessions are dispersed I know not where, but I retained one tin of *Black Bodrum Nightraiser Special*,' he said. As they waited for the coffee to brew, he opened bluntly. 'No doubt you have tragedy to report. Wynter always brings death.'

'Why did you abandon us?' blurted Orelia. *Loss has worsened me,* she immediately thought. *No words of welcome, not even a narrative; I open by blaming a friend.* 'I'm not accusing,' she added quickly. 'I just want to understand.'

Ferensen took no exception. 'No need to apologise. I lost myself to the river – it's an addiction; the other half takes over. But thanks to my sister, I'm my old self now. So please, tell me . . .'

She had no wish to say the names out loud, but Ferensen's understanding gave her strength. 'Hayman Salt is dead. An artist called Everthorne, who loved me, is dead, and I fear for Fortemain too.'

Ferensen poured the coffee. 'Fortemain. That is grievous news, but yes, he would be the first casualty.' *A roll-call of the victims of my inertia,* he reflected.

He waved over her guide as he reappeared. 'Orelia, allow me to introduce Gabriel. Gabriel, this is Orelia. I trust you both absolutely and we need shared minds in this complex matter.'

Orelia lacked the will to protest, or even to probe. Without a word, Gabriel sat beside Ferensen and she continued her story.

This time she did not hold back. She told them about Valourhand, how the ice-dragon had immolated Salt, the unexpected mixing-point beneath Rotherweird's marshland, Madge Brown's true identity, the paradox of Bole resurrecting Wynter by killing him, the transportation of Bolitho's observatory to Lost Acre and the mysterious open-air temple.

Ferensen's eyebrows rose and fell, but he did not interrupt. Gabriel sat impassively, with no sign of incredulity.

Once finished, she drained the richly scented coffee.

'So Wynter has Bole's knowledge and Bole has Wynter's appearance,' said Ferensen. 'There may be a weakness there, with so many personalities loose in the one mind. Did they discuss an end objective?'

'The retaking of Rotherweird,' replied Orelia.

'And anything beyond that?'

Orelia shook her head as the tears came suddenly.

'We need more wood for the fire,' Gabriel said, tactfully walking away.

Orelia whispered to Ferensen, 'Bole stole Everthorne's appearance – he seduced me.' She wiped a sleeve across her face. 'I feel abused. Stained.'

Ferensen, a sufferer himself, knew the art of comfort: directness, no soft banalities.

'Was he tender?'

Orelia looked up at him, surprised by the question. 'Yes, very,' she replied, remembering the houseboat, the rugs, the charcoal glowing in the grate, the gentle tilt of the hull.

'Bole does not know tenderness. What survives of Everthorne made love to you. That's all you need to know.'

Orelia pulled herself together, pulled a piece of paper from her pocket and unfolded it. 'What about this? Does it mean anything? I found it in Bolitho's observatory.'

Gabriel returned and built the fire while Ferensen studied Bolitho's enigmatic notes – or, rather to him, Fortemain's.

'Jones' presence here is no surprise.' Ferensen lowered his voice. 'When he brought young Vixen Valourhand to me with her poisoned leg, I knew instantly he had endured the mixing-point. More to the point, when Salt came to my summer entertainment, I realised Jones shared Salt's peculiar aura. Both have played the Green Man.'

'That means Jones is over a thousand years old,' muttered Orelia.

Gabriel broke his silence. 'My parents knew him, and my grand-parents before that. God knows what he's seen over the centuries – and learned.'

'Gabriel owns the land where the white tile sits,' explained Ferensen, 'as did his family before him.'

Ferensen's revelation reassured Orelia. It made sense of Jones' unknown origins, his secrecy and 'play the fool' cover, and his rush to the marsh.

Above their heads, occasional birds had given way to occasional bats. Men, women and children appeared from a passageway above them, some of the adults with bows in hand.

'A sign of the times, alas,' said Ferensen, looking at the weapons.

Orelia suddenly felt homesick. 'I miss my shop,' she said. 'This is the Christmas season – and I've piles of stock to clear.'

Ferensen said gently, 'You're the one witness who can bring Wynter down. You wouldn't last two minutes. They think you're dead, which is not an advantage to throw away lightly. Better to enjoy a Witan Hall Christmas. They're as rare as the purple emperor. We've done it three times in four hundred years – once for a flood, once for a great freeze and now for Wynter's return.'

'You'd best show me round then,' replied Orelia. 'And I'll try to make myself useful; not that child-minding is my forte.'

4

'I return to my own'

To Rotherweirders facing the inexplicable, a stranger promising explanations exercised an irresistible draw. The town's bakers, every family's first port of call, were primed; the curfew was lifted and the Apothecaries flocked from their stronghold.

The name spread as children skipped through the streets chanting the Rotherweird 'Winter' nursery rhyme. The jagged caissons of ice which had so disfigured the river had lost their hard edges to the early sunshine and subsided. Even the sky, bluer than not, bestowed approval. A semblance of tranquillity had been restored.

An early morning post-Winter Solstice sightseeing trip gripped the populace, who traipsed between the vanished observatory, the tower in Market Square, the mysterious octagonal building which had replaced the church and the Hall of the Apothecaries, because Wynter was reputed to be staying there. They wondered what he looked like, this intangible presence who had filled the vacuum left by the spoiled election.

Fanguin knew The Understairs better than most, having taken a keen interest in his poorer charges when a form master. One, now a rickshaw driver, hailed him from the press outside the Hall of the Apothecaries.

'They won't let anyone in, Mr Fanguin.'

'Well, there's a surprise.'

'It's guarded as well as locked.'

He was right: Apothecaries stood at every entrance, although without their lightning sticks. One strode forward. 'Doctor Fanguin, please follow me.'

His admission to the main entrance rewarded an impatient crowd with another talking point: a dismissed schoolmaster welcomed to the inner sanctum of the Apothecaries?

Scry, her back to a blazing fire, greeted Fanguin as he placed his specimen box on the table in the Great Hall.

'Let me guess,' she said. 'They're not creatures of this world.'

'Some are, some aren't. I found *porcellio scaber* and several moults of *oniscus asellus* in a supporting beam – that's two of our five common woodlice, so not so unusual. They suggest the tower was built here. But the fringe of the hole was not.'

'Just the fringe?'

'I used a fishing rod. Lower down, the ferns and moss are Rotherweird through and through. It's as if the top of a cake has been sliced off. There are pulleys below, and vacuum devices, all of local manufacture. The opening in the ground is the exception. It's alien.'

'Very good, Doctor Fanguin. To your hole we can add a vanishing church and observatory.'

The door behind Scry swung open to admit an ascetic-looking man with silver hair in a dun-coloured cloak over the pied clothes of an Apothecary. Despite heavy boots, he moved like a dancer. He exuded experience. If this was Wynter, he had survived hibernation for more than four hundred years with no apparent ill effects.

Fanguin did not hold back. 'I know who you are, and I know what you did.'

Scry, half enraged and half taken aback, glared at Fanguin, but Wynter silenced her with a raised hand.

'You're the victim of a false narrative which I shall shortly refute,' he told Fanguin.

'How false?' responded Fanguin aggressively.

'The inverse of the truth – call it mirror-writing.' Wynter smiled. 'Before long you and I will visit the other place, and like Darwin, we'll unravel her secrets. Now do forgive me, but I've a gospel to deliver.'

Wynter turned on his heels and withdrew, Scry following as if attached by a lead.

Darwin? Wynter, the Elizabethan, could not possibly have absorbed so much so quickly, could he? And yet Scry's deference appeared to authenticate his identity.

Sister Prudence's stern voice intervened. 'Miss Scry said to leave your finds. She'll send further instructions later.'

'I'd like to study them somewhere secure,' said Fanguin, hoping to investigate the inner warrens of the Apothecaries' Hall.

'I'll see you at the Town Hall,' replied Sister Prudence, pointedly showing Fanguin the door.

Above their heads in the Master's Chamber, Scry's proposals fell on stony ground.

'I do *what?*' hissed Thomes.

'It's already organised: six Apothecaries either side of the inside entrance to the Parliament Chamber in a line.'

'Like a guard of bloody honour?'

'As a guard of honour.'

'He's done *nothing* for this town. He's clever, knows some science – all right, quite a lot of science – and he's clearly studied our history inside out, which incidentally makes him a criminal.'

'Trust me,' she replied, 'it's to your benefit.'

Scry chastised herself for overlooking a fundamental question. Worshipping Wynter's memory had conditioned her to see his return as the crowning objective – but what thereafter was the mission for the New Age of the Eleusians? *The Roman Recipe Book* had been filled to the last page long ago.

Maybe his address to the town would provide enlightenment.

5

Filling a Void

The Apothecaries on duty at the Parliament Chamber were, as instructed, firm but courteous. Sister Prudence took the lead. 'Here, Mr Snorkel, Mrs Snorkel. Pride of place goes to our former Mayor, but no interruptions, please.'

Despite smarting from his overnight incarceration, the Snorkels took their seats. His men still dominated the committees of government, and Rotherweird would not tolerate a stranger for long. Novelty wears fast in politics.

Scry showed similar *politesse*. 'Mr Gorhambury, we regret your detention, but it was necessary in the interests of public order.'

'I reserve my position,' replied Gorhambury stiffly, but *what* position? The *Popular Choice Regulations* ended his powers on 'Election Day', not, regrettably, on a conclusive election result. He was the Town Clerk again: from pumpkin to gilded carriage to pumpkin, a victim of lax seventeenth-century draftsmanship.

Another provision troubled Gorhambury: '*In time of war or crisis, where the Mayor is absent or otherwise seriously impaired, the Town Council may elect a Mayor for no less than three months and no more than a year, at the expiry of which period an election must be held.*' The Mayor was absent, in a manner of speaking. The *Regulations* and the return of Wynter dovetailed like a Master Carpenter's joint. What next?

The Guild Masters, Rhombus Smith and the senior Judge were greeted and placed with Gorhambury in the front row. Fanguin, in the second row, glanced round the Chamber. Hayman Salt had perished two nights earlier, attempting to frustrate the ice-dragon, but where were Orelia Roc, Gregorius Jones, Jonah Oblong, Vixen Valourhand and Marmion Finch?

The central platform looked set for a coronation. Snorkel's ornate chair stood alone in the centre as if awaiting a new incumbent. Apothecaries held high multiple tube-lights arranged in pleasing colour combinations around the central dais. Fashioned under Scry's direction, they created an optimistic, almost festive, atmosphere.

And yet . . .

Wynter entered between the two lines of Apothecaries without show, but the atmosphere shifted from expectation to suspicion, even resentment. Eyes narrowed; lips curled; feet shuffled. An outsider had come to lecture Rotherweird – *by what right?* Even the Apothecaries, normally insensitive to opinions other than their own, exchanged anxious glances. Had Scry's influence led Master Thomes astray?

Wynter faced this hostile reception with his usual unfussy calm. 'Please be at ease, ladies and gentlemen of Rotherweird. My name is Geryon Wynter and I return as a founding father to explain these threatening and unique events.'

'You look like a stranger to me,' hissed Mr Norrington, a baker known for his volubility over the counter, and everywhere else.

'Hear, hear!'

'You will find my precise likeness carved in oak on the top of the central pillar in the portico of Escutcheon Place and your future told on coins beneath your feet.' He raised an arm slowly. 'I am not the stranger you think I am.'

The baker's two sons hurried out of the Chamber, their instructions predictable and predicted.

Snorkel supporters from the Town Hall now joined in wagging their fingers like disapproving parents. 'So where's our church gone, Mr Wynter?'

'And what's in its place?'

'I cannot answer that without history,' replied Wynter, which prompted Gorhambury to leap to his feet.

'Then *no*.'

'You mentioned coins,' interrupted Bendigo Sly, Snorkel's leading eavesman. 'Where are they?'

Scry watched and admired; Wynter danced to nobody's tune.

He answered a different question, to hook the crowd. 'They're prophecy coins, to be interpreted rather than spent – they're minted in finest gold, in keeping with their importance.'

That magic monosyllable 'gold' struck deep.

'I said, *where are they?*'

'You did and I heard, Mr Sly, but I prefer your interest to your avarice.' The shift in tone of voice was faint, but discernible.

The audience wondered how a stranger could read Sly so well. 'But as you ask,' Wynter continued, 'Market Square has a central hexagonal cobblestone, which I call the heart of the town. Lift it.'

Three men left with Bendigo Sly on this new mission, just as the two breathless boys returned. Relishing the attention, the baker's sons delivered their report.

'His face *is* there, on the column, just as he said.'

'How do you mean "*his* face"?' asked the baker.

''ere and 'ere,' said the eldest, tapping his cheekbones and eye sockets.

'And the 'air,' added the other, 'it's that 'igh on the 'ead and swept back.'

'Freshly carved,' said Norrington. 'It's a trick.'

His two sons shook their heads. 'It's old wood, Pa, for real,' said one.

'Grey and cracked like the rest of it,' added the other.

Across the Chamber, Mr Blossom, the portly Master of the Metalworkers, rose ponderously. 'Perhaps you can tell us why *The Thingamajig* shattered?' he asked.

'No flash and no bang must mean no bomb,' ventured Wynter, as if he had been there. 'Did anything else happen at the same time?'

'The quake!' cried a mix of male and female voices.

'So Nature herself is your saboteur. The forces that moved the rock under your feet shook the stones above your head, turning ballot-balls into cannonballs.'

'More hokum,' cried the baker. 'Whoever heard of an airquake?'

'He's a fraud,' jeered a member of Snorkel's circle.

'But a clever one,' Snorkel whispered to Mrs Finch on his left.

'*You* would know,' interrupted Mrs Snorkel, irritated by her husband's insatiable interest in Mrs Finch and her *décolletage*. She glanced across, but, for once, the Herald's wife was ignoring her admirer's attentions. She appeared transfixed by the newcomer, who was dismissing a threatening surge from the aisles with a raised right hand.

'We also have an unexpected visitor. Mr Fanguin will explain.'

Reacting to Wynter's informed benevolence and his own resurgence in status, Fanguin was beginning to doubt Ferensen's narrative and the Elizabethan trial record. Perhaps Ferensen had abandoned them for fear of the truth emerging? But he remained wary; Wynter was almost *too* informed.

He ascended the dais, collected his specimen box from Scry and chose his words carefully. 'I've never met Mr Wynter before today. But I *did* find a most unusual creature in the grass by the new tower in Market Square.'

Fanguin returned to his place. Wynter slid open the glass lid. A mantis-like insect, big as a fist, clambered out on stilt-like legs. It stalked the tabletop, head swivelling full circle. Momentarily, it disappeared, blending exactly, a chameleon mantis, before rejecting disguise as unnecessary.

Ooohs and *aaahs* swirled around the Chamber.

'I call it a mantoleon,' said Wynter, 'but beware – this miniature scout may have a giant parent.'

More disbelief: an unusual creature, true, but small – Fanguin the disgraced biologist must have provided it himself. The mantoleon abruptly halted its exploration of the tabletop. Wings sprouted from its thorax and the insect took off, swooping along the rows of seats with a scissory hum. Several stood, vainly swatting at the insect with sticks and umbrellas, until it soared high into the roof and smashed through a high window. Shards of glass sprinkled the audience below. The mantoleon had taken flight.

'That's a troubling sign,' said Wynter. 'I do believe it was counting you.'

Cries of outrage greeted this analysis. Sister Prudence gave a curt hand signal to the Apothecaries surrounding the rostrum. Wynter was losing his grip.

'This outsider is behind all this!' cried Norrington, prompting a second surge towards the platform, but Sly returned just in time and pushed his way through the crowd, followed by his three assistants, who were carrying a small chest of oak banded in iron. Sly flourished the cobblestone with a rounded hexagonal head, which he had lifted from the centre of Market Square. They placed their findings on the table beside Wynter.

'Where you said, like you said, but the chest won't open,' said Sly.

Those who had left their seats stopped in their tracks. Snorkel scowled. He and his forbears had always controlled the importation of gold. By rights, he should be opening the chest, not this interloper. But the depth of Wynter's planning troubled him. He would not be a pushover.

Wynter held up the chest like a communion chalice.

'A most intricate and ancient lock, but as you do not accept me *yet*, let someone you trust describe it. Mr Gorhambury . . . ?'

Gorhambury succumbed to the compliment and examined the chest from all sides. 'The oak is tightly fitted and the iron strong. The discolouration suggests great age. I shall ask Mr Blossom to describe the lock.'

The Master of the Metalworkers waddled up, happy to be making a second contribution. He gave Wynter a wary look, peered at the lock with a magnifying glass, applied a screwdriver for some minutes and delivered his verdict. 'The chest is ancient and finely made, but our Guild and the Woodworkers could rustle one up with no trouble. The lock is a different matter. It is keyless, of Rotherweird manufacture, late sixteenth century. Most unusually for its time, the rotating numbers have been protected from grime and rust by a glass panel, which I shall now remove.'

After a brief pause he continued, 'The wheels, numbers one to nine, still rotate freely.' Mr Blossom could not resist a display of arithmetical expertise. 'The odds of chancing on the right combination at the first attempt are, of course, one in ten thousand.' He rolled the numbers. 'Not my lucky day.'

'Ask Clever Clogs,' cried the baker, poking a finger at Wynter.

'Yes, sound advice indeed, you should always ask me. As I said, the chest holds prophecy coins. And as I am your future, we can expect the combination to be the date of my arrival: 2-2-1-2, the day after the Winter Solstice.' Wynter spoke with such certainty that the click of the sprung latch came as no surprise.

'Mr Blossom, be so good as to describe the contents.'

The Master of the Metalworkers produced each coin with a flourish and laid them on the table in a line.

'Unmistakably gold,' he said, after examining one through octagonal tortoiseshell spectacles, 'and little need for spit and polish. Eight in all, with Mr Wynter's head on all but one.'

'No, *seven*,' replied Wynter without even looking.

'I *can* count, Mr Wynter.'

Wynter's face whipped round, the first disconcerted action in a hitherto polished performance. He flipped the coins like a croupier turning cards. There were eight, and one coin did indeed lack his likeness. He gave a dismissive aside – 'They are for *you* to interpret . . .' – and marched out.

The Apothecaries, taken by surprise, followed. Scry remained, gripped by curiosity: what stories might the prophecy coins tell?

Pandemonium ensued. The Goldsmiths claimed ownership, as did Sly for the last incumbent Mayor. The Master of the Toymakers proposed equal division between the Guilds, hardly a solution with eight coins and twelve Guilds. Rhombus Smith proposed the Herald, but a quick search revealed that Finch was neither in the Chamber nor at home.

Scry shook her head at this crude focus on ownership. She peered at every coin within reach and listened for every clue. Wynter's face appeared in varied poses and expressions: *I rule you in all my moods.* The images on the obverse were more cryptic.

As physical manhandling broke out, Scry hammered the table with her fist and shrieked, 'Silence!' Two coins tinkled on their return to the tabletop.

'You brought this Wynter in,' shouted back the baker, 'you and the Apothecaries. Why should we listen to you?'

'You're an oaf who should know better,' she retorted. 'Buildings vanish, machines explode, new buildings rise from the earth – and you dismiss the only person who offers an explanation. As to the coins, the Town Hall archivist should have custody. Do you agree, Mr Gorhambury?'

Gorhambury rose to the challenge. 'Under paragraph 3(5)(vi)(b) of the *Treasure Trove Regulations*, all valuables excavated within the town precincts – other than books – belong to the Town Hall. And in terms of personal custody that means our archivist, Mr Jeavons.'

Gorhambury in appearance embodied the essence of a town clerk. Jeavons matched his role as exactly. The short stature, beaky face and tapering fingers implied the delicate touch required for handling old municipal records. He wore a purple velvet jacket over a green waistcoat, both adorned with brass buttons embossed – for no particular reason – with hunting horns. Pince-nez sat askew on the bridge of an aquiline nose.

'Make way for Jeavons, make way for Jeavons,' he squeaked. From his pocket he produced a clutch of velvet pouches with woven silver drawstrings. He lovingly placed each coin in a separate pouch while delivering a mini-sermon on the demands of his office.

'Research requires concentration; concentration requires no distractions, and no distractions means solitude. I shall post my conclusions on the Town Hall noticeboard on Christmas Eve.'

With his anti-climactic announcement, the archivist left with the tiptoe walk of a burglar.

Gorhambury followed close behind. In his experience, gold and foul play tended to operate in tandem.

With more muttering than rational discussion, the Chamber dispersed.

Outside, the weather dithered, patches of blue striving to repel thickening cloud. It remained bitterly cold. Fanguin and Boris, blowing their hands between exchanges, could find no explanation for the worrying absence of their friends. They moved on to their reading of the morning's events.

'That eighth coin changed his face like a glove puppet, temperate summer to tropical storm,' said Fanguin, noting that his wife was heading back to the Hall of the Apothecaries – to mix Elizabethan pre-prandials, presumably.

'Wynter can't have buried them,' reflected Boris. 'He'd been executed in the mixing-point before Market Square even existed.'

'He knew . . .' Fanguin corrected himself. 'He *thought* he knew their number and their messages.'

'He and Bole pre-planned it. The coins are there to ease his return to power.' Boris paused. The coins were assuming real importance. 'The obverse must predict what he will bring to pass. He wishes to be king and shaman.'

'But who added the eighth? Ferensen never mentioned coins

to me. And, assuming we believe him, he never returned to Rotherweird until Midsummer Day.'

'I trust you're not falling for this rigmarole.'

Fanguin ignored the gentle rebuke. 'Morval Seer, marooned in the body of a spider, is obviously out. That leaves only our good friend Fortemain, alias Bolitho.'

Boris dissented, more on instinct than rational grounds. 'I think Fortemain favours direct action, when not indulging in celestial science. Remember he recalled Oxenbridge to thwart Wynter and became a moleman: both practical steps. This feels more like someone on Wynter's plane, combating his use of myth and mystery with a touch of the same.'

Defeated by one puzzle, they moved to another.

'If you're right, Boris, the coins will tell us what Wynter's planning. How well do you know Jeavons?'

'Well enough. Leave him to me.'

'I did see two of them. Number three had a hand seizing a snake; and number seven a body climbing out of a grave.'

'Hardly encouraging,' replied Boris. 'I saw a more seasonal touch on number four: a sprig of mistletoe.'

'Curiouser and curiouser,' replied Fanguin.

6

The Foreign Coin

Wynter walked back to the Hall of the Apothecaries at a brisk pace. He, or rather Calx Bole, whose knowledge and experience he had absorbed, had buried the coins at dead of night, when Market Square was nearing completion, four centuries ago. Had Rotherweird allowed study of her history, citizens would have known that a Master Carver had proposed a hexagonal stone to represent the heart of the emerging town. He admired the sophistication of Bole's planning, but Bole's memories held no explanation for this headless intruder.

Thomes hastened alongside. He had been in thrall to Wynter by the end of dinner the night before; now his support was wavering.

'You had them and you lost them – and why release that grotesque insect? Cheap stunts never work here.'

'Do you know the meaning of the word "revelation", Master Thomes?' Wynter spoke the word 'Master' as if it were the junior form of Mister.

'I do believe I do,' replied Thomes testily.

'I don't mean rabbits from hats, I mean a true Revelation: a transforming truth, a new god, a new history obliterating all that has gone before.'

'I have a word for the source of such revelations,' responded Thomes. 'A megalomaniac.'

Wynter would not be goaded. 'Be useful, Master Thomes. What do you make of the coins?'

'I know Jeavons. He's a fastidious perfectionist. Most gold substitutes are magnetic; gold is not. He has age-tests for everything from bronze to paper. He'll sniff you out in no time. We're not stupid, Mr Wynter.'

'I would never have returned here if you were. Now, best not to irritate, Master. I asked for your opinion.'

'You got them there somehow.'

'Did you see the coin with a name?'

Thomes had. It made no sense. 'Escharion.'

'There's no such word,' muttered Wynter, for once sounding fretful.

'How would you know?' asked Thomes.

'I read ancient Greek, and I speak it. I could converse with Achilles. As it's not a real word, it must be a mix of words to describe something unique. "Eschatos" means last in Greek, and "eschatology" is the study of death or the soul or the final destiny of man.'

'What about the "-arion" bit?'

'*Clario* is Latin and Middle English for trumpet, and an organ stop with similar qualities.'

'Just what I thought,' said Thomes in a know-it-all voice. 'Nobody would invest so much effort for a concept. It must refer to a rare and valuable object.' A thought struck him: Wynter or an agent of his had placed the seven coins in their underground vault in Market Square. They were numbered, so the seven coins illustrated the story Wynter wished to tell about himself, no doubt with the props and supporting cast already in place. But the eighth had been an unwelcome coda, hence Wynter's anxiety.

He could not resist a deft prod at Wynter's vanity. 'Escharion will come at the end, when you least expect it,' he added with a smirk.

'At the end – *at the end*, Master Thomes – your parents must have neglected your prayers! A world *without* end – that's what we all aspire to. Only no man or god has ever delivered such a thing.'

Master Thomes found the reply oddly reassuring. Madmen never last.

Wynter returned to his room. Toying with the townsfolk had served his myth and his purpose: an immortal, unrecognised, returns to claim his birthright. Their scepticism would deepen to belief later. Yet a new mind in an old body demanded rest after its first outing. On the bed, Scry had laid out a white shirt and black trousers. She had measured him in the morning, down and across, as if for a coffin. She had not lost her gift for decisive action.

After an hour of dreamless sleep, he woke. A splash of white caught his eye. A writing desk, raked like a schoolboy's, held a single sheet of paper. The writing, its ornament as precise as a baroque trill, he recognised as Calx Bole's. Yet Bole was dead and he, Geryon Wynter, had absorbed Bole's knowledge and experience. The message was unsettling:

My pen I give to you that shall succeed me in my pilgrimage.
Escharion is an intruder, placed by the enemy, so hunt it down.

Or had he written it – at least physically? *My pen I give to you.* Who else could replicate Bole's script so exactly? The implications, layers on layers, unnerved him. The town and its denizens had held no surprises, because he had acquired from Bole a unique centuries-deep navigational guide – but had he acquired more than knowledge? What of Bole's own will and ambitions?

He shrugged off the concerns. Bole had been an exemplary servant in every way, hence his self-sacrifice. Some cerebral misfire had caused this aberration. It would not happen again.

Like a splash of rain on the forehead, dripped from an over-head tree, an image came unbidden: a cage swinging beneath the mixing-point as a lithe young woman slipped from it into the grass, naked, leaving a monstrous creature behind her.

A desire rooted, germinated, blossomed. He must have his chronicler back.

7

Actions and Reactions

That night Jeavons completed his assay on the coins. He wrote a detailed report for the files and a pithy version for popular consumption.

A gentle knock on the door announced Madge Brown, as ever courtesy itself. 'On behalf of the Artefacts Committee, Mr Jeavons, I'd like to draw the first coin, if I may. You might use one in your public report.'

Normally possessive of his materials, Jeavons succumbed; if only Mrs Jeavons were so polite. Brown had brought pen and ink. She drew slowly and precisely, the contours conveyed by subtle shading.

'I would release one at a time in their numerical order,' she said. 'You'll get more attention that way and it's high time your department was given due recognition. And it'll take me time to do the lot.'

Jeavons purred.

Across the street, Snorkel, in earnest conversation with Sly, was deploying less diplomatic language. 'Where's that fucker Finch when you need him?' Snorkel leaned over a long table in the study in the Mayor's grace-and-favour apartment, voted to Snorkel by a well-packed Finance Committee within weeks of his first election. His pudgy fingers flicked out a long scroll. 'There are no Wynters on the electoral roll in my time, or my father's. He's a ten-carat impostor and the coins are a set-up. It's time we played tough, or you and I, Sly, are going to have our bums royally wrenched from the butter.'

Snorkel summoned a flunky with the vigorous shake of a silver bell and barked, 'Get the box from the fridge.'

Sly offered comfort. 'He has not done enough, Your Worship. The Guilds won't wear him. Nor will the people. He's an outsider, for God's sake.'

'So was that bastard Slickstone.'

'You saw him off.'

'Then I was Mayor, now I'm not.'

The flunky returned and handed over a slim wooden box wrapped in a cloth which smoked like a living presence.

'Keep it in your freezer until the *moment juste* arrives,' Snorkel told Sly. 'An anonymous gift. Indeed, Sly, this handover is not happening. If you're ever asked, you were given it by the North Tower for safekeeping.'

'To be deployed when?'

'If and when conventional means fail. You'll know.'

Sly disliked the grime of negotiation, but it had to be done. 'Your Worship, Mrs Sly has a cultured eye for fine jewellery, which requires occasional acts of munificence.'

'The Snorkel Foundation supports well-chosen investment.'

'Ruby earrings, to be exact, four hundred guineas.'

Snorkel turned to the flunky, a man in his fifties, a retainer of the old school. 'We did not hear that, did we, Dawson. Mrs Sly should set up a charity for rheumatoid fishermen.'

Sly avoided the Golden Mean as too conspicuous for a man with the future in the crook of his arm. Potential labels for his modest place in Rotherweird's Index of Notables came and went: *Henchman (see*

Snorkel); *Fixer (see Snorkel)*; *Eavesman (for Snorkel)*. He scowled. There had been material benefits, but little recognition.

A new label caused him to lengthen his stride and stand tall: *Sly the Kingmaker*.

8

A Visit to the Butcher

Rotherweird's premier butchers lay west of Market Square, close to the first stairwell to Aether's Way. Sides of beef and cured hams hung from hooks above delicacies in rows of trays – pâtés, black pudding, sweetbreads, kidney, hearts and liver, and a rich variety of sausages; a mosaic of blood and skin, each pithily described on spiked wooden tallies.

Following the quake, a click had afflicted the refrigeration unit, as if a rotor were chaffing the mesh. Mr Cutts, for all his vigour with a cleaver, was a punctilious observer of the *Meat Hygiene Regulations*. He woke as its rhythm appeared to change. Would the rotor fracture? Visions of losing his stock to contamination on the very eve of Christmas assailed him.

Twice he checked his descent on the stairs. The click had now acquired an accompaniment, a grating squeak, like a knife on glass.

'Horace, what *are* you up to?' muttered Mrs Cutts into her pillow.

As his gaze rested on the shop below, Cutts froze. An unnatural grey-green triangular skull bobbed outside the shop-front window, illuminated by the gas-lamp across the street. A mask, he would have said, only this skull had eyes, flipping open and shut, and viscous saliva dripping from its jaws.

The threat to his livelihood ousted any sense of caution. He ran down the remaining stairs, waving his arms and crying, 'Piss off!'

The next words tailed away as the skull acquired context. At least eight tall, spindly legs with spurred joints supported a long-ribbed body, all the colour of old bones. The monstrosity resembled the insect let loose by Wynter in the Town Hall the previous morning – but magnified beyond measure. Mesmerised, he shuffled closer. The window's glass had been cut as if by a skater's blade, so explaining the squeaking noise. The chiselled line formed a perfect equilateral triangle, *the shape of the creature's head.*

The realisation came too late. The skull-like face on its prehensile neck hurtled forward and decapitated the unfortunate Mr Cutts in a shower of glass, before gorging itself on this alien's magnificent larder.

In a nearby alleyway, Scry restrained her posse of Apothecaries.

Welcome to Wynter's world: heroes against monsters and lessons learned in blood. Tonight's gospel would be clear: you listen to the Master.

Random barn owls apart, the markings for Rotherweird's night music fluctuated between *pianissimo* and silence. The violent percussion of falling glass and Mrs Cutts' screams woke neighbours far and wide. They emerged, took stock, retreated, and re-emerged with sticks, cricket bats, pruning shears and even frying pans.

Still Scry waited. The Apothecaries behind her, mostly young, looked anything but heroic. She divided them into two groups of six.

'Go up Plato's Alley, where you'll find Mr Wynter, then head down from Market Square. We move up from here. The joints are its weak spot, but be sure to leave the kill to Mr Wynter. If anyone falls, recalibrate your conductor-stick to connect with your new neighbour.' Scry felt liberated. Delivering dry prophecies paled beside making them come good in His cause.

Wynter heard more than he saw from the anonymity of Plato's Alley, a narrow footpath between back-to-back houses which turned at right angles into the Golden Mean just south of Market Square. This first prophecy coin was not without risk to him and the whole enterprise, but thrones are for risk-takers. Answer the sphinx, challenge the suitors, slay the Nemean lion and whomsoever or whatsoever the great cosmic clock places in your path. Well, not quite in this instance; Bole had arranged tonight's challenge.

A clack on the cobblestones announced the Apothecaries trotting towards him.

Think Argonauts, he mused, *think the Geats in Beowulf's mead hall, think Ulysses' crew: all givers of life to gild their master's legend.*

Fanguin arrived at the Golden Mean clutching a rope, to find bodies and ripped animal carcasses disfiguring the street. Around him, makeshift weapons were making little impression on the chitin-hard casing of the mantoleon's limbs and body. Applying fired pitch to the creature's legs did no better.

Jones would have been Fanguin's first choice of recruit, Valourhand the second, but neither were there, so he chose a young man from The Understairs, a former pupil. Strong and nimble, Brocas, a cobble-layer by trade, evaded the mantoleon's lunges with a matador's grace.

'I've an idea,' shouted Fanguin. 'We wrap the rope round a back leg and then you run around and around, keeping it tight. Then we truss him up like Gulliver.'

Brocas looked unconvinced.

'It worked with a giraffe, according to a book I read. Just keep to one side in case it kicks.'

The rear legs anchored the mantoleon, which helped Fanguin's first stage as the creature could not reach directly behind, but running the rope around the forelegs in full sight was fraught with peril. However, others quickly grasped the strategy and bravely did their best to distract the beast.

Scry scowled in disapproval. Fanguin's ingenuity was threatening to unravel everything. She rushed her team up the Golden Mean as Wynter, looking down the road, simultaneously reached the same conclusion.

He switched on his conductor-stick. 'Follow me,' he ordered, and the two groups closed, lightning arcing between their sticks to create an inescapable cordon. The crowd of jostling attackers backed away, Brocas included.

Three Apothecaries fell, but the broken arc quickly realigned and started cutting through the creature's joints like wire through cheese. The mantoleon threshed and shrieked, only to crumple as Wynter delivered the *coup de grâce*, severing its head with a single strike.

Think of skeleton warriors born of the dragon's teeth, think of Medusa, think of Grendel; think of Jason, Perseus and Beowulf – *and* think of Wynter.

The onslaught of extremes of image, smell and experience – the monster, the violence, the horror, the fear and the excitement, the iron tang of fresh blood, a victory against the odds – found release in a deafening outburst of applause as the survivors shook their weapons and cried 'Wynter ... Wynter!' Windows opened down the Golden Mean like a grotesque advent calendar as protruding women and children joined the chorus of praise.

One figure did not cheer. She knelt by the mantoleon's body, her half-open dressing gown revealing a white nightdress beneath, both speckled with blood, red and green. She picked up a hatchet from the cobbles and hacked two spurs off one of the creature's legs. She walked to Wynter and offered one with both hands.

'Your trophy.'

There was more cheering, but still the woman did not smile.

High priestesses don't smile, thought Fanguin. *This is role-play*. In the half-light and incongruous setting, he could not place the woman. She was neither young nor old, with dark *intense* hair coiling down her neck.

Fanguin moved closer, recognising the woman as she turned, walked north up the Golden Mean and disappeared. It was Mrs Finch. Her petty snobbery had turned feral.

Magisterially, Wynter moved among the bereaved and the wounded, offering thanks for their sacrifice and consolation. Gorhambury, unobtrusive in a grey overcoat over a grey and white striped nightgown, more escaped prisoner than Town Clerk, administered the practicalities, summoning stretchers and doctors, clearing the debris.

The next morning Jeavons placed on the Town Hall noticeboard his assay report, declaring that the seven numbered coins had been minted centuries ago, by the same hand. The eigth was of a similar vintage, but from a different smithy.

Beneath, there appeared a meticulous drawing of both sides of the first coin, Wynter's head on one, on the other the Roman numeral I above a strikingly realistic representation of the mantoleon, its head floating free of its body.

All as foretold.

IN TOWN

I

Checks and Balances

Boris managed to assemble six Guild Masters for a meeting in *The Journeyman's Gist* at eleven, an hour before noonday opening. The other five declined. Bill Ferdy provided coffee, the Bakers an assortment of *patisserie*.

'We'll get nowhere without all of us,' said the Master Mixer. 'Only a united front will stop the Apothecaries. I'm all for Wynter, but those bastards are riding on his coattails.'

The Mixers had long loathed the Apothecaries for stealing their rightful name.

Boris held fire. After the prophecy coins and the town's deliverance from the mantoleon, Wynter had become the favoured candidate for the vacancy left by the spoiled election. If only Orelia had not disappeared. During her electoral campaign, she had listened to the Guilds, unlike Snorkel and Strimmer, and her stock remained high. Plan B required delicate presentation.

Master Silversmith took over.

'I've consulted the walking encyclopaedia,' he said. 'In time of emergency, which I take to include earthquake, a monster and an exploding ballot box, the Guilds can elect a temporary Mayor, provided ten of their twelve Courts are unanimous.'

Boris too had consulted Gorhambury. The Silversmith, whether by accident or design, had neglected the small print. He dropped in the critical words casually as if adding a pinch of salt to a stew.

'But only on terms which protect the people's fundamental rights and privileges under this constitution.'

'What does that mean?' asked the Master Silversmith suspiciously. *'You're* Deputy Mayor? Is that the plot?'

'God forbid,' replied Boris. 'But we need to keep the constitutional checks and balances. Wynter is an outsider. You never know.'

He had sown the seed. He sat back, allowing others to claim the idea, and ordered a round of Sturdy.

'How about a Council with a right of veto?' suggested the Master Baker.

'There's a problem there,' intervened the Master Mixer. 'The Apothecaries would dominate. You saw what happened on the Island Field. We'll be enjoying Prim's hospitality ourselves in no time.'

'That's a risk we'll have to take.' The Mistress Milliner, the only woman present, had silver hair and a mind as precise as her stitching. She turned to Boris. 'Master Fireworker, this Council is your suggestion. What do you say?'

'Wynter is an honorary Apothecary. He stays in their Hall. They provide his personal guard. The Apothecaries cannot sit on the Council.' Boris had memorised the Regulation. *'No person and no representative of any Guild may sit on any Committee or other body where they have a general conflict of interest and must withdraw from any vote or debate in which they have a particular interest.* If we impose that condition at the outset, Wynter has little option but to accept.'

'Very Gorhambury. Very right and proper,' commented the Mistress Milliner.

'What about the others?' asked the Master Baker.

'A Council without the Apothecaries! They'd be here like a shot – and all in favour – if they knew.'

Nobody disagreed. Bill arrived with a tray of pint glasses and swapped them for the empty coffee mugs.

Boris stood. 'A toast to checks and balances,' he said.

They followed suit, hands lifted high.

The Mistress Milliner added a salutary coda under her breath.

'Remembering there's theory and there's practice,' she murmured.

2

Advent Windows

Outsiders had Advent calendars; Rotherweird had Advent windows. Every property, The Understairs included, entered the ballot for twenty-four different addresses, chosen by the spin of a barrel and then supplied in strict confidence to the appointed artist. On production of a municipal 'Advent warrant', the proprietor was obliged to tender the topmost window of their tower or house, where a backlit blind with a suitably seasonal illustration would be installed for display during the hours of darkness. Adults and children scoured the streets in search of every evening's new window through to Christmas Eve.

In recent years, however, interest had diminished, for Snorkel, fearful of satire, had appointed an artist whose saccharine images had only grown in dullness and repetition.

For Gorhambury, in a childhood blighted by poverty, the Advent windows had acquired a near-mystical significance and he deeply resented their descent into banality. During his interregnum, he 'retired' the artist, Gilbert Gibbins, and appointed Ember Vine, Rotherweird's best-known single mother and sculptress. Ember in turn engaged her sixteen-year-old daughter Amber at a guinea a day, in part to keep her from mischief and in part for her left-field ideas.

Vine opened with a baffled dodo emerging from a speckled egg with a motto above the number 1: *The last shall be first*. The second of December moved operations to The Understairs, an attic window in a teetering block off Hamelin Way festooned in balconies.

The tenant, a young Town Hall cleaner, plied Vine with coffee and advice. 'The balcony blocks the view, I'm afraid, and we can hardly move it.'

'Come on, Mum,' said Amber, 'this is a dimensional puzzle and you're a sculptor.'

In the single room, shelves bowed under the weight of home-made mechanicals, including a jack-in-a-box.

Ember smiled. She had it. 'Can you do me thin wire, a good spring and a clockwork timer?'

On the following evening and thereafter every half hour from dusk to midnight, an illuminated jack-in-a-box face sprang out and over the balcony, then retracted. The features were unmistakably Snorkel's, caught in an attitude of surprise. His habitual rudeness to the lowly had rebounded.

Word spread and the traditional draw of the Advent windows revived.

Number twenty-three, the top floor of a tower overlooking Aether's Way, brought a different challenge. They climbed eight flights of bare boards to a single door on a pinched landing. Ember knocked twice without response, but when Amber tried the door, it opened. They entered a large all-purpose space: bedroom, kitchen-ette and study. Ember turned on the gaslights as Amber rotated on the spot in the middle of the room. She had fashioned a detection game for these visits to unfamiliar rooms.

'Single occupier, female and fit . . .' she started.

All safe conclusions, given the row of polished shoes and the skipping rope.

Ember's turn; she rotated too. 'She's mathematical, practical, one of the Summoned, and tidy to the point of mania.'

In support of this last proposition, she pointed to the perfect alignment of shoes and the child's bear, nose and ears much repaired, sitting dead centre of the bed. On the study table, screwdrivers and metal pieces had been sorted by type and size like stowed cutlery.

'*One of the Summoned* – I challenge that,' said Amber.

'It's the print.'

A single etching of a German university, gothic spires illustrated in intricate detail, hung above the study table, again dead centre. It bore a date, 1684, an obvious breach of the *History Regulations*, which no resident would dare to make.

Amber ran to the wall beside the door, peering at a row of horizontal pencil lines grouped close together at head height. Dates had been recorded in numerals beside them.

'She measures herself every week.' She pursed her lips. 'I think she's getting smaller, or at least she's afraid she is.' Now intrigued, Amber skipped over to the calendar beside the bed. 'She's ticked the days off until the twenty-first, then there's nothing.'

'The Winter Solstice,' said Ember Vine. 'Election and Earthquake Day.'

'And she studies spheres,' added Amber.

Ember declined to speculate on potential connections between her own anonymous commission to sculpt a sphere and their absent hostess. She unpacked her brushes and paints, spread the white blind open on the floor and opened her mind. She liked an Advent window to reflect the room behind it.

'Be a dear and brew us some coffee.'

With pencil first, then brush, an image formed: a woman's face, shrouded in a blue cowl, looking down with only the bridge of the nose and upper eyelids visible; the hint of an oval face.

'Who's that?' asked Amber, flicking the kettle's oscillator.

Ember had no idea. 'A Madonna looking down?'

Amber gave her mother an appraising look. The previous twenty-two days of December had been unremittingly secular.

'It just came,' her mother added.

On a shelf an exquisite porcelain rose with green stem and leaves and a carmine bloom rested on a sheet of paper.

'Where's Spring Steps?' asked Amber.

'It's a back street in Hoy, close to the church.'

'Something matters at number three.'

The kettle started to bubble – only to stall as the temperature plummeted. Amber looked to the windows, front and back, but both were firmly closed. The tongues of gaslight dimmed. She felt an occupying presence – *her* bed, *her* bear, *her* shoes and *her* room.

Oblivious, Ember's brushes dipped and skipped across the blind-to-be at unnatural speed. Amber had a fleeting view of foreign landscape, black-and-white, flickering like old film. The usual disciplines, time and space, had lost their grip.

'She's here,' whispered Amber. 'She's warning us.'

Still the artist's fingers danced. Only the image mattered: the town must *know*.

All change.

The kettle piped its song; the gas-lamps resumed a steady light. A dimensional fracture had healed.

Ember examined her work, a young woman with enough detail to tantalise, not enough to identify.

'You did feel that?'

'Feel what, dear?'

'You saw nothing?'

'I saw what I painted.'

'She's dead, Mum, *unnaturally* dead. I saw her in silhouette, disappearing in mid-air.'

'Say nothing to anyone,' replied her mother.

They hung the blind, installed the timer-light behind and, in deference to the prevailing tidiness, washed and dried their mugs.

On Advent window twenty-three the town was divided. One camp dismissed it as obscure and bereft of its predecessors' wit.

The other lauded the cowled face as thought-provoking and refreshingly spiritual.

The following morning Ember Vine visited *Baubles & Relics* to discover that Orelia Roc, her chosen confidante, had also vanished.

Where now?

3

A Hollow Christmas

Christmas, a time of healing, drew the people in. Every year Guilds and cottage industries achieved novelty from mechanicals to indoor fireworks, from high fashion to Vlad's newest brandy. In addition to the Advent windows, seasonal carvings adorned windows, balconies and staircases inside and out.

On Christmas night three life-sized mechanicals, bare-armed caricatures of countrysiders, each with a mattock or hoe in hand, jerked into life at the Ten-Mile Post, commencing their journey to town. Their robotic tread was scheduled to end in Market Square at dusk on New Year's Eve. Each by tradition carried a capacious casket, filled by countrysiders with fruit, vegetables and seed: their homage to the town. Their kneecaps had a polished sheen from years of rubbing by the town's populace in search of luck for the coming year.

But other human rituals had been derailed. There were no last-minute visits to *Baubles & Relics* for stocking-fillers, and no church. Religious Rotherweirders paradoxically took this last setback in their stride as a miracle yet to be explained, but the agnostic majority, who attended only on feast days, bemoaned a lost fixture in the social calendar. The sealed octagon presented nothing but unpleasing stark modernity.

Wynter moved among the townsfolk, amiable and austere, not pressing his case.

Early on Boxing Day morning, Jeavons released Madge Brown's

drawing of the second prophecy coin: Wynter's head on one side, the Town Hall on the other.

Refuse me if you dare.

The last meeting had ended in acrimony, Wynter spared violence only by the diverting arrival of the prophecy coins. But his starring role in the mantoleon's defeat had transformed the dynamics. The scapegoat had turned saviour and was not, in truth, an outsider at all.

Wynter positioned himself well away from the Apothecaries this time. Gorhambury was to put the motion. Outside, Market Square was packed, with The Understairs well represented on this public holiday.

Oblong had spent Christmas at the Polks. Miss Trimble's canoodling with Boris, not to mention their magnetic attraction to mistletoe, had irked him, mostly as a reminder of his own unattached state, although Bert's children had provided compensation.

He had held back his 'exclusive' until after lunch, as soon as the children had dispersed.

'I went to *The Journeyman's Gist* straight after the election,' he started.

'You breached the curfew!' exclaimed Boris in mock outrage.

'Ever so brave,' added Miss Trimble, patting Boris' thigh.

'Geryon Wynter was there and I met him, pretty well one to one. He was surprisingly charming – well, compared to Strimmer.'

'Did he give anything away?'

'Only his wish to address us.'

The subject stalled as Bert hammered the table with both fists. 'Now, now, this is Christmas. No politics!'

Oblong's diary recorded these events in mundane terms (*turkey and crackers, bread sauce from Miss Trimble. Beware Vlad's plum brandy, odd hallucination*). He had stayed over Christmas night in a hammock in the Eureka room. Peering from the main window he had glimpsed two silhouettes on an adjacent roof, both coated and scarfed. One was unmistakably Boris, but when the other turned, Oblong blinked and blinked again in disbelief. A wide-brimmed hat floated free of the shoulders: Boris was standing beside a man with no head.

He opened the window for a better view and the apparitions vanished.

4

A Warning Ignored

As an excitable town was heading for the Parliament Chamber for a final decision on the Mayoralty, an ominous warning sounded from the heavens in Market Square. A disembodied voice, recognisably that of the Town Crier, Portly Bowes, spoke from a clear blue sky:

> *Who forged his golden coins and why?*
> *True prophecies can also lie,*
> *Guinea pigs, we spin and choose –*
> *Heads he wins and tails you lose.*

Despite its repetition from every corner of the Square and the ethereal quality of delivery from thin air, few gave the cryptic message weight. They suspected a South Tower trick, and, more to the point, where had Mr Bowes been when the mantoleon had struck?

Oblong made his way to the middle tier of the Chamber. He saw no sign of Everthorne; he half-hoped the artist, with his good looks and creative energy, had returned home. More worrying, Jones and Orelia were still missing.

Gorhambury fiddled with the knot on his tie. Wynter had engaged with the people. He had not lobbied and offered no bribes. He had put his own life on the line. Might Ferensen's narrative be askew? Had Sir Veronal Slickstone, Sir Henry's murderer, been the true villain all along?

He rose to his feet. 'Ladies and gentlemen, we have no Mayor.

That is the background to today's extraordinary assembly – and I use the word "extraordinary" in the meaning allotted to it by paragraph 6(5)(ii)(b) of the *Procedural Regulations*—'

A familiar cry emerged from the stalls. 'Get on with it, Bor'em-very!'

'I am getting on with it, you silly man. These are matters of moment.' Gorhambury forged on. 'A motion has been tabled by eleven of the twelve Guilds, as follows: "*To appoint Mr Geryon Wynter of no fixed address as the Mayor of Rotherweird for one year subject to terms . . .*"'

Norrington, the baker and Wynter's opponent at the last meeting, had not lost his voice. '*What* terms? We're handing power to a stranger. He could be anyone.'

Gorhambury flipped the flap on his jacket pocket. His dry diction for once betrayed impatience.

Gorhambury evolving, noted Oblong, *assertive almost.*

'I was coming to the terms, *obviously*. The motion stipulates a Council of Guild Masters, excepting the Apothecaries, with a right of veto over all appointments and any change in the law.'

Placing a tomato beside a pallid chameleon would best describe the transformation in Thomes' complexion. He left his seat and descended to the floor wagging a finger at Gorhambury. 'How dare you exclude us! We are *the* Guild. It's grotesque, preposterous—'

'That's a challenge for the proposers to answer,' replied Gorhambury primly.

Poor choreography afflicted the movers of the motion: three Guild Masters stood up and each simultaneously launched a riposte.

'One at a time,' intoned the former Town Clerk.

A sequence of 'after yous' consigned the issue to the Master Mixer.

'Mr Wynter stays with the Apothecaries. Miss Scry, an honorary Apothecary, spoke for him at the last meeting. He has an obvious debt. There is a glaring conflict of interest. We stand by our motion.'

'Bully for you!' cried the baker.

Gorhambury halted Thomes with a raised finger. 'Any amendments must be read to all, reduced to writing and placed with me for numbering. Those wishing to speak will queue by the rostrum, unless they have a point of order.'

'Amendment 1: delete "*except the Apothecaries*"!' boomed Thomes, plucking his goatee in rage.

The amendment duly made its way to Gorhambury's desk.

Wynter watched and waited, memorising every speaker's name, profession and stance: supporter, floater or opponent. The invitation would surely come, and it did, from the Mistress Milliner.

'In an election, candidates address us on their programmes. How enlightening if Mr Wynter would do the same.'

Lambs and lemmings, thought Wynter, unable to resist in his mind blending the more esoteric faces with birds and beasts, but he played the rules, walking to the back of the line of would-be speakers, only for those in front to make way. It was *him* they wanted to hear.

'Men and women of Rotherweird, I shall do whatever you ask, on whatever conditions. I shall serve you all, high and low, with due humility. I shall engage both with the Council's collective wisdom and with those without a Guild. I seek no payment, as I am a man of means. Consider it a marriage: *with all my worldly goods I thee endow.*'

'Marriage is for life,' growled Snorkel in his wife's ear, earning a resigned nod by way of response.

'I would welcome a neutral lodging, so as not to disturb your former Mayor in this festive season ...' added Wynter.

Madge Brown, Gorhambury's introvert Sunday evening companion, unexpectedly rose to her feet. 'Point of order, Mr Gorhambury. As Assistant Librarian and Secretary to the Artefacts Committee, I can report that the Manor is available for Mr Wynter. On our Committee's advice, the contract of sale with Sir Veronal stipulated that upon his absence for six consecutive calendar months, ownership would revert to the town – as it did on the Winter Solstice.'

Strimmer clenched his fists. Sir Veronal had pledged the Manor to *him*.

Snorkel, ignoring protocol, stood up. 'How's that for foresight?' he asked rhetorically, with a sweep of an arm. 'I get the Manor refurbished at Sir Veronal's expense for your benefit!'

The hoped-for applause did not materialise. Snorkel was yesterday's news. Geryon Wynter had put his life on the line for the town.

Wynter slipped in a coda, menacing only to Oblong, with his knowledge of history. 'Where there was one monster, there may be more. As a matter of urgency, we need to improve our arms and we need a defence force.'

Nobody dissented, and those bereaved by the mantoleon's assault applauded. Amendment followed amendment, each approved by a forest of hands. Inside and out, heels clattered floorboards and cobbles, a drum-line beneath the chorus of 'Wynter, Wynter'.

Wynter repeated the mayoral oath. Miss Brown presented the Manor's key on a velvet cushion, adding to Gorhambury's puzzlement. There had been no meeting of the Artefacts Committee since November – and how had she acquired the key? The cushion struck him as a *louche*, subservient touch. Had Brown gone rogue?

Two announcements closed the meeting.

Wynter declared, 'I shall address the Chamber on policy on New Year's Day.'

Gorhambury concluded, 'I remind you that Mr Snorkel as retiring Mayor will make his *envoi* speech from the Town Hall balcony at noon on New Year's Eve. It is customary to bring a charged glass for a concluding toast.'

'Out with the old and in with the new, that's his slogan,' hissed Snorkel to his wife. 'But I'm not finished yet.'

To Scry, the cards had fallen almost too well, including the timing of the Manor's transfer. A warning whisper chaffed like a stone in a shoe: Wynter had miraculously absorbed the town's geography, the names and inclinations of her inhabitants and her constitutional rules. An earlier self-restoration might explain the phenomenon, but Wynter revered his own legend. He would never countenance a failed prophecy. She shelved the concern: after all, he was the most remarkable man she had ever encountered in almost five hundred years.

Only the town's modern historian watched the proceedings in horror. He shut his eyes, catching in thought a tang of salt and an offshore breeze. Dunes unfurled left and right, their slopes criss-crossed with abandoned palisades, here a sandal, there a broken javelin. The giant horse gazed longingly at the town gates, skin gold and azure blue, ears pricked, the four wheels poised to run: a gift beyond gifts.

It was as if.

It was as if.

5

The Manor Reclaimed

After waves of applause and an occasional vulgar slap on Wynter's back, the crowd dispersed to the ritual Boxing Day lunch of warmed-up leftovers. The Apothecaries wended their way back to their Guild Hall, Thomes at the head in his personal rickshaw, fulminating at the compromise amendment which permitted his Guild to join the Council only if its interests were directly engaged.

'Might Mr Wynter like a view?' Madge Brown raised a key in each hand, like a pose from a coin, rich in symbolism. She took the lead with modest, tidy steps, in keeping with her modest, tidy appearance.

With mounting irritation – the return to the Manor should be *her* moment – Scry lagged behind.

At the outer gate, Brown halted. 'Former glory – isn't that what you're here to restore, Mr Wynter?'

She turned the key with a dainty flourish. Wynter shuffled through to be engulfed by emotion – the Manor, his palace, home to his rule, with the added spice of Nona and Estella beside him, the latter blissfully unaware of the former's presence. Hitherto, he had felt afflicted by blandness. Now he felt *himself*. On a similar winter day, centuries ago, he had walked this very path to take his destiny with the earth still fresh on Sir Henry's grave. Here too he had been marched to his trial and death sentence – all as planned. These were *his* memories, nobody else's.

Time had not turned the line of the path and Slickstone's planting had mimicked the Elizabethan garden precisely. Only one feature disfigured the scene.

'The wall is grotesque,' Wynter cried. 'It throws unnecessary shadow.'

'Have it down then,' replied Miss Brown, 'but it may have its uses.'

'You're speaking to the Mayor,' hissed Scry. 'Give me the keys and run along.' She added a chilly, 'Thank you.'

Brown did not obey immediately. She had a wry birdlike quality and an infuriating resilience. She walked on to the entrance porch. 'The giants' fire is lit, the kitchen provisioned and the master bedroom prepared. You will, of course, need staff.'

She directed her remarks to Wynter as if Scry were not there.

The giants' fire – so the Eleusians had termed the hearth in the Great Hall with the huge stone men supporting the mantle. Brown had inadvertently snagged a memory.

She inserted the door key, turned it and handed both keys to Wynter.

'I assure you, Miss Brown, we will restore former glories,' he said.

Still she did not leave, instead ushering him into the Great Hall.

'Sir Veronal Slickstone did not give us loyalty, but he did have taste,' Brown said. Slickstone's paintings and tapestries still hung *in situ*, the sixteenth century dominant: a traitor turned interior decorator. She added *sotto voce* as she turned to leave, 'By the way, you may receive a disagreeable visitor in the very near future. But I recommend hearing him out.'

Wynter turned to Scry the moment Brown left the room. 'Well, Estella, we are back.' He sounded different, his old self.

'After you, Master,' she said with a tug on his sleeve. They wandered around the Great Hall, the setting for so many past triumphs: Scry's childhood and the most audacious scientific household in the world.

'I sat here,' said Wynter, curling his fingers round the back of the chair.

'No, no,' intervened Scry, 'that was Calx Bole's chair. You were always here, dead centre.'

'Of course, I was, of course – time's tricks!' exclaimed Wynter, unsettled by the error. 'Let's explore.'

They did so, Scry noting spotless surfaces, fresh soap in the bathrooms, a generous lunch on the hob and a pair of slippers to size beside the master's bed. The foresight of the Artefacts Committee was uncanny.

The haunting stillness, like a school in holiday time, muted the ecstasy of their return. To break it, she led him to the attics.

'My cell,' she said, 'where Nona and I wove the history of the Eleusians. A penance, we told Oxenbridge.' Scry paused. Her breathing stumbled in the excitement. A dull gunmetal-grey tube hugged the wainscot. She wrenched off the lid, extracted the tapestry and rolled it out in the centre of the room. The colours shone, untouched by time, and it was Scry's turn to be surprised by the potency of memory. She felt every dive of the needle, every tug on the thread, all those years of false repentance.

Wynter enthused over the tapestry. 'A penance – it's a New Testament!' He pored over the detail: his lunch with Sir Henry, Sir Henry's death, the experiments, the arrest, the execution – all there, *faithfully* rendered by a joint venture between his two most faithful acolytes.

'You shared the work, but I say this corner is you and that corner is Nona.'

Scry found the mention of Nona's name dispiriting. She rose to the bait. 'How so?'

'Take *this* Calx Bole and *that* Calx Bole.' The difference was palpable, even in wool – her Bole was corpulent, a toad-like figure; Nona's had an energetic intelligence.

Wynter did not press the comparison. 'Now let me share a secret with you.' He ushered her back to the Great Hall.

'This was the court room. I stood there manacled before pygmies: *Sir* Robert Oxenbridge, Mr Hubert Finch. Yet right beside me ...' Wynter walked towards the corner of the room and stood, his face close to the panelling. 'Observe, linenfold pattern as you'd expect from dull Sir Henry; but here, we have Eleusian carvings.' With a flamboyant gesture, he ran his fingers over a succession of monstrous heads and tails, before stooping to turn one and slide another.

Four panels swung out to reveal a spacious cavity. They placed the contents on the table. Wynter surveyed them, satisfied but slightly puzzled: a tray bearing nine tiny glass cruets with a scroll sealed with wax, a single phial made of old glass filled to the stopper with a luminous green liquid, a book and a velvet sack with drawstrings.

Scry recognised the cruets from Wynter's Last Supper, when every surviving Eleusian had given blood.

Wynter handed her the scroll. 'The town has a blood bank, to which all adults contribute, so matching was easy.' He smiled. 'You'd expect our Eleusian descendants to be well represented today, and so they are.'

On one level, she understood: the new order would honour the old. Descendants must be preferred. On another, it made no sense: Wynter had entered the Manor today for the first time in more than four hundred years. How could he have arranged all this?

'I need a household, including guards. Concentrate on those in The Understairs. They'll be more malleable.'

'And the sack?' she asked.

'A childhood memento of no consequence,' he said. 'But this' – he lifted the phial to the candle and then to the window – 'I do not remember.' The specks of light came and went like glow-worms in grass. 'When we've eaten, send for Doctor Fanguin.'

'And the book?' asked Scry.

Wynter held out the spine. The title declared its purpose: *The*

Roman Recipe Book II. The frontispiece held the same introductory words as its predecessor: *I was bound bearing mysterious recipes*, an anagram of *Geryon's Precise Bestiarium*, but the pages were yet to be filled.

'We need our artist back,' replied Wynter.

'Rotherweird lacks artists, Master.'

'I mean Morval Seer.'

'But surely she—?'

'She has served her time, as I have.'

Over lunch, Wynter for the first time declared ignorance. 'What's in the tower?'

'I assumed it was part of the plan.'

'Not that I know of,' replied Wynter, 'and the same goes for the structure which has replaced the church.'

'Both are sealed.'

As she spoke, Scry realised such work would take centuries if done by one man. She had been excluded from so much, and even Wynter, it now appeared, was not omniscient. 'How was it done, Master? Who managed your return?'

'A mixing-point managed my return.' Wynter cut a pear into exact slices and changed the subject. 'You recall the man Ferdy, in the tavern?'

'Everyone knows Ferdy.'

'Ferdy's ancestor harboured the changelings when they escaped, including Vibes and the beautiful boy. They have been dealt with, as has Fortemain, by you, dear Estella, but a Ferdy lives on.'

'Not this Ferdy, surely?'

'The sins of the fathers are the sins of the sons.'

'We can destroy him whenever you want,' said Scry.

Slivers of pear skin lay draped over the rim of Wynter's plate like petals, pared to match. 'That would be humdrum. But let us talk science.'

And so they did, Wynter probing Scry, not vice versa, teacher turned invigilator. Particle physics and dimensional theory dominated the questions. Wynter vigorously rejected notions of multiple time dimensions, but parallel physical dimensions intrigued him. She scribbled equations and he followed suit, jabbing at the complacent armour of the latest learning. Could you leave one universe and opt for another? If you could, links must exist. Could they be severed or re-forged? More equations covered their paper napkins as they moved on to Madge Brown's immaculate cheese selection.

'Lost Acre is faithful to our time and season,' he said hammering the table, 'but she is locked into this valley. Why? And how can we exploit it?'

Neither could yet offer an answer.

6

True or False?

When Fanguin arrived, he found the Manor Wall gate ajar. He had walked this path just once before, to Slickstone's party, as an unemployed has-been. But this time Scry had paid him handsomely for his work before Christmas and his presence – with his best microscope – had been requested by the new Mayor.

But I will not succumb, so testified the scalpel taped to his right leg. This man had inflicted unimaginable horrors on orphans and his own students, so what might he do to Rotherweird? Law had passed due sentence centuries ago.

The ornate iron door knocker rose and fell twice.

The door swung open.

'Doctor Fanguin, do follow me.'

In the Great Hall, Wynter presented Fanguin with a stemmed glass of chilled white wine. 'A breath of summer in winter,' said his host. 'I owe you a history lesson. Let's start with a provocative question: how did we Eleusians acquire the stones?'

Wynter's directness stormed Fanguin's barricades. And the question had bite. Wynter might have stumbled on the quarry of coloured rock as Oblong and Valourhand had, but how had they found the perfectly circular stones which alone could manipulate matter?

'You've not met him, then?' added Wynter.

'Met whom?'

'Lost Acre's human ruler, who has been there since God knows when. How else could my late servant Calx Bole have learned to shapeshift?'

Fanguin gawped, another question with bite. On reflection, the complexity of such a feat did indeed seem beyond Elizabethan capabilities.

'Yes, we experimented with birds and animals – but wouldn't you have done in our position? But shapeshifting!? That was one of the hedge-priest's blighted gifts.'

Hedge-priest! He had seen sarsens and sculpted flowers in the passages beneath the town, and everyone knew the ancient statue of a dark druid in Grove Gardens.

Fanguin launched a flurry of questions, all answered succinctly by the perfect witness.

'Who killed Sir Henry?'

'Slickstone, or rather, Master Malise. He was a psychotic child from the start.'

'Who imprisoned Morval Seer in a spider's body?'

'Slickstone – she refused him.'

'Who collected the orphans?'

'Slickstone.'

'Who led the experiments?'

'Calx Bole did the human experiments in my guise, encouraged by the hedge-priest. I was unaware until too late. I don't deny responsibility for attempting what the mixing-point did anyway, merging the local fauna.'

'Your trial record portrays you as defiant,' Fanguin pointed out.

'Oxenbridge was a fool. The world experiments on living things to advance. And the mixing-point grants immortality. I did discover that for myself – with a mayfly in a box. But I did not corrupt children.'

'Why should I believe in this druid of yours?'

'Ask your friend Gregorius Jones.'

'He's unavailable.'

'Pity – all right, try another question. As you know, when the dark star comes, the fabric of Lost Acre becomes unstable, and, believe me, the instability grows with every visit. So, who saved Lost Acre in 1017, and the millennia before that?'

Fanguin, having no answer, changed tack. 'What about the Furies? I mean your friend Scry, or rather your pupil, and whoever the other one is.'

'Girls will be girls.' Wynter refilled their glasses. 'Prodigies both, each strove to outdo the other. I don't know whether they discovered the trick for themselves, or if the hedge-priest taught them.'

'Where is Bole?'

'He is no more.'

'What of the third woman Eleusian?'

'Time caught up with her.'

'And our new architectural arrivals – the tower and the octagon?'

For the first time, Wynter looked troubled. 'I know nothing of the tower. The octagon replaces the church, so we assume it connects to worship in some way. But neither are my doing.'

'And your resurrection?'

'I never died. I had a half-life. The details are distressing, but I lived through the centuries, absorbing scientific knowledge. Test me; any time, any place, anyone.'

Fanguin hunted for an issue of little import now but significant in its day. 'Who did Leibniz argue with about what?'

Wynter smiled. 'Leibniz claimed to have discovered calculus independently of Newton, not that it was called calculus then. It started as a polite debate in 1699 and twelve years later sank into mutual abuse. Both men were difficult. I can give you years, dates, and who supported whom and why and I can even tell you what the two protagonists looked like, having met both.'

Like the twists of a kaleidoscope, presumed facts reformed, some becoming clear, others blurred and unconvincing. Fanguin felt disorientated by the welter of forbidden history. 'Why have you chosen to tell me all this?' he asked at last.

'You've the intelligence to see it's credible, and I need scientifically minded allies.'

'To do what?'

'To repel the enemy. You've not been to Lost Acre. The dark star is disintegrating and nobody knows quite what will happen. The hedge-priest is looking for a new dominion and probing our defences. The mantoleon was just the beginning.'

'Frankly, Mr Wynter, I do not believe you.'

'Frankly, Doctor Fanguin, I do not expect you to – not immediately. The hedge-priest gave my servant this remarkable phial. I'd welcome your views.'

Fanguin placed his microscope on the table, dipped a sterile nail varnish brush into the liquid, smeared a glass slide, drew up a chair, peered, shook his head in wonderment and peered again before delivering his verdict.

'Imagine Brownian motion, only magnified many times over. The chips of light vanish and reappear without any journey in between – like oversize atomic particles.' Fanguin moved to his conclusion. 'It's sap, the blood of a tree, but a most unusual tree.'

Wynter gazed at Fanguin, the distinctive ear lobes and set of the eyes, and that fierce intellectual curiosity. He had liked his forbear, a quiet, studious boy.

'You will appreciate Lost Acre more than most,' said Wynter. 'Please take the phial home, report any further discoveries and record all time spent. I pay expertise by the hour.'

As Fanguin made for the door, Wynter gestured back at the Great Hall. 'This house was in its time revolutionary: multiple chimneys, foreign glass, plastered ceilings, a staircase wide enough for two to pass and rooms assigned to specific activities. Someone, somewhere, always has to be first.'

Fanguin left, half confused, half excited.

*

Wynter sat before the fire, savouring the wine's taste, smell and texture, before rising to open a second alcove behind the linenfold panelling. The boxes of Rotherweird gold guineas remained neatly stacked, gathered by Bole over the centuries for the good work to come. What a servant he had been!

He moved to the table, picked up the velvet sack from the first alcove and loosened the drawstrings. He inserted a hand and one by one extracted each elmwood human figure, followed by the ship, the two clashing rocks, the fleece, the comatose dragon and the bronze giant Talos. He never touched a face, too respectful for that, but held between thumb and forefinger the toys of his childhood. He aspired not to be an Argonaut or even the hero Jason. No, he must join the gods who played with them.

A thought came, arriving oddly, like a posted message. *Explore the garden.* Candle- lantern in hand, Wynter took the rear entrance, noting again Nona's thoroughness: dead leaves had been cleared, the late pruning done, summer's growth tied back against the winter winds. Unlike Estella, Nona did her work without expectation of thanks or praise.

Another prompt, another message, drew him to the hexagonal brick tower which had once housed the Eleusians' familiars. Wynter caught a rustle, like a broom sweeping flagstones, high up, even though the tower had no upper floors. Most of the familiars had been winged; his young charges had flown them from gauntleted fists like falcons. But they could not have survived Oxenbridge, surely, let alone the ensuing centuries.

Wynter drew the bolt and tiptoed in, lantern thrust in front.

Tidy creatures, he thought; their dried excrement formed a sculpted tower in one corner. He looked up at the unfamiliar faces looking down, owls more than anything else. Feathery faces swivelled, eyes blinked: a hint of human expression.

As the largest dropped to the floor, a name came.

'Strix?'

The creature's lipped beak squawked, calling the others down like an attentive class, and Wynter guessed they could understand, but not speak, a common trait among the mixing-point's creations.

'Your time approaches, my children. But remember: never fly by daylight, and never be seen in the Manor grounds.'

A fresh haunch of meat hung from a butcher's hook on a pulley high on a cross-gable. Bole's preparations had been truly exemplary.

Wynter prided himself on his hearing and his stealth. The former gift caught the catch of heels in the gravel path; the latter caught his visitor at the main door. Dark hair like a gorgon's coiled down to a jade dress and heavy shawl. She turned. Early forties, he guessed.

'You said to come.'

The woman who had presented the spur from the mantoleon's leg exuded the same intensity, even without the gore. She looked taller than she was. Think Medea, one of the elmwood figures on the table.

He showed her into the Great Hall.

She ran a finger along the tabletop, the chairs and the banister. 'The place is spotless. Are you served by ghosts?'

'A grateful town, I imagine.'

'Miss Brown goes in and out, but nobody else. It's meant to be locked.'

An inquisitive mind, noted Wynter. 'And you – Mrs or Miss?'

'Fennel.'

'Fennel who?'

It was like squeezing blood from a stone: front teeth chaffed her lower lip, a first sign of weakness. 'Finch,' she muttered defensively.

Wynter's predatory instincts surged: Finch the usurper. The sins of the fathers are the sins of the daughters.

'You're a *Finch*?'

'I am *not*. I was married to one, a pedant, dry as a biscuit and all that's wrong with this town. The Herald knows the past, but rules nothing. The Mayor rules but knows only the present. It was not ever so.'

Very inquisitive, thought Wynter. 'How do you know about the past?'

'I've a key to the *archivoire*. It didn't occur to the pedant that I might be curious. Think of that delicious, forbidden fruit – the *past*.' Fennel paused. 'I've frittered years away, working the Snorkel household for no return. But you, Mr Wynter . . . you are different.' She seized his hands, inclining her head in a gesture of fealty. 'You must . . .' She struggled to escape the triteness of Snorkel's social vocabulary – receptions, soirées, parties. 'You must unleash an event.'

'I understand my predecessor did just that.'

'It was extravagant, but dull. People came and left as themselves. Your event will redefine them.'

'How?'

'I'll draft an invitation. I understand service, Mr Wynter. You ingratiate with generalities; you serve by attention to detail.'

With that unexpected epigram, Fennel lowered her head as if before an altar and saw herself out.

7

Servant or Master

Nights had hitherto brought black-out, but here, in the four-poster in the Manor's master bedroom, his former bedroom, he dreamed.

He is among his toys, myth and reality blending. He lifts a fleece stitched with golden prophecy coins; he sends the Argo through the closing rocks; he sows the mantoleon's teeth and his enemies die – Norrington the baker, Snorkel and Thomes. He enjoys the sorceress' embrace, Medea wearing the face of Fennel Finch.

But the Argo's return is not a hero's landfall. The bay is dark with spillage: soulless towers in concrete and glass nuzzle the clouds and the inhabitants are glassy-eyed, afflicted by drift. He inhales the reek of a failed species.

Brow freckled with sweat, Wynter awoke to a new message on a single page beside the bed in Bole's writing, one word:

Doomsday

'Servant or Master'

8

Of Transport and Tears

The guineas in Fanguin's pocket jangled conveniently as he passed Vlad's on his journey home. A bottle of whisky under his arm, he bounded past the amended note on the hallway table (*Remains of flan in oven*) and up several flights of stairs to his study. He had a theory to test.

He divided the sap into two tiny glass cruets. The strange particles of light in the viscous liquid still shone and danced. With a pair of tweezers, he dropped an iron filing in one cruet, only for it to vanish and reappear, almost instantly, in the other. He repeated the experiment after dipping the filing in red ink. Same result.

Conventional sap, through xylem and phloem, transported nutrients from places of production and storage to places of use, but this liquid could transport alien physical objects through glass. The oaky flavour of the whisky made a suitable toast for the revelation. He felt young again, in his prime.

Another discovery followed: the immersed filing was emitting low-level radiation. The activity mildly increased if you placed two filings close to each other. Instinct said this mattered, but he could not articulate why.

He reached for the whisky, then uncharacteristically paused. The sap had fragrance, not honeysuckle or rose, but something deeper; its effect was a clearing of heart and head. He resealed the cruets. An alarm bell rang, but Fanguin ignored it; his eagerness to share these breakthroughs with Wynter displaced any thought of his friends.

Scry too returned home, glad to be free of the Apothecaries and, more particularly, Gurney Thomes.

She cut the crusty red wax sealing the scroll which identified those in town with Eleusian blood. The paper felt old and the ink had a brownish tinge. The writing, unmistakably Bole's, had been reduced to the miniscule to accommodate the crowded names and multicoloured lines linking each to one of the numbered but uni-dentified blood samples. In more than five centuries the Eleusians' bloodlines had blossomed. She had a rich cohort from which to choose her recruits.

A few absentees reassured her – no Snorkel and no Thomes. Of those present, two names, in particular, did not surprise, such were their scientific gifts: Strimmer and Fanguin.

Yet she remained uneasy. Genetic testing of this refinement was a recent art, and Bole could only have accessed Rotherweird's blood bank in town. She had hunted down and killed his familiar, but she had never seen him.

As she opened the desk drawer for a clean sheet to record her selections, a signature caught her eye: Madge Brown's letter from October. She re-read it.

Two numbers, 7.49 and 8.49, have appeared during the cleaning of a portrait (of their Founder) owned by the Apothecaries. As The Clairvoyancy sells almanacs and works on mystical numbers, we wondered if you might assist on their significance. Our chair thinks they may be co-ordinates, indicating the whereabouts of other lost artefacts.

The following morning Scry inspected the minutes of the Artefacts Committee at the Town Hall. They contained the barest of refer-ences to the cleaning of the Founder's portrait, with no mention of the appearance of the mysterious numbers. She also noted a passing reference to the Manor and the unresolved issue of what to do with Sir Veronal Slickstone's chattels after his disappearance, but nothing more.

Madge Brown had directed her to the portrait and the clue which held the timing of Wynter's return; she had restored the Manor to Wynter; she had addressed him with an easy informality.

Her unease deepened. Miss Brown merited a closer look.

9

Without Precedent

Gorhambury returned to his lodgings in The Understairs feeling all at sea. The *Regulations* did not cater for a Town Clerk's appointment under an emergency Mayor. He liked men who eschewed chicanery, played by the book and put town before personal interest. In short, he preferred Mr Wynter to Mr Snorkel. Yet the Fury, the mantoleon, *The Dark Devices* in the *archivoire*, Finch's abduction and Sir Veronal's disappearance pointed to a dark past threatening the present.

He chased the residue of his Christmas pudding around the plate. It had a crusty, unappetising appearance.

'Reginald?' said a familiar voice from the other side of his front door.

With a sigh he ambled over. 'Please don't call me Reginald, not on the landing. Neighbours may misconstrue.'

Madge Brown did not enter. 'I'm sorry about Christmas.'

'Don't be. I had a day off.'

Gorhambury's Christmas dinner had been like any other Gorhambury evening meal, with the added adornment of a solitary cracker, an oddly challenging exercise with the same person pulling at both ends. He had daringly worn a polka-dot tie, his solitary gift to himself, and a strawberry-coloured paper hat with a gold rim from the cracker, whose resemblance to a crown had induced constitutional unease. Madge Brown's failure to visit had brought mild disappointment, leavened by relief. He experienced the same ambiguous reaction now.

'By way of apology I'm buying you a festive drink at *The Journeyman's Gist*. No, Reginald, don't argue – Ferdy is holding a table. It'll all be very discreet.'

'A quick half,' he muttered.

'See you there then,' replied Madge. 'You've ten minutes to spruce up.'

Twenty minutes later, Gorhambury sat sipping his half-pint of Sturdy as if it were tea. 'Sprucing up' had involved dispensing with his waistcoat and pocketing a coloured handkerchief which had been his father's.

'Your amendment was a bold initiative,' he said with a hint of rebuke. He might have said the same of her drink, ginger wine, in his experience a wolf in sheep's clothing. 'Your Committee hasn't met for a good forty-nine days.'

'Sorry. I should have forewarned you. But imagine the consequences of not doing so. The Snorkels refuse to leave. Mr Wynter shacks up with the Apothecaries. I acted properly, Reginald, indeed, thoughtfully . . . with an eye to the town's best interests.'

Gorhambury winced. 'Please, Miss Brown, *not* Reginald, not here.'

'*And* the Secretary to the Artefacts Committee has emergency powers.'

This was true, another *Regulation* passed in the mists of time for reasons unfathomable.

'What's done is done,' muttered Gorhambury.

Twenty minutes of strained light conversation ensued before Madge Brown made a surprise announcement. 'I shall be away for a time.' She drained her glass with indecent abandon. 'I've an ailing mother in wider England and my sister has done more than her stint. We're swapping places. You'll find her a different kettle of fish, but just as competent.'

She stood up and patted Gorhambury on the crown of the head. 'I'm off to pack. I'm sorry to go in these exciting times, but then, a change is as good as a rest.'

She stooped and whispered in Gorhambury's ear as she passed, 'Watch out for Persephone Brown.'

In an alcove around the corner Oblong sat opposite his own unexpected companion.

'I'm a friend of Orelia Roc's,' said Ember Vine.

'Ditto.'

'She's missing, and I don't know where or why.'

Oblong's weakness for impressing attractive women led to a maladroit choice of phrase. 'I'm afraid I was out for the count.' He paused before explaining, 'I mean, the election.'

'How odd; I'd expect our only modern historian to be present at such a rare event – indeed, unique, as it turned out.' Hide in plain sight: Ember felt at ease, surrounded by people cocooned in their own conversations. 'I confided in Orelia my peculiar commission: to carve the constituent pieces of a sphere from some very strange rocks. And she confided in me, up to a point.'

Oblong, not a natural spy, dropped his lower jaw at the word 'sphere'.

He looked like a fish at feeding time, which reassured Ember. *He must know more. Candour for candour*, she decided. Holding nothing back, she ended with her ghostly experience with the Advent window for the twenty-third of December. 'I checked the tenant. She was one of the Summoned – a Miss Pomeny Tighe.'

Oblong's jaw sank further. With the better part of two pints of Sturdy working at his synapses, inhibitions evaporated. With Finch, Jones, Valourhand and Roc missing, they needed new recruits. 'I shouldn't be saying this, and I fear you will be shocked . . .'

'I'm an artist. Only unnecessary shyness and deliberate untruths shock me.'

Oblong told the story, helped by Ember oiling the relevant valves with a third pint of Sturdy.

'Wow,' she said, not doubting a word. To her artist's eye, the disparate pieces fitted, coherent despite the grotesquery. 'I have a potential lead from Tighe's rooms – an address in Hoy.' She showed him the piece of paper.

Oblong reacted with incredulity. 'Miss Tighe came straight from Germany. How could she know anyone in Hoy?'

She echoed his unease. 'It lay under a fine porcelain rose – not a Rotherweird piece. Why bring such a delicate object all this way? My daughter said Tighe's ghost was warning us.'

'I'll give it a gander,' replied Oblong, affecting a cavalier jauntiness. 'Nobody notices when I leave town, not even my class.'

Vine the sculptress and painter read well the tension lines which underpinned faces, the false smiles and the true. She stood up and took him by his forearms. 'You need passion in your life,' she said as she left. 'Don't resist when it happens. And do find Orelia.'

'Fat chance,' he muttered, alone again with his drink.

Old History

1563. Lost Acre.

They are in Lost Acre. The guards have gone and the light is failing. Wynter has held the girls back. They huddle together, feeling vulnerable as winged creatures drift in their direction from the woods below.

'No worry, we're safe with him,' says Wynter.

'With whom?'

No need to reply; the old man strides uphill over the sward without any other visible weapon save a dark, twisted staff. His robes shimmer. Estella and Pomeny see an anachronism, but Nona senses an ancient power more potent even than Wynter's. There are rings on his fingers, pinpoints of stone.

'You progress but slowly,' says the old man. Wynter bristles, but here the hedge-priest is master. 'Maybe your women crave special gifts,' he adds. 'I will show you, Mr Wynter, another time, but not now. Dusk is dangerous and they are too young to know, *yet*.' He appraises the girls, his eyes resting a fraction longer on her, Nona feels. 'I will, of course, require a small indulgence in return.'

He escorts them to the tile. Their would-be pursuers veer away. Here this man is king.

'You've passed a studious week in a studious season, but remember, my children, that knowledge is but the wherewithal. Without imagination you can never reach for the stars. Put down your pens and listen.' Wynter stands, his back to a blazing fire which ousts the darkness of the Autumn Equinox. In the Great Hall he tells his seated audience of Persephone, a life half spent in the over-world and half in Hades. This very day, he reminds them, marks her return to the Lord of the Dead.

Nona has imagination more opulent in measure than Estella. The story infiltrates the core of her being, the thought of a queen moving between two worlds and two gods with a seasonal divide. She muses on Lost Acre and the Rotherweird Valley, and on the hedge-priest, pallid as Hades, God of the Dead, and yearns to be a modern, living rendition of the myth.

IN AND OUT OF TOWN

I

Keeping Up Appearances

As on her previous visit, Madge Brown alias Nona Lihni walks from the U-Bahn stop. Nobody offers a lift to this nondescript figure with lace-up shoes, tan stockings and mousey, unfashionable hair.

Far away, the snow line holds. Close by, frost gathers as a hooked moon rises. It is past midnight, with little traffic.

She vaults the roadside wall. Behind it runs an avenue of mature poplars, branches held close and vertical. She climbs the tallest, round and round, as if ascending a helter-skelter.

At the highest point her weight allows, she leans out, feet braced against the trunk, holds the posture, then falls like fruit – but, unlike fruit, she transforms, sprouting claws, wings of dark leather and a beak of tortoiseshell. She skims the clinic's roof and finds the expected row of skylights. Such places favour them, for sunlight rekindles thoughts of resurrected youth.

She lands and is herself again. Instruments from her dowdy handbag unpick combinations, immobilise alarms and open locked doors and cabinets. She removes her own file before rifling the rest for the desired statistics. She would like to be a dancer. She craves both beauty and grace. She has had her fill of fustiness.

Dr Obern's clientele is dominated by vacuous dolls . . . but she finds an exception. Too tall for the ballet, the notes confess, but the photographs portray a woman of feline beauty. The oversize breasts demanded by a rich, bullying husband will not infect the genetic profile. She notes the card's number. A huge fridge holds reserves of skin and plasma. Matching file to phial, she transfers the latter to the small cold box in her bag.

She loathes this place. On her last visit Dr Obern treated her as inferior, as if her looks and search for dowdiness lacked class. He had shown no interest in her past or personality, only her money. Immortals do not tolerate such slights. She returns to his study. Behind the desk sits an espresso machine, all chrome and gold, with a spotless mug inscribed in a self-indulgent script Herr Doktor Direktor. Beside it, a Perspex container holds capsules of coffee; only a few are left. A hypodermic from her unremarkable bag injects a single capsule. The tiny hole will not leak, and the chosen toxins will inflict agony before they kill.

She lets herself out the back, re-locking and re-arming the alarms as she goes.

Now to the mixing-point and the birth of Miss Persephone Brown.

2

Wynter's Blade

The morning after Wynter's accession to the Manor, a sentry selected by Scry barred the way through the Manor gate with his halberd. 'I don't know you and you're not on the list.'

'I've lowdown for Mr Wynter.' The middle-aged man fingered a long skinning blade attached to his belt which appeared to account for his clothes: a rabbit-skin jacket, a waistcoat of moleskin and rough-cut leather trousers. Unshaven, of average height with over-prominent eyes and a permanently curled lip, he had a raw, discomforting presence.

'Your name, sir?'

'What's it to you?'

'Everyone gives a name. My orders are most particular.'

'Carcasey Jack.'

'Interesting jacket, Mr Jack.'

'Am I in or am I not?'

'Up the path, knock twice and do what you're told.'

At the Manor's front door, a second guard admitted Carcasey Jack to the Great Hall. At the table sat an older man with silver hair fitting the new Mayor's description.

Jack had no interest in small talk. 'I'm Carcasey Jack and your dowdy friend said you'd have more of these.'

A golden guinea spun gently on the table.

Wynter, seated and surrounded by papers, did not move. 'Look up, Mr Jack.'

Carcasey Jack tilted his head, revealing a centre bald as a monk's tonsure. A strange owl-like bird perched on the rafters, large, with odd skin, unlike any bird he had ever seen or snared. 'Strix will have your eyes out in seconds if I ask. So, you sit down; you call me Mr Wynter, sir, and you make your case for whatever you want.'

Jack fingered the handle of his knife.

'I really wouldn't,' added Wynter with a smile.

Carcasey Jack sat down, his body twisted towards Wynter.

Long ago, across a court room, Wynter had adjudged Bole useful on sight. He reached the same judgement about this man, although for different reasons. The knife at his waist had skinned and sliced for pleasure as much as work, so his face said, and the living as well as the dead. Carcasey Jack would fill a glaring vacancy. For the moment he would hear him out.

'I've lived out there, but I'm no countrysider. I'm better than that. I hanker for life in town. So when your woman jangled her coins, I said I'd come, and I have . . . Mr Wynter, sir.'

'To offer me what?'

'A location.' Jack licked his lips. 'The countrysiders' refuge, their biggest secret; nobody tells it but Carcasey Jack.'

Wynter's fingers danced along the tabletop. He had hoped to surprise them in their homes, but if they were gathered in a single place, he could harvest the children and dispose of the rest much more easily.

'But first my price. I want a nice place in town. I want money. I want respect.'

'Let's add a position of authority with power over others.' Wynter paused. 'I sense you're good at elucidation.'

Few would grasp such an elliptical observation, but Jack did.

'Extracting useful information? Oh I'd be good, very good indeed.'

'One condition: you serve *only* me.'

Carcasey Jack did not hesitate. The stranger had the aura of a born ruler. He had seized the town and needed Carcasey Jack to hold it. A void within him began to fill. He had at last found a cause and purpose.

He reached for his knife, cut an X across his right palm and offered his wounded hand. 'Done,' he said, 'Mr Wynter, sir.'

That evening Denzil Prim, Head Gaoler, received a visit from Scry.

'You've been promoted, Mr Prim.'

'Happy where I am,' replied Prim. 'Home sweet home.'

'It's meant to be a prison.'

Prim replied by parroting Thomes' words on the eve of the election. 'Hall of Correction sounds more redemptive.'

'We need lookouts on the walls. You'll organise the rota. You get the same pay, but shorter hours and fresh air. You've been underground too long. Your assistant is also relieved, and the guard's flat is to be vacated.'

She handed Prim two letters, the termination and re-appointment. Prim was muttering a protest when an unfamiliar man loped out of the shadows. Prim styled himself a connoisseur of the criminal classes, despite encountering little worse than drunkenness and minor affray. For once, he recoiled. The intruder had a sadist's face. His precious cells, places for reflection and the gentle workings of conscience, would be transformed to a charnel house.

'You wouldn't be questioning Mr Wynter's orders?'

The voice had a needling quality. Unwilling to fight, Prim attempted a dignified withdrawal. 'There's admin to finish.'

'The letter says "now", the letter means *now*.' The man took a step closer. He smelled faintly of iron.

Scry watched them, a weasel playing a rabbit.

'All right, all right,' mumbled Prim, assembling his possessions.

After Prim's departure, Carcasey Jack peered into the first cell. 'No manacles?' he said. 'You can't do anything without manacles.'

3

Last Chance Saloon

The gathering in Snorkel's grace-and-favour reception room exuded enraged desperation. The language varied from the petulant to the threatening.

'The Foundation's transfers are frozen, Sidney. He's got the fucking bank onside.'

'He's docked our charitable status.'

Outrage greeted the news, even though the Coracle Technique Society had never met, and its sole officers, recipients of the Foundation's Grant, were the speaker and his wife.

'The bastard has only been in post three days.'

'He's only been *here* five days.'

'He hasn't a clue how government works.'

In a corner Sly watched, listened and reflected. *Has Snorkel the flair to reclaim his fief or is this the keening whine of yesterday's men?*

His master's pudgy fingers drummed a side table. 'There's a saying about dirty linen. Such complaints aren't easily aired.' A glum silence greeted this unassailable truth. 'But bring Wynter down and the good old ways resume. For that, I need ammunition.'

'The Manor is buying supplies with old coin. That's illegal.'

'It's a misdemeanour, not a crime; I need proper dirt, real or manufactured.'

A member of the Artefacts Committee chipped in. 'The Brown woman had no business giving him the Manor. The Committee *never* endorsed it. We've been watching her and she's been in and out ever since. The whole arrangement stinks.'

The revelation troubled Snorkel: the nondescript Madge Brown in league with Wynter? It defied common sense.

The baker, Norrington, Snorkel's placeman on the Victuals Committee, added a different perspective. 'We don't know enough because he doesn't tell us enough. Sprinkle in questions, Mr Snorkel: who were his parents? Where was he born? How does he know Scry and the Apothecaries? That's where the real crookery lies.'

Snorkel felt a surge of inspiration: Wynter *had* missed a fundamental. He embraced the baker. 'I had a Plan B, but now we don't need it. We have him, hook, line and sinker.'

4

Envoi

The ornate high balcony on the Town Hall façade held near-mystical status. Built for permanence in stone, not wood, it enjoyed a commanding view over Market Square like a pulpit in the forum. Here, once in their lives, newlyweds could address their friends at the conclusion of the civil ceremony, and from here outgoing Mayors trumpeted their successes (and, very occasionally, acknowledged their disappointments) when welcoming their successors at noon on New Year's Eve.

The supports, which dominated the view from below, had a rococo look, puff-cheeked *putti* blowing musical instruments, their limbs entwined with fronds and grapes. Perhaps in deference to the matrimonial role, here alone in town the monstrous did not feature. A small platform on legs had been placed on the balcony to enable Snorkel to look over and down on his audience.

Atmospherics smiled on the occasion: it was hat and scarf weather, but there was no risk of precipitation with scudding clouds grey only at their centre. The town turned out, goblets in hand, charged with wine as Gorhambury had requested.

Villains are unduly eulogised on death, so now at his secession the populace put aside Snorkel's venality.

Carcasey Jack followed his new master's orders and stayed away, as had the Apothecaries. Strimmer attended in the hope of incident. Wynter kept his distance, positioning himself at an inconspicuous ground-floor window. Scry stood nearby with a notebook for recording any significant audience reaction.

On the balcony above, Snorkel, in a green herringbone tweed overcoat, opened expansively. 'Citizens – once my people, still my people – welcome. I have so many thank-yous: for your appreciation, your forbearance, even your constructive criticism. I see so many potential Mayors – yes, you, sir; you, sir; you, sir.' Snorkel's finger danced from man to man; no chance of a 'you, madam', not with his world view. 'So it pains me that at a time of such turbulence for our beloved town an unheralded arrival has seized this once great office.'

Unheralded – the word had special connotations in Rotherweird. Gorhambury's right hand flew to his mouth. In the blizzard of events and legal conundra he had missed the most basic regulation: paragraph 1(1) of the *Citizen Registration Regulations*. A Mayor had to be a citizen, and a citizen had to be registered.

Snorkel careered through the breach. 'Where was Mr Wynter born? To whom? And where is our Herald? Vanished! Coincidence? Hardly! We have a cuckoo in the nest, ladies and gentlemen.'

Snorkel scratched his neck before continuing, 'So, it's time for . . .'

The sentence subsided into meaningless chunter as his cheeks pumped in and out and his breath plumed. 'I've been . . .' he gurgled as his limbs danced, propelling him forward onto the balustrade. The crowd shuffled back in horror. Snorkel waltzed, arms flailing for balance, but in vain—

He toppled and fell.

Blood and brains spattered the cobbles.

Mrs Snorkel screamed.

All around the square, arms dropped in shock, spilling wine, and a disbelieving crowd waited for *someone* to do something.

Fennel Finch looked on, her handsome face as hard as stone. It had not been her doing, but she wished it had. *His enemies shall fall; his friends shall be exalted.*

'His limbs danced'

Gorhambury yelled for a stretcher.

Strimmer betrayed no emotion, but his mind was racing. Mors Valett, the town's undertaker-cum-coroner would examine the body and find no wound beyond the impact of the fall. He would find no poison in mouth or stomach. If he was quick, a blood test might reveal traces of neurotoxin, but the masking agents would soon take effect. The sliver of ice would have melted already.

He had been careful, delivering the insulated cold box to Snorkel's private premises at dead of night. He had used gloves and left no note, but the weapon's sophistication, if found, would point to the North Tower's involvement. What he had not anticipated was this twist: Snorkel's chosen assassin must have turned on his – or her – master.

Ever pragmatic, Strimmer moved away from the unanswerable to the ballistics. Snorkel could not have been shot from below. His attacker had to be at or above the same level, and quite close. Identical slim towers with slit windows decorated the front corners of the Town Hall. Facing a fifty-fifty choice, Strimmer chose left, his tread determined rather than hurried. A side door at ground level stood ajar. A middle-aged member of the Town Hall staff was guarding the entrance, her face grey with shock.

'Anyone been up here?'

'Only Mr Sly, checking for troublemakers. What's happening to us?' she asked.

'Cuckoo in the nest,' replied Mr Strimmer, 'like Mr Snorkel said.'

She twitched her head in warning. From an adjacent door, Wynter emerged.

Strimmer played his usual sardonic self. 'Some *envoi*,' he said.

'Fit men do not jump off balconies unaided,' replied Wynter. 'Any suggestions?'

The woman drifted away, uncomfortable in the presence of political heavyweights and troubled by the pertinent questions Snorkel had posed minutes before his fall.

'Probably not a song-and-dance routine gone awry – how about patronage dies, promises for past services are broken and enemies made? Or maybe someone didn't like his speech and where it was going.'

Wynter ignored the jibe and called the woman back. She answered his questions carefully. Snorkel had looked tense, but in no way ill. She had heard him practising; there could be no question of suicide. His closest associates had been in the crowd. Only Mrs Snorkel had been in the room behind him. He had intended to toast the crowd and, no, she hadn't seen the goblet fall. So, yes, it must still be up there.

'Please secure it,' said Wynter. Once she had gone, he turned back to Strimmer. 'Did you dislike Mr Snorkel?'

'We shared the joshing camaraderie of political opponents,' replied Strimmer.

Wynter's riposte surprised not only Strimmer, but Wynter himself. 'I believe you knew a Mr Robert Flask.'

Strimmer had regularly abused Snorkel in Flask's company, but how could Wynter know that? He watched Wynter's retreating back with renewed hatred. The man was truly dangerous.

Wynter felt a parcel of memories break free and release. He saw and heard fragments of conversation between Strimmer and an unattractive man called Flask in *The Journeyman's Gist* and a realisation dawned. He held in his head not only Calx Bole and the artist, Everthorne, but others too.

5

The Rogue Mechanicals

Throughout the day, trade burgeoned in the coffee shops on Aether's Way, the urge to communal discussion fuelled by the sequence of dire events and a dearth of answers. Was Wynter cause or solution? Expectations for his promised New Year speech had risen to fever-pitch.

New Year's Eve still had one card to play. As daylight failed, the townsfolk lined the Golden Mean for the arrival of the mechanicals, cheering every staccato step as the trio entered the gate with characteristic punctuality. A former Mayor might have suffered an unpredictable and violent end hours earlier, but rituals bring reassurance. At the centre of Market Square, three children, chosen by ballot, moved forward to open the caskets of rural produce – only for Wynter, in full Mayoral regalia, to raise a restraining hand. Pulling on a pair of heavy leather gauntlets, he moved to the central figure and flicked the clasp of his casket. To a communal whoop of horror, a hooded serpentine head rose from the rim. Wynter seized the monstrosity and twisted the neck round and round as the creature tried to strike at his protected arms. The other two caskets yielded bloated maggots with spiny backs and a tussock of what appeared to be living grass which thrashed as Wynter balled it in his fist.

Wynter addressed his citizens with a stern brevity. 'These dire happenings are all of a piece. I shall speak of them tomorrow.'

He summoned Fanguin to collect the corpses for examination and signalled the crowd to disperse.

As metalworkers gingerly probed the mechanicals for further unwelcome surprises, voices sank to a repressed whisper. *What next?*

'Mission, Oblong!' The familiar command from a familiar voice prompted Oblong to turn. 'I've already picked the lock.'

Dark rings from fitful sleep added to the usual intensity of Valourhand's gaze.

Here we go again, he thought, following Valourhand as she half-barged and half-evaded her way through the press down the Golden Mean to *Baubles & Relics*.

Crudely cut out letters had been pasted to the window: *New Year Sale*, with a footnote underneath: *All returns to await Miss Roc*.

Valourhand strode in. 'You light the fire. I'll track down the inventory.'

Oblong stood, stupefied. 'Vixen, you're not a shopkeeper – and you'll never be, not in a month of Sundays!'

Valourhand for once deigned to explain. 'When I was slaving here over Bolitho's calculations, Orelia talked about clearing the stock at New Year and starting again. It's the least we can do.'

'Have you any idea where she is?'

'I fucked up, Oblong. Hayman Salt was her best friend and I cost him his life. And no, I haven't a clue where she is. But Roc's a survivor.' She shuffled her feet before continuing, confessing her catastrophic encounter with the ice-dragon.

Oblong, listening in silence, lit the fire, his one domestic skill.

'Why did the ice-dragon come?'

'To freeze the river and protect the town from earthquake. Bole couldn't risk returning Wynter to a ruin.'

Oblong instinctively sensed there must be more to it than that, but he judged it politic to change the subject. 'All right, a sale it is. Let's give it our best shot.'

Valourhand investigated the current display before turning her attention to Orelia's desk. 'Shit, shit, shit,' she cried, producing

Orelia's copy of *Straighten the Rope*. Although it had the same gold title lettering and lavish maroon binding as the original, these pages were blank. Valourhand reasoned out loud, 'Someone took the original and substituted this, which means the original *mattered*.'

Energised, she darted around the room, until the Bexter-Bune microscope on the table by the fire caught her eye. She peered in to discover a slide containing the tiny patch of leather Fanguin had scraped from the original book.

'Oh God,' she groaned. 'Human skin dyed maroon – it was the *binding*, Oblong, not those damned calculations! It must be Wynter's skin. He was attacked in his cell, remember. We've been fooled again.'

'But nobody was at the mixing-point,' he objected. 'Nobody but me and Pomeny Tighe.' He explained the spheres and her disappearance.

'For a dull historian, you do get up to more than your fair share,' replied Valourhand tartly. Now she too changed the subject, adjourning for further thought the troubling question of where and how Wynter had been resurrected, if not in Lost Acre's mixing-point. 'Come on, we've a lot to do.'

Obligingly, Roc's inventory recorded the acquisition costs, to which Valourhand added twenty per cent, unless she liked the piece, when she added more. Her taste was unsurprisingly idiosyncratic – walking sticks and scientific apparatus earned immediate mark-ups, but little else. She had no interest in furniture, but whimsically doubled the price of a music-box.

These humdrum tasks – bringing up the stock, rearranging the display and adding price labels – brought a measure of relief. Oblong relished the physical exercise, while Valourhand took pleasure in honest description, adding comments from the inventory which Orelia probably, and her late aunt certainly, would have left to the customer's powers of observation: *Dog owner once: see back left leg* and *Deeply scratched impression of a pig by childish pen-knife on underside.*

She added her own expertise to scientific instruments: *Excellent for an intelligent teenager, not for the pro*, and so on.

Oblong, initially hostile to the general idea, found the labels oddly engaging. Maybe her candour would attract rather than deter custom; time would tell.

Their tasks done, Oblong made the mistake of issuing a warning. 'Can I suggest you don't go snooping round the Manor. There's something about Wynter – he appears to know everything about everyone, even what's going to happen before it does.' He told her about the prophecy coins and the mantoleon's fate at Wynter's hands. 'So, beware,' he concluded.

'Now there's an idea,' she said brightly. 'It's just the night for a midnight ramble.'

The dark rings around Valourhand's eyes had inexplicably faded.

The following morning the Notice Board displayed the image of a snake gripped by a gloved hand: the third prophecy coin, all as foretold.

6

Filling the Gaps

Day by day the Manor was acquiring a household – scullions, a cook and a porter, and guards outside and in, most drawn from The Understairs. Ignored for so long by Snorkel's regime, they offered Wynter immediate loyalty. Each wore an armband displaying a dark star on a white background like a single Satanic snowflake. This abstract emblem replaced Sir Veronal's weasels wherever they could be found.

One application for cleaning duties disturbed Scry's stern countenance with a smile: *I may be short, but I'm good on the extendables and get to every crook and grannie.* The references were unexpectedly effusive.

For the first time in her life, Aggs entered the Manor.

At seven that night, Wynter sat in his familiar chair poring over his speech for the following day.

His head porter entered and announced, 'There's a man at the front gate. A Mr Bendigo Sly. He would like an audience.'

'I'll see him.'

'If I may be so bold, sir, treat Mr Sly with caution.'

'Indeed, I will.'

Sly sidled in, hangdog but alert. He carried a box wrapped in towelling.

'You've joined the unemployed, I understand,' observed Wynter without standing up.

Sly checked the room to confirm the absence of third parties. 'I'm here to appeal for clemency.'

'Clemency?' Wynter smiled, as if 'Clemency' were Sly's consort.

Sly placed the box in front of the Mayor, taking care to ensure that the towelling protected the table. Cold air misted from the surface. He opened the box. Through the steam, Wynter made out a slim metal tube and a dart-shaped indent, now empty. He picked up the tube and peered through the mouth at the fire: the interior had been rifled for accuracy. The ice must have been as hard as steel.

Toxicology and the art of delivery had always been favourite subjects. Not since the pin driven into Sir Henry's eye, a device of his own design, had he encountered such ingenuity.

'Name of poison?' he asked.

Sly blinked. He did not answer it because he did not know. 'It was meant for you,' he said instead. 'Mr Snorkel instructed me to proceed if his speech didn't do the biz.'

Wynter loathed common-or-garden slang, but he knew that to achieve extremes and eradicate scruple in your minions, you must work in combinations. He was therefore always on the hunt for that rare match where two working together generate a fiercer fanaticism than either would achieve left to their own devices. He sensed such a marriage in Bendigo Sly and Carcasey Jack.

'Who constructed this pretty thing?' asked Wynter.

'Snorkel liked to play close, Mr Wynter, but it has a North Tower feel, fancy but functional.' He belatedly answered the first question too. 'I'm piss-poor at poisons . . .' Sly shrugged. 'But I shine at intelligence-gathering.'

He's casting for the question he wants me to ask. Why not, thought Wynter.

'Who were Snorkel's cronies, Mr Sly? Who went along with this? I want the men, the women and the children.'

'I had an inkling you might ask, sir.'

Sly's list tallied closely with the names Scry had noted at Snorkel's *envoi*, but it had extras: addresses and ages, and a second tier too: their closest friends, all written in a methodical hand at odds with Sly's penchant for spoken slang.

'You start tomorrow.' Wynter stated terms, financially less generous than Sly had hoped, but not mean. 'You recruit from the defence force, but you and yours operate in the shadows. Report only to me, and make no visible move until I tell you. The greatest political sin is complacency, for it loses a winning position. That's why your former master deserved to die, and why I give you what you came for.'

He courteously showed his newest employee to the door.

Wynter felt more secure from his enemies within – but without? His inherited memory told him nothing of the Witan Hall, the location supplied by Carcasey Jack. Bole's vigilance had lapsed in terms of the countrysiders. Over the intervening centuries could they have stumbled on the mixing-point? And where was Finch, the usurper's direct descendant?

He consoled himself with the thought that many had already fallen: Fortemain had been eliminated by Scry's hand, the changelings by Nona's, and Vibes by Bole as the false Ferox. These memories had come in sleep, but with the vivid detail of the real. He had particularly relished watching the hideous dwarf, Vibes, flailing vainly with his lobster claw against the stranglehold of Bole alias Ferox in his escarpment garden.

Through Bole's eyes, now as Vibes, not Ferox, Wynter had also been shown the treehouse interior, the ventilation system and the sophisticated network of rooms. Then Tyke had appeared, Tyke the beautiful boy, the only person to have emerged from the mixing-point untouched.

An old envy flared. He had laboured hard for supremacy, whereas Tyke's gifts had not been earned. An old rage flared too: you do not defy Geryon Wynter and escape unpunished.

*

Early light, New Year's Day, brought an unexpected visitor to Fanguin's front door.

'Hurry, hurry.'

'Wha—?'

'*Hurry!*' Scry's cheeks shone like a schoolgirl's. Frequent contact had dulled the suspicion that Scry had a dual nature, half-woman, half-Fury. Fanguin, still in his pyjamas, hurried upstairs, changed and hurried back. He snatched up a specimen box on the way out. Only his biological skills could have brought her to his doorstep at this hour.

'The octagon has opened,' she announced as they hurried east. In Market Square they caught their first clear view of the town's highest terrestrial point. The structure had vanished; in its place spread the branches of a great tree, shot through with balls of vegetation.

A clutch of morning runners stood in the graveyard, the only reminder that days earlier, Brother Harfoot's church had held the summit.

The octagon's panels had opened like a flower and now lay flat like cards from a Clock Patience.

Fanguin kept the examination logical, starting with the panels: planed wood, but alien; followed by the equally alien tree. The grooved grey-green bark flaked away in his fingers. The twigs had no give and when bent, they snapped. He pinched one of the few dark buds, which also crumbled to dust. The tree was dead through and through, and the seasonal festoons of greenery were not of its making but rather that silent assassin: mistletoe. The parasite resembled the common genus, *viscum album*, with its coral-like branches, shiny leaves and plump berries. Yet this variant had a peculiarly aggressive habit, weaving in and out of the bark like a maggot through meat, and the traditional waxy white berries had a pinkish blush. Fanguin took cuttings, leaves and stalks, and gathered a handful of berries.

'A visceral death'

'Whoever did this wanted us to have the parasite rather than the host,' he murmured.

Scry agreed, privately troubled that Wynter had known nothing of the octagon or its contents. Some other force must be at work.

She probed Fanguin on a different subject. 'Do you know Madge Brown?'

'I know she gives old Gorhambury a head *massage* every Sunday night.'

Scry added this disturbing fact to her dossier on Madge Brown: she had the wherewithal to know every municipal move before it happened.

On the return journey, Scry bestowed a rare compliment. 'You know you're a descendant, Doctor Fanguin?'

'Of whom?'

'The first age,' she said.

Back in his study, Fanguin tested stalks and leaves first, but found nothing out of the ordinary. The juice of the berries, however, yielded unusually high quantities of gamma aminobutyric acid, known in the trade as GABA. The chemical had contrasting qualities – excitatory to a young mammalian brain, inhibitory to the mature. This liquid had additional elements, albeit too complex for his chemistry to unravel.

After several experiments which told him nothing new, he placed a single drop of the juice into one of the cruets of sap. The cruet juddered as sap and juice engaged in a violent reaction before settling. The juice's active ingredients had been neutralised. Remembering the filings, he brought out the second cruet and placed a drop of juice simultaneously in each. Not only did the same reaction occur in each, the cruets edged towards each other until, as before, the imposter was neutralised. To his surprise, a similar interreaction occurred between the two cruets when the juice was placed only in one. The sap's fragrance, he noted, had lost its special intensity. Damage had been done.

Fanguin settled down to prepare a written report for his new master. Wynter had warned of a hedge-priest in Lost Acre in search of a new dominion. An uncomfortable fragment of half-history gnawed away. Hadn't druids worshipped mistletoe?

7

Manifesto

The new regime brought change to the Parliament Chamber. Young men with armbands stood at every entrance door. Denizens of The Understairs sat in blocks, having, unusually, placed attendance before work commitments. Wynter had empowered them.

Behind a squint, high in a corner room which had been the night guard's cell, Sly perched with a small but powerful telescope. His note-taker sat beside him. Sly dictated only essentials: who cheered or jeered whom; who sat next to whom and left with whom; who tabled which motions with whose support. *File 1: Friend and Foe*: the first of many.

Gorhambury had spent a night in the municipal archives. Only a registered citizen could be elected Mayor, but might a breach be retrospectively remedied, and did Wynter satisfy the criteria? Had he been born to a Rotherweirder? Wynter's remarkable knowledge of every facet of local life suggested as much, as did his reaction to corruption: he had already blocked transfers to the Snorkel Foundation, revoked the protected status of suspect charities and hunted through Committee minutes for due declarations of interest, finding few. Wynter's energy had the fierceness of Virtue. Ferensen's narrative might be true of Sir Veronal, but surely not Wynter? Gorhambury disliked the Defence Force, but he conceded that recent events demanded vigilance.

Wynter had changed too. Having previously approached the

speaker's dais with deference, now he swept in, stood tall and spoke with authority.

'Out of respect for last year's candidates, I've read their speeches and found a grain of truth in each, which I propose to share.'

'Who was your mother, Mr Wynter?' growled Mr Norrington.

'Order,' cried Gorhambury. 'The Mayor assures me this issue will be addressed.'

Wynter, unruffled, resumed, 'Miss Roc had a nose for the corruption which has blighted this town. Last week I turned off the syphon; yesterday its owner died, brought down by a poison dart, ladies and gentlemen. And where is Miss Roc, the popular owner of *Baubles & Relics*? She has inexplicably vanished. Rest assured, we shall reclaim your money from the profiteers and spend it on *you*. We shall deal with those responsible.'

An unsettling mix of cheers and silence greeted the announcement. Wynter dropped his voice and crossed his chest. 'Whatever his faults, and we do not wish to speak ill of the dead, Mr Snorkel condemned countrysiders for arrogance. How right he was. It knows no bounds. Think of those three children and the monstrosities awaiting them in the mechanicals. Mr Strimmer said we should retake what is ours. I agree there too. It will be done in due time.' Wynter had not mentioned this disturbing policy to Gorhambury. 'These monsters are not made here. We must find and destroy their biological factory before it destroys us.'

'You do like to say "we", Mr Wynter, but are *you* one of us?' In the mouth of the beanpole solicitor from *Finewad & Parchling*, whose conveyancing benefits from the Snorkel regime had been immense, the question carried extra weight. 'More to the point, having regard to clause 1(1)(i)(a) of the *Citizen Registration Regulations*, are you *officially* one of us?'

'Hear, hear!' cried the late Mayor's caucus.

The wrist of Sly's note-taker ached with ceaseless exercise.

'I am a child of Rotherweird,' said Wynter gently.

'Children of Rotherweird go to Rotherweird School.'

'Wanted children do.'

'Poor Mr Wynter, abandoned like Moses in his basket!' sneered the baker.

'The tunnels, in fact, Mr Norrington,' replied Wynter.

'What tunnels?' asked the founder of the now-defunct Coracle Technique Society.

A lady member of the Sewage Committee, for whom the mysterious tunnels held a deep fascination, rose to her feet. 'There are many. We don't advertise the fact, for obvious reasons.'

Oblong leaned forward. He could see where this would end.

'We've not met. Do come up.' Wynter extended an arm in invitation.

She accepted. She whispered questions; he whispered answers, with gestures for a particular twist or turn. Finally, she gave her verdict. 'He has indeed been there, *a lot.*'

The debate continued to swing, Wynter weaving and counter-striking, but underneath the fencing an unspoken anxiety strengthened into a siren call. *Who else is there?*

The motion to grant retrospective registration passed.

8

An Unexpected Synergy

Fennel Finch hated serifs. They clogged good letters like convolvulus; they had afflicted her former husband's script and Sir Veronal's invitation to the Manor. By contrast, she had endowed the names on the cream-coloured card in front of her – Geryon Wynter and the Manor – with monolithic permanence. The sting lay in the bottom left-hand corner.

Dress: No admission unless unrecognisable.

She had consulted Sly. Wynter yearned to separate Rotherweird's wheat from the chaff, and that meant garnering intelligence on everyone. This condition would serve that purpose.

As she drafted and discarded, more menial staff counted and cleaned the cellar's contents, all bequests from Sir Veronal: crystal glasses, the finest cutlery, ornate plates, silver bowls and candelabra. Alongside them, glassmakers and metalworkers added the dark star and eradicated the weasel, an armorial putsch.

Down the passage Wynter brooded. Entertaining the populace troubled him. Opening the Manor's doors might dissipate mystique, and Slickstone, his most colourful former pupil, would be hard to outdo. And should would-be gods be entertainers?

When Fennel's draft arrived on a salver, he placed it beside Fanguin's report. His forehead furrowed. Their thinking combined somehow. He sensed opportunity.

He scribbled: iron filings, aura, unrecognisable, escharion. *Hunt down the last prophecy coin* had been Bole's message. *It's an intruder placed by the enemy.* Bole should know, as he had minted and buried the others. But by *which* enemy, and to what purpose? The peculiarity of the word 'escharion' suggested a connection with Lost Acre.

A stratagem was forming. He summoned Fennel Finch. 'How can our guests be unrecognisable?' he asked.

She wore a simple pleated woollen dress belted with a shawl: the priestess look. A hooked object hung from her belt. 'I won't admit them unless they are.'

'You'll be refusing half of them – there'll be a riot!'

'They'll do anything to come. You'll see.'

'What about their voices?'

'The South Tower sells a distortion device. You attach it under the tongue. We'll distribute them before arrival, so they *will* be unrecognisable. They'll talk to whomever attracts them and they'll say whatever they think. You and Mr Sly will learn much.'

'You've budgeted for a single invitation.'

'The Town Hall noticeboard addresses every adult in town.'

'Suppose I want to reach someone out of town.'

'You have only to ask.' She did not fidget. Her fierceness was oddly still.

'I want two heat-proof cylinders to hold paper versions. They must glow in a fire, declare my name.' He paused before adding, 'We're after enemies as well as friends.'

'Pique their curiosity? Oh yes, how neat.'

9

Caveat Emptor

Baubles & Relics' New Year Sale defied expectations, despite the proprietor's absence and despite being by the usual rules of commerce an object lesson in 'how not to do it'.

Valourhand maintained the candour of her labelling: 'Wonky means wonky. You'll be sitting on a bargain or the floor.'

She cajoled: 'Madam, if someone caressed you three times, you'd expect a proposal, so I expect an offer.'

She invented: 'That ancient bamboo landed the largest pike ever recorded. What's a rod without a lucky reel?'

She mitigated: 'Scratches, sir, on a tabletop, are the scars of good living. Embrace them. Who wants to live with a monk?'

She used Oblong as a minion and occasional male model. Of a moth-eaten deerstalker: 'Relax. If it looks good on him . . .'

She even versified:

> '*After the death of a Mayor,*
> *Buy a new chair.*'

She sold.

'The place looks rather forlorn,' observed Oblong at closing time.

Everyone had taken their purchases with them, afraid that Orelia Roc might never return and that Valourhand – who had insisted on immediate payment – might prove unreliable when it came to delivery.

The few survivors huddled together in the middle of the shop surrounded by an ocean of bare floor.

'You mean, didn't we do well.' She gestured at a tall figure lurking by the front window. 'We might be about to do better.'

Oblong gulped. 'It's Wynter, Geryon Wynter, *the* Wynter.'

'So, let him in.'

Wynter had exchanged his Mayoral regalia for a long overcoat.

'I don't think I know you,' said Valourhand frostily.

'If memory serves, you missed all three of my addresses to the town. I'm Geryon Wynter, your new Mayor. I trust Miss Roc is well?'

'There's a side table, a rackety sofa, a chamber pot, a lamp in need of wiring and a stuffed infant crocodile. Take your pick.'

Wynter declined the invitation. He strode to the rear, picked up the ledger and thumbed through.

'Hey, that's not yours.'

'I don't have to own a book to browse it, Miss Valourhand.'

He was focusing, Oblong noted, on the 'E' entries.

'We're out of egg-timers,' added Valourhand facetiously.

Wynter ignored her, shifting his attention to the shelf above Orelia's desk with its reference books on furniture and *objets d'art*, again the 'E' entries.

'Have either of you heard of an escharion?'

Wynter wrote the word down and gazed into their faces like an inquisitor.

Valourhand suffered a jolt of self-rebuke. She must rejoin the game. Her manner changed in a trice. 'Why do you ask?'

Annoyingly, Oblong answered. 'The word appears on a coin, one of several buried beneath Market Square. I don't think Mr Wynter was expecting it. They all had his head on them, save this one.'

Valourhand tried again to draw him out. 'Maybe it's a book.'

Wynter shrugged. 'It's unknown to the British Library.'

Oblong recalled his discussion with Ember Vine about Pomeny

Tighe's room. The address in Hoy had been placed beneath a *china rose*. Wynter's cryptic presence called to mind the Eleusians' penchant for anagrams, and a realisation dawned. The letters of china rose rearranged to 'escharion'. Calx Bole again? But if Calx Bole knew, Wynter knew, and he would not be wasting his time here. And if Scry knew, again, Wynter would know, surely. Riddles of this kind had been an Elizabethan trait throughout: fashioned by the brilliant children for amusement, they had become a favoured means of adult communication, or so Oblong reasoned.

That left a sole suspect: the third Eleusian woman, the second Fury, about whom they knew little.

'Guinea for your thoughts?' asked Wynter, now staring intently at Oblong, whose expression betrayed his breakthrough.

He improvised. 'If not a title, it can still be a character or place. I'd say Milton or Bunyan – how about a fallen angel?'

Wynter looked amused. 'A thought, Mr Oblong. I'm obliged.' He turned to Valourhand. 'Talking of *Paradise Lost*, do you ever go to the wider world?'

'They order, they pay, we supply. There's no need.'

'Who are they?'

'Governments, factions, middlemen . . . whoever.'

'And is what your North Tower supplies the stuff of Paradise?'

Wynter had found a loose rivet in Valourhand's formidable armour. 'I just do the defensive work,' she said, defensively.

'Which makes an aggressive technology less easy to defend against and therefore more lethal. But that's not my question. Do they not deserve each other out there? Have they not thrown away the opportunities? Have they not failed?' He paused. 'Do they not deserve to be punished?'

Oblong gasped at the hypocrisy. This man had murdered and maimed innocent children. 'And what would you have us do?' he countered.

'Eight of the Ten Commandments are "don'ts".' Wynter paused.

'So be active. Honour the worthy, make an example of the rest.'
The smile turned luxuriant.

> 'Hurled headlong flaming from the ethereal sky
> With hideous ruin and combustion down
> To bottomless perdition, there to dwell
> In adamantine chains and penal fire . . .

'*Paradise Lost*, Mr Oblong, a favourite quotation – good night to you both.'

'Intriguing,' said Valourhand as the door closed, 'and not what I expected. He's more layered than Slickstone.'

'He's a cold-hearted killer – and he knows about Orelia.'

Valourhand raised an eyebrow. Oblong the detective would not do; she must nip that ambition in the bud. 'You sound very sure, but then I suppose historians are never wrong.'

'The way he asked after her was false.'

'I deduce that he doesn't care; no more, no less.'

'Why mention her at all, then?'

'Duh! It's *her* shop. He's the Mayor and he's ingratiating himself, that's what Mayors do.' She awarded him a Wynter-like stare. 'So, what about this escharion? Your brainwaves are rare, Oblong, so best to share.'

'You've withdrawn from public life, remember?'

'Bunyan, my arse.' Oblong gathered his coat and scarf, while Valourhand continued, 'And another thing: we're to believe he was resurrected ten days ago. Not only has he memorised every street and person in town, he's read and learned *Paradise Lost*, which appeared a hundred years after his death. Something doesn't fit.'

10

Midnight Ramblers

Valourhand's declared 'retirement' lasted twenty-four hours. After signing off the ledger for the *Baubles & Relics* sale, she visited the open octagon. Torch-beams flickered in and out of the dead tree's branches as Apothecaries harvested the swathes of mistletoe into waiting sacks. An electrified silver wire cordoned the site. Other Apothecaries rose and stooped, like waders on sand, using tweezers to pick up fallen berries.

The following morning, she walked to the Manor. Two young men clutching spears tipped with fresh steel were guarding the open gates. Another man sat in a cabin, snug to the wall, a large book on the table in front of him.

The guards were not hostile and the scripted reason for their arms was comforting enough.

'We're in contact with the walls and the gatehouses. Orders of the Mayor; the next creature won't catch us by surprise.'

Less reassuring were the armbands, the acronym RDF (Rotherweird Defence Force) embroidered on their shirts, their instructions to 'move on' and the way they flourished their shiny new weapons.

That night, in full vaulting regalia, black balaclava and adhesive gloves, she effortlessly accomplished two demanding leaps from the school to a high gable overlooking the Golden Mean. She had added a sling-line to her repertoire to bring balconies into play when roofs could not be aligned, a common obstacle in districts dominated by towers. To her dismay, two sentries were patrolling from the Gatehouse to Market Square and another two the town walls. What had happened to the ancient freedoms? Why shouldn't a young woman be free to cavort among the rooftops?

She re-mapped her route. Crossing the Golden Mean would be too risky, so she would tackle the octagon first. Using the sling-line as much as the pole, she made her way to a narrow alley which abutted the cemetery. By the splaying silhouette of the dead tree, two black caps bobbed together and apart: Apothecaries on guard. Of the mistletoe, there was no sign. They clearly intended to keep all berries well away from the populace. But why was this parasitical crop so valuable?

She removed from her backpack a wheeled clockwork toy-cum-firework of her own design which she called 'The Distractor'. She released two timers, one for motion and one for ignition, and then the brake. It careered past the Apothecaries, emitting an intermittent luminous glow and an eerie low whistle.

The mantoleon had conditioned even hard-nosed Apothecaries to expect the fantastical: one pointed, the other loosed an arrow and both pursued it down the slope towards the cliff-face.

Valourhand had only a few minutes. *Ignore the obvious places; they would have searched those already.* She crawled around the bole and there, pinched between a root and the ground, she found two berries attached to a single stalk.

The Distractor exploded with a deafening and provocative 'tee-hee', the cue for Valourhand to run.

An arrow thwacked into a beam at the alley's mouth at head-height – not a warning shot; they meant to kill. Mercifully, the Apothecaries lacked initiative as well as accuracy. Having been ordered to guard the tree, they dutifully opted to resume their previous positions while she followed a labyrinthine ground-level route to Market Square via The Understairs.

The Golden Mean sentries had a similar mindset, mechanically turning back from the mouth of Market Square, whether coming from north or south. After a quick sprint as their backs turned, she launched herself from street to balcony to roof to Aether's Way to balcony and she was on her way again.

The Manor posed a different challenge because the wall obscured the likely line of patrol. Landing on the open lawn risked instant detention, or worse, but now her earlier reconnaissance paid off. The gardens beyond the gates lay in darkness, which meant that the cabin was presently unoccupied. She cleared the wall and landed like a cat on the cabin's flat roof.

A single sentry following the wall faced away and soon passed from view. The front porch would be guarded, or at least the front door would be locked. She left the pole resting against the wall, zigzagged her way to a side wall, snagged her line on a drying room's low chimney, abseiled up and repeated the process to gain the main roofline.

Finch held the Manor's plans in the *archivoire*. On the night of the Herald's abduction, she had sneaked a glance in the hope of paying Slickstone a visit when the opportunity arose. Her brief encounter with Wynter at *Baubles & Relics* had confirmed that anywhere other than the master bedroom would be beneath him.

Kill Wynter. She patted the stiletto strapped to her right boot. Then it would all be over and Hayman Salt avenged. She navigated the gullies until the master bedroom was directly beneath her. Sir Henry Grassal's arms had been set in the wall above, too inaccessible or too faded for Wynter or Slickstone to trouble to efface them.

Securing her line on the nearest stack, she bounced down the wall, freezing when the sentry came into view. A small catch and pulley catered for ascent and descent, although gravity made the former exercise slower.

She bounced down to the double window. The left side was open, but obstructed by curtains of heavy damask. She had overlooked that possibility, having no time for such fripperies herself. At least the pole and rings were wooden, less likely to rattle or squeak. In a tiny gap, candlelight flickered. She glanced down. The lavender bushes set in the patterned brickwork bed would not break a fall.

The unexpected light unsettled her. If he were awake, her prospects looked bleak, but she had no interest in retreat. She let her legs drop to bring her body flat against the window. At a stretch she could grip the curtain, but she would still lack the traction to move it. She raised a boot, extracted the stiletto and stabbed through the curtain close to the rings. This time she had the leverage. The curtain drew back.

She bit her lip to contain a scream: Wynter in a white nightgown stood two feet away, staring straight at her, motionless, save for his face, which was twitching like a dreaming dog. Inexplicably, he made no move. She might as well have been invisible.

The eyes looked, yet did not see, reminding her of a pithy missive from Rhombus Smith, introducing overnight stays for the upper forms: '*Should you encounter a glassy-eyed pupil roaming the passages, assume he or she is a sleepwalker. They'll think they're somewhere else, so do not wake them; just lead the victim back to bed with kindness and stealth.*'

Not this one, he's getting steel between the ribs.

She worked out her entry: squeeze through sideways, roll forward to the floor and strike.

Then he moved, his left hand lifting a piece of paper, the right hand a pencil in a brass holder. He wrote laboriously, like a child struggling with dictation, three words only. He held the paper in front of him, so close that Valourhand could read the large, clumsy letters: *Thy aged girls*. If a reference to the female Eleusians, it seemed pointless: Wynter must surely know of their continued existence. Above the letters, someone had drawn two trees, one facing up and one down, with conjoined roots. The fine line was at odds with the clumsy writing.

Valourhand hesitated. Some deep mystery was playing out. Might killing Wynter make it insoluble? And, with Bole still out there somewhere, leave them more exposed rather than less? After all, riddles and deep-laid plans had hallmarked Bole's handiwork to date.

She never reached a conclusion for a flying creature pummelled her shoulder from behind, knocking her clear of the sill. The stiletto toppled to the ground, where it stood impaled and proud, an infant Excalibur.

Working the pulley, she accelerated her descent, swinging from side to side, head twisting to locate her assailant.

A flash of white over the ramparts closed at bewildering speed. Spun upside down by a second blow, strong as a flailing arm, Valourhand flapped like a beetle on its back. An owl-like creature hovered feet away with feet extended, part talons, part toes. An avian predator, but with human elements too. *It's aligning my eyes*, thought Valourhand. Stripped of any means of physical counter-attack or defence, she tried the only available option.

'I'm a friend,' she mouthed, still inverted.

Not these words, Valourhand was sure, but something else stalled the intended assault. The creature circled her dangling body before darting away at the same breakneck speed.

She righted herself, reached the ground, retrieved the stiletto and released the remote catch. The line spun round the chimney and scraped along the slate roof before falling at her feet and rewinding. She glanced up. The curtain had not changed position, nor had the light from the candle behind it.

That moment of final inspection nearly cost Valourhand her life. Two sentries, spears levelled, sprinted from the shadows, young men, as fast as her and no less determined. She had taught them both in the past, but old bonds had sundered. Her stiletto lacked the reach for attack, so she swirled the sling-line about her and brandished her blade, knowing neither would, or indeed could, halt their charge.

Miraculously the owl-boy, minutes earlier her attacker, now saved her, flitting between her pursuers, flapping around their faces, shrieking and diving, inducing hesitation as well as distraction. She rushed to the cabin, seized her pole and vaulted the wall. In minutes, she had reached the security of Rotherweird's roofscape, sentries and owl-boy alike vanished from view.

She allowed herself a moment to take stock.

The owl-boy had saved Wynter from her, and her from the sentries. The face, though foul, had exuded intelligence, surely a creature of the mixing-point. She formulated her theory: somehow the owl-boy knew that she, like Wynter, had been to the other place and therefore that either of them might have the stones and the knowledge to unravel his tangled being. Therefore, both of them should be preserved.

But for Wynter's behaviour, she had no explanation. Sleepwalking rarely afflicted adults, and never in her experience did its sufferers write unconsciously. Moreover, the curt message – *thy* aged girls, not *my* – suggested a third party communicating with Wynter, not Wynter with himself.

If Bole – who was he now? Where was he, and how was he pulling the strings? Bole had bested them at every turn so far, ever leaving dark questions with no answers in his wake.

Below her, a solitary vehicle hurried from The Understairs towards Market Square. Valourhand had not seen the like in Rotherweird before. Painted black all over, it had four wheels, not three, solid sides and roof, with two doors and a running board at the rear. Its pace and stealth indicated the vacuum technology enjoyed by the Polks' charabanc.

Valourhand decided against a closer look for fear of endangering her precious cargo, the two mistletoe berries of unusual colouring.

The Dark Rickshaw

The baker swore as he clambered out of bed. The town was going to the dogs: a usurper in power and now disrespect for the *Curfew Regulations*. The rattle of booted feet beneath his window gave way to the crump of a pummelling fist on the front door.

'Open for the RDF,' hissed an unfamiliar voice.

The mantoleon had brought horror to the streets, but violence by man on man had hitherto remained a stranger in Rotherweird.

'For fuck's sake,' replied Norrington, 'look at the hour and learn the law!'

Aggressive by nature (his chin jutted even in repose), Norrington flung the door open – to be greeted by a hefty punch to the stomach, which doubled him over. A sackcloth hood was thrust over his head and tied tight. Two men bundled him into the black rickshaw. He kicked and pummelled the walls and yelled, but mattresses affixed to the floor, sides and ceiling absorbed the blows and stifled his cries.

'You going to be quiet or not?' asked a male voice roughly when the vehicle halted and they reopened the rear doors.

The cowled head nodded, prompting the removal of the hood. He was at the mouth of the prison. They marched him into the gloom, where another man with a bald crown and jagged teeth awaited them. He wore a leather apron and smelled of excrement and death.

'You have displeased Mr Wynter.' The lower lip curled down as he spoke. The voice had an unpleasant grating timbre.

'Who's this? You're not from the town – you're another unregistered interloper. How dare you . . .'

The man walked a step closer. 'The name is Carcasey Jack. I do to uppity people what others do to your bread.' Half the upper lip curled. The hand moved to the wafer-thin blade at his waist.

'I remove the crust.'

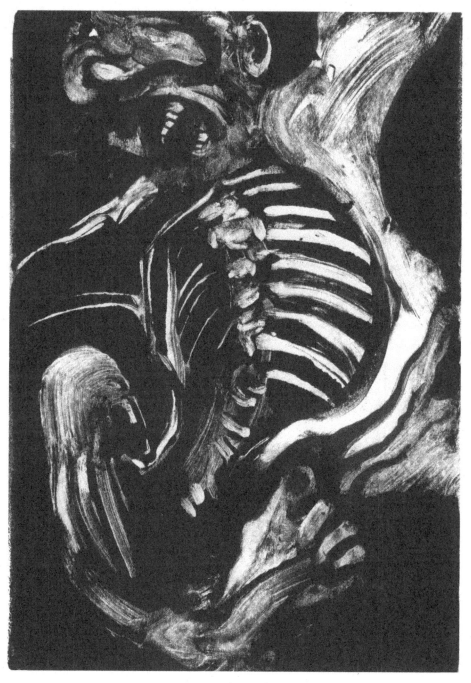

'I remove the crust.'

OUT OF TOWN

I

Spring Steps

The Rotherweird Bicycle Company, despite a seasonal width of choice, could not match Oblong's gangly physique. Thighs or knees caught the handlebars; palms rather than fingers met brake handle and gears; even the seat rubbed. Fearful of being seen by a pupil, he left early and wheeled his way until beyond the gate.

Spectators tended to aggravate his natural clumsiness, but in their absence, toes turned out and knees pumping almost at right angles, he achieved a rhythm of sorts. He reached Hoy at noon. The *Hoy Visitor's Guide*, best described as twee, identified Spring Steps as an arched passageway squeezed between two late eighteenth-century houses opposite the church. On the map it led nowhere.

The genteel Georgian houses, all symmetry and elegance, would not have shamed a cathedral close, with their elaborate railings painted black, topiary, generous sash windows and ornate porches with fanlights shaped like the setting sun.

The archway, flanked and almost obscured by a pair of bay trees in tubs, shaped to the last leaf, sheltered an earlier age. In the shadows behind, at the opposing corners of the arch, lurked an angel and a demon in stone, the former holding aloft a flaming sword and the latter brandishing a trident.

Oblong squeezed past. The map had not lied: there was an alley, stone-built and little wider than Oblong himself. It turned left, right and left past gardens to which it gave no access, to end at a single iron gate festooned in padlocks. The name *The Aberration* wound through the iron railings. He peered through, recoiled and peered again. Beyond a modest garden, a solitary half-timbered tower-house, Rotherweird-style through and through, had been tucked in between its well-bred neighbours. Even the carvings were there, riffs on oak faces and animal grotesques.

A post-box bore an unchallenging monogram:

AC

There was no bell, no knocker, and no way of announcing himself that Oblong could see. A solitary light shone from the topmost window. He had come too far to retreat now.

'Hello-o?'

No curtain twitched, no door opened, no window shifted; nothing.

AC. A rummage in his memory summoned an alliterative title, an old book Fanguin had bought from Bevis Vibes at the Hoy Book Fair some years ago: *The Vagrant Vicar*. The author, a local antiquary, had the striking name Ambrose Claud – and he claimed to have visited the Rotherweird Valley.

The memory sharpened his wits. The gate had two supporting piers, an odd mix of undressed stone, five small, perfect, light-coloured squares, others with one straightened edge. The mortar looked unconvincing. He pressed a random light stone without effect. He pressed harder and it clicked. He counted twenty-one of the straight-edged irregulars. He had vowels and consonants – but how to reset?

Answer: a single hexagonal stone where he should have expected it, between the hinges. He pressed, and then, treating the stones as tiles in alphabetical order from left to right, entered A-M-B-R-O-S-E-C-L-A-U-D.

To his astonishment, a bell tinkled on the tower's first floor, then the second, then the third.

No person came, but a dog did. Unflattering words came first –

mongrel, misshapen cur – but gentler ones followed swiftly: intelligent, stealthy, *large*. He looked, sniffed and nuzzled through the railings. Oblong could relate to dogs. They liked to be liked, not fawned over. A pat on the head was as good as a handshake.

The dog trotted back, returning with a young man with prematurely white hair. The right shoulder hunched from time to time, the face jerking up too, almost as if he were addressing an invisible parrot. He was lean, almost handsome, eyes limpid with a tinge of anxiety or sadness.

He smiled as he opened the gate from the side opposite the hinges. The padlocks were a mere deterrent.

'Ambrose the Unlucky,' said his host, offering a firm handshake.

'Sorry?'

'Ambrose the Thirteenth – do come in.'

A Rotherweird-style front door led to a Rotherweird-style hall panelled in oak, Rotherweird's building material of choice. But the eye did not rest on structural features. The walls, Rotherweird-style, held no pictures, but unlike Rotherweird, positively heaved with history. Brackets and shelves in various styles sported pots, plates, spears, fragments of mosaic, glass cases filled with coins, and much, much more. Many had notes pinned or fixed with tape or sealing wax, the script often faded to near-invisibility.

Oblong peered at the captions as they passed: *Purchased, Ambrose VI, Derbyshire*; *Unburied, Ambrose III, Sussex*, and so on. The furniture in the hall and on the upper landing was no less burdened. He had chanced on a dynasty of jackdaws, collectors of artefacts nationwide.

'The house is a beach for time's jetsam,' said Claud jovially. 'Every piece has a story and the cacophony can overwhelm at first. So, let's find a quiet space.'

He skipped down a short passage. 'Quiet space' meant a tidy, unexceptional kitchen, if old-fashioned, where a fire glowed in an old cooking range.

'How about a name?' he asked.

Oblong blushed. He had been overwhelmed by his surroundings and the unexpected warmth of the welcome. 'I'm so sorry – how rude of me – I'm Jonah Oblong, Rotherweird School's modern historian.' Oblong's head suddenly jerked around the room as he sensed an additional presence.

'I feel it too,' said Claud. 'You've been to the other place, but not in the mixing-point, just like me – Cur, however, has been in both. That's not my choice of name, I must stress, but his. Cur stands for cursed. There's a boy in there somewhere.'

Cur sat beside Oblong as if in affirmation.

'Forgive me if I take stock,' stuttered Oblong. 'What on earth have you been doing in the other place?'

'Every Claud goes on reaching majority. It's our initiation, if you like. You have to bring back one example of its distinctive fauna. I chose an oversize bird's egg. For most of us, once was enough, but Ambrose I made a habit of it.'

'Ambrose I?'

'Ambrose the Audacious,' said Claud, 'the fifteenth-century founder of the dynasty. He was a priest and built a chapel west of town. It's still standing, but no longer in use.' Claud moved to the range. 'Nothing ousts chill like hot soup – all right with you? And I propose wine in the interim; it's that kind of day.'

He poured them each a glass, a deep ruby-red, as Oblong struggled to assimilate the flood of revelations. The current Ambrose was not an immortal from the mixing-point, but the dog was. Valourhand had mentioned a canine survivor from *The Agonies* which she had called the Mance.

'Have you had Cur long?'

'He's a family friend, he comes and goes. Ambrose III found him, or vice versa.'

That figures date-wise, thought Oblong. *He's one of Wynter's creations.*

'But what brings you here, Mr Oblong? We like to keep our collection secret.'

'The word "escharion" and a china rose.'

Claud looked pensive but he made the link immediately. 'So they're at it again. Anagrams, riddles; that's the trouble with child prodigies, they never really grow up.' He refilled their glasses. 'Bring your wine, you might need it. We're moving from object clutter to literary clutter.'

During the ascent, Claud pointed out a Saxon torc in a glass case labelled, *Bought from Geryon Wynter by Ambrose III, Rotherweird Valley*. 'Wynter had no money when he first arrived.'

The top-floor library, an *archivoire* in miniature, explained Claud's knowledge of these arcane details. Events, personalities and transactions had been slavishly recorded over the centuries in chronologically ordered and numbered volumes. Oblong fleetingly felt peeved: he had fancied himself as Rotherweird's secret chronicler, but he could never compete with the illicit records of generations of Clauds.

'The escharion first appears in Ambrose I's fifteenth-century annals,' Claud explained, pulling down a small volume of great age. 'He's the priest, remember. No Chaucer, but no slouch either, despite his scansion. Here we have Caxton's printer's mark.'

Cur sat down opposite them beneath the only window, head and ears cocked, as Claud opened the book and held his thumb above the verse.

> 'At the gaytes of Spring,
> When trees are hoar white strewn,
> Escharion must heat the seed of winter
> Lest all men die in bitternesse.'

Claud paused not for effect, but to weigh the consequences. 'Mind if I write it down?'

'By all means, but it's for your eyes only.' For camouflage Oblong scribbled the verse in the notebook which housed his own literary endeavours.

'Perhaps you'd like to see the escharion,' Claud added.

Rendered speechless in this house of surprises, Oblong bobbed his head. Claud took down a much larger volume entitled *Ambrose Claud on Rarer Ferns*. The inside pages had been hollowed out.

Claud removed the instrument and presented it on the flat of his hands like a waiter proffering a plate.

Oblong had never handled such an exquisite object. Despite its age, the silver held its patina, a fitting medium for the monstrous details entwined with geometric patterns of high complexity which snaked through the two pipes into the one mouthpiece.

'Have you blown it?' asked Oblong.

Claud chuckled at the *double entendre*. 'No and no,' he said. 'I believe it's to be used once and once only. We Clauds did not settle in Hoy for bridge evenings, croquet and cream teas. Here we can keep an eye on the valley without your restrictions – or so we thought, but it became a dark secret, imprisoning generations. The collection, and the knowledge it holds, is too dangerous to sell and too precious to destroy.' He paused, as if weighing the conse-quences of his family's self-assumed burden, then sighed. 'Please take it to Rotherweird.'

'But the Eleusians planted that clue – that's just what they want us to do.'

'Maybe they're less in control than they think. "*Lest all men die in bitternesse.*" Suppose all does mean *all*. If you ever pop into our family chapel, you'll get my drift. There were, maybe still are, hedge-priests in the other place, from way, way back. One of them gave this to Ambrose I, and no doubt for a reason. Mr Wynter isn't the only player in the game.'

Old Oblong would have turned bashful and rejected the request, but he had changed, and Cur was watching closely. Also, he took this particular Claud to be a force for good.

New Oblong accepted.

Claud wrapped the escharion in a velvet bag.

Over soup, then cheese, they discussed history, including the ifs and buts of the Roman withdrawal from Britain, a subject wholly off-limits in Rotherweird.

At the gate, Claud delivered a last surprise. 'What I'd really like to be is an honorary citizen of Rotherweird. But that's a right to be won, I suppose.'

After watching Oblong around the first corner, he turned for home, but Cur did not follow him.

'Off again,' he said to the dog, more statement than question. Cur loped down the alley and waited, before moving off again. Claud inhaled deeply to clear his head. It was beginning to freeze again. He judged his visitor maladroit and pedantic, not unfamiliar vices in the Claud family, but with compensating qualities: decency, persistence and a willingness to take risks. Had he said too much or too little? He had held nothing back concerning the escharion, but he had omitted the friendship between his father, Ambrose XII the Astronomer, and Professor Bolitho. Too much knowledge is a dangerous thing.

Anxiety about taking the escharion to town in easy reach of Wynter and a craving for sympathetic company diverted Oblong's descent. Unsure of the way from Hoy, he trusted to instinct and luck and veered right halfway down the escarpment. The frail beam of his front lamp bounced along the fringes of a narrow lane. Huge oaks pressed like closing sentinels, dusk drained to darkness, horizons closed in and he lost his bearings.

Fortune more often than not abandons the brave, but tonight she stayed. Oblong swerved around a corner and joined a more generous uphill road which he instantly recognised from previous visits.

A familiar address halted his relieved descent from the Ferdys' front gate to the house.

'Unexpected pleasure, Obbers, but may I say, you've a mighty peculiar silhouette on two wheels.'

'Thanks, Jones – but what are you doing here?'

The gym teacher held a churn in one hand, a sack of winter vegetables in the other. By way of reply, he placed both on the ground and steered Oblong towards a wooden outhouse shaped like a hull with gun-ports.

'You have to hear this.'

Jones prised a shutter open, crouched and listened. Oblong followed suit. Inside the hen-house a familiar voice was concluding a night-time story.

'Now, my fluffies, having relished the sad tale of *The Thrush, the Weevil and the Apple*, tomorrow Finchy-boy edges closer to the drumstick with *The Fox and the Canary*. G-olé!'

Jones whispered, 'It's bizarre, Obbers! They adore Finch-speak, and Finch adores them. They can't stop laying.'

Finch reversed out of the hen-coop, displacing a rooster from his right shoulder as he closed the door. He carried a pail half-filled with speckled brown eggs.

'They cluck at the good bits,' said Finch, greeting Oblong with his free hand.

'We'll be constipated for life at this rate,' muttered Jones.

Inside, three armchairs faced a roaring fire.

'Where are the Ferdys?'

Jones eyed the velvet bag in the crook of Oblong's arm and fell silent, leaving Finch to field the query. 'We *think* – and we *hope* – that Bill's in town for appearances and the missus and the brood have scarpered. It's Wynter, the long arm of history, you understand. He has special uses for children.'

'Fled where?'

Finch shrugged.

Initial badinage faded into serious narrative. Finch shared his tale first: his underground odyssey, the rising tower, the monstrous sac where the observatory had been and his return to the moleman's kingdom.

At this point Jones took over. His delivery had the clipped brevity of a soldier's despatch. 'Orelia and I ran across the marsh. We got to the cell where they kept Finch. The rock wall had opened. There was a scream, a woman's scream. I went that way, Miss Roc to the opening in the wall. I found Fortemain's dead body, speared by a trap, with Miss Seer standing beside him.' Jones added an unexpected poetic touch. 'Inconsolable. I returned to the rock wall, but it had closed, back as before. I heard nothing beyond. We buried Fortemain with full honours, telescopes across the chest, in a barrow fit for a king.'

'You're saying Orelia was behind the wall?'

'I can't be sure,' said Jones.

'The North Tower can blow away rock, surely.'

'Maybe what's in there is meant to be hidden. Maybe there's another way out.'

'You left her!' protested Oblong.

Finch turned surprisingly stern. 'Cool it, Oblong. Jones rescued Morval. Hindsight, dear boy, is the historian's luxury. Put yourself there and then, in the moment, before you judge.'

Oblong relented. 'Sorry, Jones, that was unfair.' Belatedly realising that the three chairs had already been in place when they entered, he changed the subject. 'Morval is here?'

'Upstairs and feverish, but slowly on the mend,' said Jones wearily. 'She's been to hell and back.'

'Her speech isn't that easy to follow,' added Finch.

'A tad rich coming from you,' said Jones, the old breeziness magically restored. 'Now it's Obbers' turn.'

Oblong related Pomeny Tighe's tragic end in the mixing-point, the mantoleon's raid, the accession of Wynter, Snorkel's unexpected and unexplained demise, the clue in Pomeny Tighe's room and his trip to the Clauds' family tower in Hoy. He quoted the Chaucerian verse by Ambrose I and produced the escharion as his final flourish.

'Some rooty-toot,' muttered Finch, turning the instrument in his fingers before raising it to his mouth.

'No!' cried Jones. 'Cover it up and put it away.'

Finch blinked. Gallantry and heartiness, Jones' default position, had shifted to *gravitas*. *Odds are it's the truth peeping through when people go out of character.* He obeyed Jones' request.

'You've seen it before?' asked Oblong.

Jones half-retreated. 'Maybe I did, a long time ago, and maybe I didn't. But I wouldn't trust it.' He added a casual rider. 'Did this Claud fellow mention druids or hedge-priests?'

'The escharion came to Ambrose from one of them, but nobody knows when.' He paused: a tangent, but it seemed relevant. 'And Ambrose III knew Wynter.'

'A fifteenth-century druid – is that what eating dock leaves does for you?' exclaimed Jones, back in default mode.

Jones laid the table for three and a tray for one, while Finch made a mushroom omelette with unnecessary panache. Oblong carried the tray upstairs to the Ferdys' bedroom, which Jones and Finch had assigned to Morval for its curative view.

She was not in bed. She had sniffed out every inkpot, brush and paint-box in this artistic household and had also found receptive paper, homemade by Mrs Ferdy, in one of the many outhouses. Like a rainbow of all colours, the paints ran in an arc from white on the left to black on the right. Her golden hair flooded the chair back, fanning out wider than her shoulders. Nothing moved but arm and fingers.

Oblong placed the tray on a stool and peered over her shoulder. He had expected a symbolic work-in-progress, an earthing of her grief. Instead, the scene had the instant impact of recent events, perfectly rendered: Jones leading Finch leading Morval through the fields at dusk, the particular meadows irregularly streaked with snow after the first half-thaw, the dead sheep lying in the lee of a hedgerow. Their clothes were their clothes, likewise the posture –

Jones ramrod-straight, the taller Finch stooped, the light-footed Morval. He felt oddly humbled. He knew dates, events and dynasties, but she held a true mirror to what had been.

She turned and smiled. Too often beauty creates distance – stand back, admire, but do not touch – or the false proximity of desire. To Oblong, it merely exacerbated the devastating damage she had suffered and prompted an urge to heal her.

'Your supper,' he stammered. So banal, he attempted an artistic critique. 'It's them, it really is. You're a chronicler.'

'*The murrion flock . . . the pelting river . . .*' she replied.

'Quite so,' stumbled Oblong, suddenly feeling himself an intruder – this was her bedroom, her studio, her private space. Yet he had made a tentative connection between Morval's cryptic words and an observation by Gorhambury after his fleeting visit to the spider-woman's lair. After supper, Finch handed over his notes of Morval's ramblings and the connection strengthened, prompting a grim conclusion. He would have to return to the other place: only an understanding of her symptoms might yield the workings of a cure.

The day had not exhausted her surprises. As the three men gazed into the blazing embers, the iron grate tinkled and sparks flew as an object fell down the chimney. They all craned forward. A cylinder glowed in the embers, the writing on its side stencilled in fire: *Geryon Wynter invites.*

Jones hauled the cylinder out with the tongs and doused it under the tap. Finch, master of documents, unfurled the scroll inside.

'It's a party at the Manor, Valentine's Day, addressed to any adult resident here – but you have to be unrecognisable. Voice disguisers will be provided at the gatehouse, apparently.'

'How on earth do you make yourself unrecognisable?' asked the self-consciously conspicuous Oblong.

'My dear boy,' said Finch, '*every* Rotherweird home has a dressing-up box.'

*

In the early hours, with the fire dead and the men asleep, Morval slipped downstairs. Chimneys don't rattle without reason. She read the scroll on the table with no sense of danger or self-preservation. Such an event had to be recorded, *ergo*, she must be there. Only her solitary gift had kept her sane when trapped in the spider's body. Thereafter the loss of speech and, after its recovery, coherent language, had only accentuated art's anchoring role.

The young man who had brought her supper intrigued her. All her life she had been surrounded by men and women with prodigious talents and self-certainty. Even the spider had been a predator *par excellence*. Oblong's hesitation struck her as virtuous. His odd physique had character. She hoped he would do something memorable deserving of preservation in paint.

A Bard in Lost Acre

Oblong followed the precept that dawn to early morning was the safest time to visit the other place. He rose in the early hours and left a note thanking Finch and Jones for supper and their company. The escharion he placed beneath the bed in his temporary room.

He reached the white tile later than he would have liked and survived his entry, but it was painful and more dislocating than usual. Once in, however, the open meadow was unusually quiet. The dark star, all but burnt out, had declined to a mere smudge. The survivor of the original impact, creator of these two parallel worlds, was now itself approaching extinction.

He reached the great tree and scrambled down to the stream and over it before blundering into a silvery wire: a fragment of the spiderwoman's web. Minutes later, he caught the gleam of a brass door-handle. He hurried in, closing the door behind him.

Hips and ankles met hard edges as he groped for surfaces in the darkness. He found a rattling box and beside it a tall cylinder: matches and a candle. The wick flared and homely details emerged wherever he looked – half a bottle of Vlad's best brandy; glass and cutlery for one laid on a round oak table; a single tap with a bronze bowl beneath; dry grass, flints, kindling and wood tidily stacked; arrays of pans, saucepans and oil-lamps. He ran a finger along the tabletop, gathering a smudge of dust. He heaved a sigh of relief. No one had been here since Valourhand's summertime visit.

The room was pleasantly warm despite the season and the bare stone flags. He traced the heat source to a flagstone with an iron ring by the back wall which lifted to reveal a smouldering red eye deep in the ground: a permanent oven. Beside it, with a space in between, a like slab opened to a cold store, a blue glow sulking beneath the stone shelves. Lost Acre's mysteries ever multiplied.

He explored further, holding the oil-lamp aloft like a miner. A warren of passages spread wide and deep, opening into a variety of chambers, some fair, some foul. A larder crammed with body parts lay next to a chamber with a circular skylight in the roof. It housed an easel, piles of spent and half-spent tubes of paint, wooden boards, a palette, cut canvasses and scores of brushes. Miniature studies stood propped against the wainscot and along the easel-rail: flowers, implements, details of costume. The large bulb-shaped door confirmed that Morval painted when the spider-half of their composite body slept. He prayed the converse was true, when the spider was at work in his butcher's room.

The room felt incomplete: there were too many expended materials for the work on view, even to Oblong's inexpert eye. Behind the easel, he found another door: no handle, and fitted so close that only a hairline declared its presence. It took a while to locate the hidden mechanism, which only opened when pushed dead centre. Fortemain must have constructed it for Morval centuries ago.

Oblong walked in, oil-lamp held aloft, and stopped in amazement. The chamber had the impact of a chapel frescoed by a Renaissance master. The scenes flowed into each other, divided only by hedge or wall. Dead centre, where a tabernacle might have been, stood the largest image, Rotherweird Manor, festooned in roses and espaliered fruit trees. Leaning on a stick, a benign figure peered out. Ordinary scenes – baking, apple-picking, fishing, classes outdoors and indoors – rubbed shoulders with the more obscure. Men, women and children from peasants to the privileged had a startling clarity, with no hint of caricature or invention. They were *real*. Morval must have always painted what she saw – or rather, remembered seeing – not what she felt, but her observational powers were so acute, the distinction mattered little.

Oblong identified Wynter and Bole without difficulty, for they dominated the left-hand wall. Wynter, tall and cadaverous, wore an easy, superior look, while Bole skulked in the background, deferential, even obsequious – but, oh, how he *watched*. The more Oblong studied him, the more disturbed he became. In an adjacent scene the adolescent Slickstone, instantly recognisable by his modern self, wore his attributes for all to see: cleverness, intolerance, cruelty and an immutable self-belief. Bole, by contrast, remained an enigma. The other Eleusians ignored him, but he did not ignore them.

The mixing-point was there, the great tree and the monsters. On his rare appearances Morval's twin brother, the youthful Ferensen, was always alone with Nature. She had only painted Fortemain from behind, his head lifted to the heavens, as if to protect him from later detection. He found Estella Scry, that heavy jowl no less distinctive in youth, sitting beside another Eleusian woman, as Wynter taught from a lectern. Behind, as ever, Bole watched. The dynamic felt disturbed; undercurrents were at work. Scry looked suspicious, not of Wynter, but of Bole and of the other woman.

The opposite long wall furnished a striking antidote: an undulating landscape with one season melting into the next, sections for day and night in each. Everywhere the valley's ordinary people busied themselves with ordinary tasks, with no sign of the Manor's inhabitants. That thought triggered another: Morval had excluded herself. He could understand why. Painting her body as it was would have been too painful.

But Oblong was wrong; she had not flinched. On the otherwise undecorated rear wall, at the base of the doorway, easy to miss, she sat in a meadow, a bag of painting materials beside her. Her mouth half open, her hands gestured towards the doorway. She looked incredulous, and in conversation, but with whom?

On the other side of the doorway, a man in ragged leather and primitive sandals occupied the same bank. Despite the luxuriant dark beard, there was no mistaking the nose and set of the forehead: Gregorius Jones! Not so far away, Wynter was conversing earnestly with a druid-like stranger. Whether his flowing robes were white with black folds or vice versa, Oblong could not be sure.

These tantalising discoveries threatened to distract him from the true purpose for his visit. He backtracked to the kitchen and followed the rear passage to the black tile, which was still dead, and the mosaic of the young Ferensen on the ceiling. On the way back, he found the recessed shelf which Gorhambury had mentioned and let out a whoop of triumph. A very early *Collected Works of Shakespeare* nestled among the library books. It bore a publication date of 1632, at least sixty years after Morval Seer's imprisonment in the spider's body. The frontispiece boasted a print of the dramatist in a splendid ruff.

Excited now, he hurried to *A Midsummer Night's Dream*, written some twenty years after Morval's entangling with the spider. He did not know where the text came, just that it did; nor did he know the full context, just those two short phrases which Morval had spoken in the Ferdys' bedroom: 'pelting river' and 'murrion flock'. Connections engulfed him – the sustaining beauty of the language, achieving in words the vividness of Morval's painting of their journey, and the chilling fact that Titania's speech concerned the horrors of winter:

> *Contagious fogs; which falling on the land*
> *Have every pelting river made so proud*
> *That they have overborne their continents . . .*
> *. . . The fold stands empty in the drowned field,*
> *And crows are fatted with the murrion flock . . .*

The lines had been marked with tiny ink dots beneath the text. Here Morval Seer had maintained her sustaining contact with the English language. On recovering speech, these fragments had been her starting point. He found other passages from Finch's note similarly marked – themes of darkness and suffering, but hope too.

Objective achieved, he hurried back to the white tile, the priceless early folio wrapped in a square of leather from one of the many larders.

'All according to plan,' he announced to himself as he stepped on the tile, only to emerge high on an escarpment in an unfamiliar glade of yew trees, deep in shadow and frost. Like Orelia before him, he was greeted by Gabriel and escorted in the same gruff manner by the same route to the Witan Hall. He arrived shaken by the journey's dizzier moments but unharmed.

Once again Ferensen strode across from the huge fireplace. 'Our pet historian, if I'm not mistaken.' He did not shake Oblong's hand but embraced him like a comrade-in-arms. 'Welcome to the endgame,' he whispered as he did so, before adding a social touch. 'Here, Mr Oblong, the cider is usually better than the beer.'

Tankards filled, Oblong shared all he knew, ordering the revelations according to impact. Ferensen's early reactions mixed the humane and the pragmatic. Stricken by the death of Pomeny Tighe ('the kindest of the three'), he treated Wynter's lightning rise to power as inevitable. 'He's had centuries to prepare,' he observed. Fanguin's adventure with the mantoleon cheered him up. 'Tying up its legs! He's a chip off the old block.'

The way Ferensen looked alternately at him and the embers suggested he knew worse was to come. As delicately as he could, Oblong related the death of Fortemain.

For a time, they said nothing. Ferensen poked the fire and crossed himself.

'When the best are lost, the ordinary must do their best,' he said at last. 'And is there news of my sister?'

As Oblong fumbled for words, Ferensen found a prompt. 'You've a package stuffed down your jacket, Mr Oblong, and to judge from the shape it's neither toothbrush nor nightshirt. Let's start with that.'

'I found it in the spiderwoman's lair.' Oblong showed Ferensen the Shakespeare folio, explaining how the candle of human language had kept Morval sane. 'I shall cure her, Mr Ferensen, you have my word.'

Sometimes the correlation between the old man and Morval's youthful beauty stretched understanding to breaking point, but at others, as now, the bond between them seemed wholly natural.

Ferensen placed a hand on Oblong's. 'You do that, Mr Oblong, please do. But now it's my surprise.' He called over Oblong's guide, who was sitting at the Hall's main table. 'This is Gabriel, the best forester we have. He knows every inch of the escarpment, every tree in the valley. I sometimes think he *is* a tree.'

Oblong wanted to say, 'He's as verbally forthcoming as one!' but restrained himself.

'Would you kindly find our second last new arrival?' Ferensen asked Gabriel, who disappeared without a word.

When he returned with Orelia, Oblong stumbled to his feet and opened his arms. Like writing to the bereaved, words could not do justice. 'Oh,' he said as they hugged each other.

'Oh yourself,' she replied.

Oblong conjured a spontaneous banality. 'We had a sale for you at *Baubles & Relics* – we got rid of all that back stock, just as you wanted.'

Caring for other people's children had been hard work, suspending her grief more than assuaging it, but this knock-back to reality engaged Orelia's old self in a true healing moment.

'Who got the chair with the carved arms and the jammy leg? And the jar with the blue lions?'

Oblong struggled for names, but he could describe most of the purchasers. His account of Valourhand's sales patter lightened the mood, while bringing home to him just how much the shop mattered to Orelia.

Ferensen observed the exchange and said nothing: this was the right way round, light before dark.

Finally, Orelia asked, 'So, what other news?'

Oblong combined his own narrative with those of Jones and Finch. Fortemain's death did not wholly surprise Orelia, for the woman's scream had implied disaster. 'But there's no trace of Bole anywhere,' Oblong concluded.

'There wouldn't be,' explained Orelia. 'Bole strangled Wynter, so acquiring Wynter's appearance and character, while preserving his own knowledge; just as he did with Vibes and Everthorne.'

'Everthorne!'

Orelia told her story simply and well, withholding only her afternoon of passion with the false Everthorne. She had confessed this error of the heart to Ferensen and that was enough.

'So it's the two trees which connect Rotherweird and Lost Acre, or rather their roots?' said Oblong when she had finished. 'The hedge-priests must have discovered it and marked all the known access points with tiles.'

'But suddenly they're rerouting us,' added Orelia. 'Rootwork was among the words Fortemain wrote down and left for me in the observatory.'

'The problem is coming out, which suggests it's the other place's tree which is ailing.' Gabriel's mellow voice and powerful physique belied his stillness. He spoke without turning his head or moving his arms and hands.

Orelia peered at him, but Ferensen dispelled her unease. 'He knows all we know, as did his father and grandfather before him. The white tile is on his land.' Ferensen paused. 'We have a more immediate problem.' He produced a slim canister from his pocket. It contained a slip of paper, which he unfurled. 'It's an invitation to the Manor from Mr Wynter, whose name appears on the side when heated. It arrived via the chimney.'

'The Ferdys got one too,' added Oblong.

'An Unrecognisable Party – irresistible,' said Orelia, now desperate to return to town.

Ferensen grimaced. They were missing the graver implications. 'Did Morval read it?' he asked.

'Not that I know of,' replied Oblong, 'but by now she may have.'

Ferensen prodded the fire again. With each thrust of the poker, he posed a question. 'Who's Wynter really inviting? He must know no countrysider will come. Who's his aerial postman? What's the point of such a party? Why does he think whoever he's after might be here or with the Ferdys? And how does he know about the Witan Hall?'

Gabriel answered the last question. 'Carcasey Jack, most likely. He left home for town. He mutilates animals for pleasure and would do anything for the right coin. *Anything.*'

Ferensen did not dissent. 'Betraying the location of the Witan Hall is a capital offence out here. So it must be a bagful of coin. Wynter will be wary of the Apothecaries. He'll want his own men where it matters.'

Oblong offered reassurance. 'But he couldn't attack here. He hasn't the manpower.'

That struck Ferensen as true, and nor did Wynter know the terrain as they did. But he felt uneasy, without being able to articulate why. 'He has eyes in the dark, though.' Ferensen's own eyes seemed to sink in, as they always did when remembering the experiments he had failed to prevent. This particular victim he had blanked from his mind for centuries. The falling canister had brought him back. 'Strix, they called him.'

'An owl-like bird of ill omen,' added Oblong in his schoolmasterly voice. 'It fed on human flesh.'

Orelia glared at Oblong. *God, he can be clumsy.*

Oblong belatedly changed tone. 'Sorry, Ferensen, you were saying—?'

'Strix was Wynter's pride and joy. He put a local boy in with a huge owl he'd bought in London.' He paused. 'The point is, Strix would know if a house harboured someone who'd been to the other place. He'd be able to sense it.'

'If Wynter has Bole's memories, he knows you're still alive,' said Orelia, remembering Ferensen's stand against Slickstone at the mixing-point. 'Bole was Ferox then, and he spared us both. We know why he spared me – but why you, his arch-enemy?'

Ferensen paused as a horrible truth dawned. It would be as in the old days. It was Morval whom Wynter wanted: she had painted for Wynter to save him then, and she would do so again now. 'We *must* keep Morval away from him – he'll do nothing of note until she's there to record it.'

A heavier question hung unanswered. Were Bole's Herculean efforts merely a bid to re-run the Eleusian days? Had Wynter returned for no more than another round of experiments, another *Roman Recipe Book*, and in time, inevitably, another Oxenbridge to end them?

The conversation meandered, but with a hard subtext: *We cannot move because we do not yet know the game.*

Oblong, accepting Ferensen's advice that the Ferdys' house would be a journey too far at this hour, stayed for supper. With the children consigned to their dormitories, peace descended on the Witan Hall. By way of light relief, Oblong recounted his first arrival in Rotherweird – the tantalising glimpses of the town through the mist, his bizarre interview, Rhombus Smith's evident dislike of Snorkel, how Miss Trimble had seemed so formidable, when in truth she was kindness itself, how Boris had greeted him with a song:

> 'Not all those who wear velvet are good,
> My child,
> Beware those who like silver, not wood,
> My child.'

Ferensen closed proceedings. 'Tonight, Mr Oblong will add a new first to his expanding list. He will sleep in a hammock.'

Old History

These are the halcyon days before the arrival of the other children and long before Wynter. The Seers imbibe knowledge like water as Sir Henry ignites their peculiar talents.

Today Morval has a rendezvous with a boy from the woods at the stone bridge at the margins of the Manor's grounds.

'You can call me Morval now,' says Morval. 'It's my new name.'

'It sounds noble to me. I liked the old one.'

'You must meet Sir Henry.'

'I don't have the words, do I. Not for you neither. What are you learning in there?' Coram Ferdy hops from foot to foot. His ragged breeches look incongruous beside Morval's embroidered dress.

'All sorts. We study botany and anatomy and—'

'You speak different.'

Morval, though still a girl, feels the pain of estrangement. He is slipping away from their present into their past.

Hieronymus joins them from beneath the bridge. 'Ferdy,' he says, 'I can show you an insect which lives underwater and uses tiny stones for armour. Want to see?'

'I got to help in the fields,' shouts Ferdy as he runs off.

For no apparent reason, Morval cries after him, 'We'll look after you. Promise.'

*

But they do not, or cannot, ten years later, when it matters, when Ferdy's being is twisted with the owl's into Strix, and his mother hangs herself from the great oak at the end of the meadow.

1563. November. The Rotherweird Valley.

Dankness pervades the Rotherweird Valley. Trees drip, fires sputter and the prodigies turn fractious. The girls play the boys against each other. Classes suffer. Diversion and separation are called for.

Wynter's black library includes *De La Pirotechnia*, an Italian volume which betrays the secrets of gunpowder manufacture. He will lead the boys in experiments with iron tubes and a generous supply of sulphur, charcoal and saltpetre. The girls he entrusts to Calx Bole, who chooses a mounted expedition to Hoy, taking Wynter's horse for himself and moorland ponies for the rest.

The mist is spectral. Any old path chronicles a history of journeys. Unbeknownst to them, this one has carried Brothers Hilarion and Harfoot in and out on their first visit to the valley.

The girls, save for Morval, giggle on discovering their destina-tion: a chapel in a nondescript meadow on the Hoy side of the escarpment. Bole and Wynter avoided even the short climb from the Manor to Rotherweird's own place of worship. So why here?

'Have we been that wicked?' asks Nona-to-be.

Estella-to-be points at a leering stone grotesque. 'It's the Potamus!' she cries.

Bole ignores the barb. A verger opens the arched oak door. Darkness greets them with that distinctive cold which stone walls nurture in sulky weather. Bole distributes torches, but there is nothing remarkable until he walks down the aisle and raises his flame to the chancel arch.

Terrifying images stare back. Men and women fall, interlaced with fire, water and frost; heads twist at unnatural angles; feet splay, and with them fall cities too, towers and arches, beams and tiles, and the earth is cracked with veins of black. There are neither demons nor angels, only a single bearded man in white, standing dead centre with His chosen few around him. Behind them an Arcadian landscape, uncannily reminiscent of their own valley, rises to the rafters.

Morval not only sees, she hears the cataclysmic noise of final destruction.

Nona drinks in the scene. This is ultimate power, the infliction of final judgement. Doomsday.

'Consequences'

IN TOWN

I

A Clairvoyant Looks Back

A mizzling rain muzzled the town. It was a morning for firesides, board games and books. Estella Scry took advantage, commencing her investigation at the Town Hall.

'Might I see the membership list for the Artefacts Committee? I may have stumbled on something significant.'

A batty irrelevance, more like, thought the woman at Reception, who disapproved of *The Clairvoyancy* peddling superstition to the suggestible. Nonetheless, every citizen had a right to ask and the right to know. The woman reached behind her and opened the ledger on the counter top, revealing the names and addresses in neat alphabetical order.

'Pen?' asked the woman.

'No need, I memorise,' replied Scry.

Madge Brown; Floor G, 1 Myrmidon Coil. Scry's nostrils twitched: a high floor in an insalubrious backwater, hardly the natural roost for the town's Assistant Librarian. Above Reception hung a wall chart with the name of every municipal employee adjacent to a window for presence (green) and absence (red). Madge Brown was one of the few spotted red like a sold picture.

'Is the Committee Secretary on holiday?'

'She's on compassionate leave, helping out a sick relative in wider England.'

Scry shrugged. 'It can wait.' She had cultivated her image for a purpose. Dressing prim and respectable kept the less well-off at bay. *The Clairvoyancy* attracted the disdain of the better-off for its tackiness, including those who in secret visited her rooms at night for discreet insights into their future. Only from the Apothecaries had she of late garnered attention and respect.

Where the Golden Mean abutted Hamelin Way, at the centre of a whorl of mean houses, stood a pencil-thin tower with a wooden ball on the summit, the whole resembling an inverted exclamation mark: 1 Myrmidon Coil.

The building had single doors on a succession of exterior landings reached by a snaking staircase. Scry judged the accommodation too pinched for family quarters, with only two windows to a floor at best. She winced at the crudity of the carvings and the rickety state of the steps.

Floor G and its single flat nestled beneath the lip of the roof's gutter. The curtains were drawn and the door locked.

Scry's handbag was an accomplished liar. It housed the natural accessories to her dress – a hand-mirror, a comb, a purse and a handkerchief from an emporium on Aether's Way tastefully embroidered with her initials – but it also contained the burglar's complete wherewithal. She inserted a tiny scope into the keyhole and peered through. A Quondam III, a rare pin-tumbler lock, confronted her, hardly standard security for an Assistant Librarian. She inserted a tension wrench at the bottom of the key-hole and a pick at the top. Ten minutes, more trial than error, and she was in.

First impressions could not have been more conventional. Construct a room for Madge Brown and this would be it: dowdy clothes and sturdy shoes tidily arranged, a card index on the only table with a bookbinder's vice and instruments beside it, shelves stacked with novels by outmoded writers from the turn of the last century remaindered by the Library Committee, and a single virginal bed. Above a mean fireplace hung a fine carving in oak, flat to the wall, of a woman with a vine climbing one leg and a leafless thorn the other.

On closer inspection, oddities emerged. Above the door on a small shelf stood a head-and-shoulders shop dummy swathed in brightly coloured scarves and a jaunty hat, wholly alien to Madge Brown's public mode of dress. Also incongruous for their flamboyance were the fine gold earrings shaped like pomegranates in the solitary jewellery box.

Between two bookshelves a ladder led to a trap door, a conventional feature in Rotherweird for allowing roof repair without scaffolding. Scry put down her handbag and ascended. A generous skylight illuminated a spinney of grey rafters and a flue for the seven fireplaces below. The skylight's frame opened outwards but also slid upwards on runners, facilitating access to the lead flashing at the tower's rim. Scry leaned out.

At that moment she knew.

When her other self, she launched from human feet but returned to land on talons, pockmarking the outer rim of her tower. Here too the flashing was scored like a dart board.

A poisonous brew of half-memories, jealousy of her erstwhile friend, loathing of Bole and unanswered questions engulfed her. Struggling to impose order on the implications, Scry staggered back onto Madge Brown's bed – or rather, *Nona*'s bed: Nona, who was closer to Wynter than she, Nona, confidante of the repulsive Calx Bole, Nona her fellow Fury, Nona the agent (surely) of Wynter's resurrection, Nona the riddler, Nona, who had somehow shed her former appearance.

Fresh wounds opened. She recalled her exchange with Madge Brown in the Manor's Great Hall, when Brown had avoided being left alone with Scry. The aura of the mixing-point would betray her. By the same token, Wynter must know her identity and be party to the deception.

Rage, and a desire for understanding, impelled Scry to a more intrusive search. Within minutes secrets wriggled free of the innocent exterior trappings.

The books had been filleted: the contents were very different to those declared by their innocuous titles: works on multi-dimensional physics, the science of the phloem and xylem, parasitology and, incongruously, mythology, both Norse and classical.

Among the bookbinding instruments, she found fine brushes, a jar one-quarter filled with a resinous substance and a tube of paint marked 'old gold'. Brown had tampered with the portrait of the Apothecaries' Founder before calling her in to investigate.

Scry scowled. *I've been Nona's puppet throughout.*

A desk drawer yielded a brochure, an alpine scene featuring a meadow overwhelmed with blue lupins, a modern building in traditional materials and the words *The Obern Clinic: We Judge by Appearances.*

Nona must have been a unique visitor, Scry mused, *a woman who wished to be dowdified.* In the same drawer she found a letter from Italy with a terse message:

It is done. Tancred E

The writer had added a miniature portrait, a good-looking man whom Scry instantly recognised as the artist, Tancred Everthorne, the most conspicuous of the Rotherweirders from the wider world who had been summoned for the election. *What* had been 'done' by Everthorne? Why was Brown in contact with an overseas Rotherweirder of no obvious consequence?

She peered at the letter. Of all the Eleusians, Bole and Nona had relished riddles the most. Artists rarely sign themselves by first name and initial. She sensed a hidden layer. She shuffled the letters. *Decanter* emerged from *Tancred E*, and with it a word association: Flask had been the town's previous modern historian and had disappeared just before Slickstone's arrival. For decanter read Flask? If Nona and Brown were the same person, could Flask and Everthorne be so too? The image of the corpulent Bole danced in her head. To survive, he must have been immersed in the mixing-point by Wynter – but with what companion and to what effect?

One stark fact dwarfed the plethora of questions: she had been excluded from almost everything, relegated to a tiny cog in Wynter's great machine.

But she left in better spirits. Nona had always underestimated her, heavy-featured Estella. Now she was on the scent and they did not know it. Only one question tortured her: was Wynter their accomplice, or another of their puppets?

2

Île Flottante

North of the town where the river turned south, a small bay held a rich supply of flat stones, a favourite haunt for children who liked to skip them across the water towards the far shore.

'Nine jumps,' cried the boy immodestly.

'Mine went further,' countered his competitive sister.

Their friend, a more contemplative personality, sat on the bank and watched. 'The water's gone scarlet,' he said, pointing.

He was right: a sliver of colour stained the shallows. Brother and sister kicked off their boots before wading out to investigate. The shape resembled a giant crimson sponge, rolling from side to side in the current. It had followed the line of the deeper water before snagging on a belt of shingle.

The children back-stepped, arms waving in horror, lost for words.

The boy on the bank rushed across.

The blubber had a human ear.

The news reached Gorhambury, who hastened to the North Gate, only to find it closed. 'I hear there's been a fatality. I wish to see the body.'

'Mr Sly's orders, sir: no access until it's dealt with.'

'Mr Sly has no status to give orders.'

'Mr Sly acts for Mr Wynter.'

'In what capacity?' stammered Gorhambury. Established procedures governed the exercise of the mayoral prerogative, even in times of emergency. The sentry, disappointingly untutored in the constitutional niceties, maintained his immovable attitude.

Gorhambury changed his angle of attack. 'What happened?'

'He's been skinned from shoulder to toes. Mr Sly says there's a new monster on the loose.'

'Where was he found?'

'In the river below Grove Gardens – but I can't say any more, Mr Gorhambury, really I can't. "Close your lips like a clam," said Mr Sly, "or we'll scare the populace."'

How unusually thoughtful of him, thought Gorhambury.

'Who is he?'

'The ears indicate Mr Norrington, the loudmouthed baker on Aether's Way – the one who does the feisty orange macaroons.'

Gorhambury hurried back to the Town Hall and summoned a Council meeting. In accordance with the *Regulations*, he notified the Mayor in writing. An amendment tabled by Madge Brown at the recent meeting called by Wynter had stipulated that the Manor should be the venue: the Parliament Chamber should not house an arm of the executive. At the time Gorhambury had nodded sagely in agreement. Now doubts bubbled to the surface. The town's carefully calibrated checks and balances were looking increasingly askew.

Lavishly hung with Slickstone's imported paintings, the Great Hall made an intimidating setting for the first meeting of the eleven Guild Masters, nine men and two women, who constituted the Emergency Mayor's Advisory Council. The flickering light from the candelabra and a well-built fire accentuated the strain on their faces: pursed lips, shaking heads and fidgety hands. But they had their notes and questions prepared.

Sly entered, accompanied by several armbanded servants. An iron circle with vertical iron spikes on its rim was lowered from the eaves; candles were impaled and lit and the device was then raised high like a halo over Wynter's empty chair at the head of the table.

The entourage withdrew and still Wynter made them wait. Sly returned to align with fastidious care a pen, a pad with lines of tidy notes and a small brass bell. Gorhambury, Scry and Strimmer arrived as Sly withdrew. Scry sat at a chair with its own small table, suggestive of a secretarial role. Gorhambury, surrounded by *Regulations*, inhabited a larger table near the fire. Strimmer lounged in an armchair beneath the main window, some way from the Council table.

Wynter entered last and alone. He wore a white silk shirt, a stark contrast to a dark waistcoat which almost reached his knees like a chasuble: Church and State conjoined.

'Welcome to the Great Hall,' said Wynter, courteous as ever, 'and our first Council meeting.'

'Point of order, Mr Mayor,' said the Master Baker. 'Why is she here?' He twitched his head in Scry's direction. 'If you'd been to her shop, you'd understand our concerns.'

Wynter smiled, quite unruffled. 'I understand some think Miss Scry too close to the Apothecaries.' Surreptitious glances met and moved on. The Mayor was surprisingly well-informed, and his candour equally unexpected. 'Miss Madge Brown, secretary under the *Regulations* to all governmental bodies not covered by the *Regulations*, is on compassionate leave and so Miss Scry has most kindly agreed to deputise. However, the point need not detain us.' Wynter tinkled his bell.

Jaws dropped, mouths gaped and hands stilled as a young woman loped in like a panther. She had a classical beauty: aquiline nose, generous mouth, tawny eyes and a lithe, graceful figure. She wore her dark hair up, exposing a slender neck. She was dressed in the colours of autumn and winter: an ochre skirt, berry-red blouse and a darker ochre shawl flecked with white and red.

While the Mistress Milliner pondered how best to clothe such an elegant frame, the male Guild Masters affected only casual interest, each anxious not to appear voyeuristic before their peers.

Strimmer showed no such restraint. Not since Pomeny Tighe had he encountered such a magnetic sexual presence. Her skirt was tastefully but teasingly short. In his own estimation the town's most skilful predator, he resolved that this gazelle of a woman had to be his.

He walked forward and pulled back her chair.

She almost ignored him, but not quite. She knew the game. She promised a special hunt, and a special kill.

Wynter made the introduction. 'A few preliminaries. Mr Polk is here as Master Fireworker, but as his position is secret, he will be leaving by the rear entrance. Miss Brown's sister, Persephone, from wider England, is standing in for her sister. She is fully briefed and a registered Rotherweirder. Thank you, Miss Scry, for helping out. I trust there are no objections.'

Scry had had no warning, but she played this most unpleasant surprise as if she had. She rose, placed her pens in her bag, smoothed her pleated skirt over her thighs and, in marked contrast to her successor's lightness of foot, trudged out.

Wynter opened proceedings. 'The South Tower is to be complimented on producing phials of antivenom to combat the mantoleon's lethal toxins. They'll be distributed to every household. We'll be ready if, God forbid, there's a next time.'

'On the question of "next time", Mr Norrington was one of our best,' said the Master Baker.

Wynter qualified the compliment. 'One of our best bakers, certainly.'

Scratch, scratch. Persephone Brown's pen danced across the page: speaker left, utterances right, like a play script.

'I have prepared a draft bulletin.' Persephone Brown read it aloud, the voice husky but musical. 'Mr Norrington was found in the river beneath Grove Gardens, the victim of a fatal attack by a clawed creature during the hours of curfew. His political contribution has been as noteworthy as his *patisserie*. Condolences are offered. Countrysiders are implicated. Counter-measures will be taken.'

'Such a creature would leave tracks,' observed the Master Baker suspiciously.

'The river and the marsh have washed them away.'

'Below Grove Gardens would be below the prison,' observed Boris.

'What are you insinuating?' asked Wynter, his voice now silkier.

'A monster within, or a monster without – or both. I make no assumptions. Who runs the prison?'

'Mr Sly – he did much work for the late lamented Mr Snorkel. He is a steady hand on the tiller.'

'Slippery, more like,' muttered the Master Baker.

Attuned to farming the wind of change, the Master Tanner, formerly one of Snorkel's men, timed his entry to perfection. 'I'm more interested in the future. The Mayor is right to focus on counter-measures. I propose increasing the Home Guard and investigating where these countrysiders hang out – how many there are of them, and what other fell creatures they're cooking up.'

Persephone Brown parroted the Master Tanner's proposal, then asked, 'Those for the motion?'

Subject to an amendment from Boris ('*may* be cooking up'), the proposal was carried unanimously.

Strimmer meanwhile was imagining Persephone free of her berry-red shirt.

The Mistress Milliner changed tack. 'We've all seen the octagon's strange contents. Why has the mistletoe been taken by the Apothecaries?'

'Mr Strimmer?' said Wynter, passing the question.

Strimmer, jolted back to reality, took the opportunity to impress Persephone Brown. 'It's an alien and virulent species, sent to infect us. As head of the North Tower I have the expertise, and the

Apothecaries have the most secure research premises. If Mr Wynter and I hadn't moved quickly, the birds would have got there first, eaten the berries and infected the whole neighbourhood. Imagine the consequences of that.'

'Thank you,' said the Mistress Milliner. 'I understand.'

'Next, we have our pending victory celebration, otherwise known as the Unrecognisable Party.'

Unease flickered across the Councillors' faces at this odd characterisation of Wynter's event.

Unabashed, Wynter continued, his cheeks reddening as his delivery grew more passionate. 'All worthwhile victories have casualties – and ours will be toasted and celebrated. Their sacrifices will be recorded. Remember the Argonauts lost at sea, torn apart by the Cyclops. Remember Beowulf's men, taken by the monster Grendel – they are part of legend now, and so too our brave men and women.' Fanaticism gleamed in his eyes.

'He weaves his own legend,' Ferensen had said.

True colours showing through, thought Boris.

But the moment quickly passed. Wynter's voice settled back to its usual silkiness. 'Fennel,' he said.

The one-time doyenne of Snorkel's *soirées* made her entrance in a priestess-like green shift with dark hair tied back and a claw from the mantoleon hanging on a gold chain about her neck.

Persephone Brown's pen hung in mid-air. This apparition had not figured in her calculations, nor Bole's, she felt sure.

Fennel Finch was staring at Wynter with near-religious reverence.

He half-responded in kind, a stark reminder to Persephone that Wynter had a will of his own. But a new piece, even on a crowded board, provided opportunity as well as risk, the more so if its shape and reach were as peculiar as this one's.

She resumed her secretarial pose, eyes down and hand poised to write.

*

In a passageway outside the Great Hall, Scry took advantage of the fact that nobody stood between her and the nearest back staircase. She had used it as a child, as an Eleusian and later as Oxenbridge's prisoner.

Up a flight to the next floor, along the corridor and down half a flight and she was standing outside the master bedroom. She knew Wynter's domestic rituals; it was too late to make the bed and too early to turn it down. She eased the latch. As on the ground floor, local furniture rubbed shoulders with Slickstone's high-class antique imports, including the magnificent four-poster bed. Two pieces of paper had been anchored beneath the bedside lamp. Scry could make out fragments of words on the top piece beneath an image. The half-familiar handwriting was too modern and free to be Wynter's, and the image too fine for his modest draughtsmanship.

Did she want to know?

Uncharacteristically, she dithered before deciding she did.

A mirror image of two trees, conjoined by their roots, one facing up, one down, decorated the top piece, but the profile of their branches differed, as if drawn from life. The inverted tree bore an uncanny resemblance to the one in the other place. Beneath it appeared the words THY AGED GIRLS in a fumbling script. Nonetheless the handwriting closely resembled Calx Bole's, whereas the drawing looked professional. The words' mildly mocking tone did not feel like the description Wynter would apply to his beloved Eleusians, although the pen responsible, nib still smeared with dried ink, was lying next to the note.

She moved to the second piece of paper. It contained the single word *Doomsday*, again in Bole's writing, like the note found in Wynter's room in the Guild of the Apothecaries on his first morning back.

So many players on one bedside table!

That very multiplicity, and the conjoining of the tree, raised a possibility so repellent that she could barely entertain it. She slipped downstairs and set off from the back door to the Town Hall.

In the Great Hall, Wynter had seized the initiative. 'Ladies and gentlemen, I consider it important to soothe anxiety with good news. We have recovered a tidy sum from the Snorkel Foundation, which I shall be redirecting towards structural improvements, including in The Understairs, whose young men have provided such staunch assistance in these dark times.'

'Excellent suggestion, Mayor,' said the Master Tanner, and nobody dissented.

'There is one final matter,' said Wynter. 'We can do without baseless warnings being delivered from the heavens, as I understand occurred after the last Parliament Chamber meeting. They tell me the voice belongs to the Town Crier, who has inexplicably disappeared. We shall post a reward for information as to his whereabouts.'

Wynter turned to Boris. 'You're the expert on aerial transport. Any ideas?'

'The South Tower produces voice-dispersal devices. The Crier isn't called "Portly" for nothing. He's certainly not built to fly.'

'This isn't funny, Polk,' said the Master Tanner sternly.

'Indeed, it is not,' replied Boris.

With that exchange, and after a few parting pleasantries from Wynter, the first meeting of the Rotherweird Council adjourned.

Wynter sat alone with Persephone Brown. 'It is you. You're so different, I did wonder.'

'Test me.'

Wynter took her to the window and pointed. 'What was there?' he asked.

'An oak bench, and ivy festooned the wall. I liked to read Robert Recorde's *Arithmetic* there in the summer. I especially liked the title of his second volume – *The Whetstone of Whit.*'

Wynter smiled. 'She was a ballet dancer, I can tell.'

Nona's eyes narrowed a fraction. This was not Wynter speaking. He had never seen a ballet dancer in his life. It must be Bole, or Bole's experience. 'A life of practice and exercise – such dull memories! But only twenty-eight years of them, and I suppress them with ease.' She wondered quite how Bole and Wynter had merged, for her strategy had made certain assumptions.

Wynter obligingly took the cue. 'I write notes to myself at night. I dream of unimaginable places. Of course, my erstwhile servant is still on call to help.'

'But your will is intact – you are yourself?'

'I am as I look,' replied Wynter.

Nona detected a hint of *uncertainty* in his voice.

'And Estella didn't look suspicious – of me or you.'

'She's not, which is why we always preferred you, dear Nona. She's dutiful and devoted, but ponderous.' Wynter could not resist returning to what worried him most. 'Did Calx share with you any plan or ambition for my return?'

'Only his desire to serve you.'

Wynter judged the reply fractionally too quick and marginally too clever. He ventured a more testing question. 'What's in the tower?' he asked.

Nona's eyes narrowed. 'Bole constructed it.'

'Quite so, but he hasn't deigned to share its purpose.'

'I imagine,' said Nona slowly, 'that Bole can't just flood your mind with knowledge all at once. Give him a little time.'

Wynter changed the subject. 'I have a problem with the countrysiders: they're holed up in an inaccessible place in the woods. They're fully stocked and watered and we haven't enough men to force them out.'

Persephone freed her hair, revelling in her new looks. 'Leave it to me, Mr Wynter. I've spent much time in Lost Acre. It has many secrets, one of which will fix this problem perfectly.' She gave the word 'fix' special emphasis.

Wynter raised both eyebrows. 'Just wait until my party is done,' he said.

She translated his condition with ease: he wanted his chronicler back first. Waiting was a small price to pay. 'Of course,' she said, and changed the subject again. 'I too dislike the Town Crier speaking out of the blue. It's presumptuous.' Unseen voices from the heavens had a divine feel, which should not be a privilege for the common citizen. 'However, I know how it's done and I'm sure the North Tower and the Apothecaries can deal with it, if I might be your message-bearer.'

Scry reached the Town Hall just before closing. 'Have the Summoned left for home?' she asked the same unwelcoming woman on the reception desk, who looked down her nose and sniffed.

'Most of them – they do have jobs, you know.'

'What about the artist, Mr Everthorne? He looked rather a dilettante to me.'

'Well, he *was* in a hurry,' the receptionist admitted. 'He didn't check out and he left all his paints and brushes behind.'

'How careless of him,' replied Scry, as if the news were expected but also unwelcome.

Outside in Market Square, Strimmer accosted Persephone Brown. 'As Head of the North Tower, I'd like a copy of the minutes. Why not drop them in to my rooms?'

'You can inspect them at the Town Hall.'

'You're quite a contrast to your sister.'

'In what way?'

Strimmer grinned. 'Shall I start from top or bottom?'

'Tread carefully, Mr Strimmer.' She turned and walked away, skirt swishing left and right.

Strimmer leered after her.

Persephone Brown smiled to herself. She had played the sibyl once and she would not do so again. He had been warned.

She slipped into Hamelin Way and hastened on to the Hall of the Apothecaries, where, through a combination of charm, will and the impact of the unfamiliar, she gained speedy admission to Master Thomes' study. As Madge Brown of the Artefacts Committee she had endured Thomes' withering rudeness. As Persephone Brown, she induced a very different reaction.

He stroked the fleshy folds of his neck and, piggy eyes gleaming, invited her to share his mid-morning coffee and raspberry butter-milk cakes. 'I have an excellent private cook,' he added.

'Mrs Fanguin.'

The piggy eyes narrowed.

'It's our business to know,' she added with a winning smile. 'I've come from the Council.'

Thomes spluttered, his napkin freckling with spots of white coffee. 'It's an outrage excluding us – a bloody outrage.'

'It's a privilege, Master Thomes. In the Council, the Guilds must answer to each other. They don't ask about you because if they did, you'd be entitled to be there. That lets you get on with your business – and Mr Wynter's business – unmolested. Who wants to be accountable?'

Thomes licked the edge of a cake. Penelope Brown excelled her dingy sister in all departments. 'What can we do for you?'

'We need a flying machine.'

Thomes' napkin mopped up more spluttered coffee. 'A what?'

She pushed over a sheaf of papers. 'Copy that, if you'd be so kind, and then improve it.'

Thomes read through the confidential prototype licence applica-tion, a necessary step for testing any invention, and the supporting plans. On reaching the applicant's name, he shook his head.

'Have you ever seen a Polk prototype?' he asked sarcastically.

'This one works, *and*' – she took from her bag a pencil and a tiny pot. She opened the pot and dipped the pencil. The point disappeared, but it still drew – 'it'll be invisible. The Apothecaries can watch the world unseen.'

Thomes' spirits rose. 'I see, I see: the eye in the sky, the hawk in the dark.'

She put pencil and pot away and rose gracefully to her feet. 'Once you've downed Polk's rival machine, of course.'

3

Payday

Sly, having no wish to be seen, took a rickshaw to the prison. Wynter's coin jangled pleasingly in his pockets. Mrs Sly would be most appreciative.

Carcasey Jack's legs, sprawled across the front desk, greeted him. The toecaps of his boots, crisscrossed with cuts and scrapes, had the same aura of violence as the rest of him. 'I don't like unemployment,' he growled, picking his nails with a thin-bladed knife.

'The pleasure of a job well done wears off,' Sly agreed, 'but you must wait a while.' Sly put the success of his political slogans down to a mastery of metaphor. 'Mr Wynter is a patient fisherman. He needs time to bait the line.'

Jack took up the analogy. 'So when's he casting the next fly?'

'The Unrecognisable Party is my hunch.'

Carcasey Jack guffawed, a guttural croak like grinding stones. 'Unrecognisable! Only I do "unrecognisable".'

Sly peered into the passage leading down to the cells. He knew nothing of history, but he had worked out the recipe for sustaining power long ago: carrots for those you need, stick for the rest. Snorkel had only been good at carrots, but Wynter excelled at both. Wynter would last.

He placed Jack's wages on the table. 'Remember what it's for, Mr Jack. No chitchat out of school. Be a shadow.'

Jack flicked his legs off the table with a surprisingly agile grace and stood up, his ginger-grey stubble almost rubbing against Sly's chin. 'But I can talk to you, yes? I deserve a Guild all to myself, don't I, Mr Sly? Carcasey Jack, the Master Skinner.'

Sly mustered a strained grin and departed. Thank God he served the intelligence side of Wynter's needs and not the physical. After five minutes with Jack, he felt in need of a long, hot bath.

4

None of Your Business

Valourhand knocked. She received no response, although she knew he was in, for the high study window glowed in the gloom of a heavily overcast morning.

She pounded the oak again and this time she heard a clatter of footsteps.

Fanguin flung open the door. He looked uncharacteristically sober and alert for the hour. 'I'm busy, Valourhand, up to my ears.'

'Fanguin, I need your help.'

'It's Doctor Fanguin, actually.'

'You can be the Margrave Fanguin for all I care, I still need your help.' She opened her palm, showing the single mistletoe berry.

'Where'd you get that?'

'Where do you think?'

'It's municipal property.'

'It's toxic, and it must be here for a purpose.'

'It's unusual, certainly – and it's under full investigation. Leave it to the experts.'

'Why are the Apothecaries involved?'

'It's toxic, just as you said.'

'Fanguin—'

'*Doctor* Fanguin . . .'

She glared at him. 'What's got into you?'

'My talents have at last been recognised. I'm the town's new head biologist. Give me the berry and I'll share our findings in due course.'

Valourhand looked shocked. 'You're working for Wynter!'

'No more than the North Tower or the school or the sanitation department,' he parried.

Valourhand carefully returned the berry to her pocket. 'This will end in tears, *Doctor* Fanguin,' she said, turning away.

On her way home, she dropped in a note at 3 Artery Lane. Oblong might be the most irritating man in Rotherweird, but his feeble mind did house a gift for unravelling Elizabethan riddles.

On the Golden Mean she caught up with Boris on his way home from the Council Meeting. He looked pale.

'You heard about Norrington?' he asked.

Valourhand gave him a hard stare: *I don't do gossip.*

'The baker: he was skinned alive and dumped in the river below the prison. As Prim has been relieved of his duties and we've a new Head Gaoler, you may draw your own conclusions.'

Valourhand did. She steered Boris into an alleyway before describing the house with the dead dog, the dead hens, the manacles and the skinning knives, and the centuries-old golden guinea lying on the floor.

'Now you understand the perils of being caught,' Boris said when she had finished.

'Caught doing what?' she asked.

For the moment Boris sidestepped the question. Only Valourhand's unique talents suited the delicate mission he had in mind, but Norrington's fate had given him second thoughts.

He introduced the subject obliquely. 'The mistletoe is now in the joint custody of the Apothecaries and the North Tower. As neither of them have any known interest in botany, we can assume those berries have properties of particular use to Wynter.'

Valourhand clenched her fists. 'I hate to say it, but Fanguin – sorry, *Doctor* Fanguin – is helping them.' She paused. 'I have two berries and I've tested one. It has the oddest properties. The question is – what are they using the mistletoe *for*?'

'We've done a recce,' Boris divulged, 'but we've not been very successful. The skylights are made of smoked glass. And we can't land to open them.'

'You've *flown* over the building?' She was struggling to keep up. 'How?'

'Well, the Hoverfly has.'

'What's the Hoverfly?'

'My latest prototype.'

The Island Field had witnessed numerous test flights by Polk prototypes, most proving that da Vinci's more inventive drawings were rarely practical.

'Without being seen?'

'Remember Snorkel's bust and the invisibility paint? The Hoverfly has added stealth. But it can only land on a level surface and a rope dangling in mid-air tends to get noticed.'

'Bugger Snorkel's bust, Boris! Your bloody paint nearly killed me and our modern historian.' She recounted the knife attack by the invisible woman on Lazarus Night. 'They're not stupid. They have the paint themselves, so they'll know what you're up to. You and the Crier are in more danger than I am.'

'But the people are refusing to listen,' Boris said plaintively. 'We hoped a voice from the aether would do the business.' Boris had developed an avuncular fondness for Valourhand, whose exceptional virtues outweighed her minor vices. Nonetheless he decided to take the plunge. 'If you could get there under your own steam, open one skylight or cut a hole – and just look in. And I mean just look in, nothing else. And if you go, it has to be the night of Wynter's party. Those thugs from the RDF will be elsewhere.'

Valourhand had not the slightest intention of repeating her Slickstone protest, and in any case, she hated parties as all froth and no substance.

'If the weather plays ball,' she said, 'I'll give it a go.'

OUT OF TOWN

I

Mr Fluffy

Oblong left the Witan Hall early the following morning. Orelia wanted to join him – 'I'm not playing the witness who's never called' – but in the end, she had been dissuaded. Oblong had pointed out that without Salt's key to the hidden side door in the outer wall they would have to enter the main gate where they would be registered. The mantoleon had served its purpose by allowing Wynter to raise security levels everywhere in town. Nor was Orelia exactly inconspicuous. She would be in Wynter's clutches in no time.

Oblong had his own dilemma. Though desperate to help Morval recover normal speech, he also felt honour-bound to share Claud's information with Valourhand. Her off-piste thinking might unlock the mysteries of the escharion. He had left his bicycle at the Ferdys', so he decided to compromise by spending a night there before returning to town.

After losing his way twice in dank weather and poor visibility, at dusk he caught the tell-tale glow of the windows and the ghostly silhouettes of the poles and strings of the hop-fields. Smoke curled from the chimney.

He opened the front door without knocking – and froze.

Before him stood a pantomime man-size cockerel with a wobbling crimson comb and multicoloured feathers sprouting from his rear. Beside the cockerel stood a chess-like red-purple bishop with mitre and crozier.

'Mr Fluffy,' said the Bishop, introducing the cockerel.

'Bishop Gregorius,' responded the cockerel, genuflecting.

In the shadows Morval was sitting beside an open chest over-flowing with costumes.

The heads came off. 'Well,' said Jones, 'what do you think, Obbers?'

'I'm not convinced,' he admitted, 'especially Finch.'

'The point is,' Jones said, '*we'll* know who we are – but nobody else will.'

Oblong, slow on the uptake, voiced his reservations. 'I'm not sure you should be going – and, if you do, who's looking after Morval?'

'You are,' they replied in unison.

For the moment Oblong did not argue. 'All right. You sort out your adjustments. I need time with Morval.'

Finch, despite the absurd costume, turned serious. 'Where have you been?'

Oblong explained, omitting only his visit to the spiderwoman's lair.

Excitement greeted the news that Ferensen had entered the lists once more. 'Did he say anything about the escharion?' asked Jones intensely.

'I didn't mention it,' Oblong admitted. 'I kept it secret, as you suggested.'

Jones relaxed and announced, 'Come on, Finchy, time to feed the chickens.' They ambled out.

How the hens might react to a costumed rooster did not detain Oblong. He called Morval over to a chair by the fire. He did not mention the book from the spiderwoman's lair, fearful of what that memory might do, opening instead with one of the lines she had marked. 'Who's the "fatal bellman", Morval? Hunt in the past for me.'

Morval's face worked. She had memorised the words for a reason. *It was the owl that shrieked the fatal bellman.* She dived into her memory and stammered, 'C-Coram Ferdy.'

'The murrion flock . . .'

'Winter. Yes, Wynter.'

'What did Wynter do to Coram Ferdy?'

When Morval shook her head in despair, Oblong rebuilt the fire. *Take it slowly.* 'Wynter called him Strix, yes?'

'They fed him to the sky with an owl,' Morval replied, a complete sentence. Oblong had broken through. 'Our friend Coram.' She stared into the flames. '*Words are easy like the wind; faithful friends are hard to find.*'

In her face Oblong saw guilt. She and her brother must have failed to save Coram Ferdy. He took her hands in encouragement. He had never yet seen Morval in full smile; now he did, but with the unblocking of pathways came anxiety.

Croaked more than spoken, words flooded out. 'There's a book wherein men may seek the light of truth. *Weaving spiders come not here.*'

Oblong felt this *mattered*: she was mixing lines and plays and adapting them. He chastised himself for his schoolmasterly urge to unpick the references and concentrated instead on what she was trying to say.

A book, what book? The Shakespeare?

Morval's hands slipped from his and she slumped in her chair, exhausted. He would have to leave it for now.

'*The dear repose for limbs with travel tired,*' he said, pleased at finding an apt quotation.

She smiled again, a more intimate smile, stood up, kissed him on the forehead and walked upstairs.

He wanted to follow, but in talent, looks and richness of experience he was but dust compared to her. Instead, he stayed by the fire and pondered Wynter's legacy – such darkness and so little light.

Two days later, at mid-morning, Finch, Jones and Oblong sat round the Ferdys' kitchen table, discussing the immediate future. Outside, Morval Seer was absorbed in a series of cloud studies.

'Jones and I have classes to teach, and term's about to start,' Oblong pointed out.

'Mine teach themselves mainly,' added Jones, 'but their physique requires constant attention.'

'I'll look after her,' said Finch, 'no worry. But I do have to go to this party.'

'It's a Saturday,' said Jones. 'Only the first class of the day is down to me. At a double-quick sprint, I can relieve Finch with plenty of time. Just do the training, Finch: get those spindly thighs pumping. I'm sorry Wynter will miss my party moves, but there we are.'

Oblong placed the Shakespeare Folio on the table. 'She's on the mend,' he said. 'I'm leaving this behind. Study the marked passages and you'll find conversation easier.'

Finch, it appeared, already had. '*Better to be king of silence than slave of your words*,' replied the Herald theatrically.

After lunch, Jones ran back to town, while Oblong cycled. He brought the escharion with him, having decided to hide it beneath the floorboards of his flat. He had only days to prepare a new syllabus and to complete his reports. He envied Jones his cavalier approach to Form VIB, who chose their own syllabus. Jones' reports were famed for their brevity: a system of plus and minus signs appended to only two entries covering all subjects: Health in Body and Health in Mind. The marks for the first invariably dictated the marks for the second and alone attracted occasional additional compliments: 'memorable back flip', 'genius on parallel bars'. If the unsportsmanlike tried, that's all he asked.

Oblong felt obliged to display his greater powers of discernment.

A single letter awaited him at 3 Artery Lane, in Valourhand's distinctive spare manuscript.

In sleep Wynter holds a piece of paper. It illustrates two trees conjoined and carries the words Thy Aged Girls. Can your ferocious intellect assist?

Oblong was too intrigued by the challenge to consider the source of Valourhand's information. His parents had wrestled over the crossword every Saturday breakfast, exchanging clues and answers while he struggled with their pointless complexity. Yet for Elizabethans, codes and riddles threaded the language of power from Walsingham to John Dee. Elizabeth herself had had a private cipher. Coded communications had cost Mary Queen of Scots her head, and others too. Shakespeare and Ben Johnson played with the order of letters. Wynter would have relished the secrecy, but so would his acolytes, with their feverish intelligence and conceited desire for an exclusive language. No doubt Bole too had been driven to compete, even to excel.

Oblong regarded Valourhand's note as a living challenge from history. He climbed the stairs with letters swirling in his head, conscious of his one advantage. Unlike Valourhand, he knew from Orelia that Wynter's drawing represented the two great trees and their shared multi-dimensional root system which governed the passageways between the Rotherweird Valley and Lost Acre.

His ruminations stalled as he reached the landing to find his outside door ajar. Footsteps shuffled inside.

He had no weapon. He crept into the silent gloom of the hallway, fists clenched.

As he lit a match, a vice-like grip seized his left arm from behind and spun him round. 'Gotcha!'

The strong but bony hands fleetingly brought the Fury to mind – until a familiar voice cackled, 'Who's not been sleeping in *his* bed?'

He turned puce. 'I was . . . um . . . visiting.'

''Course, that's how romance starts, with *visiting*.' Aggs dug Oblong in the ribs. 'Bravo, I say.'

'I was doing a good turn.'

'Aggs the super-sleuth says you bin gone at least three nights. That's a good sign in my book.'

Oblong dug himself ever deeper. 'I went to Hoy on an errand.'

'But did you stay the night in Hoy, you old devil?' Aggs opened the kitchen door, revealing three jars on the sideboard. Mercifully, she changed the subject. 'I takes you to be a dark marmalade man, chunky and reserved.' Her fingers gripped a jar, loosened the top and twisted, but then her face transformed from *bonhomie* to grief.

She put down the jar and let her arms fall, crying, 'What's happening to our town, Mr Oblong? And where is Mr Salt? My first client, 'e was, boy and man.'

'He's dead, Aggs,' Oblong said quietly.

'I guessed. You know from their rooms. The spirit goes a-wander.'

'He fought, Aggs, as we must.' He gave her a clumsy hug.

'I also knew 'cos he sent me somat through the post, a tiny box, what he never does. There was a note . . .' She snuffled into a duster. 'It said, "It's of good and bad effect, but more good than bad".'

'*It?*' asked Oblong.

'You knows how I like flowers.'

He did. On their late summer journey to dine at Ferensen's house, Salt had delighted Aggs by naming every wild flower they had passed.

'Salt said it's the seed of the Midsummer flower and rare as rubies. It's to do with that walking tree what came at the Fair.'

Oblong had forgotten that Aggs had been one of the privileged few to whom Ferensen had given the antidote to the Hammer. She and Fanguin had sat together watching the arrival of the Green Man during his play at the Midsummer Fair.

'He said *not* to plant it,' she added.

Aggs' jaw jutted. She was holding something back – just a trifle, but he felt sure, a significant trifle.

'And . . . ?'

'What goes around comes around,' she whispered. The chin jutted once more. *Subject closed.*

'Don't give it to me,' Oblong said. 'I'm overloaded at the moment.'

'No worries,' replied Aggs bluntly, 'I ain't. Mr Salt was a dark marmalade man. You live up to it.' She gathered up her coat and made for the door.

'I need inspiration,' said Oblong suddenly.

Aggs doubled back and opened Oblong's not-so-secret drinks reserve. Her finger floated over a new arrival labelled Bonny New Year. 'That one,' she said, 'is my *Ginger Grenade.*' She grinned. '*Ginger Grenade* puts Vlad's in the shade. You want perspiration, go for it.'

After Aggs' departure, Oblong wrestled with his priorities. He had a backlog of mundane tasks; he was missing Morval Seer acutely, and he had made no progress with the escharion. A hedge-priest had given it to a Claud and a Claud had done business with Wynter. The note under the china rose had led him to Hoy and to Claud, but who had placed it there?

He had played chess as a teenager. Inattention to the wiles of the enemy and over-concentration on his own position had been a weakness – but who now was the enemy? Wynter had acquired Bole's knowledge, but what of his will? Writing messages in his sleep suggested a drip-feed from servant to master. Bole alone had masterminded the destruction of Slickstone – so what other strategies had he conceived between Wynter's death and resurrection?

As for Madge Brown, Scry's fellow Eleusian, he could hardly confront her without a shred of evidence.

Oblong placed Valourhand's note beside the as-yet-unopened bottle of *Ginger Grenade*. He did two hours of reports before sketching out a syllabus based on the nineteenth century's greatest inventions: the steam train, the light bulb, the internal combustion engine, the telephone, the rifle – only to realise that Rotherweird had prospered without any of them. He reverted to the collapse of royal power from the nineteenth century onwards. That might at least sow seeds of scepticism about Wynter's ambitions.

His hard labour done, he pulled the cork, poured himself a generous glass, *digestif* turned *aperitif*, and started on Valourhand's challenge: the meaning of *Thy Aged Girls*.

Aggs was right: the liqueur had quite a kick. Half an hour passed before he realised that he was exploring from the wrong end of the telescope. Plenty of word combinations emerged, but none made useful sense, which took him back to the drawing. 'Think of two trees with conjoined roots, think myth,' he told himself firmly. Then it came, *The Yggdrasil*: Thy Aged Girls reshuffled.

His literary dictionary confirmed the answer: *In Norse mythology the holy tree* Yggdrasil *is the centre of the universe with roots extending to different worlds.* Another reference struck him particularly: *On the coming of the comet and the twilight of the gods, when the world will be engulfed by fire, the tree, though sorely damaged, will be the source of new life.*

He raised a glass to himself. He would enjoy telling Valourhand that his 'ferocious intellect' *had* assisted.

But there was a darker undertow in the Apocalyptic tone, not dissimilar to the poem by the early Ambrose Claud, and he wondered what it signified to Bole.

2

The Cost of Taking the Shilling

'Have a look at these with these alongside.' Bomber pushed two paint sample cards across the kitchen table towards her husband, followed by a pile of carpet samples. 'I'd go for *eau-de-Nil* and sailor's grey: not too cold and not too warm. Our hall should be a temperate zone.'

Fanguin was elsewhere. 'We allow three dimensions for physical space – length, height and depth – and another for time. But now there are papers which canvas ten dimensions at least. My iron filing has to be somewhere between one tray and the other. Or does it?'

'Fanguin, you're not concentrating.'

'I am finding it difficult,' he snapped.

'Painters and carpet-layers get booked up. January is a good time.'

'I dislike the conjunction of magical sap and toxic mistletoe juice. Why would both turn up at the same time?'

'I can't imagine. There is another grey. They call it slate, but it's more pigeon to me . . . this one.'

'All the way up?'

'Obviously all the way up; we don't want to live in an angel cake.'

'How much is the carpet?'

'We're not skimping, not after all these years.'

'Sap, mistletoe and Wynter: they all arrived in the same delivery. Is that sheer coincidence? I'm privy, Bomber, to other information. All's not what it seems in this town, whether he's good or bad.'

'Don't bite the hand that feeds. I've heard him talk science – even the Apothecaries were in awe. We're lucky to have him. More to the point, *you're* lucky to have him, *Doctor* Fanguin.'

Fanguin pushed the tea away. 'I need a proper drink.'

'Not until . . .'

Fanguin looked at the carpet samples. 'I'd go for the grey carpet and blue-green walls – pigeons dipping their beaks in the Nile.'

Behind closed doors, fancy costumes were dug out and examined and, if selected, adjusted to best disguise the wearer. The town's haberdashery shops and especially *Titfertat* (hiding the head being the most demanding task) conducted a roaring trade in accessories, although not, to their chagrin, in more profitable finished articles, for the very order would compromise anonymity. In Rotherweird, high fashion had never been the exclusive preserve of the rich. Necessity mothered invention in poorer households, where sewing, knitting, crocheting and weaving had always flourished. The Understairs might exude decay in buildings, but not in dress, unless one judged only by the cost of materials.

The Slickstone party had been exclusive. Wynter's was to be brazenly inclusive.

The Apothecaries decried such frivolity. Beneath the smoked-glass skylights of their research buildings, they distilled the juice of the mistletoe, straining away impurities and any trace of skin or pips. Strimmer, an expert toxicologist, led the analysis. He had never before encountered such a brutal natural substance. The Manor sent down a phial of sap and Fanguin's paper. Strimmer had no time for biology, but the violence of the chemical interaction explained why the mistletoe's host had been so *very* dead. He adopted Fanguin's name for the juice, *Visceral*, a play on *viscum album*, the European mistletoe.

Apothecaries were swarming over an adjacent roof, ostensibly repairing timbers and tiles but in fact installing hinges to provide an exit for the peculiar machine taking shape below.

*

In the Fanguins' front hall, walls had been stripped and cracks filled and smoothed for replastering. The old stair carpet had been removed and the banisters re-fixed, sanded and varnished with the first coat. The astringent smell reminded Fanguin of a laboratory.

With the Council's blessing, the Rotherweird Defence Force had swollen in number, its new recruits attracted by the generous pay. The Town Hall lowered the state of emergency, despite Norrington's sad demise, releasing some guards to join the workers in clearing driftwood and shoring up the damaged riverbank.

Neither Oblong nor Valourhand had any involvement in these activities.

Between frenzied – on Oblong's part, at least – bouts of academic preparation, they met at 3 Artery Lane. Valourhand had insisted on seeing the escharion.

'Two pipes with one mouthpiece: two trees with one stem?' suggested Valourhand.

'Talking of which . . .' Oblong seized the entrée as he refilled their glasses. '*Thy Aged Girls* – it's Bole again – another bloody anagram. It's *The Yggdrasil*, otherwise known as the life-tree in Norse legend. It has roots in two worlds at least.'

He earned a compliment in Valourhand-speak. 'Very occasionally,' she replied, 'you surprise me.'

After much debate, she summarised their conclusions. 'Wynter has absorbed Bole's accrued knowledge and skills and that includes Everthorne's draftsmanship. He uses them all the time. But Bole has a plan and that still has to be sold to Wynter: hence the nocturnal messages. Since only Bole could have constructed the octagon – he has a carver's talents too, remember – we can take it the mistletoe's toxic juice is part of his grand design, whatever that might be. The escharion connects with both Wynter and Lost Acre, which makes the Doomsday theme very troubling. Why would Wynter wish to harm Lost Acre – or Rotherweird? Or maybe he wants to change the passageways between the two worlds? That would explain why the tiles rerouted you and Roc.'

Oblong added another player and, with her, another complication. 'There's Madge Brown to reckon with too: it was she who attacked us on Lazarus Night. She was happy to leave Orelia to starve. She destroyed the changelings.'

Valourhand said nothing. She remembered the attack on the changelings all too well. For weeks she had indulged in emotional self-surgery, striving to excise from her memory the young man she had chased from Bolitho's play by the Winterbourne stream all the way to the changelings' burning home.

Oblong corrected himself. 'Well, except for the Mance, the dog-boy I met at Claud's house in Hoy. He's still alive.'

Valourhand still said nothing.

'I should try and smoke Madge Brown out somehow,' he suggested.

Finally, Valourhand broke cover. 'What about Tyke?'

'Nope. There's been no sign.'

'They want him dead,' she said with a rare trace of emotion. 'I know they do.'

In the event, Madge Brown found Oblong first, not that Oblong knew it.

Oblong embraced the hospitality of *The Journeyman's Gist* in January more than any other month, in part out of sentiment, for January had been the month of his first visit after taking up his post in Rotherweird. He also liked the blazing fire and the cosiness it engendered, in contrast to the frenetic press at the bar in summer. Tonight, the end of the holidays had drained custom, leaving free chairs aplenty.

He sat next to the fire, pad open in front of him, the left page crammed with crossed-out lines and abortive beginnings. Morval's winterscape had been haunting him: the travellers with their heads down, oblivious to the corpse of the sheep half-camouflaged in the ribbons of snow. A poem he admired described Icarus falling into the sea unseen by a ploughman on the cliffs and the sailors in boats nearby. How could he do justice to Morval's oddly similar image? Make the fleece golden, perhaps?

'Mr Oblong?'

He raised his head as other heads turned too, drawn by the striking young woman standing in front of him. The gold of her cider winked in the firelight: a match to the autumnal yellows and browns of her dress. She had a natural elegance.

'Did they stare at you when you first arrived?'

'They sure did.' *Not for the same reason*, he thought, but did not say. 'It does wear off,' he added.

'Sorry for intruding.' She gave his pad a wry smile. 'I'm Persephone Brown, Madge Brown's sister. I'm here to deputise and I wanted a *very* quiet word.'

'Where's Madge?'

'Our mother is unwell, although it's more in mind than body. We thought a change of nurse might revive the failing circuits.' She glanced around the room. 'Would it disturb the muse if we moved out of the stalls?'

'If only the muse were here,' replied Oblong modestly as he snapped his notebook shut.

They walked over to a lonelier table, well away from the fire.

She lowered her voice. 'There's another reason. Madge felt threatened by your new Mayor. She said you and friends of yours had an inkling of the truth – that it all goes back into history, which is why I should confide in you.'

Oblong downed a generous gulp of *Feisty Peculiar* as he strived to get a grip. *Madge Brown's sister?*

Persephone sipped her cider and continued, 'She mentioned the other place – she said there's a plan for the Spring Equinox.

Mr Wynter will be there – and he has to be stopped.' She paused. 'Oh dear, is this all nonsense to you?'

Oblong's senses jangled. Persephone Brown had the same aura as Pomeny Tighe: she herself had been to Lost Acre.

'Yes and no,' mumbled Oblong, filling his hand with nuts.

Persephone did not let up. 'Come on, Mr Oblong, you've been there – Madge said so. Or are you denying it?'

Oblong spluttered a mix of beer, spittle and nuts half into his hand and half down his front. She dabbed his shirt with a handkerchief. He blushed, deep crimson.

'Been *where*?' he stammered.

'There's a tile with a white flower incised on its surface. Madge took me once, years ago.'

Befuddled by data and drink, Oblong dropped anchor at square one, articulating what many had thought but only Strimmer had said out loud. 'I have to say you're not remotely like her – Madge, I mean.'

'Well, that's hardly surprising.'

'Oh?'

'She's adopted and I'm not. You wouldn't know, Mr Oblong, but if a young Rotherweirder is orphaned in the wider world, the nearest Rotherweirder takes them on. It keeps loyalties intact. All is recorded in Escutcheon Place.'

Apparent lies assumed the subtler colours of possibility. Oblong saw no alternative but to take the encounter at face value. 'I'm sorry I doubted you.'

'I'd be suspicious if you hadn't.'

'Did Madge mention mistletoe?'

'The Council Meeting discussed it. But no, she didn't, well, not quite no – she said Gorhambury resisted its traditions.' She added a wink.

Oblong winced. Gorhambury retreating before Madge advancing with a sprig of mistletoe conjured an image of instant *vérité*.

'Oblong and Persephone'

She picked up their glasses. 'Let me oil the wheels. I feel so much better for sharing this.' She did not wait for Oblong's protest but moved straight to the bar.

Oblong subjected the account to scrutiny. *Fact*: Madge Brown had been at Wynter's resurrection. *Surmise*: Madge Brown had been hoping to interfere, but had had the powerfully built Everthorne to contend with. *Problem*: Orelia had given little detail of Brown's role, focusing – understandably – on Everthorne. *Fact*: Madge Brown had left town. *Question*: Why she would leave if she were Wynter's henchwoman, now of all times?

The interval dispelled the intensity, but Persephone Brown continued to exude a surprising certainty for a relative stranger to the town's affairs.

'I'm in the perfect position to keep an eye on Wynter,' she concluded. 'I'm sure he won't suspect.'

Persephone Brown worked her way from *The Journeyman's Gist* southeast to Rotherweird School. In the corner of the first Quad the sign on the music teachers' staircase listed the Precentor's rooms as occupying the ground, first and second floors. The Head of Music languished in cramped accommodation under the eaves. He administered only to boys. The Precentor served the town.

She knocked on the Precentor's door. She had an order and a commission to place: three short period pieces admirably suited to the occasion. For a reason she could not explain, she added a wildly different fourth, as a *coda*. Like an impulse buy.

OUT OF TOWN

I

Therapy Time

Orelia recorded a ninth Beatitude: *Blessed are those who devote themselves to children who are not theirs.* Steep slopes and adverse weather gated all but the eldest, but Megan Ferdy had a compensating genius for organising diversions while keeping control. Supplies were plentiful; morale and discipline the challenges. Other countrysiders came and went, Ferensen gave lessons on outlandish subjects, performed party tricks and told extravagant stories, but Megan provided the constant commanding presence.

Orelia took to volunteering for the grimiest tasks to dull the edge of grief.

On a glorious day not long after Oblong's departure, Ferensen took her aside at breakfast. 'You should take the air. You need to replenish yourself. The trail to the left is best.' He handed her a telescope. 'And this can only improve the experience. It won't cloud over until ten to one, or thereabouts.'

'A walk can't rewrite the past,' she muttered.

Ferensen shook her gently by the shoulders as if waking her up. 'A good walk can rewrite almost anything.'

She would not have taken instructions from anyone else and did not want pity, but she found Ferensen's counsel hard to resist. He rarely offered advice, but if he did, he meant it.

Orelia dressed in her old clothes. The view from the verandah dazzled – winter in her finery, a sky shorn of cloud and air so still bird-calls carried from miles away. She followed Ferensen's recommended path into deep shadow where hoarfrost mimicked light snow to a small platform, the perfect vantage point. Ferensen's telescope had an array of catches and buttons which delivered narrow and wide views with differing magnification. She could make out the town, far away. *Baubles & Relics* lay beneath the towers, out of sight, untenanted and bereft of stock.

Downcast, she turned back. *Walks rewrite nothing.*

'That's barely a stroll.' Gabriel emerged only yards away, twirling a thumb stick.

'I suppose Ferensen sent you.'

'I'm capable of making my own decisions. I'm on my way to the valley. It starts with a steep scramble. I like to use the trunks.' He swung his way down the slope. Had he asked her expressly, she would not have followed, but given the initiative, she did. Frozen leaves crackled beneath their feet and she fought for breath in the cold, but the effort was restorative.

They joined a lower path and a gentler descent.

'The first flowers of spring,' said Gabriel, flicking the hazel catkins as they passed. 'Wood-ear favours the elder,' he observed, tapping a fungus lightly with his stick. He had an economical way of speaking which Orelia rather liked. A mile on he stopped beneath a stand of Scots pines. 'They're one of my favourites: high up, and wait for the colour to show.'

A single busy note from several voices drifted down from the canopy above. She aligned Ferensen's telescope; the inner mechanism whirred, drawing her up to the treetops and the finch-sized birds attacking the pine cones. One cone fell at her feet, then another.

'Plum waistcoats for the men, parrot-green for the women,' Gabriel said, adding, 'For once in the bird world, both sexes are equally smart.'

'What's wrong with their beaks? They're twisted—'

'Nothing is wrong and everything's right. Crossbills are purpose-built for twisting the scales of the cones to get at the seeds.'

As they moved into meadowland, Orelia looked across to a bowl of beeches above a tumble of thick undergrowth. They were close to the white tile, which lay on Gabriel's land, according to Ferensen.

'Superficial familiarity labels the bizarre as commonplace,' Gabriel said. 'We give birds and insects names, which makes us think we understand them, when in fact we don't. Lost Acre's creatures have no names, so it's all outlandish, but we're first cousins, really.' He led the way across a bridge made of two lopped tree trunks. He gestured at the meadow ahead. 'Elms flourished here once, but alas, no longer.' His pointing hand moved. 'And that's me.'

The oak timber frame and the cob walls fashioned from earth and straw conferred a natural camouflage. Only the chimney was brick. In a shaded corner by the front door stood Hayman Salt's *Darkness Rose* in its pot, carmine blooms hanging freely, impervious to winter's grasp. Its twin had opened the way for her escape from the sealed rock chamber beneath the marsh.

'She's living proof that benign life forms exist in the other place too,' Gabriel said, the tiny thorns retracting as he ran his finger lightly along a stem.

'You've been there, haven't you?'

'Rarely,' he replied, without elaborating. He opened the front door. At the far end of a large front room, a stone sink and an iron cooking range provided the kitchen basics. A shelf held old Vlad bottles with new handwritten labels overlaying the printed originals.

Several fine pieces of furniture caught the eye, including a walnut marquetry writing table. Archaeological finds and carvings adorned the walls. A fire had been laid on a generous hearth.

'Please don't light it,' she said on impulse, so strong was the memory of Everthorne lighting the fire in the houseboat, the first step in her seduction.

'There's no need,' he replied. A tiled stove stood discreetly opposite the front door. 'Peat bricks burn slow as a snail with almost no smoke.' He lifted the metal lid and added more from a wicker basket. 'Open fires are for high days and holidays.' He handed her a key. 'My workshop is out the back. I'll brew up some coffee.'

Orelia rebuked herself: he had no barn, livestock or arable crops, so he had to have a skill.

The outhouse resembled the main building in materials. The oak beams jutting from the roof corners had been carved with motifs from Nature.

Inside, diagonal lines of sunlight shot through gaps in the heavy shutters. One caught the tube of an astronomical telescope, a high-end South Tower model. Furniture parts hung from ropes slung between the beams: arms, legs, chair-backs, stretchers, both unadorned and ornate. Wood shavings littered the floor.

'I'm disorderly,' he said. 'When I feel like carving an arm, that's what I do, whether it's needed or not. Still, repair work keeps the wolf from the door.' He smiled at her puzzled reaction. 'Oh yes, I have customers in town. I'm cheaper than the Guild.'

It's not only that, she thought, *you're as good as their best.*

Gabriel opened the shutters. Mallets and chisels hung in size order above a long work-bench. He described each wood like a personal friend. 'Yew and ash bend. Beech polishes well – all my tools have beech handles. Box is for inlay. Sweet chestnut stains the fingers. But elm and walnut are best.'

Orelia warmed to the way he spoke of what he liked or loved; she had not heard him utter an unkind word – a weak trait maybe, but a welcome one. 'I had a remote ancestor who carved wood. His name was Benedict Roc,' she said.

'I know – *the* one and only Benedict Roc. He always signed his pieces. They're rare and valuable.'

Suddenly clues cohered: the refilled Vlad bottles, the telescope, the tile's proximity . . .

'You knew Professor Bolitho,' she said, a statement, not a question.

'He'd come here to take his telescope to the other place. He brought humour, learning and a new cocktail every time.' Gabriel's weatherworn face broke into a smile. The hard near-monosyllabic carapace was splintering. 'Saint Elmo's Fire is my favourite.'

What about the Darkness Rose, *the archaeological finds, the interest in Nature – and another visitor to the other place?* She sensed the jetsam of another town personality. 'What about Hayman Salt?'

The thaw continued. 'Sometimes they'd come together. I called him The Jolly Grumbler – not a good name for a pub, but that's what he was.' The light in his face faded. 'Now you say they're both dead.'

Orelia understood: Gabriel had many acquaintances, but very few friends.

He shrugged, closed the shutters and led her back to the house. Pouring the coffee, he opened up further. 'I didn't drag you here to show off my livelihood. There's something I'd like you to have.' He extracted a chart from a desk drawer. 'I did this for Salt – for this Christmas.'

The chart mapped the trees within the immediate curtilage of the town, including the Island Field, the banks of the Rother and the first outlying meadows. A numbered key marked species and Gabriel's estimate of their age.

'Why give it to me?'

'It's for your shop. You sell furniture and you know your wood, I imagine. With this, you can spin a yarn about where every piece came from.' He paused. 'And because Salt was your friend.'

The chart had striking precision. She had walked those banks many times.

'Do hang it,' Gabriel said quietly.

'Thank you. I will.' Outside, the shadows had shortened. 'I must be getting back,' she said. 'Ferensen was right about the benefits of exercise.'

'I'm not very good with children. I've no idea what they're

thinking.' He had an odd circuitous directness, perhaps the hallmark of a solitary life, but she had no doubt what he meant.

'You're staying, then.'

This time he replied with an action, equally clear: he took down an empty miniature and filled it from a larger half-full bottle. 'For the climb,' he said. 'A dash of *St Elmo's* – and every inch of your rigging will glow.'

She laughed. 'I have so many thank-yous,' she said, 'for the chart, the pick-me-up and the company.'

Gabriel hesitated. He felt an urge to explain, but indirectly. 'My father was Michael; his mother was Uriel and my great-grandfather Remiel.'

'Right,' said Orelia after a moment's thought, 'I get it, you're all named after archangels.'

'It's an absurd conceit.' Gabriel drained his glass. 'Archangels are messengers, but we were mere guardians of the way to the other place. Going back, we've used all seven names. The eldest child always stays here: you get the property, but the duties come with it. Now we're not even guardians, just observers.' He put the glass down and sighed. 'Of course, there is one true archangel left.'

Now Orelia was lost. 'And who's that?'

'The eighth and mightiest: Lucifer – that's how we saw Wynter then, and it's how we see him now. We suffered the most. Remember what he did to the Seers, *our* brilliant children, among many others.'

Orelia tried to imagine this rural outpost in the late sixteenth century, its forced discovery of the astonishing mystery on its doorstep and the enormity of what Wynter had done. No wonder they had given their appointed protectors mystical names.

'Fortemain stood up to him and ended the First Age and we shall do the same for the Second,' Orelia said firmly.

'We shall certainly try,' replied Gabriel as Orelia drained her glass. Outside, she trailed the carmine flowers of the *Darkness Rose* with her fingertips before heading off across the meadow. Gabriel stood by his doorway and watched.

In her contrary mood, she found it a more supportive gesture than if he had waved.

The following morning, for good or ill, Gabriel discovered a surprising absentee. The *Darkness Rose* had vanished, roots and all.

IN TOWN

Corps de Ballet

Slickstone had spared no expense in converting the disused stables at the rear of the Manor into a long row of offices. Panelling, floorboards, chairs, tables and dressers were scrupulously in period. Persephone Brown observed the transformation with satisfaction. It had been part of their strategy to have Slickstone's wealth fund the Manor's long-overdue restoration before his come-uppance.

She tracked down Fennel Finch in the last corner room, next to Sly's office.

Her reception was frosty. 'Hands off Mr Wynter,' said Fennel as soon as her visitor had closed the door.

Persephone greeted the snarl with a smile. 'I wish you luck. He's a fascinating enigma, but too ancient for me.'

Fennel's shoulders lowered slightly. 'What can I do for you?'

'I'm to circulate a report to the Council on party preparations. You're my first port of call.'

'I'm your only port of call.' Fennel delivered her summary with a business-like air. 'Unrecognisable means just that. Guests will be hidden from their front door to their arrival at the Manor – I've commissioned every rickshaw in town and they're being fitted out with canvas sides and ceilings. Circuitous routes will be taken. Voice distortion devices will be issued before arrival. All costumes will be inspected. The numbers are about right: some aren't coming, but many are.'

'What about countrysiders?'

'It's the same for everyone. The Gatehouse guards will be blind-folded and voice devices will be fitted at the Gatehouse.'

Meticulous, yet fanatical beneath. *This is a woman to watch*, Persephone decided. 'Thank you,' she said. 'That's more than enough.'

But Persephone did not leave.

'Anything else, Miss Brown?' asked Fennel.

'My sister said Mr Wynter had a programme for the future, but she had no idea what it was.'

Fennel frowned. 'Your sister had extensive contact with Mr Wynter in a very short time. And Master Thomes showed me a most unusual instruction from *her* to him: a hundred syringes! Mr Wynter had no idea when I raised it. Someone is playing games.'

Persephone feigned amazement at her own communication. 'Madge does run ahead of herself sometimes, but I'm sure there's rhyme and reason to it. Protective measures, perhaps?'

'Protection against what?'

'Against whatever the next monster may bring?' Persephone glanced at the claw hanging from Fennel's neck.

Snorkel's suspicious death had fuelled a wealth of conspiracy theories, and her old social circle, habitués of Snorkel's *soirées*, had cold-shouldered her for cosying up to the new Mayor. Persephone Brown's pleasant manner induced her to voice a growing concern which she had hitherto kept to herself. 'I find Mr Wynter admirably decisive, but occasionally confused,' she said.

'That's what Madge thought – but it's hardly surprising after a life in the tunnels.' Persephone shivered theatrically, leaned over the desk and whispered, 'Tell you what, let's keep each other informed. Neither of us want Snorkel's cronies back.'

Fennel gave Persephone an appraising look. 'Done,' she said.

Back in the long passage, Persephone gritted her teeth. She was Persephone after all, a goddess, and with the month of March, her

month, fast approaching, she had found herself mired in dispirit-
ingly menial preparatory tasks.

Without warning, she underwent an alchemical change.
Persephone alias Nona spoke no French, but words in that language
tumbled into her head and her body responded.

She executed two *coupes en tournant* into a high *grand jeté en tournant* followed by two *posé* turns into a *temps levé* in first arabesque.
Quite some *enchaînement*! If only she had an audience greater than
the visored suit of armour lurking in the alcove at the end of the
passage. She felt exhilarated as her old self resumed control.

Nobody knew who she was, *yet*, except Wynter, for whom she
had a question. She found him in the Great Hall, working through
Sly's latest intelligence report.

She closed the inner door. 'Why this party?' she asked.

'I'm hoping to attract some unwelcome guests,' he said.

'I don't see Ferensen coming.'

'Probably not,' he agreed.

'Who then who matters?' Persephone paused. 'Oh yes, you want
your chronicler back.' Wynter's lower lip rose at one corner. She had
half an answer. Then an ancient memory returned, a creaturing day
when nothing had gone quite right. 'Not that boy, the one who . . .'

Wynter's reserve fractured. He rose to his feet, angry in an
instant. 'He's *arrogant*. He aspires to divinity.'

'He's just a freak who survived the mixing-point, that's all. He's
the exception who proves the rule. So what?'

'He defied me. He brought Oxenbridge in. He rescued the
changelings.'

'He's still a beautiful boy – is that it?'

Wynter returned to his chair, calmed down. 'It's simply a question of due punishment,' he said.

If only, thought Persephone, *if only*. But she played along.

2

Dressings Up and a Dressing Down

Finch set off for town after an early lunch.

Jones had declared solidarity. 'You are a tribune of the people. You have duties. We're with you in spirit, Finchy.'

Morval offered a warning as she clasped both his hands, her speech less fractured than usual. *'In disguise, the enemy may do much.'*

Finch recognised the dangers: Slickstone had murdered Mrs Banter, Orelia's aunt, for the crime of being related to a member of Wynter's execution party. Why should Wynter be more merciful to a man whose ancestor had supplanted him? Yet he hurried on, his costume tucked under his arm. Finch, the fastidious keeper of records, had turned devil-may-care.

After Finch's departure, Jones sat by the fire with Morval as the afternoon light bled away.

His route to a cure mixed candour and directness. 'How did he fight, the spider?'

She scuffed the floor with her foot and snapped her teeth. Jones nodded.

'Entangle and stab, I understand. There's a gladiator who fought like that. We called him the *retiarius*. He wielded a net for a web and a trident for a sting.' Jones paused. 'But he couldn't draw for toffees.' He smiled at her. Her appearance had barely changed since their first meeting in Wynter's time. He wondered what her parents had been like. He wondered if she wondered.

Morval reached for the log basket and placed a strip of bark on the fire. Gregorius the Roman scout noted an oddity: they had been burning ash, whose distinctive diamond pattern bore no resemblance to this furrowed surface. Before he could comment, smoke billowed from the fire like incense. As he inhaled, his eyes closed, and his mind drifted into a distant past. He was walking the hill above his childhood home. His sandalled feet released the fragrance of herbs, oregano and wild thyme. Warmth bathed his face.

Morval moved away from the fire and rifled through the Ferdys' costume box. She had already made her choice: a multicoloured shift in autumnal colours with an equally anonymous mask. She packed them in a sack with selected art materials.

She regretted the heartache her disappearance would cause her friend Gregorius, but she had to be there. She had to *record*.

Once outside, she ran at extraordinary speed, mostly upright, occasionally dipping an arm to the ground. A cruel line jangled in her head:

> '. . . *beauty blemished once forever's lost,*
> *In spite of physic, painting, pain and cost . . .*'

She ran on regardless.

No Apothecary went or wished to go to the Unrecognisable Party, save for the Guild's Master. Curiosity and frustration gripped Thomes in equal measure. The Guild's exclusion from the Council rankled, despite Wynter's reassurance that it left them with a freer hand. Snorkel's body had been cremated with indecent haste and now Strimmer and Scry were boxing for prime position. Last but not least, Wynter had commandeered his cook for the day and he had run out of marshmallows. He could not afford *not* to go, which left the thorny question of costume.

He consulted Sister Prudence. 'Vulgarity will reign!' he whined. 'I wish to be a beacon of dignity.'

'Beacons stand out, Master. We don't want Wynter to know you're there. It strikes me that disguise should be like recognition: you start with the face.' Sister Prudence produced a grotesque rubbery mask, a double face like Janus. One half had an aquiline nose and beige hair falling to the shoulders; the other sported a bald high-domed forehead with white hair flying from the sides as if electrocuted. Unworn, the features concertinaed. 'There's an ingenious fastening system to hold the two halves together at the neck,' she added with her usual calm practicality.

'It's obscene,' Thomes hissed. 'It's like the seven dwarves rolled into one.'

'Actually, it's Newton at the back and Einstein at the front. Your costume unites the two. You're a walking unified theory of everything.'

Bowled over by a surge of vanity, Thomes seized the mask and barked, 'Mirror! *Mirrors!*'

'This goes with it.' The costume maintained the divided theme, with split trousers and shoes which faced both ways. Only the arms belonged exclusively to Einstein, the one who looked forward, naturally.

Had the costume lacked quality, the result would indeed have been a horrendous muddle, but Sister Prudence had paid the head seamstress at *Raganuffin* handsomely and it showed.

'As it happens,' said Thomes, pirouetting in front of three mirrors held by junior Apothecaries, 'my own physiognomy exhibits the best of both.' He added his grudging stamp of approval. 'It'll do.'

Only the weak expect gratitude. Sister Prudence continued unabashed, 'I have persuaded Mrs Finch that any Apothecary is above sartorial checks, while implying that no Apothecary is likely to go. I have prepared two rickshaws, to disguise your route. Listen and learn, Master. Mr Wynter is too good to be true.'

*

Bolitho's funeral had encouraged Valourhand to reduce people to chemical elements. Common elements readily attached themselves to each other and viewed a party as a golden opportunity to exchange their trivial energies. The rarer types in her Periodic Table were loners: Bolitho, Salt, Ferensen and Finch. Her judgement on Jones had moved with better acquaintance from dull as hydrogen to a more elusive element. He could be gregarious and distant, energetic and wary, dim but occasionally insightful – whether by accident or design, she could not yet tell. The Apothecaries she placed in the second rank, as both common, in that they were all the same, but rare in their refusal to engage with others.

Oblong she classified as a unique element: *Moron*. If he provided the promised distraction for her party-night mission, she might review.

Only Tyke ranked in rarity with herself. He would be alone somewhere, nursing, like her, his own agendas.

Scry strove to exorcise her theory, but it had taken root too deep, so horrific were the implications. Her love of Wynter had sustained a vigil of centuries. She had sowed the omens for his return; she had moulded the Apothecaries to his purpose. Indeed, the clues in their Hall had appeared to confirm that she alone was the instrument of his resurrection. In *The Journeyman's Gist* he had greeted her as his long-lost saviour. Bole and Nona were no more: Wynter had said in so many words.

Lies, lies and more lies, *if her theory were true*.

The loathsome Bole was manning the tiller, and Nona the pretty, Nona the clever, had been Wynter's chosen instrument.

If her theory were true.

The man she loved on the surface was the man she loathed beneath.

If her theory were true.

She had not been engaged in the arrangements for the party. *If her theory were true*, and Bole and Nona jointly held the conductor's baton, the party must be another play in their wider game.

So she would go. *The Clairvoyancy* held in its reserve stock a costume for Lazarus Night which she had never brought herself to sell. Only a student of classical myth like Nona would make the connections: the white robe for neutral and implacable judgement; the dagger and whip in the belt for retribution.

She would be Nemesis.

'You look ridiculous,' said Bomber.

Fanguin did. His foam bosom lurking beneath the white and blue frock, the rural blouse, dainty shoes, the wig, the mask and beribboned bonnet did Bo Peep few favours.

'It says fancy, it says dress, and it says unrecognisable,' he pointed out. 'I pass with flying colours.'

'"Fancy dress" does not mean "a dress". Especially not for a corpulent male of a certain age.'

Fanguin pirouetted. 'Ankle to knee has always been my strong point. This might come in useful too.' Fanguin flourished Bo Peep's crook. 'Anyway, what are you wearing?'

'I'm not.'

'Don't tell me you're ducking out. Freebies galore and in the Manor – it's an unmissable piss-up.'

'Drink needs ballast, Fanguin, as you should know better than most. I'm overseeing the kitchens. I've a class of twenty with a multitude of tasks and differing abilities. If the evening's to work, I've got to get the best out of them.'

The material benefits had reconciled Fanguin to his wife's work for the repulsive Apothecaries, helped by viewing her as an independent contractor whose employment was occasional. But overseeing the Manor kitchens sounded uncomfortably menial and carried a risk of long-term commitment. His doubts about Wynter had also sharpened. There had been no comeback on his reports, as if his revelatory analysis had told Wynter nothing new. Ferensen's dark narrative was returning to view.

'You don't think twice about working for Mr Wynter?' Fanguin asked casually.

'You didn't. Why should I?'

'I work for the town, where the Mayor is unavoidable,' replied Fanguin defensively. 'The point is, we know precious little about him.'

'He's one of us – and I thought you cared for orphans, Godfery?' Bomber's hands went to her hips, always a bad sign. 'When Snorkel treated you despicably, I supported you through thick and thin. I knew there'd be one more chance and there was, and you took it. Throw it away now and I'm off.'

Bo Peep sat down, disconsolate. Familiar demons began to whisper: when between the devil and the deep blue sea, best have a drink and hope the answer floats your way.

Gorhambury had been allowed a five-minute audience with the Mayor on a private matter.

'Your Worship, I wonder if I might be excused the full rigour of your party?'

'Mr Gorhambury, it's an invitation, not an order.'

'I know a code is a code, but I don't feel the Town Clerk's position is compatible with fancy dress or anonymity. I would feel myself a spy.' *Or a clown*, he thought, but did not say.

Wynter rose from his desk. 'My dear Gorhambury, Council members come as themselves for that very reason. You may too. Consider it done.'

'Thank you, your Worship. How very understanding.'

Snorkel would have humiliated him. If Wynter were a wolf in sheep's clothing, the clothing could hardly be more attractive. He walked home with jaunty step, wondering whether to give his polka-dot tie an outing.

*

Orelia's admiration for Miss Trimble, the School Porter, had deepened. Managing children *en masse* demanded application and patience. One regime did not fit all. Some relished the experience as an adventure; others, uprooted from their homes, languished.

More than a month had passed without a move from Wynter, but she knew it would come. On the evidence of past history, only the young with growing cells could be melded successfully in the mixing-point with other life-forms. Had adults been suitable, Wynter would have used them in the Eleusians' first age. Bole would know that with Social Services, computerised records and street cameras you could no longer trawl cities for orphans and remain undetected. They would need the home-grown.

Ferensen had tried to dissuade her, but, for better or worse, it was time to face her would-be killers and the Unrecognisable Party would get her close. Her first stop therefore: the ottoman in the basement of *Baubles & Relics* which housed the Roc family costume collection.

The Mance slept during the day in an abandoned lean-to in Augean Alley. By night he wandered, noting and memorising highways and byways. He had not been back to town since his immersion in the mixing-point centuries earlier.

He located the property described by Tyke as an 'ally's home', only to find it deserted. He caught the scent of enemies too, including the Fury-woman who had killed his friends and destroyed his home with her infernal arrows. Near the prison, he caught the iron smell of the torturer of animals who lived by a bend in the river. He read the invitation on the municipal noticeboard.

Rotherweird had fallen under Wynter's spell once more.

To protect or attack? That was one question.

The other engaged his divided being:

Now what to do,
Four legs or two?

Valourhand had taken to dropping off notes for Oblong at 3 Artery Lane as if his actual company were unbearable. Predictably peremptory in tone, they had the virtue of precision. Take the latest:

> *Enclosed is how you may divert the guards at the Apothecaries' research facility on the night of the Unrecognisable Party, 7 p.m. precisely. The building is 117 paces south-southwest from the Hall. If you don't show up, I'll do my best alone, but expect to be arrested, &c. I'm assuming you're not dim enough to be a party animal and prefer to be useful.*

Oblong had been in a quandary about the party. He had felt isolated at Slickstone's reception and hated the thought of dressing up, but he was the town's only historian and nothing bettered first-hand observation. The problem of costume decided him: the invitation prohibited the use of Great Race costumes to preserve anonymity, and he had no other. Like it or not, he had another Valourhand *rendezvous* to look forward to.

3

Return of the Natives

Finch arrived at the South Gatehouse at dusk. The sentry, sporting an unfamiliar armband, extended a cordial greeting. 'Mr Finch – long time, no see.'

Finch improvised with a half-truth. 'I got caught by the quake. A tower went up and I went down.'

Recent events had raised credulity levels. Since the Herald was barred from the hustings, Finch would have been in town – and there was a circular gap at the base of the tower, so why not?

'We've a new Mayor, Mr Finch, and monsters have been on the loose. The evidence points to those effing countrysiders. Even the New Year mechanicals were infected with *creatures*. Which makes it puzzling as to why Mr Wynter has asked them tonight.'

Finch played dumb. 'Asked them to *what* tonight?'

'His Unrecognisable Party – it starts at seven. It's at the Manor – Mr Wynter has taken up residence there. Can you imagine not having the first idea who you're talking to?' The sentry ushered Finch into the Gatehouse. 'This may sound kinky, Mr Finch, but orders are orders. Perhaps you'd be so kind as to blindfold me, seeing as we've got to guarantee their anonymity should any come.'

The sentry presented a strip of dark cloth and Finch obliged. While the man struggled to get his bearings, Finch pocketed a voice detection device from the basket by the door.

He took the sentry by the arm and led him to his stool. 'If I may

ask a favour in return?' he said. 'Please don't tell the Mayor I'm
back. I'd like to surprise him.'

'Well, my orders are to report your return . . .'

'Heralds of all people should surely announce themselves,' replied
Finch.

'As you put it that way, mum's the word.'

Finch wrapped a scarf around his face. As he headed through
empty streets to Escutcheon Place, unease laced with guilt assailed
him. Hostile forces had seized the town, while he had dawdled
at the Ferdys'. His ancestors would have put their constitutional
duties before the pleasures of chicken farming.

Orelia arrived at the South Gate in a large coat, face masked by
a scarf and hair held back in a functional countryside hat. The
blindfolded guard delivered his rehearsed text like an automaton.

'Whoever you are, dear countrysider, do not speak. You're to
enjoy the anonymity afforded to all party guests. Take a voice
distortion device from the table in the room behind me and place
it beneath the tongue. Change there too, if you haven't changed
already. I assure you I'm in the dark.'

Orelia ignored the instruction to change, but did take a device.
The Golden Mean was deserted, its shops closed and windows
curtained or shuttered. The bicycle rickshaw bays had emptied.
Glancing back, she glimpsed an old man standing stock-still beyond
the bridge on the Island Field. The white hair and grizzled beard
suggested great age, as did the supporting staff, but the figure's
upright stance exuded dignity and strength of purpose. It brought
to mind Cinquecento statues she had once seen: Christ dressed as
beggar, or John the Baptist perhaps.

She turned away and followed the Golden Mean. The front
window of *Baubles & Relics* came as a shock. Her beloved shop
looked like a plundered tomb: bare but for a small pile of rejects

in the centre of the floor. Once inside, she drew the curtains before lighting a small fire. She kept the gas-lights low.

Valourhand and Oblong had left the ledger on her kneehole desk. The sales had been meticulously recorded and the takings left in a cash-box in the drawer with an explanatory note in two hands:

Hope margin of 22.23% satisfactory. V.V.

and beneath:

Doubled the money on the stuffed parrot! J.O.

Thank God for friends. She descended to the basement, rummaged through the costumes and made a quick decision in tune with her solitary state. She tied back her hair, whitened her cheeks, changed and found a suitably neutral mask.

She would go as a nun.

4

Visceral Reactions

Doom's Tocsin chimed the half-hour: 5.30 p.m. and imminently party-time. From her rooftop refuge, Valourhand watched the town stir into life like an ants' nest kicked by a boot. Rickshaws scurried to and fro, their routes haphazard but all terminating at the gates of the Manor. Modified umbrellas with long draped sides concealed guests from their doorways to the waiting rickshaws.

Guests arrived in such a state of excitement that few heard the rebuke from a disembodied voice in the skies above the Manor, and those who did dismissed it as another prank by an unhinged Town Crier:

> *'Unrecognisable you are,*
> *Monstrous your children may become,*
> *Go dance like planets round a star:*
> *Only the deaf to sense are truly dumb.'*

Valourhand gambled that while the rickshaw drivers might look behind as well as forward, they would hardly look upwards, and there were no pedestrians in sight. The greater risk lay in the rickety beams and balconies of The Understairs, hitherto rarely visited in her aerial rambles.

Conditions were good, clear but not cold enough yet for ice to form. She reached the Square which held the Hall of the Apothecaries without incident. Predictably, the Guild had ignored the curfew within the curtilage of its own buildings. Sentries were stationed at each end and along the sides of the main research building. Every ten minutes they marched up and down, spinning on their heels like well-oiled mechanicals.

The distance from surrounding buildings and the absence of chimneys ruled out use of the snag-line, leaving her no choice but to pole herself up from street level. Everything depended on Oblong's diversion. *But where the hell was he?*

The answer: gangling down Hamelin Way two minutes behind schedule. Hopefully his clueless appearance would not provoke suspicion.

Oblong tried not to look as if he were looking, but snatched upward glances revealed no sign of Valourhand. She would hardly be wearing fluorescent colours, but a glimpse would have been reassuring. He chose the sentry at the rear: he had the bleakest view and would probably be the most junior, a key element in his strategy. He had prepared for the mission by stalking the streets to catch the rare moments when Apothecaries conversed with each other. 'Brother' and 'Sister' had been their invariable mode of address.

'Evening, Brother,' he said with breezy *bonhomie*.

Oblong had failed to factor in the simple fact that Apothecaries *only* engaged fraternally with each other.

The sentry's withering look translated as *I'm no brother of yours.*

'I have a problem,' continued Oblong.

He won a second withering look: *Clearly you do.*

'Um . . . I found something which might interest the Guild.'

Valourhand fidgeted in irritation. *Stop gassing and play your card.*

At last Oblong had drawn a flicker of interest. The sentry extended a gloved hand. *Show me*, the gesture said.

'It's precious,' whispered Oblong. 'I need more than one of you, for security's sake.'

The sentry summoned his nearest colleague, they exchanged whispers and the same hand extended.

'It's precious,' Oblong repeated, 'and also potentially dangerous.'

After more whispering, the second sentry moved to the front of the building and called over another colleague, who had a superior air.

Valourhand cursed. The fourth sentry, still at his post, was blocking her chosen route, and any attempt to lure him away would be a move too many. She scuttled across to the other side, keeping the pole down as best she could.

Oblong produced a tiny envelope and tipped a berry, waxy white with pink cheeks, into the palm of his hand. Black hats dipped, rims touching. It could be 1605, mused Oblong, with Catesby, Fawkes and Rookwood in earnest discussion. How many barrels of gunpowder would they need, and where best to place them? Over the hats he glimpsed a slim figure running across the open space. It planted a pole and disappeared.

Mission accomplished.

Only something was wrong. The senior Apothecary peered at the berry, then wet his finger and rubbed the skin. The blush disappeared to reveal a berry of *viscum album*, as common in trees as dandelions in grass.

He grimaced. *Bloody Valourhand has set me up!* The lead sentry smacked him hard in the face with the flat of his hand. Caught off-guard, he stumbled. A hefty kick took his feet away and he fell hard onto the cobbles.

The sentries chuckled and returned to their posts.

Valourhand watched Oblong limp back down Hamelin Way with a smidgen of sympathy. She allowed time for any suspicions to dissipate. The Apothecaries' boots resumed their metronomic beat before falling silent. They stood facing outwards.

The three skylights were too dirty to see through. They glowed, but one less intensely than the other two. She pressed her ear to the glass – silence. She tentatively concluded that the building comprised two chambers, one was bigger than the other, and not even Apothecaries worked on Saturday evenings.

She cut the putty from the single pane above the smaller chamber, lifted it with a suction pad, fastened the snag-line to a beam on the inside and made her descent. A glance confirmed her deductions. Gaslights turned low cast a milky light on a bare room, with no Apothecaries in sight.

A workbench held a bottle, a tiny syringe and a short branch whose cut ends had the whiteness of living wood. On a desk, a ledger listed complex measurements of force and distance. Tucked in at the back was a short report in Fanguin's writing.

'Imbecile,' she muttered to herself.

Severely twisted iron brackets had been piled in a corner. Dislodged masonry and plaster lay along the wainscot on the front wall. Holes in the walls marked where the damaged brackets had once been fixed. One remained intact, fixed high on the back wall. It secured another cut branch, pointing across the room.

She checked the bottle. One or both of the branches had been injected with Visceral.

Old words came to mind: *Yggdrasil, Ragnarok, Doomsday*. She found the experiment repugnant: injecting the juice of a vicious parasite into living tissue, not in pursuit of a cure but for destructive effect. The end objective remained elusive.

She retraced her steps and re-fixed the pane. Instinct told her not to risk another entry. She drilled a small hole in the next pane and lowered her scope through. A large craft was in the course of construction. She could make out vacuum coils, rotors and several seats. She manoeuvred the scope round to a trestle table, on which rested two tins labelled *Invisibility Paint – Secret*. Boris had better beware.

Fortune assisted her escape: two rickshaws from the direction of the Hall of the Apothecaries pulled up. As soon as the sentries rushed over, Valourhand vaulted back the way she had come. After changing at the Undercroft, she made her way by conventional means and a roundabout route to 3 Artery Lane to find Oblong slumped in an armchair dabbing a bruised cheek.

'Sorry about that,' she said. 'But you took it like a man.' Coming from Valourhand, the phrase did not have its usual complimentary ring. She would have laid out all three.

'Not my finest hour,' mumbled Oblong, but he cheered when Valourhand recounted her discoveries, even if they did little to advance an understanding of Wynter's precise objectives.

'That godawful party is about to kick off,' she concluded.

'Oddly,' said Oblong, 'I saw a nun walking up the Golden Mean. She had a mask, but the figure . . .' His other cheek blushed. 'She reminded me of Orelia.'

'*What!*'

Why was Valourhand being so slow? 'Orelia *Roc*?'

'You let her go?'

'I wasn't sure. She was unrecognisable . . .'

'She's the only one who can bring Wynter down – he thinks she's dead, but once . . .' Valourhand paced the room, stopped dead and made an announcement. 'Right, Oblong, you have to go. You have to look after her.'

'Why don't you go?'

'I haven't a costume.'

'Nor have I.'

'Well, go and find one. It's a Manor, for God's sake. There must be *something* you can wear.'

'It's been closed for more than four hundred years.'

'Slickstone was dapper as a peacock and his kit's still there. Go for it – just avoid the main streets. There's a curfew, don't forget.'

Oblong shook his head. Enough was enough.

'Follow me,' added Valourhand, not for the first time.

He took a swig of Aggs' Ginger Grenade and gave in. 'You're right.' The thought of Orelia in Wynter's hands had reinvigorated him. He also wondered why Valourhand was holding back. After all, she had nearly paid with her life for her colourful protest against Slickstone at his party.

He decided that she must be planning a final confrontation with Wynter, but she knew this was not the time.

She led the way through a maze of alleys and cut-throughs, most of which Oblong had never noticed before, until they emerged from a tortuous back street near Aether's Way into a small space dominated by the northwestern section of the Manor wall.

'Right,' she said decisively, 'over you go.'

'I beg your pardon?'

'You're not going in the front way, *obviously*. I squat. You stand on my shoulders. I stand up. You put one foot *there*, your hand *there*, the next foot *there*, and you're in. There's a convenient woodpile on the other side.'

Oblong resembled a daddy long-legs struggling up a pane of glass, yet he managed, albeit at the cost of grazed knees and a torn trouser leg.

Valourhand ambled half the way back to her rooms, then reconsidered. The traitor in their midst had to be reminded of his loyalties, which meant returning to the Undercroft, then another rooftop journey. As she stepped clear of a puddle with the furred-mirror look of the beginning-to-freeze, the ice-dragon came to mind, or rather, its perfection, the cause of her fatal hesitation which had cost Hayman Salt his life.

But the mixing-point did not deal in perfection. The riddle worried away at Valourhand as if it mattered.

Oblong staggered across the lawn at the back of the Manor, conscious of his grazed knees, bruised cheek and sore ribs. He was by now a familiar figure in town, so it was no surprise when a young woman from the kitchens hailed him. He recognised her as one of the more boisterous recent School-leavers. Her parents had optimistically christened her Serenity.

'Mr Oblong, you've no costume, you're recognisable and they won't let you in.'

He found the glint in Serenity's eye unnerving. Running a class had developed his sixth sense for mischief-makers.

She looked him up and down and turned solicitous. 'I know just the thing – come with me.' She led Oblong into the passage at the rear of the Manor. 'Mr Sly's down there – you'd best avoid him – but there's your man.'

Oblong swivelled, but could see nobody to right or left.

'*Him.*' She pointed.

There, in an alcove, stood a suit of armour, complete with visor and silver-plated shoes.

She looked rather pleased with herself. 'Nobody will know who you are – and you won't need a voice distortion device either, not in that tin can. Just keep statue-still, all right?'

Obediently, Oblong froze, not sure whether he had been rescued or trapped. She had quick hands and in no time she had fastened on pauldrons, rerebraces, vambraces, gauntlets, greaves, tassets and sollerets.

'Now for the *pièce de résistance!*' she said with a noise which Oblong could not quite place – an exhaled breath of satisfaction or a repressed chuckle? She stood on the pedestal where the armour had been, leaned forward and placed the bassinet over his head.

'I hope you're pleased.' She offered him a make-up mirror from her pocket.

Oblong made several discoveries. Armour does not enhance movement. *Thank God, this isn't a dance,* he thought. His view of the world resembled that of a man immured in a postbox. Holding a glass in gauntlets would be testing, and drinking even harder. His nose had been reduced to a sharp cone-shaped protuberance with holes like a colander.

As abruptly as she had appeared, his assistant vanished.

Each step clanking, he turned with painful slowness to adjust his view – and chanced on good news: a sword rested against the wall.

He had the wherewithal to defend Orelia.

Morval Seer assessed her chosen section of the town wall. She translated patches of loose mortar, a buddleia stump and a protruding piece of rock into handholds, footholds and a route. At the core of her being, tiny vestiges of arachnid DNA still coiled with hers.

She scuttled up and set off along the rooftops to the Manor's enclosing wall. Unlike Valourhand, she had no need of a pole.

5

Who's Who?

The Precentor tapped his baton on his left kneecap and peered down from the gallery at the Great Hall. Five minutes to doors opening, ten minutes to the Mayor's entry. Around him sat his consort, trumpets gleaming and wooden viols aglow.

From beyond the doors a peculiar hubbub grew in volume and intensity as from an aviary of metallic birds. The voice distortion devices did no credit to the musical qualities of the human voice.

Encouraged by the handsome cash advance on a generous fee, and the fact that the music on the stands before them was timeless and the main piece English – the consort had practised hard. At last they had a Mayor with taste. The acoustics – the curtains, the wood, the carpets and the people – would do the music justice.

High across the room, almost at rafter-level, a movement caught the Precentor's eye. An insignificant balcony with no visible means of access peeped from beneath an equally insignificant window. Spikes stuck out from the tiny balustrade like perches. He could not fathom their purpose. In disbelief he watched a slight figure in a mask and a costume which blended with the Great Hall's mix of stone and oak ease through the window.

He rebuked himself. The conductor's art requires *immersion*, not distraction. It was not for him to reason who or how or why. The great doors would shortly open. His hands, and the minions they commanded, would shortly hold the stage.

*

On the other side of the door, guests were gathering fast. The idiosyncrasy of the invitation had raised the town's sartorial imagination to new heights.

In contrast to Sir Veronal Slickstone's grand affair, the Mayor had set out to put them at ease. First arrivals would wait for the last before the doors opened; everyone would enter together. A marquee, warmed by a system of heaters, covered the front lawn. A quartet drawn from Rotherweird School's best played in one corner; the School's gymnastic elite, their skills honed by Gregorius Jones, displayed in another. Champagne cocktails loosened tongues and inhibitions.

Wynter also had a legend to weave. Two blackboards had been set at either end of the marquee.

One displayed drawings of the fifth and sixth prophecy coins which respectively portrayed a human figure emerging from a grate and two masked dancers. *All is ordained.*

A map headed *The Mayor's Lost Years* had been clipped to the other blackboard. It showed in detail the subterranean world of Wynter's supposed childhood. A parenthesis declared: *Verified by the Sewage Committee.* The robotic voices thrown by the distortion devices jabbered in fascination as guests, Bo Peep among them, jostled for a better view.

Fanguin wished he had Everthorne Senior's map to hand, but the lay-out did resemble the company's two journeys to Escutcheon Place, although, unsurprisingly, the more sensitive access points were missing, including the Library and Escutcheon Place.

An elegant figure dressed as Herne the Hunter (or Huntress) fielded questions with the aid of the tip of a bow.

'What did he live off?' asked a merman.

'Fish – there are streams, here and here. He fashioned a net from discarded string.'

'How did he see?' asked a unicorn.

'Good question – he had an unknown benefactress, who dropped candle ends and matches through a street grate, this one here, almost daily, for years. If you're her, let yourself be known.'

Fanguin clicked his shepherdess' crook on the blackboard leg. He needed a trap question. Herne had an elegant poise which did not equate with any known members of the Sewage Committee.

'Where did Mr Wynter surface?' Bo Peep asked.

Herne's hesitation was fleeting, but discernible. She pointed in the approximate direction of *The Journeyman's Gist Underground*.

'Here roughly, but entry is barred for the moment. The tunnels are not only labyrinthine; they're insecure after the recent seismic activity.'

Fanguin deduced that Herne worked closely with Wynter, knew the tunnels and could not risk a lie. He or she had chosen the entrance which was furthest from any place of significance while finding a plausible reason to keep anyone from entering.

Strimmer's interest in Herne had a different focus. He had noted the strength in the calves and the grace of those legs before. Now clad in powder-blue tights, they belonged without doubt to Persephone Brown.

Strimmer's costume had been designed as a man on the prowl: a flowing black robe had been embroidered with a line from Mephistopheles in Marlowe's *Doctor Faustus*: *I came here of mine own accord*. His mask wore a lascivious grin above a rich priapic beard. Strimmer's sexual frustration had sharpened since Pomeny Tighe's inexplicable departure. His many other conquests bored him.

An end to his famine beckoned.

Scry sniffed behind her mask. The aura of Lost Acre infected the air like the odour of fresh paint – but from whom? She seethed too. These cheap and showy lies about Wynter's childhood belittled his legend. But she had only to wait. Once an exhibitionist, always an exhibitionist: sooner or later Nona would show herself.

Orelia engaged with nobody, and nobody engaged with her. Such were the advantages of taking the veil. Guests apologised for the lightest nudge. She had last seen Wynter naked and vulnerable, offering his head for strangulation. This extrovert enterprise suggested self-confidence regained. She thought of Bole, so long a servant and now a master. She had no wish to see Wynter, but knew she must.

'Ouch,' gasped Oblong as a waiter bent his armoured thumb over the base of his wine glass and inserted a straw through one of the holes in his bassinet's visor, poking an eye before finding the mouth.

Step by step he shuffled across the lawn, using his sword to prevent a fall. He held his drink high with the free hand. The din of conversation roared like tinnitus in the confines of the helmet. On turning to survey the guests, the straw abandoned the glass.

A boiled egg with velvet breeches slapped his thighs in hilarity. 'You've drawn the short straw there, sir.'

''oove it eese,' replied Oblong.

'Come again, Sir Knight?' Humpty Dumpty put his head to the bassinet, inducing near darkness.

''oove the ucking aw,' replied Oblong.

Unhelpfully, Humpty Dumpty merely inserted another.

In this ark of the bizarre, he alone had achieved absurdity, but absurdity, he consoled himself, furnished the best cover. Nobody would suspect his serious intent, although even there the obstacles mounted. On his next rotation, he counted three nuns in near-identical habits. Which one should he defend?

As his consternation grew, Oblong grew hotter and hotter, until runnels of sweat ran from forehead to cheeks to torso. He felt like a turkey baking in foil.

He reached for an inaccessible handkerchief to wipe his inaccessible brow and panic took hold, raising his body temperature still further.

Would he be trapped for life like the man in the iron mask?

6

Open Doors

The Precentor had a double door cue: the opposing entrances to the Great Hall and the gallery above.

As the former opened, a quartet within the consort – three viols and a harpsichord as *basso continuo* – played Pachelbel's *Canon*, a piece of dignified restraint. It induced a modicum of silence, even wonder.

On the other side of the gallery door, Gorhambury strained to keep track of the music. Behind him stood the Guild Masters, excepting the Master Fireworker and the Master of the Apothecaries, in full fig, with the Mayor at the rear. As the Pachelbel subsided, Gorhambury opened the doors. The stately motion of the Precentor's baton came to rest, but fleetingly. A rhythmic accompaniment from strings, oboes and recorders filled the Hall, to be joined at the moment of Wynter's entry by the trumpets with a blazing welcome which could only be described as royal.

Chests puffed with civic pride. The counter-tenors entered next, their high notes pure as glass.

> 'Sound the trumpet, till around
> You make the list'ning shores rebound . . .'

Purcell's short anthem gave time enough to create a stage for the Mayor. He stood dead centre of the gallery, fingers clasping the balustrade.

'Welcome, ladies, gentlemen and whoever else. This Manor preceded the town. It is the source of our independence and greatness.'

Wynter's nostrils twitched with self-satisfaction. He recognised the auras of Scry and Nona-Persephone, but complex cross-currents implied the presence of more guests with experience of the other place. He had baited his line well – but whom had he hooked, and which were they? If Sly had done his job, answers would come soon enough.

'Circulate, speak your mind, explore and learn,' he continued, 'and above all: enjoy yourselves!'

As he sat down, Wynter saw a slight figure on the high balcony installed centuries ago as a roost for the Eleusians' fliers. The head dipped, rose and dipped as hands pale against the camouflage of the costume moved up, down and across. An artist at work. He tilted back his head in a moment of ecstasy: his chronicler was back. How Morval Seer could have managed the ascent did not matter; her feat bore testimony to his enduring fascination, even for his enemies.

He summoned a waiter. 'Place a man outside beneath that balcony and *don't* let her escape.'

The waiter hurried out, puzzled as to how the Mayor could read gender through disguise and at such a distance.

Orelia watched Wynter, mesmerised. She had stowed away so much, burying deep the pain and visual images from the platform in the great tree underground. Now she saw once more Everthorne disappearing before her eyes and becoming Wynter.

She turned her face to the wall.

Sly's backroom rivalled the Great Hall for hubbub and concentration of people. Data engulfed his hard-pressed deputy.

'Two bishops, a highwayman and a wine bottle.'

'Someone in robes with a whip and a dagger.'

'A devil.'

'Two gondoliers.'

'Slow down,' shouted the deputy. 'I have to cross-refer.'

He flourished the rickshaw drivers' list to make good the point.

'A nun.'

'And a Mother Superior.'

'Make that two nuns.'

'And two jesters.'

'No, one's a clown.'

'Fuck!' exclaimed Sly. His elaborate system had a flaw. They had three lists, two of which – Fennel Finch's and the rickshaw drivers' – were complete, but their descriptions differed. One man's ghost was another man's senator. 'Have we *any* certainties?'

'A giant cockerel.'

'One old geezer in a sheepskin waistcoat with a stick – he's not on any list that I've seen,' added another.

'Maybe he's the wizard.'

'No, *he*'s got a starry conical hat.'

'If he's an old man with a stick, he's recognisable and shouldn't be here,' hissed Sly. He had never liked the idea of an Unrecognisable Party and liked it even less now.

The original informer elaborated. 'The geezer's mask melds with his face somehow, and the stick is living wood. He's not talking to anyone and only drinks water.'

Sly hammered the desk with his fist. 'Call yourself an *intelligence* service? You're a shambles. Get a grip!' He pointed at his most reliable agent. 'Start with a head count and we'll take it from there.'

'I've a swaying knight in full armour,' added a new arrival, 'and an Einstein-Newton two-faced clone.'

'No and no,' said the deputy after checking his lists.

'*Full* armour?' exploded Sly.

'Actually, boss, it's the suit from outside your door.'

Sly hammered the table a second time. 'Get the fuck out there – listen and serve. Report only disloyalty to the Mayor, all right, no common chitchat. And keep an eye on that damned knight.'

As the room emptied, Sly stared at the ceiling. 'We deserve a pay rise,' he said.

He had one consolation. All exits had been locked, every window and door. Armed guards were patrolling the first floor and every staircase. The snatch squads were in place.

When the unmasking came, all would be revealed.

In the Great Hall and the adjacent rooms, including the library, partygoers exploited their anonymity. Suspicious spouses pried into lunch hours; would-be investors probed target businesses and Snorkel's old acolytes explored the new Mayor's current standing.

Others asked about themselves, including Fanguin, whose stock question – 'Any idea if Fanguin is here?' – elicited mostly downbeat reviews.

'A free piss-up? Of course he's here.'

'He'll be the first to fall over.'

'I'd put money on that idiot knight.'

Several added that he did not deserve Mrs Fanguin, or her cuisine, and one even blamed the mantoleon's appearance on his interest in insects.

As Fanguin's mood darkened, his cocktail intake increased.

Scry was shadowing the knight when a waiter sidled up and whispered through the visor, 'Tell me who you are and I'll fix that drink.'

Behind the armoured back, a straining Scry caught only fragmented words.

'. . . Ona . . . long.'

Nona all along! The bitch must know she was listening. The height did not fit, but Nona had been adept with stilts. The shoulder blades looked to be the weak point, but she must not be caught.

Bide your time, bide your time, she muttered, retreating a little.

Strimmer discovered that Herne had the gazelle-like qualities of the hunted, which only increased her allure. She had given him the slip several times before he cornered her in the library. 'Fancy a chase tonight?' His hand strayed to the small of her back as he leaned over and whispered, 'Or even a rut, Persephone?'

The lightly antlered head gazed doe-eyed at Strimmer. 'Be at the Pool of Mixed Intentions at midnight,' replied the metallic singsong voice.

'Won't that be a tad cold for what we have in mind?'

'Cold? You think so?' Her turn to lean over. 'Really, Mr Strimmer.'

Finch worked his way to the library for different reasons. Books are acquired for show or for rarity or in hope. Their mere presence on a shelf might tell little, but a well-thumbed page or chapter offers a window to the owner's soul. Bookplates confirmed that Sir Veronal had created this particular library, a treasure trove of rare first editions, ancient and modern.

A fine marquetry desk had been separated from its chair and pushed to the wall to make room for guests. A solitary book rested dead centre, a pen beside it at a perfect vertical. Its last reader had been fastidious, or the Manor's cleaner was. Finch glanced at the book shelves, but they were full, with not a single gap. *A recent acquisition*, he concluded.

A giant cockerel with literary leanings felt incongruous, but Finch opened the book nonetheless. *The Elder Edda from the Codex Regius* declared the title page. The foreword introduced a collection of poems and prose pieces from Norse myth derived from a twelfth-century manuscript discovered in 1642. The ink on the manuscript dedication looked fresh: *To Geryon Wynter from Nona*, above the words *Caveat Redemptor*.

The wordplay on caveat emptor discomforted Finch. The collection had not surfaced until after Wynter's death, so it must be a recent gift. But who was Nona? And why beware the Redeemer? Orelia's narrative as relayed by Oblong placed Madge Brown as Bole's accomplice and co-architect of Wynter's resurrection. No other candidate came to mind.

'Of interest?' asked an unidentifiable mechanical voice.

Finch spun round. Herne faced him.

'Old books are always of interest.' He displayed the title page.

'Do we consider myth part of history?' asked Herne.

The question put Finch on his guard. Ordinary townsfolk did not think that way. The study of old history was banned, but the reading of myths and legends was not; end of story.

He played along. 'People believed them once, so perhaps we should.' He decided to chance his arm: Herne had been fielding questions about Wynter's fabricated childhood, so she must be close to Wynter. 'Odd dedication, though – it almost looks as though we should beware of Mr Wynter.'

'Or Mr Wynter should beware of someone else,' suggested Herne.

Finch replaced the book.

With a startling fleetness of foot, Herne glided through a knot of guests and out of the library.

Master Thomes found the whole event nauseating. Worse, he had been victimised by trivial people.

'Weighed down by gravity, Isaac?'

'Eyes in the back of your head, Albert?'

Music, drink and costumes – not to mention the *cost* – represented Mammon at its worst. A degenerate blows down a brass tube and everyone swoons. Only the Apothecaries could curb these vices. *Black and white, sheep and goats: this is the true moral landscape; no in-betweens.*

Thomes did grudgingly concede that his cook had excelled herself. The beef carpaccio with cheese crisp had been delectable. He had consumed five – but then, nobody knew who he was, save the Almighty who would surely overlook one venial sin.

Oblong changed his strategy. He slipped into an inconsequential passage within earshot of the Great Hall and became a suit of armour. He stood stock-still, holding the pommel with both hands by his waist with the sword tip between his feet. He ignored all ribaldry and attempts at conversation. He had chosen to be on call, rather than risk the two-to-one odds of defending the wrong nun. Beneath his shell, the temperature eased and he dozed, despite the social activity all around.

Orelia maintained her vow of silence, helped by the presence of two other near-identical nuns, who made her actions less conspicuous. She had explored the back stairs at the Slickstone party, but this time they were blocked by an armed guard. Waiters and waitresses varied in their movements; some kept to the kitchens, but others diverted to a passage at the back of the Manor before reloading their trays.

She headed backstage, redirected by passing waiters to the Ladies. She followed their instructions, then doubled back. Nobody accosted her and waiters chatted freely in her hearing – nuns could be trusted.

She caught a few tantalising snippets.

'Can't wait for the prize-giving.'

'I've got my target.'

'There's quite a number.'

A vampire passed by and on impulse, Orelia raised her crucifix. Was role-play taking over, or had she missed her vocation?

The vampire felt a parallel urge to sink her false teeth into the nun's neck, but she hurried on to see Sly.

'Maybe your former husband is one of them,' Sly suggested.

'He can't be.'

'Why not?'

'He's dry as dust with no imagination and he's never dressed up in his life. It makes you wonder who Mr Wynter is really after.'

'Well, you're about to find out.'

The Precentor's third cue arrived: three words on a single piece of paper, two for a piece and one for an instrument: Lully's 'Gavotte' and 'trumpet'. He tapped the shoulder of the nearest trumpeter, who made her way to the gallery, where she sat at the front to one side. The string section duly struck up the dance, while two waiters and waitresses demonstrated its essentials. Lully's 'Gavotte' had a gentle formality which encouraged the audience to join in.

A throng of guests, ushered back from outlying rooms, swept Orelia back to the Great Hall.

'I don't suppose you're allowed to dance?' said a passing conjurer, moving on when she shook her head.

She took an inconspicuous position close to a curtain and well away from the centre of the room. A jester with an odd forward-leaning posture, as if poised for a tumble, worked himself in front of her. Her backstage reconnaissance had suggested one of the two jesters on view was an unexpected guest. Her apprehension grew.

Wynter did not join the dance but reappeared in the now empty gallery, flanked by a guard and the single trumpeter. Sly sat down behind him.

Orelia sensed the opening of a final Act and the closing of a net. The thought ripped away her flimsy wishful thinking. She had no evidence to deploy against Wynter. Worse, any public accusation would reveal the existence of Rotherweird's mixing-point – *if* anyone even believed her, which was improbable when they would find only a solid wall of rock. What a fool she had been to come. Best opposition did not call for petty acts of defiance – she needed to be there at the endgame, whenever that might be, when Wynter would not expect it.

On her tiny balcony Morval Seer was adjusting quickly to a new medium. She had never used pastels before, but oils and water-colours needed too much paraphernalia for this confined space.

Wynter watched her with a *frisson* of pleasure. *Just like the old days.*

Downstairs, a passing waiter urged, 'On the dance floor, please, Mr Cockerel.'

Reluctantly Finch obliged, musing on leadership as he trudged to the Great Hall. Was the wider world any better? Had anyone devised a ladder which encouraged talent *and* decency to ascend? Consider Rotherweird's recent helmsmen: Snorkel, Slickstone,

Thomes, Strimmer and now Wynter. Only Rhombus Smith, the Headmaster, had talent and decency. Could the first Finch have done more when bequeathing power to the first Mayor all those centuries ago? He doubted it. As a rule, it's the biggest rat who wins a rat race.

Nearby, a waitress took Einstein by the hand. 'Come on, Twinkle Toes, give us the light fantastic!'

'I will not,' he growled, but a figure dressed as a playing card grabbed him by the arm and whirled him into the dance. He had been press-ganged.

Oblong suffered the same indignity at the hands of a fortune-teller. In a state of near immobility, he raised alternate feet and, when energy reserves allowed, tapped the floor with his sword like a Morris dancer. Through the tiny holes of his bassinet, he glimpsed Bo Peep, displaying more vigour than timing. His temperature, having subsided, began to rise again.

The old man with the thin green staff did not move – *would* not move, despite being cajoled and almost manhandled. Something in his manner decided the waiters against forcing the issue. Two nuns joined the dance too, but Orelia also stood firm. The jester in front of her stooped out of sight as a waiter passed.

Wynter did not allow the gavotte to drag on. It was time.

The single trumpet sounded.

'Ladies, gentlemen and whoever else, it's time to award our costume prizes. I cannot be accused of favouritism, as I have no clue who inhabits them. We have bouquets and magnums of Vlad's best, six prizes, which I shall announce in reverse order.'

Unease infected the room: Wynter the costume-prize-giver felt as unnatural as a military children's entertainer. His evident excitement at the exercise and the presence of Sly behind him jarred. Orelia sidled towards an exit and to her alarm, so did the jester. She should have realised that Wynter would have costumed placemen too.

'The combed cockerel comes sixth. Remove your mask, sir, madam or miss.'

Finch eyed the doorways where armed men had appeared, discreet but strategically placed. *Do it with class*, he decided.

He opened one arm in a flamboyant gesture and announced while removing his headpiece, 'I give you a headless chicken.'

Astonished silence gave way to applause and then to wild cheering. They had missed their Herald. Finch blushed; he had never grasped his own popularity.

Wynter squinted as Sly whispered, 'Take the credit.'

'It's good to have you back, Mr Finch,' he said gracefully.

Sly noted yet again Wynter's remarkable grasp of town personalities – he had not furnished the Mayor with a physical description of Finch, nor could the Mayor have ever met him.

'Escutcheon Place could do with some flowers,' replied Finch with equal grace.

Wynter returned to Sly's list. 'Mr Newtonstein,' he shouted, as if announcing a monster.

An incandescent Thomes pushed away a waitress who offered to assist with his mask. A light titter greeted the unveiling: the Master of the Apothecaries in party gear!

Thomes refused the prize to a mild undercurrent of disapproval, but he did not attempt to leave. His antennae told him more was to come, for Wynter's face had changed, anticipation giving way to disappointment. *Why?*

The Mayor's voice turned surly. 'Sir Knight,' he barked.

Oblong did not hear the call, nor had he heard the music stop, or noticed that those around him were standing still. Like a demented mechanical, he continued to tap his sword while raising one foot after the other.

Fanguin, intrigued to know the occupant's identity, tapped the bassinet with his crook. It rang like a bell and Oblong reeled.

Now or never, thought Scry, and stabbed sharply with her dagger, a backhand blow as she was facing the other way – but Oblong wobbled at the critical moment and the knife glanced harmlessly off his back.

He felt it, though. Spinning round to confront his assailant, his shod heels caught, he lurched forward and crashed to the floor. The ancient leather ties on the bassinet snapped and the helmet rolled away.

'Evening, all,' stammered Oblong from his prone position.

Wynter gaped and guests cheered, more in *Schadenfreude* than appreciation. No entertainment bettered an outsider making a fool of himself.

Wynter's disappointments continued with the unmasking of Bo Peep. Fanguin cradled the magnum of Vlad's best whisky like a newborn baby.

Wynter cursed. If only these idiots had played by the rules and declared their costumes! Behind him, Sly recalled the earlier confusion between nuns and Mothers Superior, for he had counted three habits when both pre-party lists had shown only two. He began to hunt them down as Wynter declared the winner of the second prize.

'The Old Testament prophet – yes, that's you, sir, with the stick.'

The old man did not move.

Wynter leaned over the balustrade as his interest quickened. 'Come for your prize, sir – unmask yourself.'

The prophet walked forward to the centre of the Hall. The walk was young, the stance equally so, but the face? Close up, a waiter recoiled: a mask, and yet somehow, *not* a mask. The furrows and colours had the grotesquery of overstatement: too vivid, too deep – and too *waxy*.

'Get candles,' yelled Wynter, ignoring Sly's call for restraint.

'It's your party, your Worship. Gently does it.'

'Closer – *closer*,' Wynter called.

Waiters held a candle to either side of the old man's face, with another in front. The guests surged round for a better look. Even the Precentor abandoned his position.

Still the prophet did not move, even when his face began to run and drip.

Orelia watched in horror as rivulets of coloured wax ran from cheeks and forehead, spattering his shoulders like a sconce. *Surely not Ferensen? He had insisted he wouldn't come.*

Patches of skin and fine features emerged: high cheekbones, the outline of an aquiline nose and the bloom of youth. The beautiful boy had come: Tyke, the classical God of Mischief.

Wynter's face transfigured from disappointment to a savage smile. Only Sly's advice maintained a degree of composure. 'Do we know this intruder?' he cried.

'No,' yelled the guests, like a pantomime audience.

The ravaged wax over a glimmer of beauty gave Tyke a near-demonic appearance.

'He's a countrysider – a spy – *an enemy*! He's prospecting for our weaknesses. He's counting our numbers,' Wynter crowed.

The guests backed away. Wynter anticipated danger. Tyke's mere presence, his peculiar virtuous stillness, must not be allowed to work its influence.

'Take him away,' he ordered, but no force was needed. Tyke walked slowly towards the nearest exit.

'Change of mood needed, your Worship,' prompted Sly, who had no idea who the human waxwork might be. His capture visibly mattered to his master, but must not mar a hitherto successful evening.

'And now,' announced Wynter, striving for calm, 'the first prize goes to . . . the jester.'

Sly signalled to the Precentor, calling for a burst of music.

Orelia's mind raced as the wind section delivered a fanfare. Was the jester friend or foe? Each prize-winner to date had been a non-conformist – Fanguin, Oblong, Finch, Tyke and Master Thomes.

The jester, bent low, was edging his way towards the same doorway as Tyke. Orelia weighed the choices, gambled and followed.

But Sly had also seen the jester on the move, with a single nun in tow – the dissident nun, surely. He leaned forward to Wynter's ear yet again.

'Correction – we have a joint first prize! The jester and the nun – *that* nun,' added Wynter, pointing.

Orelia did not get far.

'Sorry, sister, you're going nowhere,' said the guard, levelling a halberd at her stomach as he turned and unlocked the door for Tyke to pass – only to yelp in pain, drop his halberd and clasp his ankle. The jester, now on all fours, burst through and Orelia elbowed her way after him.

'They won't get far,' Sly whispered to his master.

'He fucking *bit* me!' yelled the guard.

'The countrysiders don't want our prizes!' Wynter shouted. 'But do we care?'

His triumphant tone only half-reassured his guests. Sly gestured frantically at the Precentor: *Play something, play anything.* But the Precentor had eyes only for Herne.

She twitched her 'antlers': his final cue. Viols gave way to violins, flutes and oboes multiplied. A loose, luxuriant melody swept the room. The music had lurched from the seventeenth century to the nineteenth, 1894 to be exact, and a ballet from 1912.

Herne shimmied forward, tossing bow and quiver to a waiter. The body bent to the music and the music bent to the body. Guests parted to give her space. By an irony lost on Wynter, his guests succumbed to countrysider music *par excellence*: *Prélude à l'après-midi d'un faune.*

Persephone barely knew what had possessed her, but the sea of admiring faces entered her soul. The strange names which had prompted this display returned: *Debussy, Nijinsky, Diaghilev.* She bathed in the attention she had always craved.

Strimmer ogled every move from behind his mask. Midnight at the Pool of Mixed Intentions would be unforgettable. Roll over, Pomeny Tighe.

Wynter was less impressed. The Unrecognisable Party should adorn *his* legend, not hers. He hastened from the room as the solo dance ended to a wave of rapturous applause.

'Who's the old man, then?' Sly asked him, struggling to keep up.

'He defied me once. He's about to discover the price.'

'He's not from here, I could see that much.'

'He's a nothing.'

Sly held grudges. He understood. With revenge, they dissolved.

'Don't you want to say good night to your guests?'

'I want to interrogate my prisoner.'

So, not quite a nothing, thought Sly. They hurried down to Sly's office, only to find the door locked.

Sly knocked with his fist. 'Open for his Worship.'

Tyke's arms had been tied together in front of his stomach. The running wax had re-congealed, making him look grotesque, a victim of torture. His stick rested against the back of the chair.

'Untie him,' said Wynter. 'He doesn't do resistance.'

'You sure, your Worship?'

'Do it.'

They untied him gingerly, but Wynter was right, Tyke made no move.

'Leave us alone,' Wynter ordered, 'you too, Mr Sly.'

The room emptied. Beneath the wax the loathsome boy was still untouched by time.

'We meet again.'

'For the last time?'

'That's for me to decide.'

'Indeed, it is.'

Tyke had not changed. He still had that maddening know-it-all indifference to what awaited him – and that damnable country burr. Any creature fashioned in the mixing-point by the Eleusians was his to claim. Tyke's freakish immunity to physical change did not make him an exception.

'You are *mine*, Tyke. *I* preserved you – *I* gave you immortality.'

'You should not have killed Mr Vibes. You should not have killed my friends.'

This confusion between Bole, Nona and himself amused Wynter. It was as if he had lived all along.

'Apologise for your treachery and serve me; then I might be merciful.'

'Mercy is not yours to give.'

'You think not?'

Wynter tapped the door with his fist and Sly hurried back in with his retainers.

'Mr Jack is hungry for work. Tell him to take as much time as he wants.'

As ever, Tyke did not resist. He picked up his stick and followed his warders out.

Backstage, Orelia had no time for music. She entrusted her hopes to the jester. Fragments of costume flew from him – ruff, striped breeches, harlequin jacket and white gloves – to reveal a doglike beast, unmistakably from the other place. Now on all fours, the half-animal charged through the legs of the staircase guard, throwing him off-balance; Orelia's follow-up knocked him over.

The beast appeared to know his way, avoiding the obvious staircases and the guards. *The gift of scent*, Orelia assumed. He bounded up a remote flight into a small attic room with a skylight accessed by a short ladder. She shinned up and opened it as cries and clattering feet closed from below. To her surprise, the canine misfit nimbly climbed the ladder after her. Once out, he slammed the skylight shut. Above them, the sky had cleared; swathes of stars peered down. A light frost glistened on the slates.

Her companion moved towards the middle of the roof.

But they were not alone. Elizabethans and moderns alike seek symmetry in a house. As they emerged on the roof, a parallel skylight opened to their left, releasing guards who pointed, flourishing their weapons.

Her companion loped towards them, oddly heedless of the danger.

'No,' she yelled, her distortion device still in place, 'don't do this for me.' She muttered an old lyric by way of a prayer: *You gotta get me out of this place.*

Miraculously, the gods were listening. A disembodied rope appeared from nowhere. The beast leaped, grabbed it and clambered up with alacrity. She lifted her habit and ran towards the lifeline. Had the enemy rushed her, she would not have made it, but the troubling sight of a half-dog suspended in mid-air induced a temporary freeze. Orelia hesitated: the rope had no visible means of support, nor did the beast looking down at her.

A familiar voice shouted from the night sky,

> *'Don't be a dope,*
> *Just use the rope.'*

She took the Town Crier's advice. As soon as she gripped the rope, it yanked her skywards. She hauled herself up onto what felt like a spar-shape length of wood. The unseen craft wheeled away.

From below the guards could see only a woman, a freakish half-dog and a coil of rope against the night sky.

Orelia's right arm juddered up and down: a welcoming handshake from an invisible man.

'Is that you, Portly Bowes?'

The mind of Portly Bowes, the Town Crier, had versified long ago, a consequence of weight of work and an otherwise solitary life. He prepared his bulletins assiduously, but instant conversation invariably sailed close to doggerel.

'*Now we fly, and soon we dock,*
Roc meet Mance, and Mance meet Roc.'

Unsure how to thank her companion, she reverted to stereotype and patted the Mance on the head. He nuzzled her back. The machine yawed like a ship despite the absence of even a breeze – Polk technology, surely.

Bowes appeared to read her mind.

'*Your host is no Leonardo and may be no saint,*
But he makes the most of invisibility paint.'

Invisibility, what a bitch, thought Bowes, one idea for *six* syllables.

No Leonardo indeed, thought Orelia, trying to resolve felt surfaces into a visual reality. Da Vinci's airships had elegance and symmetry; Boris Polk's resembled a cat's-cradle of struts, string and vacuum technology coils.

More serious questions jostled for attention. Hopefully, she had maintained her anonymity, but any re-opening of the shop would betray her presence and bring instant arrest. And what of Tyke? Wynter clearly hated him, so what had Tyke to gain by coming? A *danse macabre* was playing out.

The vessel landed between two gables on an outbuilding of *The Polk Land & Water Company*. Boris flagged them in like an airport attendant. Miss Trimble handed out glasses of Vlad's best brandy, a bone for the Mance and a warm overcoat for Bowes. They adjourned through a window, down the stairs and across the courtyard to the main house, where Bert and a blazing fire awaited them.

'On account of the paint Portly has to be starkers in flight, which isn't ideal in mid-February,' Bert explained. 'He warms up quickly, though, don't you, Portly.'

'I have cladding and padding
For aerial gadding,'

responded Bowes.

'I haven't thanked you,' said Orelia, still shivering.

'Thank Ferensen,' replied Boris. 'The Hoverfly and the presence of our good friend the Mance are all down to him.' Boris paused. 'I've told Angela and Portly all there is to know. If we'd educated more like minds earlier, we might not be quite so isolated now.'

'Fair enough,' said Orelia, and she meant it. 'Remember Tyke?'

'I never met him, but I know you have. He helped look after the changelings for centuries.' Boris paused. 'The Mance said Tyke would go to Wynter's party and that he wouldn't try to escape. He said that was his way.'

Orelia patted the dog's head again. 'He was right,' she replied before pulling up. 'Did you say "*said*"?'

'Speaking is a horrible effort for the poor lad, but he can *in extremis*. He will miss Tyke horribly.'

'But he saved me and left Tyke to Wynter.' She swallowed her words.

The great dog sat like a sphinx before the fire, back legs splayed straight behind him.

Boris acted as his advocate. 'They were orphan boys from the mudflats of London. Vibes was decent, but Tyke was special: a mirror to everyone else's shortcomings. Tyke looks after himself, always has.' He turned to Orelia. 'Can I ask a favour? Your gear is unsettling. It makes me feel I should go to confession.'

That was the thing about Boris: he made you smile without trying. As Orelia removed her headpiece, Bert exploited the change in mood. He disliked protracted conversations on serious topics. You ended up chasing your tail and exhausting the capacity for action.

'Let's play Racing Demon,' he suggested.

And they did. The participation of a half-invisible man doubled the fun. Cards landed or whisked away without warning and all the while the dog-boy continued his quiet communion with the fire.

A frenetic forty minutes of game-play sharpened brains and induced a decision by Boris.

'We have to move the Hoverfly, and we have to do it tonight.'

'But it's invisible,' said Bert.

'And solid. Search our premises and you'd find it in minutes. And Wynter suspects me already.'

Before discussion could turn to the pilot for this mission, the front door reverberated.

'Can't they read?' moaned Bert, gesturing through the window at the sign on the courtyard's railings which proclaimed: *NO RICK-SHAW REPAIRS AFTER SEVEN.*

Bert stumped to the door to find a bedraggled figure outside in need of personal repair. Pink marks and bruises grazed his forehead and cheekbones. His left hand and right foot were still encased in mediaeval armour.

'Sorry,' said Oblong. 'One damn thing after another. I hoped you might have the tools . . .'

'It's Sir Jonah,' Bert bellowed over his shoulder.

Miss Trimble was first to the rescue. Flushed by drink and card play, she looked gorgeous – but yet again the damsel was rescuing the knight.

'Butter,' she said, 'or fat.'

'Pliers,' added Bert.

'And keep him out here or he'll swell in the heat.'

The courtyard of *The Polk Land & Water Company* had witnessed the launch of the Hydra, the resurgence of *The Thingamajig* and puddles splashing under the feet of an invisible man. This ranked alongside. Oblong sat on a wooden stump for chopping firewood, groaning as others extricated with difficulty his trapped fingers and toes. From the upstairs windows Bert's children watched gleefully.

Oblong was building a legend as permanent as Wynter's, not that he knew it.

Released, he joined them by the fire. 'Why does it always happen to me?' he asked.

'You walk into it,' replied Orelia.

'You could have bloody helped.'

'I didn't know it was you until you keeled over.' Orelia descended into giggles. 'You should have seen his helmet. Straws kept getting stuck, and—'

'In that case the man needs sustenance,' intervened Miss Trimble firmly.

'Yes, yes, of course, sorry,' stammered Orelia.

Oblong ate his supper, absentmindedly stroking the head of the Mance.

'He was the jester,' Orelia explained.

'Good boy,' said Oblong, patting his head.

They described the party for the benefit of the Polks, Bowes and Miss Trimble, before Boris returned to their present problem.

'We need a pilot to move the Hoverfly somewhere out of harm's way, and *now*. Only problem is, it means a night out of town.'

'I'll do it,' said Orelia.

'To be blunt, you're our witness and you're not expendable. And Portly, you're the town's heartbeat.'

Miss Trimble reluctantly declined. 'I work Sundays,' she said. 'I'd be missed.'

'We would too,' said Boris. 'There's a Council meeting first thing tomorrow and Bert's on Sabbath repair duties.'

'What you need,' said Oblong glumly, 'is an expendable outsider.'

A connoisseur of children, Miss Trimble knew how to encourage. 'No, no, we need someone intrepid who's up for a knightly quest.'

Oblong took the bait, hook, line and sinker. 'I know the saying. Black rickshaws come in threes. I get floored by an Apothecary, locked in armour – and now this. *Avanti!*'

The presence of Orelia and Miss Trimble combined with a desire to compensate for his undignified arrival drove Oblong to undue bravado. Despite Boris' best efforts, he declined to take his controls lesson at a sensible pace.

'I'm not an idiot, Polk – that one up, that one down.'

'The coil switch, otherwise known as the ignition?'

Oblong fumbled.

'This one – just press for on and off.'

'Yes, yes, got it.'

Boris tapped him on the shoulder. 'There's no parachute, so pay attention.'

'Two levers and a switch aren't rocket science.'

'You're forgetting the steering column. Here, treat it like a joystick. But remember the course is set.'

Orelia stepped in. 'And it's useful to know where you're going. There's a meadow three hundred yards due east of the white tile. There's a well-hidden house in a bend of the river – that's where Gabriel hangs out. I suggest you park it there.'

'I'm dropping in on the Ferdys first. Just to see everything's all right.'

By which Oblong meant, *to check on Morval.*

'If you must,' said Boris, realigning the steering column.

'Right, come on – Wynter could be at the gates any minute. *Avanti!*' Oblong pressed the ignition and threw the up lever.

'Gently!' yelled Boris as Oblong's body hurtled skywards before levelling off and heading in a westerly direction.

A single syllable drifted back. '*Yikes!*'

'I wouldn't enlist as his guardian angel,' said Boris.

'And he's hopeless at heights,' added Orelia, recalling earlier chapters in Oblong's hapless adventures.

The children however cheered wildly, much as Form VIB was wont to cheer Gregorius Jones.

'But somehow he muddles through,' said Miss Trimble with the judicial finality of a school report.

'The white tile'

7

After the Lord Mayor's Show

A flurry of guards arrived after Tyke's removal with less satisfactory news.

'The nun and the jester escaped.'

'We did our best.'

They paused for fear the Mayor would think them mad.

'The jester turned out to be an unusually dexterous dog, unless it's a costume within a costume.'

To their relief Mr Wynter did not flinch. 'What of the nun?' he asked.

'Good legs,' giggled a guard.

'And the Herald?'

The question escaped an answer for Herne stormed in, removing her mask and crying, 'You've sent the old man to prison. We all know what happens there. It's a big mistake.'

Sly interrupted her. 'Miss Brown, this is not your business.'

Herne's fingers clasped and unclasped. 'I want to see the Mayor. Alone.'

Wynter's inner voice, hitherto silent, delivered an urgent warning. *Stand your ground.* Why should Nona care about Tyke? Tyke had been party to Oxenbridge's return. He was one of *the* enemies. Nor did he like insolence in front of others. 'Mr Sly is right. This is not your business.'

'Harm him and you'll regret it,' hissed Persephone Brown.

Wynter turned cold. 'Your position is noted.'

Persephone reflected. She recalled Tyke as he had been at the party and a detail struck her. Maybe her worry was needless. 'Thank you. Point taken, Mr Wynter. It won't happen again.'

Finch had dallied as close to the rear passage as he dared. Another guard passed the other way. *Time to extricate myself*, Finch decided. The guards inside knew his party-wear, but those outside might not. He joined the last guests, replacing his cockerel's head as he did so.

'What is it now?' barked Wynter tetchily.

The new arrival hopped from foot to foot. 'She gave us the slip. The woman on the balcony, I mean.'

'*What* woman?' asked Sly suspiciously.

Wynter's cheeks, flushed by the confrontation with Tyke, turned ashen. He flicked Sly's question aside with his hand. 'How can anyone escape a twenty-foot drop?'

'I've never seen anything like it – honest to God, she ran across the wall *sideways*, hands and feet all crooked like . . . like a spider.' The guard paused. 'I made it up to the balcony – she left a memento. Or maybe it's a thank-you?'

The single sheet held sketches of heads, none larger than a Rotherweird sixpence, all in pencil and pastel. They had Morval Seer's unmistakable brand of dispassionate accuracy. Uncannily, she had picked only significant heads despite the disguises: the cockerel, Herne, the nun, the jester and, of course, Tyke's waxy face – and his own.

Wynter liked his own likeness. He looked imposing. He knew her method. The act of sketching would root the images in her memory; later, she would paint up the full scene, compressing the night's events into a single picture. He hoped it would be in oils. His anger cooled.

'Now we know what brings her to water, it'll be easy to catch her next time. Understand this, Mr Sly: real rulers have chroniclers, and the best attract the best. Have it framed.' The thought brought to mind another ruler of sorts. 'Where's the Herald?'

'You heard the applause, your Worship. He's an oddball, but held in high regard. We had to let him leave.'

Once clear of the Manor gates, Finch dived down an alley, removed the voice distortion device and tossed it down a drain. Others passed by, mostly couples still in costume, then the night swallowed everyone except him, a pantomime cockerel heading for a cold bed and a mansion crammed with books which only he was allowed to read. Wrapped in disappointment at his failure to influence events, he did not register the figure emerging to his left until the last moment.

'I thought vampires avoided crossroads,' he said with quick good humour. The costumed spectre cruised up to him without acknowledging the *bon mot*. He felt a sharp pain, not in the neck but his right upper arm, as it passed.

'Goodbye, Mr Finch,' said a voice, still disguised, and his assailant turned and ran off into the dark.

Laughter with a metallic edge echoed back.

Finch found a gas-lamp, removed his head-piece and freed the injured arm. A thin greenish line zigzagged down from his shoulder and a necrotic black shadow was already spreading from the wound. He fought to keep his breath even. His hands were quivering.

I can't treat this. Rotherweird's doctors all lived at the other end of town and in any case, they were probably still wending their way home from the party. Names came and went, all acquaintances, but no friends. Then he had a thought – someone he had admired at a distance, someone who lived nearby.

'Reprieve me,' he said to the heavens, 'and I'll do my bit.' He tied a handkerchief above the wound and staggered on.

At a safe distance, Fennel wiped away the viridian stickiness at the point of the mantoleon's claw before making her way back to the Manor. The night was still young and she had much still to accomplish.

*

Finch made his destination, but only just. His right leg dragged; his right arm had stiffened; his breathing was ragged and hallucinations assailed him in the form of miniature mantoleons snapping at his face and hands.

His good arm yanked once at the bell pull – then he collapsed.

Inside the house, a wooden owl flapped its wings and hooted. Only one property had such an original device for announcing visitors.

'Amber!' yelled Ember Vine on finding a body prone on her doorstep.

Amber recognised a tone more urgent than the weary pitch used by her mother for teenage rebuke and ran to the door.

'Get a syringe from the bathroom and the antivenom from last week. Hurry, *hurry!*'

An emergency! Amber needed no encouragement to abandon her homework: the atomic weight and boiling-point of the first ten chemical elements. *If only the casualty were a little younger.*

Her mother impressed with her decisiveness. She had always treated herself when over-vigorous sculpting inflicted cuts, burns and even acid damage.

Ember had seen the wounds inflicted by the mantoleon during the fight in the Golden Mean, when she had fought with a furnace tool.

'We must get the wound below the heart,' she said as they manoeuvred Finch's unconscious body. 'And away with that tourniquet – it's quite the wrong idea.' Amber, keen to contribute, tied her hair back in readiness. 'No, no, no – you only suck out poison in romantic novels.'

Ember injected the antivenom.

'Vampoleon . . . Vampoleon . . .' Finch repeated the word several times before subsiding back into unconsciousness.

The black rickshaw boasted cushioned sides, floor and ceiling, sound-proofing adaptations requested by the Town Hall and implemented by the Apothecaries. Screams and violence in the course of state business should be private matters.

But Tyke did not scream; he sat quite still. His guards sounded more likely to come to blows, one corpulent and benign, the other thin and less so.

The latter spat in Tyke's face. 'You bastard. You *countrysider* bastard.'

'He's not been charged,' said the corpulent guard, 'let alone tried. You shouldn't act just on the Mayor's say-so.'

'Fuck off, or you'll be next.' The lean man turned back to Tyke. 'You're dead meat where you're going. Hear that, wax-face?'

Carcasey Jack preferred firelight to gaslight for serious work. The redder flame burnished the skin. He ambled to the prison entrance, where he examined Tyke as a doctor might, from tapping a clavicle to kneading the scalp. He seized a torch and held it close.

'He's dripping like a pork chop all over our nice floor,' he said, dripping too, with the sweat of anticipation.

His assistants scraped off the wax with tin plates and dinner knives.

'Now he's *sincere*,' crowed Jack. 'You don't get it, do you? *Sincere* comes from without wax. *Sine cera.* Jack the learned, Jack the quick. And such a *pretty* boy.' Jack sliced off the sheepskin waistcoat with a flick of his knife. 'Take him down, lads. Into the bowels we go.'

Tyke waved the gaolers away and started the descent unaided. *Just show me the way,* the gesture said.

Jack's knife spun around his wrist like a circus trick. *Where to start, oh, where to start?*

8

Fly-by-Night

Oblong froze, petrified. At least at the top of the church tower on the day of the Great Equinox Race he had had bricks and mortar to cling to. To be suspended well above the treetops like a wingless angel was the stuff of nightmares.

His fumbling arms missed the altitude levers and the steering column. The Hoverfly maintained the westerly course set by Boris and Oblong's inaction might have brought it to perish on the escarpment, had not a familiar sight stumbling through a meadow brought him to his senses. Concern and curiosity triumphed over vertigo: he got a grip, physically and mentally, and lowered the craft to a safe but amateurish landing.

He ran through the damp grass. 'Aggs? What the hell are you doing here?'

Swathed in a blue duffle coat, scarf and balaclava, Aggs looked frozen and lost. But the sight of an employer restored her wits.

'I could ask the same of you, Mr O. It's way past your bedtime.'

Oblong put a hand to her cheek. 'You're . . .'

'Frozzled,' interrupted Aggs. 'We ain't as staminous as once we were. And dogs run wild out here, Mr O.' She paused to blow on her hands. 'And 'istorians.'

'Well,' explained Oblong, 'I'm delivering this craft, only you can't see it. I can give you a lift if it's on the way.'

On realising that Oblong was speaking the truth, rather than under the influence of her *Ginger Grenade*, Aggs transformed from a bedraggled bag-lady to an expert on stealth machines.

'Well, if I ain't an Austrian, it's a Polk Peculiar. You lurkin' out there, Mr Bowes?'

Oblong, prone to underestimate the resources of cleaning ladies, stammered, 'He . . . he's stayed in town.'

'Criers don't spout from the 'eavens unsupported. Then there's that paint what Mr Polk brewed up. Two and two, Mr O, makes what? Four-sight!'

'And where would you want to go?' asked Oblong, bumbling about the meadow in search of the craft.

She watched him, shaking her head. 'Like chair feet in a carpet,' she said, walking straight to where a patch of indented grass gave the game away. Her hands, sensitised by decades of wipe and polish, skated over the unseen surfaces. "ere, 'ere, 'ere and 'ere,' she said, finding the levers and experimenting. The Hoverfly lifted and turned in a circle. 'All aboard for Toyland!' she cried.

Aggs suffered from vertigo's opposite: a passion for heights. Her fatigue succumbed to ecstasy as the craft rose and fell like a fairground pony, although under her adroit handling the undulations were gentle, controlled.

'Ferdy residence?' said Oblong.

'Most convenient,' she replied.

Aggs landed the vessel in the orchard behind the house with the grace of a butterfly. Smoke coiled from the chimney.

Jones lay slumped half-asleep in front of the fire, an empty plate and tankard on the floor beside him.

'Show me a bachelor what clears up his own mess!' Aggs cried.

The rebuke broke Jones' reverie. He staggered to his feet and recharged the fire. 'Aggs, Oblong – to what do I owe this unexpected pleasure?' His voice lacked its usual *brio*.

'What's up, Jones?' asked Oblong as Aggs addressed the debris left by Jones' meal and Finch's lunch.

'I'm so sorry. Morval gave me the slip.' He picked up a fragment of bark from the hearth. 'This stuff knocks you out for hours – worse than a Bolitho special. Did you go to the party?'

'I got bullied into it by Valourhand. I didn't see Morval – but then, I didn't see much of anything. Don't laugh, Jones, I got stuck in a suit of armour. It happens.'

Jones nodded sympathetically.

'Wynter was arresting people at the end – Orelia escaped, but he got Tyke and maybe Finch. It was all an elaborate trick. God, I hope Morval's all right.' To spare Jones and control his own anxiety, Oblong changed the subject. 'Aggs, I trust you haven't come all this way just to tidy up after Jones?'

Aggs, coat and balaclava off, sleeves stripped to the elbow, dipped into her cleavage. 'Right, Mr Misery-Ree,' she said to Jones, 'you got to buck up cos this ain't no snowdrop.' She produced a small tortoiseshell box as if it held the keys of the universe. A single tear rolled down her left cheek. 'It's from the late, untidy Mr Salt.' She paused. 'There's a catch with the catch.'

Her crabbed fingers played with the sides and the base and the lid sprang open. She handed the box to Jones.

He tipped it up and rolled the single seed on the flat of his hand. The perfect sphere, a mahogany skin blistered with tiny green spikes, settled. Jones gazed at the seed with an expression which paradoxically suggested intense concentration and private faraway thought. His fist closed and darted to his pocket.

'You keep the box,' he said, handing it back to Aggs. 'That's what Salt would have wanted.'

Oblong belatedly remembered his appointed destination.

'Aggs, you take my bedroom upstairs. It's second on the left – and it's tidy. I've a final visit to make.'

Aggs' hands flew to her hips. 'Mr O, you ain't fit to fly a kite.'

Before waiting for a reply, she put on her balaclava and coat.

Nobody had mentioned the flying machine to Jones, but he showed no interest. He was still standing there, stock-still.

Aggs took his hands. 'Mr Jones ain't never let nobody down, and 'e ain't starting now,' she said firmly.

'Bye, old friend,' added Oblong. 'See you on Monday.'

They left, and in minutes, in Aggs' capable hands, the invisible Hoverfly rose once more.

Inside, Jones held his hands to the fire. Outside, frost gleamed. He felt himself in the grip of Nature's polarities. He had an uncomfortable intuition as to what he was expected to do with his bequest; why else would Salt have chosen him of all people?

He put on his jersey and overcoat and set the fireguard.

Once outside, he resorted to his old cure for those dark moments when the Fates were baying at your heels.

He ran and ran and ran.

Age may drink at the Fountain of Youth, but the hangover is often deep, long and quick to strike.

Aggs had, in the space of a few hours, braved unfamiliar meadows in pitch-dark, piloted an invisible flying machine and carried out Hayman Salt's last wish. Unsurprisingly, she fell asleep at the wheel.

Oblong leaped to his feet as the craft slewed right and secured Aggs to an unseen spar with her scarf. She mumbled, 'poor Salt', 'poor town', and, intermittently, Ferensen's name. Her head slumped, but her breath still steamed.

From time to time, a bird would skim past; an owl, he assumed.

Orelia's destination had sounded clear enough, but trees, river and meadows lost their distinctive line at this hour and height, all much of a muchness. He brought the machine low, but the house Orelia had described eluded him, until a tang of woodsmoke betrayed a roofline lurking between trees. He brought the machine round to the adjacent meadow. Beyond, a crescent of beeches decorated a crest above rough ground. They were not far from the white tile.

'Not long now, Aggs,' he said, anxious about his passenger, whose breath had lost vigour like a kettle going off the boil.

Two shapes emerged, one aerial and one terrestrial. A misshapen bird arrowed past and from the near-invisible cottage, a doorway glowed. Through it a single figure strode towards them.

He gave Oblong's hand a firm but cursory shake. 'Good to see you again,' Gabriel said, 'but I expected one of you, not two.' He picked up Aggs like a sack of leaves.

'I picked up a hitchhiker,' Oblong started, but Gabriel maintained his sense of urgency.

'Be quick, Mr Oblong. There are owl-boys about. You're lucky to have had Panjan as an escort.'

They hurried inside and Gabriel carried Aggs to what Oblong took to be a bedroom, where they lit the firewood in the modest grate. Aggs did not resist blankets and eiderdown.

'Get the green bottle by the fireplace downstairs,' Gabriel asked brusquely, 'and a glass from the rack.'

In this cottage with worked wood everywhere, Gabriel looked even more arboreal, with his long limbs, luxuriant beard and that deep voice with its creak-in-a-storm quality. His delivery, and indeed his manner, reminded Oblong of Ferensen: no-nonsense, but somehow friendly.

'Who's the walrus?' asked Aggs, instantly restored by the dose of St Elmo's and a friendly masculine presence.

'He's Gabriel and you're plain Aggs,' explained Oblong.

'You're very splendid and not at all plain, Aggs, but you do need warmth and sleep,' said Gabriel.

'*Do you remember an inn, Miranda, do you remember an inn?*' sang Aggs after another swig.

'It won't last,' whispered Gabriel, and it didn't. Snoring overtook speech as they reached the bottom of the stairs. 'Barn owls sound rather like that,' he added. 'Keep your coat on – and I do hope you've eaten, because we're going in.'

'In where?'

'The tile has settled down and that means change. Forewarned is forearmed.'

'What about Aggs?'

'Panjan will watch the house as he watched your flight. He's not to be trifled with.'

Oblong noticed a note from Boris on the table – no wonder Gabriel had been there to greet them. 'Pigeon-post is quick,' he confirmed, handing Oblong a long blackthorn thumb stick. His own stick held a globe-stone at the end, so they would have light if they needed it.

He locked the door and did not say another word until they reached the tile. Gabriel knelt and ran his palm over the tile's surface and the surrounding ground. 'Best I go first,' he said.

Oblong grinned as Gabriel disappeared. His stock was rising. Valourhand had not trusted him to follow through the underground tile; Gabriel did trust him, even on the briefest acquaintance. He stamped the ground impatiently as the tile recharged.

This time his disembodiment delivered a new experience, a journey more than instant travel. He was borne along as if by a current or a wind in the high air. Other insubstantial matter drifted past.

The hyaline of drifting glooms ... he half-thought as he staggered from the tile. A few yards away Gabriel was bending over a tussock of grass. Damp tickled Oblong's cheeks, neither rain, nor fog, just floating moisture. They had arrived in the usual meadow, but fuzzy pinpoints of pale blue light dotted the open landscape.

'Mere worms, I call them,' said Gabriel. He shook his stick and the globe-stone flared. 'I've never seen them in such profusion, and I've never seen the vegetation so yellow. It's the decay which attracts them.'

'Did you float on the way?' asked Oblong.

Gabriel fielded the question seriously. 'It's a dimensional shift –

Bolitho foresaw the effect but couldn't say what might follow. He's a terrible loss.'

Oblong cursed his slowness. The St Elmo's cordial had to be a Bolitho concoction. Salt and Bolitho had both visited Lost Acre, and Gabriel knew them both.

'We must check the tree,' added Gabriel. The globe-stone's light bobbed along, closely mirroring the glow of the mere worms.

Oblong followed in silence.

The tree resembled a giant with head and shoulders lost in the clouds. The upper branches and the mixing-point were invisible. Peppered with mere worms, the undergrowth retained the same sandy colour.

'*The Yggdrasil*,' murmured Oblong.

'It could well be. I believe the Danes raided this far, so maybe they had a skald with them – and maybe he went in and understood.'

'Skald?'

'Rather up your street, Mr Oblong. Skalds were poets, compilers of history or composers of myth, depending on your point of view. The wider world goes for the latter, but I do wonder.' He shinned up the tree trunk, leaving Oblong to reflect on his new friend. Countrysiders, it appeared, had none of the self-imposed constraints of the town when it came to history – but how could Gabriel know about the Danes?

Gabriel worked his way through a succession of branches, rubbing their tips and moving on, like a picker after ripe fruit. With startling agility for such a big man, he dropped to the ground.

'The buds are blackening from the inside, like a canker.' He patted the trunk as a doctor would an ailing child patient.

'If it dies, what happens to the mixing-point?' asked Oblong.

'And what happens to Lost Acre? What happens to *us*?'

'Valourhand got into Wynter's bedroom. He had a drawing of two trees conjoined.'

'Nature is bigger than Wynter.'

'I wouldn't be so sure,' counselled Oblong. Maybe this was Gabriel's weakness: in his cloistered meadow had he ever seen a mushroom cloud, or forests laid low, ice-sheets breaking like mirrors? Man *could* unmake what Nature had created.

'There's nothing more for us here,' Gabriel declared, 'other than to note the stillness. Everything is underground, waiting.'

The return journey repeated the eerie out-of-body experience.

Oblong felt an urge to impress Gabriel, to show he had been part of this drama, but his companion's *gravitas* prevailed until the front door, when he could resist no longer.

'Orelia mentioned a *Darkness Rose*. It seems to have gone, but I remember Salt had one.'

Gabriel chuckled. 'One and the same – Salt gave it to Bill Ferdy, who gave it to Ferensen, who entrusted it to me.'

Oblong had his way in. 'I've seen another.'

Gabriel's face changed as if this was serious news.

'Where, pray?'

'There's an earth-coloured tile, deep underground below the town catacombs. It leads to a quarry.'

'*The* quarry,' murmured Gabriel, 'not that I've been there.'

'Well, there's an identical rose where the tunnel ends, right by the tile.'

'Is there indeed?' His host sounded pleased. He unlocked the door and ushered Oblong in.

They checked on Aggs, whose breathing had a steady, contented rumble.

'Now we can indulge a little,' said Gabriel. 'You light the fire, I'll do the necessaries.'

'Necessaries' meant beer, large flat cheese biscuits like thick poppadoms, and St Elmo's to finish.

Gabriel restocked the stove with peat before resuming their conversation by the fireside. 'Legend has it, there were three *Darkness Roses*. One found Salt and two were lost. They're to be treasured for their benevolence. But legend also says they have an opposite.'

Oblong worked through the implications. 'You mean it chose to be by the underground tile?'

'More importantly, Mr Oblong, it chose to let you through.'

So it had: the canes had hugged the ceiling as he and Valourhand crawled past.

'How do you know all this?'

'We've lived here for more than four hundred years. "Guardians" would be overstating our role, but I'd accept "observers". After Wynter's fall, there had to be an early-warning system. More people come than you might expect, and not all come back. But some liked to talk. So you could say they're family legends, gleaned from Lost Acre's visitors over the years and handed down through the generations.'

'Any Clauds?' asked Oblong.

'Lots of Clauds! Mostly good, but with the occasional bad apple.'

'And Morval Seer?'

'I found Morval here last summer. I gave her clothes and I mentioned her to Bolitho.'

'Fortemain?'

'Yes, although I had no idea then. He was just a professor with a gift for exploration, cocktails and kindness. But when they met . . .' Gabriel stopped, unable to find the words. 'He brought her pencils and paints and she was transformed. I guess that talent kept her human side alive.'

Conversation drifted to the mundane, until Gabriel collected the glasses and turned practical. 'Tomorrow you can teach me how to fly that contraption. Then I'll drop you both off by the Island Field bridge. Take a bedroom at the back.' He smiled. 'Almost all your friends have used it.'

9

A Trap to Lay

Scry's six-card deal from her Tarot pack reflected both the evening's events and a tantalising but uncertain future. The four open cards spoke of the already occurred: The Fool, for her mistaken attack on the town historian; The Wheel of Fortune, for an unexpected discovery, and Justice and The Hanged Man for the assumed execution of Tyke, ever a thorn in the Eleusians' side.

The two hidden cards were more challenging. She took the High Priestess to refer to her imminent fight with Nona. The winner would be Wynter's lead acolyte. As for the other, The World – be realistic, Wynter would never return for less. But which world? He had secured the valley already.

Lost Acre's auras varied in strength, fading over time, and were hard to pin down, but she had caught a tell-tale trace from the knight's visor. Oblong had been to the other place, and not so long ago. Why?

Fellow guests had helped the absurd man shed most of his carapace, but a single armoured foot still rang on the cobbles, enabling her to follow him discreetly to Artery Lane. He had stayed only minutes and once gone, the pitiful lock on his door yielded with ease, as had the conspicuously loose floorboard which concealed the velvet bag. Scry might peddle arcane tat in *The Clairvoyancy*, but she recognised fine silver and exquisite craftsmanship when she saw it – and that tell-tale aura. This was not an instrument to blow until you knew what it did.

She shook the bag, releasing a tiny card inscribed with the single word *Escharion*, and squealed with pleasure – the name on the last prophecy coin. Now she could bait her line.

She reached for pen and ink. The invitation would require subtle drafting and her gift for forgery.

IO

The Fanguins Have a Dilemma

It had been a hard day in the Manor kitchens, with Sly forever diverting waiters to his back office, but supply had largely kept pace with demand. At ten o'clock, Bomber sent the remaining staff home. She had only the wine glasses to box up.

She had embarked on this task when Fennel Finch, now dressed in a clinging shift of green silk with her hair tied back, appeared. 'I'll finish off,' she said with a glacial smile.

'It's late, and I'm almost done.'

'You've earned your shut-eye.'

The *bonhomie* rang false, but Bomber felt outranked. 'That's very thoughtful, Mrs Finch.'

'A joy to help.'

Joy: language as false as the smile, but Bomber conceded, gathered her coat and left.

In the Great Hall, she encountered Wynter, lounging by the fire with a superior bottle of wine. He poured a glass and offered it, asking, 'Do you ever feel unappreciated, Mrs Fanguin?'

'Often,' she said truthfully.

'I offered that countrysider reconciliation – yet he refused me.'

Bomber had witnessed the destruction wrought by the mantoleon and the deformities lurking in the New Year mechanicals. 'Why do they hate us so?' she asked.

'We're achievers; they're not.' He swirled his glass, raised it to his nose and inhaled.

'But they create monsters, Mr Wynter. We can't.'

He looked oddly amused. '*Don't* doesn't mean *can't*, Mrs Fanguin. Maybe they stole the skill from us – and maybe we should retrieve it. Imagine riding a griffin or a flying horse.'

Surely he's teasing.

Wynter nibbled one of her elaborate canapés. 'Work for me. I pay most generously.'

'I'm contracted to the Apothecaries—'

'You're not, you're employed by Master Thomes. Run-of-the-mill Apothecaries don't have taste buds. Let's weigh our respective merits. Thomes doesn't do gratitude or humour. Thomes wouldn't offer you a drink by the fire.'

Too true, thought Bomber. *How perceptive, but* . . . 'We were on our uppers, Mr Fanguin and I. We owe him.'

'That explains why you took the job. It's no reason for not moving on. I offer half as much again.'

'Sentiment, I suppose.'

Wynter's manner flipped like a coin. His tone hardened. 'Sentiment! You're with me or against me, Mrs Fanguin. It's Master or Mayor. Sleep on it.'

'I'll lie awake on it,' replied Bomber diplomatically. She drained her glass, curtsied and left.

Fanguin's house key fumbled for the lock like an inexperienced lover. Once inside, his crook found the umbrella stand, the bonnet the hat-stand and his mask the bannister. Fanguin rated champagne an effervescent sonata, but Vlad's twelve-years-in-the-cask whisky was the full symphony, the real McCoy. Favourite crystal tumbler in hand, he bounded upstairs to his study, where he waved a lighted match around the nozzle of the gas-lamp with such vigour that it failed.

A feminine form launched from the darkness. 'Bloody hell, Fanguin, do you want to blow us all up?' Valourhand seized the matches and did the needful. Her eyebrows rose as his appearance registered. 'You're better in trousers, believe me.'

'Best in show,' exclaimed Fanguin, pirouetting with the bottle aloft, 'and a prize which waits for no man.' He poured a triple into the tumbler for himself and a single into a toothmug for Valourhand. 'Speaking for myself, excess fizz dries you out.'

'Which is what you need. Just tell me, yes or no, was Oblong there?'

Fanguin was not in a yes-or-no mood. He stuck several pencils in his mouth and lurched forward like Frankenstein, arms and legs stiff as spade handles.

Through pursed lips he mumbled, 'For pencils, read straws; I'm in full armour and my name begins with O.'

Valourhand did not smile. 'He was meant to be protecting Orelia.'

'Orelia?' Fanguin stumbled. '*Our* Orelia? Orelia *Roc*?' He had last seen her on Election Day, heading upriver on skates with Gregorius Jones into a maze of heaving ice. He had reluctantly accepted the town's verdict of *missing, presumed dead* when the thaw yielded no bodies.

'Sit. Listen.'

As Valourhand delivered a condensed narrative of Orelia's adventures, Fanguin felt an irresistible surge of joy.

'I gave her my lucky charm – a female St Christopher wading with Christ on her back. And she made it!' As happens with the inebriated, his mood swung abruptly from ecstatic to disconsolate. 'I've fucked up, haven't I. I've been sleeping with the enemy. I've lost my moral compass. I've been an arsehole – go on, say it.'

'You've been an arsehole.'

'I'll going to give that Madge Brown what-for.'

'Too late. She's vamoosed.'

'What?'

'She sent her sister to deputise.' Valourhand paused. 'Was there a nun at the party?'

'Nuns everywhere, half a convent's worth. There was a kerfuffle with one of them, but I didn't see much. I was admiring this magnificent label. But I think she escaped. Tell me it was Orelia.'

A click – the front door latch – escaped Fanguin, but not Valourhand.

'She's back.'

'Orelia? Where—?'

'Your missus.'

Bomber's voice boomed from below, 'Fanguin, I know you're up there. Rumour has it you won a prize. I need a swig and I need advice.'

Valourhand whispered under her breath, 'Stay with Wynter, work on the inside. That's your penance.'

Clump, clump. Bomber had a gaoler's heavy tread. She had brought her own glass and as Fanguin poured, she displayed her gift for treating all visitors, however unexpected, as welcome guests.

'Miss Valourhand – don't tell me. You helped the old fool home.'

'Something like that.'

'God knows why he dragged you up here. We've a perfectly presentable sitting room.'

'She likes the view,' stammered Fanguin.

Bomber could not suppress her true concern any longer. 'It's Master Thomes or the Mayor,' she blurted out, 'and I have to choose *tonight*.'

'Do elaborate, dear,' said Fanguin, topping up her glass.

'I must cook for one or the other – Mr Wynter won't allow two masters.'

'No contest,' said Valourhand. 'The Mayor.'

'But I'm contracted to Master Thomes, and he does so like his sweetmeats.'

'In Lent?' said Fanguin.

Valourhand ran with the idea. 'There you are – on a plate: you say you're embarrassed by his slippage into sin. Apothecaries take vows, don't they? Say there've been whispers and you're afraid of exposing him to punitive action.'

Bomber appraised Valourhand with a mix of admiration and mild suspicion. 'You're a devious one,' she said.

'And say you're joining me at the Town Hall,' added Fanguin, 'because I need watching.'

Bull's eye! Bomber visibly relaxed. 'Now that *is* true.'

11

The Pool of Mixed Intentions

Strimmer could barely contain himself. Persephone's dance had been for *him*: every curve of the faun's back, every languid stretch of arm and leg had exuded allure and erotic energy. He returned to his rooms and replaced his costume with warm clothes. Unease at her choice of venue succumbed to the prospect of a feral coupling beneath the stars, their bodies illuminated by firelight.

A leopard skin, suggestive of potency, dominated his study wall, bought from *Baubles & Relics* at exorbitant cost during Mrs Banter's reign. He folded it under his arm and set off. She, of course, must wait for him, not vice versa.

At the Island Field, he wrapped the skin around his shoulder like a classical hero, crossed the southern footbridge and followed the towpath. Persephone had kept her word. About half a mile from the Pool, he came across her head-piece. He took the vestigial antlers as a trophy. He smirked. He would be savage with her.

At the Pool the river plunged underground. Steep banks descended to reedbeds fringing a near-circular sheet of water. To the southeast lay treacherous marshland. Keen to surprise her, rather than be surprised, Strimmer skirted the rising ground before descending.

No fire greeted him, but Persephone's naked form did. She stood in the shallows, combing her hair, apparently impervious to the cold.

'*Make me immortal with a kiss,* and more than that,' he whispered to himself. He would not be bested. He removed the leopard skin, his coat, jacket and shirt.

Persephone was still wearing the bow. The string bisected her breasts. A noise drew Strimmer's eyes upwards. A small pack of agile silver-haired dogs were easing their way down the scree above her.

Persephone's voice rang across the water. 'How dare you gaze at me?'

Fragments of legend came to Strimmer: Actaeon the hunter, stumbling on Diana, goddess of the hunt, naked at her pool – and the terrible consequences.

He scrambled back up the bank as the dogs, lips curled and fangs bared, broke into a trot.

Strimmer ran like a stag, zigzagging, antlers in hand to ward off his pursuers. He ran until he could run no longer. He sawed the air with the points of bone, but the pack had been starved. They wanted blood.

They tore the tottering figure down.

'The pack had been starved'

12

After the Hunt

Persephone had been seized by the unfamiliar power of music twice now, and music had infiltrated her decision-making too – why otherwise ask the Precentor to rehearse the Debussy? She had found these spontaneous moments of dance exciting, but disturbing. She had an intruder in her head.

And later that same night, back in her bed, she dreamt music . . .

A vast theatre lies open to the night sky. An apron stage is lit by braziers. Basalt columns glimmer. Before her a thousand faces exude the warmth of rapt attention: mankind, in all its rich variety, in thrall to her.

A young man with Strimmer's face glides on stage, head jagging left and right. He pirouettes and somersaults with predatory grace: the dance of a hunter. Low to the ground come his dogs, striped like hyenas.

Movement and music are rhythmic, beyond classical. String and woodwind flow, then judder, then flow again.

Crouched in a sheath of gauze, she is all but naked. Bulrushes with plush tawny heads obstruct her view, but she knows that the watching faces wait for her.

A single clarinet uncoils her, sinuous as the stream she bathes in. The hunter is transfixed. His dogs caress her calves as they lollop to and fro. She dances as if he were not there.

Slowly old loyalties sunder; roles reverse. The hunter is hunted.

The pursuit and mauling death take time. She continues to bathe, not deigning to look. Retribution is a given.

Persephone awoke, her body spangled in sweat despite the season. She reached for a mirror for reassurance. She cocked an eyebrow, flicked a finger – her body was still hers to command, but an alien message lingered.

Art can isolate the beauty in violence and deliver it without harm.

'Begone,' she said to this squeamish intruding voice. 'You have no business here.'

Wynter lay in his four-poster bed, equally unsettled. Why should Tyke come so meekly to his doom? And why had Nona tried to save him?

He caught the shuffle of bare feet moving from the stairs to the landing outside. The door opened to admit Fennel Finch, carrying a salver with two mugs.

'They say you favour drinks from long ago. This is heated white wine laced with ground ginger, almonds and a pinch of salt. One for me and one for you.' She sat on the edge of the bed.

He sniffed it cautiously and she smiled. 'Oh yes, they had poisons too. Choose your mug.' He did, and she took a generous gulp from the other. 'You do not have forgiving eyes,' she added.

'Tell me what they are, not what they're not.'

She edged closer, examined his face. 'Ascetic, but poised on the edge of excess,' she said.

'*Never* excess,' replied Wynter.

'I said on the edge. Anyway, eyes are given. You make the furrows in the face.' She ran a finger along his cheekbone to his mouth. 'When did you last smile? Or cry out in pleasure?'

The silk of Fennel's dress tightened across her body as she twisted around to sip her drink. She ran Wynter's hand up from her hip to her breasts. He did not object.

'You smiled for Mr Snorkel too,' he pointed out.

'I gushed for Mr Snorkel. But I never did *this* for Mr Snorkel.' She paused. 'Your eyes are widening, bluer than blue.'

Protest from Wynter's inner voice only fuelled his desire. He was Master and Bole had no place here. *He* would decide.

He made room for her.

Later, in the darkness, Fennel Finch unwittingly parroted Mrs Fanguin's question. 'Tell me, Geryon—'

Wynter put a finger to her lips. 'Mr Wynter, *always*.'

'Tell me, Mr Wynter, how do countrysiders create such creatures?'

'There is a secret, Mrs Finch.'

'Fennel, *always*.'

'With children, you can fashion mythical beings. Some may fail. But rest assured, my accumulated skills are special.'

Fennel hesitated, although she didn't doubt a word he said. His face had a terrible certainty. A pagan thought overwhelmed her; the kind she had never experienced with her dry-as-dust husband. She must commit to Wynter utterly. 'I offer my son to the cause,' she said.

He interlaced his right hand with hers. *This is indeed how to propitiate the gods: the old way and the best.*

Sacrifice.

Old History

Today there is naming of streets. It is an earnest process and, since the Herald's voluntary abdication of power, democratic.

The Mayor, the Architect, the Herald, the Master Builder and the Master Carver stoop over a town plan pinned to a trestle table in Market Square. It is a breezy late spring day. The original names are printed. The five new ones announce their presence in rose madder ink, west or southeast of Market Square.

'A job well done,' announces the Mayor.

Four heads dip in agreement; one does not.

'But unfinished,' says the Master Carver, 'here, here, here, here and here.' His forefinger jabs at a tangle of anonymous alleys and snickets in The Understairs.

'Fair point,' concedes the Mayor. 'If we don't name them, they will, and I'm not having uncouth language loose in the streets.'

'I propose a classical theme,' says the Carver. 'There are five to name and five of us. I go for Myrmidon Coil.' He marks the paper accordingly. The Mayor ignores this petty breach of protocol; the Carver is rarely assertive and contributes much to the fabric of the town. The others follow: Ariadne's Thread, Augean Alley, Jason's Way and Grendel's Cut.

Later, the Mayor asks the Carver to explain his quaint choice.

'A suggestion from a lady friend and it sounded good,' he replies. On this occasion, he tells the truth. Nona has always had a way with words.

IN TOWN

I

The Morning After

'It's from Seer,' said Wynter, tapping the letter on the table.

The weak and fastidious Hieronymus Seer might have evolved into the more formidable Ferensen, but his distinctive handwriting had not changed.

'He offers a trade,' added Wynter.

'What for what?'

'No experiments, in return for the escharion.'

Persephone laughed. 'Who does he think he is?'

Wynter watched her closely. He had no idea what the escharion might be, but did Nona know? An ignorant person would surely show more interest. 'He wants a meeting in the tower. I believe you have the keys?'

'There are no keys.'

'Metaphorically speaking.' Wynter paused. 'I need all five neodymium magnets.' The revelation had come in sleep, after Fennel Finch had slipped from his bed.

'Bole told you?' Persephone asked.

'Nobody tells me anything. I just know what he knew.'

She disliked the edge to his voice. Was Wynter turning from her to Estella? Or was Estella turning Wynter against her? She could not be sure who was controlling whom. An encounter between Wynter and Ferensen, an enemy but the only other survivor from the first Eleusian Age, might elucidate. 'Am I invited?'

'He wishes to see me at midnight tomorrow – you may join us later, if you like.'

'You know the sequence?'

'I apply the magnets at the base of the tower, north face. They'll cling to their correct positions of their own accord. Then I move them: top, bottom, second top, second bottom, middle.'

'You'll have them first thing tomorrow.'

The magnets were in fact in her bag, but she had preparatory work to do.

Before Wynter could reply, Sly burst in through the front door. 'It's all going pear-shaped,' he spluttered.

'Control yourself,' hissed Wynter.

'That countrysider escaped – despite being half-butchered by Carcasey Jack' – Sly's hands were dancing in disbelief – 'then Jack goes and dies in his sleep, looking like he's seen a ghost.'

'He *what*?'

'Then—'

'Then *what*?' cried Wynter.

'Strimmer is dead. Someone or something ripped his throat out near the river.'

Wynter had little interest in the dispensable Strimmer, but Carcasey Jack and Tyke were a different matter. 'How could the countrysider escape?'

'He got out through the cell window, then God knows what he did. It's a lethal drop, miles down and jagged rocks below.'

Persephone kept her peace. She knew how.

'Take me there,' barked Wynter, 'and summon that imbecile Prim.'

Denzil Prim responded with alacrity. He had not enjoyed patrolling the town's outer wall. After twenty years in Rotherweird's subterranean chambers, agoraphobia had struck, leaving him to search out squints and places on the battlements where shadow lingered.

'Cream always rises to the top,' he said, bowing to Wynter as he entered his old home with Sly in tow. Sly delivered a warning glare: *Tone down the humour.*

Wynter ignored Prim and turned to the under-gaoler. 'Where was he kept?'

'Cell One, your Worship.'

'The deepest, the best,' added Prim helpfully.

'You'll speak when you're spoken to,' hissed Wynter, striding down into the gloom.

The under-gaoler struggled to keep up.

'Were you in the cell?'

'Only when Mr Jack called for his implements, your Worship.'

'How often was that?'

'Um ... from time to time.' The unfortunate man had no idea of the Mayor's position on the prisoner, so he trod carefully. 'Not a pretty sight,' he added.

'But he survived?'

'You can tell from the eyes. And he were breathing – well, just. Mr Jack wanted a scream or two, but he wouldn't oblige.'

'When did Jack stop?'

'Just past midnight.' The under-gaoler turned pale as he opened the cell door and stared in. 'I came back later to do the clearing-up, only to find *this.*'

They followed Wynter in. The central iron bar had been wrenched from the window's brickwork and its neighbours bent sideways until they were flat to the wall. The logic appeared irrefutable: Tyke had had an accomplice.

The under-gaoler mewed, 'It were triple-locked, your Worship. Honest, cross my heart and hope to die.'

Prim, judging this expression unfortunate, came to the rescue. 'Our tools can't bend bars like that, and bare hands neither. We're gaolers, not circus performers.'

'From the outside then,' added Sly.

The under-gaoler shook his head. 'It's a sheer drop – helluva way down.'

'Stay where you are,' commanded Wynter, tiptoeing over the bloodied flags. 'The ground is disturbed – here, here and here.' The Mayor knelt, pushed the earth with a finger. 'Get me a coil of wire,' he ordered without looking up.

Prim pulled rank. 'Bottom of my desk, second drawer, left,' he barked at the under-gaoler, who hurried out.

Rage seized Wynter. Tyke had again cheated death like a common card sharp – as in the mixing-point all those centuries ago.

The under-gaoler returned with a coil of wire, which Wynter worked into the hole. Down, down, down it went, feet deep. His audience watched, mesmerised, although, unlike him, they could not detect the unmistakable aura from the other place.

Wynter stood up and pointed at the corner beside the door. 'That hole is the furthest from the window. I suggest it's where his staff was leaning.'

The under-gaoler gabbled in bewildered excitement, 'It was, it *was* – he brought it with him and it ain't here now. That's bloody brilliant, your Worship. But . . . um . . . *how* . . . ?'

'It's a living staff. It moves, roots, and moves again.' Wynter turned to Sly. 'So we have our narrative. The countrysider had a demon wand, which broke our common iron like a biscuit. He escaped and massacred the Head of the North Tower for revenge.'

'Mr Strimmer?' gasped the gaolers.

Wynter ignored the question and moved to the window. 'What was down there?'

'Blood on the rocks,' said Sly, 'but no sign of a body.'

'Have we bloodhounds, Mr Sly?'

'Not even a beagle.'

'This place is toothless.' Wynter spat out a series of commands. 'I want a likeness drawn – I want him caught, dead or alive. Include a reward. Impose a curfew from six to six. Exempt the Defence League, and the Apothecaries when on State business. Now take me to Carcasey Jack.'

If death had come in sleep, Jack had been in the grip of nightmare. His eyes were bulging wide open and the upper teeth had torn through the lower lip. Clenched hands had frozen above his face as if warding off phantoms. The bedclothes had snared his splayed feet, but from *whom* or *what* was he trying to escape?

Wynter had never grieved for another, but now his emotions did stretch to disappointment. Moulding the perfect servant took time. Take Bendigo Sly: he had far to go – but Carcasey Jack had come ready-made.

'Mr Jack locks his door at night, and his room has no windows,' Prim pointed out.

There's no aura here, thought Wynter, examining the bedlinen. Then he pointed. 'Specks,' he said, 'like fine soot.' He walked round the bed. 'On the sheets, the pillow, the skin.'

Even Sly, Snorkel's assassin, shuddered. Rotherweird was descending into the abyss.

Jack's tools, many uncleaned, occupied a small table. Wynter picked up a tiny globe-light, shook it and peered into Jack's mouth and nostrils before handing it to Sly. 'As I thought: they're the footprints of his assassins. See for yourselves,' he said.

Standing back, Wynter shut his eyes. In his head, a macabre scene played out: Carcasey Jack, tossing and turning, unable to settle, disturbed that the wax-faced freak had not begged for mercy as he should. At last he quietened, embracing the sleep of the almost sated . . . and then, through the keyhole and under the door, they poured with their nets and stings in their thousands. They sorted themselves: loose weavers in front of tight weavers, small preceding large, before moving along the pillow and over the blanket. Legs touched legs. Eyes swivelled and locked. Spinnerets extruded their viscous polymer.

As the prostrate body snored and the mouth opened, the invaders had pounced.

Wynter ground his teeth. *Affinities.* It could only be Morval Seer. She had rescued his enemy and killed his enforcer. She had dared to declare war.

So be it.

Shocked, the trio by the body spoke.

'Blocked—'

'Sealed—'

'Silked up—'

Wynter stepped forward and chose another implement, a handy little claw which opened and closed. Deep from Jack's throat he extracted a grey furry plug. 'Spiders,' he proclaimed, deadpan. 'Legions of them.'

And here's another contrast, reflected Sly: *Snorkel would have thrown a tantrum.* Wynter harnessed his anger. He could see him already working out his revenge. There would be an eye for an eye; of that Sly had no doubt.

At the prison gates, Prim received the news he craved.

'You're on approval, Mr Prim. This is war and a time to be harsh.' He turned to Sly. 'Get Doctor Fanguin to the Manor.'

Fanguin reached the Great Hall as Wynter returned. The Mayor's enquiry wrongfooted him.

'Spiders? I confess they're not my *forte.*'

'You're a biologist, aren't you? Do they feel pain?'

Having undertaken to work on the inside, Fanguin felt obliged to play along. 'Yes, as a physiological response to unwelcome stimuli; probably no to pain as we feel it.'

'Do they feel fear in other spiders?'

'That presupposes spiders feel fear in the first place, which is hotly debated. If they do, I'd say yes. Humans smell fear, and spiders smell a damn sight better than us.'

'On the ball as ever, Doctor Fanguin.' Wynter turned to Sly. 'Find Mrs Finch.'

Fennel had settled into an upstairs bedroom with a fraction of her extensive wardrobe. She appeared in minutes, impeccably dressed and coiffed. She did not deign to acknowledge Fanguin.

'How old is this son of yours?' asked Wynter.

'Young Percy is sixteen, but older in so many ways.'

'What of his friends?'

'Only the best, of course.'

Fanguin knew Percy Finch; he had been in Form IV for a year during his tenure. He was a snobbish, cruel boy, very much the son of the mother. His parents' arid marriage and the absence of siblings had not helped.

'Doctor Fanguin wishes to conduct an experiment into the sensibilities of spiders. He wishes to use this Hall for its constant temperature. Size doesn't matter, but he needs a serious catch and he needs them alive. Well pay a shilling a dozen. Tell the Headmaster the boys are needed for special duties.'

Fanguin gulped. What to do? *I'm the spy within*, he chided himself. 'Can't wait,' he mumbled, striving for a suitable facial expression to match.

2

The Tower Opens

By eleven o'clock at night, the town was under curfew.

At the Manor gates Wynter told the guards not to follow him. 'I wish to test our security for myself,' he said.

The Tower looked even more imposing in a deserted Market Square. Before his execution he and Bole had planned much, but they had never discussed a tower. He must explore before Ferensen arrived.

He moved one of the neodymium magnets Persephone had provided across the surface of the tower's north face until it clung unaided, then repeated the process with the other four. He then slid them in the ordained sequence, easy enough as each magnet would move in only one direction. He caught a satisfying click at each journey's end as the inner mechanism responded. On the last, a door, hitherto invisible, swung open.

Wynter removed a globe-light from his pocket, shook it and stepped in. Canvas fell in folds from a central hook on the ceiling, a tent-like effect. He pushed the door to without relocking it. A camp-table faced a chair with folding legs, its seat a rectangle of seasoned leather. A pottery oil-lamp on the table had its wick intact. He lit it. A javelin occupied the far corner and a helmet, distinctively Roman, rested on a second chair.

He weighed the javelin in his right hand and found himself mumbling in Latin, as if to guards outside. Imagined campfire smoke puckered his nostrils. Outside the tent, a repair hammer chimed on a buckled shield.

Fighting to oust these alien memories, he stumbled up the stairs to the next floor: a carver's workshop. Bole had always planned to assimilate the talents of an expert carver. A name surfaced – Benedict Roc – but little more. Roc's gifts must have enabled Bole to carve the prophecies in the Hall of the Apothecaries – and to assemble this very tower. Fresh wood shavings lay among the tools; recent use had streaked the sandpaper grey.

Wynter fretted. Had he been here in sleep, or was this another coded message? At first sight, the carving on the bench, a sundered sphere, resembled work abandoned, but on closer examination, the split had been worked: a miniature wave had been cut into one face, zigzag lightning into the other.

Wynter sensed an ambush. Ferensen could never have been here and nor would he have requested this meeting. The invitation had been a forgery. He pocketed a sharp-ended awl, just in case.

He climbed again. The walls in the next room dazzled, the white unrelieved save for a single picture of a child's stick person in a peculiar hat which matched his, or possibly her, quizzical expression. The character had been rendered with black paint on an orange background. This stark floor otherwise boasted only a stool with steel legs and a steel shelf crammed with books on multi-dimensional physics. He felt the presence of a kindred spirit, an astringent mind reaching beyond orthodox scientific frontiers.

It irked Wynter that Bole's various *personae* dominated the tower's interior, with no tribute to him.

He had kept an eye on the height of each room – only one floor to go. Bole's egotistical dominance continued. He entered an exact replica of his servant's bedroom at the Manor in the first Eleusian age. He recognised the chair, the schoolboy desk, the bed, the books. Pinched and intimate compared to the Manor's master bedroom, this was nonetheless the tower's inner sanctum, the holy of holies.

Click.

The door below had opened and the sound of heavy footsteps drifted up.

They paused. His visitor was absorbing the first floor.

Thereafter the steps accelerated, floor by floor. Wynter lit the candle on Bole's desk and gripped the awl in his pocket, only to relax as a familiar figure strode in.

'Dear Estella.'

She wore black, with a bag slung over her shoulder. Her eyes blazed. She had picked up the pottery oil-lamp from the camp-table. A tongue of flame flickered in the spout. *Meet a wise virgin,* thought Wynter.

'What have you done?' she asked.

'Oh, I've done nothing of moment. *Yet.*'

'This is *you*, isn't it, this tower – it's you through and through. How could you—? *Bole.*' She spat out the single syllable.

'No, no, Estella, it is I – look at me.'

'Geryon Wynter would have shared the truth with me. Nobody has suffered more in his cause. I carried his candle alone and unaided. But that's nothing to *you.*'

'Calm yourself and listen, Estella. Calx risked his life to acquire a unique and necessary gift: he became a shapeshifter for my sake. Don't ask me how, but he did. He needed a helper, but you would never have worked with him. You called him the Potamus, remember? I had to use Calx, so I had to use Nona.'

'But . . .'

Wynter raised a restraining arm. 'On the day of my return, who came to *The Journeyman's Gist*? Who attended the First Supper at the Apothecaries? Not Nona, but *you.* You are my right hand. I've never disowned you, Estella, and I never will.'

Scry's resentments bubbled on. 'Persephone took Madge Brown's place at the Council meeting – it should have been me.' She was gambling now, presenting suspicions as fact. 'And I do know who Persephone is.'

A palpable hit – and Wynter did not take issue. Instead, he defended the move. 'I have to keep the Apothecaries at a distance as they alienate everyone else – and you're an honorary member. It's for appearances, and not for long.'

Scry paused. She had to know. 'Just tell me how it was done.'

'Dead men tell no tales.' Wynter pulled a face of deep despair. 'My skin was used in the mixing-point.'

'And then Bole killed you?'

'I believe so. Maybe he thought he could control me, but he was wrong.'

His candour restored Scry's trust. Wynter had Bole's knowledge, but nothing more. She must cement her position to keep Nona at bay.

'Mr Wynter, I've something to show you, but not here. I don't find this room congenial.'

She led the way down from Bole's bedroom. On the table in the bare white room she pulled out a velvet bag, unwrapped the escharion and handed it to Wynter. Long ago, Wynter had collected and sold ancient artefacts, everything from coins to torcs to arrowheads, but he had never seen the like of this instrument before.

'Old,' he said. 'It's older even than us.' He weighed it, felt it, read the letters. He mustered an uncertain smile. 'It's the last prophecy coin – will it signal my triumph, or my doom?'

'Both: your triumph and the doom of our enemies,' said a new voice.

Her dancer's feet had brought Persephone up unheard. Scry spun around and Wynter took a pace back. In his first life, these two had been inseparable, if competitors too.

'Who asked you here?' snarled Scry.

Persephone, beaming, spoke with a menacing calmness. 'Geryon did, didn't you, Geryon? We thought a petty forger might be at work.'

Scry knew Nona was addressing her; Wynter had as good as

confirmed it. Dr Obern's sanatorium must have provided the wherewithal.

Her rediscovered trust in Wynter evaporated. 'Why tell *her*?' she asked Wynter.

'She happened to be there – she recognised Hieronymus Seer's writing. She was concerned for my safety.'

'So I was,' added Persephone while examining the escharion. 'Pretty. So pretty.'

Scry seized the escharion back. 'You've been tricked, Mr Wynter, taken over. She and Bole planned this from the beginning.'

The accusation touched a raw nerve in Wynter, already needled by the tower's focus on Bole's multiple personalities. 'I am Geryon Wynter and I speak for myself. You serve me, both of you, as did the *late* Calx Bole.' He repacked the escharion. 'We'll assess this new discovery back at the Manor – where you'll drink to each other, and I to you.'

'We should examine the roof as we're here,' said Persephone. 'There are retractable rungs in the wall.'

She could only know that if she's been here before, concluded Scry.

Wynter also sounded wary. 'After you, Persephone,' he said, ushering her up to Bole's reconstructed bedroom.

She was right: rungs set in the wall pulled out to form steps to a barely visible trapdoor. Persephone led the way; Wynter and Scry followed less nimbly.

Stars ducked in and out of a torn sky. An erratic breeze ruffled their hair. Only a carved balustrade shielded them from the edge. Rotherweirders had been admiring from below the abstract intricacy of the carvings with the aid of a variety of optical instruments. Yet here, on the inside, abstraction yielded to elaborate real-life scenes. Persephone produced her own globe-light. On closer examination, the carvings portrayed the destruction of mankind, its habitations and inventions. Tiny faces, riven with horror and despair, screamed while houses fractured, ships sank and aeroplanes spilled passengers into space. Scry found a collapsing mine in one corner. In another, mountains heaved and sundered.

'I dreamed of this,' said Wynter. The globe on Bole's workbench and the word *Doomsday*, scribbled by him in sleep, mirrored the theme.

'Why would Bole bring you back for this?' asked Scry, moving towards him.

'An enigma, I agree, *unless*—'

He broke off as a thump and rattle brought his crouching acolytes to their feet. A long, low, iron-banded trunk resting against the balustrade had moved of its own accord. A single shaft through an iron hoop alone secured the lid. The trunk jumped again.

Scry, the closest, took a pace back. 'What the hell's in there?' she asked, glaring at her rival.

'Best not to open Pandora's box,' warned Persephone, a red rag to Scry.

'Move right back, both of you,' said Wynter.

The trunk went quiet.

'Go closer, Estella,' he ordered.

Scry edged forward apprehensively. The trunk shook violently until she bravely placed a hand on the lid and it settled, as if calmed by her touch. She looked at Wynter and at his nod, opened the lid, releasing an aura from the other place. She rummaged inside before brandishing her trophy.

'A staff – finders keepers!' she cried.

Wynter instantly coveted the dark, twisted wood. Tyke had his; Destiny was offering him a counter-weapon.

'Let me hold it?' he cried, extending a hand, only to withdraw it as shoots sprang from the wood, twined around the parapet and Scry's legs and started dragging her backwards.

'Help her—!' yelled Wynter.

'Take it,' screamed Scry, 'for God's sake, take it.' More shoots burgeoned, pinioning her wrists and ankles. Persephone could not break the iron grip, even with Wynter lending his strength to the struggle.

Scry clawed at the carved balustrade, trying to cling on, but the shoots ripped her fingers away and propelled her body towards the edge.

'Geryon ... Geryon,' she cried, 'it's Bole – Bole and her—'

She desperately ducked her head forward, having lost control of her arms, but to no avail. With a shriek, she disappeared over the edge.

Wynter peered over, waiting for Scry to transform and soar, but the dull thump of body on stone said otherwise.

Estella, there from the first, weaver of his legend and most loyal of servants, was dead.

'No,' mumbled Wynter. 'That was not meant to be.'

The shoots disentangled at a startling pace and receded into the staff. Moments later, it lay on the floor beside them, harmless as a walking stick.

'I'm not so sure,' said Persephone gently, handing the staff to Wynter. 'It's yours, Geryon: it will protect you and see us through. It's sentient, you see. It *knew*. It's a gnarl.'

'It's a *what*?' said Wynter fiercely.

'A gnarl: a rarity from the other place. It attaches itself to kindred spirits and then protects them to the last. I found it for you.'

'How did you find it?'

'I've had centuries to probe Lost Acre's secrets, but this was among the most obvious. It grew up the tree by the mixing-point.' She paused. *Should she tell him? Would it help or hinder?* Yes, she would. 'As did Tyke's staff; they're mirror opposites.' Persephone moved to even more delicate ground. 'Estella would have killed Bole sooner or later, even if that meant killing you. Maybe that's what she planned for tonight – why else go to such trouble to forge the invitation? Why choose a place nobody else can enter?'

Wynter did not respond. Grasping the staff and the escharion, he followed Persephone out.

The body lay sprawled at the base of the tower, part transformed. Scry's cheeks had turned grey; her face had a pinched look. Half-clawed toes had pierced her shoes. The shoots, now hardened to wood and binding her limbs like ligatures, had fatally stalled the metamorphosis.

Persephone frisked the body and found a short stiletto in a cloth sheath. The dulled silver blade had been smeared with thick green paste.

'See?' said Persephone.

Old Wynter, *hard* Wynter took over. 'Leave the body. We've quite a mausoleum now – Strimmer, Snorkel, Carcasey Jack, Estella – but show me a death which doesn't bestow opportunity. We enforce the curfew. We weed out the dissenters. We harden the sinews of the loyal. We find a new Town Crier.'

Persephone removed the magnets from the door. The mechanism reset and the door merged once more with the tower wall.

'And there's a world to be punished,' added Persephone with a smile, 'with our new science: *Apocalyptics*.'

'Or is it the science of mistletoe?' whispered Wynter with a smile.

'Part transformed'

3

Taking Advantage

'A minute's silence, ladies and gentlemen, for the late lamented Hengest Strimmer, Head of the North Tower, lost to us by an unexplained accident of fate,' said Gorhambury, opening the first Council meeting after the party with the precise language of *The Coroners' Verdict Regulations*.

Gorhambury, Wynter and the Guild Masters bowed their heads. Persephone Brown, sitting alone, pad on knee, did not react at all.

Exactly sixty seconds later, Gorhambury raised his head and reset his pocket watch. 'A minute's silence for the late lamented Estella Scry, owner of *The Clairvoyancy*, lost to us by an unexplained accident of fate.'

This was news to many; heads turned to face each other before dipping again.

Persephone Brown made a marginal amendment to the minutes.

Gorhambury's head and pocket watch repeated the sequence. 'A minute's silence for Carcasey Jack, head gaoler, lost to us by an unexplained accident of fate.'

With each name the Council members' reaction became more perfunctory, but this time Wynter interrupted. 'No, no, no,' he said sternly, 'these are no accidents. They're killings from outside. Vigilance must be our watchword: we must improve our armoury, double the guard and enforce the curfew more strictly.'

'What happened to Miss Scry?' asked the Master Baker.

Persephone Brown answered as if to spare the Mayor. 'One of

the guards found her at the base of the tower in Market Square. There was a rope. She may have climbed.'

'What about the tower? Suppose that's where they hide – shouldn't we burn it down? We've had nothing but trouble since it arrived,' said the Master Tanner, calculating that the proposal would appeal to the Mayor.

'Mr Snorkel's balcony was in sight of that tower,' added the Master Mixer.

'The mechanicals stopped right by it,' added another.

Persephone watched the giveaway places on Wynter's face: the corners of the eyes, the lower lip, the cheek lines, all fluttering. Bole and Wynter were facing off in a fight for control: Bole to preserve his shrine, Wynter to erase it.

Fennel Finch entered, followed by two servants bearing silver trays laden with filled coffee cups. She delivered Wynter's while supervising distribution to the others.

'Be strong,' she whispered.

The memory of Fennel's embrace ousted Bole's entreaties. *Be strong indeed.*

'We take no risks,' Wynter said. 'We'll burn it to the ground.'

The Master Woodworker vacillated: he disliked the absolutist trend of Wynter's rule and feared a scouring of the town, a division between politically acceptable carvings and the burning of any which did not conform. Like Gorhambury, he knew the power of precedent. He muttered his Guild Master's oath:

> '*Best wood cheats decay and Death;*
> *Give it life, and give it breath*'

before raising his voice. 'I have, your Worship, examined the tower through various optical devices and I assure you the carvings are truly exceptional.'

'Do you recognise the hand?' asked Wynter.

'I've asked around. He or she isn't one of ours and there's only one countrysider who could achieve that quality.'

Wynter's ears pricked up.

'He's called Gabriel.'

'How quaint,' said Wynter. 'Where does he live?'

'Near Westwood.'

Wynter ruminated. Gabriel, an archangel's name, living close to the entry to the other place? He smelled trouble, but for the moment he returned to the matter in hand. Having won his duel with Bole he felt a need for compromise. 'Very well, burn the tower, after saving any detachable carvings for further consideration.'

Persephone read out the next item on the agenda: *Desirable Distractions*.

Wynter explained, 'The people need cheering up, so we'll give them a Great Equinox Race to remember. Polk – you're the coracle expert. Find a new spin. Gorhambury will rework the rules as necessary. On the morning of the Race I shall lead a small expedition to probe the countrysiders. That should avoid my absence causing any unnecessary panic.'

Boris noted the peremptory tone of Wynter's contributions. Disturbances in Lost Acre had to date occurred on Midsummer Day and the Winter Solstice. Did Wynter's expedition herald another? But he could hardly refuse, even though Wynter's next decrees only hardened his suspicions.

'We'll take Miss Brown to record every incident and ensure a full report. In the permanent absence of Mr Strimmer, I'll take Master Thomes and a few select Apothecaries to meet any scientific challenges. Apothecaries, as we know, do not dirty their hands with the Great Equinox Race. They'll not be missed.'

Nobody dissented; the corrupted mechanicals and the mantoleon had bestowed a potentially terminal edge to the notion of scientific challenges. The Apothecaries made welcome guinea pigs.

'Excellent suggestion,' said the Master Mixer.

'That's what I call leadership,' swooned the Master Tanner.

'And quiet funerals for our three deceased,' added Wynter. 'They were unattached, after all.'

Again, nobody dissented. The power bases of the departed trio – the prison, the North Tower and *The Clairvoyancy* – shared a shadowy feel. Snorkel's position as former Mayor had merited a torchlight procession, but not theirs.

'Record time,' said Wynter as he closed the meeting, holding back only Bendigo Sly.

So much for Council meetings, thought Boris as he departed. *A performance for multiple roles has shrunk to an extended soliloquy to a captive audience.*

Wynter, ever fastidious, called for the floor to be swept and the papers cleared. Aggs managed the operation while Wynter ushered Sly to a corner.

'This Gabriel who lives near Westwood? He's inconveniently placed. He might interfere. I want him dealt with.'

'You should see his work, Mr Wynter – he can't have any time for troublemaking.'

Wynter's face held its expression like stone.

Reading the looks of your masters was a cardinal rule of survival. 'What exactly should I do?' Sly added hastily.

'Burn the place down.'

'With him inside?'

'Oh yes. If he must award himself grand titles . . .' Sly's puzzlement showed and Wynter elucidated. 'Gabriel is an angel – angels have fiery swords. So, let's play *the biter bit*. Use Thomes' machine and do it by night. We need a test run.'

Snorkel's driving force had been petty and comprehensible: self-aggrandisement protected by patronage and, thanks to Gorhambury, efficient administration. Wynter's vision had a wild, elusive edge. It made the ride more exciting; if only he knew more about Journey's End. 'Your slightest wish is my command,' replied

Sly, inclining his head as he identified another difference: Wynter inspired deference; Snorkel had not.

'Work to do,' said Boris, guiding Gorhambury in the direction of Vlad's, home to all beverages save beer. A light mizzle swept through the town. Few showed, and those who did hurried on their errands across the glistening cobbles with heads bowed as if in mourning.

Having never sought entertainment, Gorhambury had no feel for providing it. 'We could do coloured hats,' he proposed, sipping his herbal tea, 'or striped coracle poles at a stretch.'

As Boris waited for his mulled wine to cool, the air between them grew rich in competing flavours and prompted a thought. 'Right, it's always been singles or pairs, with no institutional edge. This year we'll have teams: Guild against Guild, with some extras so nobody's left out.' Boris inhaled; nutmeg and cloves jostled for supremacy over Gorhambury's lemon and ginger. 'We'll add the Scholastics for the School, the Ricketeers for the rickshaw drivers, the Misfits for the miscellaneous.'

Amendment and deletions to the *Regulations* and the Rulebook jostled like coracles in Gorhambury's head. 'The Staff for the municipal staff?' he chipped in.

'For God's sake, Gorhambury, jazz up! How about the Pen Pushers? That's what they do, after all. Each team is allowed one foursome and two doubles to defend or harass. Colours must be chosen and registered.'

Gorhambury put his foot down. 'The Municipals. I insist. We are more than mere scribes, Mr Polk.'

In the deeper workings of Boris' febrile mind, a reservation about his proposals fluttered, failed to articulate and died stillborn.

Gorhambury, by contrast, was warming up. 'We could have team songs.'

'Bold idea, Gorhambury, I'll add it.'

*

By noon that same day Gorhambury had accomplished his task; by two in the afternoon the *Great Equinox Race (Guild) Amendment Regulations*, signed by the Mayor under his emergency powers, graced the Municipal noticeboard; by four this radical departure from tradition was the talk of the town and by five, two stacks of queries and protests (the ticked on the right; the crossed on the left) forced Gorhambury to post the *Great Equinox Race (Guild) Amendment Regulations (amended)*.

The opening provisions reflected a welter of suspicion.

Stations (i.e. the assignment of the eastern or western streams as the river divides) shall be the subject of a random draw by the Town Clerk, to be witnessed by the assembled Guild Masters. Stations thus assigned shall be final.

Any new technology must be declared to the Umpire and certified to ensure a level playing field (i.e. river).

The Town Clerk (as Umpire) may not assist, join or otherwise assist the Municipals or any other team in any way whatsoever.

Arguments between Guilds equalled in intensity their internal disputes as to choice of crew, skipper, colours and team song.

Wynter smiled as amendments burgeoned. He could not have chosen a better distraction. Nobody would notice the absence of the Mayor and his select few at the Spring Equinox. He made one amendment himself, postponing the start from dawn to mid-morning: the Grand Finish and his own return should coincide.

'But they'll miss the surge,' Gorhambury pointed out.

'Don't be so sure,' replied Wynter enigmatically.

Aggs fretted for the rest of the working day. She had heard only one word, 'Gabriel', whispered in a corner by Wynter to Sly after the close of the Council Meeting, but it suggested trouble. But would she be starting a wild goose chase?

Espionage is not straightforward, she decided. By ten o'clock, her unease won through and she set off through the murk to share her intelligence with Boris.

4

The Temptation of Prudence

'I'm surprised at you, I really am,' growled Thomes.

'We'll look so aloof – and the Mixers will be there. Suppose they win.'

'Apothecaries don't mix with dross, and – *and* – Apothecaries do not *do* sport.' Thomes' piggy eyes bulged in outrage.

Sister Prudence fought on. 'Some of our younger acolytes would welcome the chance.' *Younger – the few with a flicker of life left*, she felt like saying. 'They have unspent energies.'

'No, no, no.' The Master hammered the table as if closing an auction.

'I hear there's an expedition,' she said with such calmness that Thomes took it as insolence.

'So?'

'Miscegenation – it's a subject I know about. I fought the mantoleon.'

Thomes scowled at an unintended innuendo: *While you were safely tucked up in bed.*

Sister Prudence tried to instil the concern she felt. 'I studied its shell – we're facing the unknown, Master, and who knows what else is out there? Nor do I trust Mr Wynter. Please.'

'You'll stay to mind the ship.'

Sister Prudence accepted the rebuff phlegmatically, only for her next observation to fare no better. 'The carvings from the tower were most peculiar: scenes from the last trump, and I'd swear done by the same hand as those in our own Great Hall.'

Mysteries irritated Thomes. Reason must rule. 'Poppycock. That tower is new-build. We have a copycat on the loose. You're being very difficult today, Sister Prudence. You'd do well to remember your place on the Court is up for review in the summer.'

A lifetime of dutiful service and obedience had left dissent a stranger to Sister Prudence; she had always played the music in front of her. Now, almost unintentionally, she launched a mischievous tune of her own. 'At least *I* don't have unscheduled meetings with a woman who's outside the Guild.'

Thomes' tone turned defensive and Sister Prudence discovered for the first time the virtues of a well-timed counter-attack.

'If you're referring to Miss Brown's sister, I met her to take soundings. As you don't trust Wynter, you should approve.' Thomes patted his goatee, a tic which declared machinations-in-progress or a lie just told, or often both.

'I have your interests at heart, Master,' declared Sister Prudence, as the habit of deference resumed control.

'Then act like it and mind the ship,' repeated Thomes with a nod towards his study door.

Sister Prudence paused in the passage beyond to glance through the window at the Rother. It looked sulky, she felt, its current retarded, the surface without sparkle, still stained ochre from the flood. She wondered how a river god would look – muscles twisted like cord, a rush-green beard and a torso encrusted in shells. In her youth she had tended the Guild's beehives in the narrow strip of land south of the rockface which housed the prison. She had known the river in all her moods. Then, alas, her cleverness and practicality had marked her for higher office and a Hall-bound existence.

But this restlessness was new. Geryon Wynter had brought with him danger, but also opportunity. All around the *status quo* felt precarious. She felt sure the Master had lied to her about his so-called 'soundings' with Persephone Brown, but she had also lied to him.

A crew of young Apothecary volunteers were keen to take on the town and ride the river.

Mind the ship.

Maybe she would do just that.

5

Of Webbed Feet

'Yuk, this one's all bulbous and green. Hey, stalky-eyes, ya looking at me?' Percy Finch dangled the unfortunate spider by its one surviving leg in front of his face before tossing it into the fire.

'One hundred and twenty,' cried Percy's friend, as if calling a darts score.

'Legs or spiders?' crowed Percy.

The crudity of the exchanges between the two boys shocked even Sly. Mrs Finch must have a side he had overlooked. The sooner this grotesque vigil ceased, the better it would be for everyone.

Only the fire and two tall slow candles illuminated the Great Hall. Pools of shadow hid the guards in the gallery and Sly lurking beneath the mysterious high balcony with no access. *She will come that way*, Wynter had said. What other way could there be, with all other doors and windows locked and fastened?

On went the dark charade until—

It happened in moments. A slight hooded figure slipped through the balcony window, scuttled across the wall as if on adhesive feet, dropped to the ground and advanced on the two boys.

'*They kill us for their sport* ...' said the invader, menacing in the very gentleness of her delivery.

They backed away as ordered, and with exquisite timing Sly released the cord by his right hand. The weighted net fell from the ceiling. The guards disentangled her, binding her hands, and Sly rang the servants' bell.

'We got her, we got her,' shouted Percy. 'We are the champions!'

The interior door clicked at the turn of a lock.

'Silence,' bellowed Wynter as he strode in. 'Get those boys out of here.'

Sly tossed each of them a bag of coins.

Percy and his friend gave the intruder a sidelong look as they were led away. Her movement across the wall had been unnatural, yet the face beneath the cowl had a rare beauty.

Wynter walked up close to Morval and handed the box of surviving spiders to a guard. 'Release them,' he said, 'well away from here. You see, dear Morval, I've nothing against your eight-legged friends, so long as they don't interfere with matters their petty brains cannot possibly grasp.'

'*Weaving spiders come not here*,' said Morval.

Only then did it dawn on Wynter that some elusive permanent damage had been done to his chronicler by Slickstone's vengeance, to which he had been a willing party. But what did it matter, so long as she could record his legend with her incomparable brilliance?

'Talk properly,' he snapped. 'You're not a child.'

'*I have drunk and seen the spider*,' chuntered Morval.

Wynter yanked back her cowl, releasing a cascade of golden hair. 'You don't look a day older – but that's not why you're reprieved. You work the paint as ever you did. And I know where your brother is hiding, so you'd best not disappoint.' Wynter motioned to a guard to repack her paints and brushes. 'You have your usual room, the penultimate floor, with a river view. You will join us for dinner, of course.'

Sly recalled his master's confrontation with the wax-faced intruder at the Unrecognisable Party. Now too he sensed the hand of a lost history returning to haunt the present.

'You'll finish off my party piece first. If you need materials, tell Mr Sly – just like Mr Bole in the old days. Now, as then, we'll bequeath *such* sights to posterity, you and I.'

Old History

1624. The Rotherweird Valley.

Hugo Finch is unfashionable: he likes to walk. Men and women of position prefer horse to feet for any journey of distance, to keep their garments clean and to outrun the cutpurses who occasionally filter down from Hoy. Since there is no map and but one road, and that no more than a thread of worn-away grass, he mixes exercise with exploration.

At the outer limits of his journeys he meets a raggedy man with burnished skin and the muscles of a blacksmith, who belies his ignoble appearance by speaking English and Latin with equal fluency. He goes by the lofty name Gregorius. In quick time this chance forges a friendship.

Today high summer bathes the valley in warmth and a breeze so gentle it teases the skin. He finds Gregorius in the shade near the Pool of Mixed Intentions, dangling a fishing line. A pike lies in the grass, long, sleek and armed to the teeth.

'River pirate,' says Gregorius, whose hook attaches to a wooden lure in the shape of a minnow.

'I'd like your advice,' says Finch, 'as an uninvested man. We're laying a new square in town. The Mayor and his friends wish to bury gold coins dead centre as an offering for a prosperous future. They're calling it the heart of the town. The carver has fashioned a wooden plug and built a cavity underground. They have a secure chest.'

'I've known coins to be buried by bridges for good luck. I see no harm in the idea.'

'Nor I, were the coins not so peculiar.' Finch displays the coins furtively, even in this secluded place. There are seven, each numbered, including a man with a distinctive face, a strange tree infected with mistletoe and an even stranger monster. 'I may no longer rule, but coinage remains my province. My agreement is needed, but I'd need a reason to refuse.'

Gregorius does not like what he sees: the face is Geryon Wynter's, a dabbler in the other place; the monster is of the mixing-point, and the tree has been laid low by poison. He senses guile and purpose, a strategy for a distant future.

'They lay a trail of some kind. Why else have numbers? I suggest a precaution: add a last coin of your own design, a coin which speaks of unity.'

Finch has a mind like his father's, rich in good order but short on imagination. 'Give me an image,' he asks.

'In old England they talked of an escharion, a silver instrument with two pipes and one mouthpiece.' Gregorius embellishes a little. 'They blew it to unite competing tribes. I can describe it for you.'

Gregorius does so and Finch is comforted by this symbol of togetherness. He has access to the necessary gold and Rotherweird boasts a fine worker in precious metals. He will bequeath his own little secret to posterity.

'Your line is tugging,' says Finch.

And so it is.

1650. The Chapel of St Jude, near Hoy.

In a small family chapel close to the Rotherweird escarpment, Ambrosia Claud the First kneels alone before the single statue of St Jude, patron saint of lost causes. Dusk has drained the light from the windows. A candle illuminates the saint's long-suffering face.

She accuses rather than prays. 'You have deserted me. Have I not prayed?'

The truth, and she knows it, is the converse: she has never prayed, save for herself, and then only for the right cards or dice or a man of looks or influence to turn his head. London has swallowed her life and fashioned her values. Her beauty has attracted fine baubles and a position at Court, but now, in its slow but perceptible decline, she must pay to stand still while the young saunter ahead, coiling their bodies around the ladder of advancement.

So, here she is, penniless and penitent: a true lost cause. Even her cuffs and ruff wear a jaundiced look these days.

The knocking on the chapel door is odd, two syncopated raps, delicate but insistent. Who visits a remote family chapel on the threshold of night?

A nun is the answer, although she has a secular, business-like air. 'Miss Ambrosia Claud?'

Ambrosia is not in confessional mood. Even in penury, she retains her haughtiness. 'This is a family chapel.'

'I find private places of worship more *piquant* than the grand cathedrals, don't you?'

Ambrosia has studied French; it is a Court card, after all. A *piquant* is a quill, but has a nun ever used the word in this other sense of seductive? 'What do you want?'

'I collect for the Order.' The smile sits in the eyes only. 'Relics.' The nun flicks back her cloak. A velvet pouch hangs heavy at her waist and clinks as she moves. Large coins clink, light coins tinkle. Ambrosia curses her misfortune: this is one trade she cannot do.

'St Jude has travelled all the way from Siena. He is not minded to move on.'

'I'm not here for your saint . . . fine though he is.' The postscript arrives a fraction too late. Nor should a woman of the cloth say *your* saint in such a tone.

But what matter? Ambrosia smells opportunity. She waits.

'I'm after that slither of tree you keep in the transept.'

'We guard it, Sister, under lock and key, because it's malign.'

'You're not fit to guard it for that very reason.'

Ambrosia cannot deny the undeniable. Within a few steps of the gnarl, that being the label supplied by its finder, Ambrose II, its loathing for its captors is palpable.

'Allow me to show you,' continues the nun, and she strides to the transept wall. Ambrosia shuffles close behind. The nun caresses the surface with her fingers and something untoward occurs. The wood's dark presence dissipates.

'This for that,' she adds, spilling gold coins from the pouch into her hand. Ambrosia drinks in the profile of the king's curly-haired head. It exudes power and luxury, the world she is missing.

'To relieve you of your burden,' adds the nun.

Ambrosia unlocks the lever. She cannot turn it fast enough. A trick of the light surely, but, once released, the gnarl reaches for the nun's hand, not *vice versa*.

The nun returns the coins to the pouch which she swings into Ambrosia's waiting palm. 'No need to count,' she says. 'I have a way with numbers.' The nun turns and hurries down the nave with the gnarl, conjoined almost – a transaction pleasing to both sides.

The door clicks shut as Ambrosia recalls an arithmetical truth: two negatives make a positive. Does that mean the false nun shares the gnarl's malign spirit? What has she let loose in the world? *I have a way with numbers*, her visitor had said. For four hundred pieces of gold, read forty pieces of silver? Has Judas supplanted St Jude?

Ambrosia shakes off her scruples like dust. Savour what money can buy. God loves a sinner, doesn't He?

2016. Die Graue Katze.

The alto saxophone rises, shudders in climax and subsides: his riff. Or is it hers? Here gender does not dictate or declare: men and women, many made up, converse and make assignations. Most are neither beautiful nor young, just happy to sever the mossy cords of convention.

Bole alias Benedict Roc watches. In his long experience of decadence, the Stuart Court has come closest to mastery, but the Germans do have a knack.

His new acquaintance returns from the bar with a bottle and two stemmed green-tinged glasses, a rare moment of orthodoxy. '*Trockenbeerenauslese*,' says Herr Doktor Heinrich Flasche, physicist *extraordinaire*, or better still, *Physiker außergewöhnlich*. 'Zey pick ze grapes individually once shrivelled to ze size of ze raisin.'

His accent is stereotypical German English, 'ze' for 'th' and 'v' for 'w', but his vocabulary and syntax are excellent. His unbecoming body is as ideal as his remarkable mind for the game to come.

The wine is sweet, but the balance between fruit, sugar and alcohol cannot be faulted. Bole alias Benedict Roc takes a second sip before speaking.

For his part, Doktor Flasche, aware that his appearance and intellect could be discouraging, is cheered by the attentions of this good-looking and intelligent Englishman.

'So, you're confident that parallel worlds are conceivable,' says Bole.

'More zan conceivable, dear Benedict, zey are likely, if you zubscribe as I do, to ze multiwerse – and more particularly, to membrane theory. Multiple membranes, each a uniwerse in its own right, float in high dimensions. If zey collide, which is very rare, you may get a big bang, or zomething like it.'

Bole has studied the subject long and hard. He worries that Dr Flasche's theoretical brilliance might not match the need for practical application. 'I offer a variation,' he says. 'Two membranes are joined at one tiny point. A cross-dimensional bridge occurs, the effect of a cosmic collision long ago. They share time, but not place.'

'Cosmic collision is a zound explanation for dimensional shifts and gateways. But can ze connections be zevered and with vot consequences? Zat is the burning question. You vould need a shock, you see. Zis is my expertise, you might zay.'

This mild self-compliment signs the physicist's death warrant.

They leave the club and walk the foreshore, hands on shoulders. Doktor Flasche explains that he holidays in Düsseldorf to get away from the university crowd in Cologne. It is a pleasure to meet a kindred spirit. He points at the Rhine. 'In zis town ze great composer Robert Schumann wrote his happiest vork, ze Rhenish Symphony, only to hurl himself into Old Vater Rhein four years later, also in zis town. He vas rescued, but he ended his days in a zanatorium. Such is ze hair's breadth between genius and madness.'

These are his last words.

It is after two in the morning. There are no witnesses. Exit Herr Doktor Heinrich Flasche, German theoretical physicist, and enter Mr Robert Flask, a historian without references and any prospect of employment save in one peculiar provincial town, where there happens to be a vacancy.

OUT OF TOWN

I

Habits Die Hard

Orelia had to break out. She could neither be seen in town nor face another dose of matronly duties in the Witan Hall. Oblong's narrative of his encounter with Ambrose Claud had contained a detail worth following up: the Claud family chapel, assuming Oblong had not been taken for a ride.

The Polk Travel Company's untouched copy of the local *County Guide* contained an inconspicuous Appendix N headed: Sites of No Particular Distinction. After an Ordnance Survey reference, the last entry read:

> Chapel of St Jude. Remote, forgettable, disturbing; a few brasses.
> Near Hoy; usually closed, guardian (rarely available) at Hoy,
> PO Box 71.

The paradoxical conjunction of 'forgettable' and 'disturbing' and the parenthesis suggested a cack-handed attempt to deter interest.

She wrote to the chapel's guardian as instructed and booked herself into *The Blue Lion* in Hoy.

Boris used an afternoon supply run to give her and her bicycle a clandestine lift in the back of the charabanc. Despite driving rain, she insisted on cycling from the embankment rim, reaching the inn just before opening time.

A corpulent landlord opened the door with an agreeable twinkle. He confirmed the booking.

'We're off-season, so there's plenty of room at the inn. You can have Rob Roy, Moby Dick, Long John or The Return of She. Here's the Race Card.'

The twinkle brightened on Orelia's removal of her oilskin and sou'wester.

'I do like high up,' she said.

'Well, you would, Sister,' he replied, trying not to look or sound surprised. 'Tell you what, you can have The Return of She at the price of Moby Dick.'

'Amen to that,' she replied, before reminding herself not to push her luck. She had taken care with the deception: a rosary hung from her waist, a wimple contained her gypsy hair and she wore the severe black lace-up shoes acquired for her aunt's funeral. She must hold repartee in check.

The attic room had charm. Impressionist prints and competent watercolours of Hoy's more picturesque landmarks adorned the walls and a bright kilim the floor.

After the usual unnecessary introductions – kettle, coffee, tea and milk, shower mechanics – the landlord turned remorseful. 'Oh dear,' he said. 'No Bible.'

'A change is as good as a rest,' she replied, 'and in any case I know by heart what matters. But thank you. She will Return.'

The landlord followed a golden rule: *Never ask guests where they're from or why they're here, unless they open that door themselves.* That did not prevent him speculating. *A nun on the run,* he decided from first impressions.

As at the Unrecognisable Party, her habit deterred unwanted company and attracted a display of good manners from even the more loutish regulars. The secular-minded called her Miss.

The landlord served her personally and continued to twinkle. 'Holy orders are on the house,' he said. 'Liquids only.'

'Frackle's cider,' she said. 'I like the colour and I don't like those mean-looking glasses. So, call it a pint, but if I order another, say no – and the fish pie without the chips, please.' She stacked the coins for the pie on the bar like a croupier.

Nun on the run, definitely.

She ate and drank delicately, while she watched and listened. Hoy's popular discourse lacked Rotherweird's scientific edge, but the camaraderie was still restorative. She could not reconcile this random sample of humanity with those who laid low forests, poisoned rivers and massacred their own kind in God's name. Somewhere between the individual and communal government, mankind had lost its moorings.

In the best English tradition, the weather, having frowned most of the night, was smiling by morning. A nameless narrow lane with a dead-end sign at the north of town looped west to the escarpment, where it ended in the yard of a ruined cottage with a collapsed roof. Beside it was a dilapidated car. She secured her bicycle to a tree trunk and followed an iron sign whose corroded letters read *Chapel of St Jude, 2 miles*. The grass betrayed no sign of wear; the *County Guide* entry had achieved its objective. The sun broke through, making the night's rain glisten. Early lambs tottered among ewes too pregnant or exhausted to take much notice.

The chapel had a low-slung look, with a squat tower and shallow pitched roof, although closer up, the dimensions proved to be more generous; the foreshortening had been caused by a fold in the land. The dismissive criteria in Appendix N fitted the exterior: no stained glass, no visible churchyard, no gravestones, no enclosing wall, no lych-gate, no porch and no exterior ornament of note. The single oak door had a circular black iron latch, but was locked. In her letter to the guardian, she had mentioned Oblong's name, expressed an interest in the brasses and given a time.

She was debating whether to leave when a bellow from over the hill scattered the sheep. In the far corner of the meadow stood a sturdy pole and a cross-post. The latter held a heavy ball on a chain at one end and a shield at the other. A figure in full samurai armour was jousting with the device, hacking at the shield before ducking as the ball swung round.

The warrior removed his helmet to reveal a fresh-faced young man with white hair.

'You cycle at quite a lick for a nun,' he said with a grin.

'You duck better than you strike,' she responded.

He had a schoolboy voice to match his complexion, but the sword was no toy. 'The armour is on the tight side – they were smaller then. I need to make adjustments,' he said, adding a wink to the grin as he tapped the weave of steel and bamboo strips encasing his legs and torso. 'I like the weapons of legend. What better way to keep in trim?'

'How did you get this job?' asked Orelia.

'Mine, mine, it's all mine,' he replied, gesturing at the meadow, the chapel and the sheep. 'It's true, but not much of a job. As we're not in Rotherweird Valley, we can appear on a map, but we don't in fact want visitors. Ambrose Claud the Thirteenth, at your service.'

It must have been Oblong's name that prompted this unexpected candour. Encumbered by his armour, Claud waddled rather than walked to the chapel door, which yielded to an iron key hanging round his neck.

She followed him in. The chapel had no pews or chairs, although a camp bed suggested that Ambrose the Thirteenth occasionally spent the night here. A marble altar had neither tabernacle nor candles, but the austerity was not universal. The rood screen drew the eye by its colour, subject matter and quality. Orelia shuddered. Why must doom paintings display the torments of the damned with such relish? Men, women and children tumbled into jagged rents in the earth's fiery surface. The *Schadenfreude* extended to man's inventions: water wheels, buildings, boats and primitive flying machines accompanied the human dross in their headlong fall.

'In many ways the blessed are more interesting,' commented Claud telepathically.

Indeed, they were. In the Judgement Seat sat an overweight man, a most atypical portrayal of God the Father, with books in both hands. On either side small figures, instruments in hand, measured and recorded. Orelia felt an uncomfortable tension between the doomed inventions and these apparently satisfactory faces of science. The screen had an oddly secular air.

She turned to the only other visible source of colour, a strikingly beautiful Renaissance statue in painted wood standing on a plinth near the altar.

'St Jude, patron saint of lost causes,' explained Claud. The bearded saint looked world-weary, but a slight uplift in the corners of his mouth offered the hint of hope for which he was renowned. 'The chapel is dedicated to him – not him.' Claud pointed at the statue and then at the Judge on the rood screen. The remark should have sounded sacrilegious, but it did not; this was no ordinary chapel. 'St Jude has but one rule: you have to work for his help. Put another way: if you don't play the tables, you don't give Lady Luck a chance.'

To Orelia's surprise, he handed over the door key. 'I'll be back on the eve of the Equinox at sunset. Be sure to be here.'

'You trust me?' asked Orelia. 'St Jude must be worth a pretty packet.'

'You've been to the other place, as has your friend Oblong, whom I like. And I've Gabriel's word too.' He looked into her face. 'He said hazel, and he was right.'

Orelia felt both pleased and irritated. She might have described Gabriel by his beard, but eyes were intimate territory. He had taken a liberty. Yet the pleasure of the compliment prevailed. The chapel's eight supporting pillars were each carved with an upright angel, save one whose angel was inverted.

'Do I really need three days?'

'Hardly enough time, believe me. This place is rich in history and it doesn't duck the darker side of human nature. I'd start with the brasses, as that's what you came for. They're all Clauds, Ambrose or Ambrosia – the good, the bad and the indifferent. They read like a family tree. The earliest is by the door, the most recent by the altar, as if we're creeping our way to the Promised Land. By the way, you can sing or swear as much as you like. We've just been deconsecrated.'

Ferensen knows Gabriel who knows Claud. Orelia took Ambrose the Thirteenth at his word and accepted the key.

'Keep the outside door locked and don't let anyone else in. I'll knock seven times, once for each good angel. Feel free to use the taper and light as many candles as you like.'

He walked back to the pole and removed the shield and the ball before departing with a cheery wave, leaving Orelia to disentangle his ancestors and their contributions to this peculiar place.

She established a ritual and set herself rules: she must resist distraction and complete the brasses first. Hoy provided the wherewithal in the form of twelve sheets of pastel paper, silver and bronze crayons, scissors, masking tape to prevent slippage, and a duster to buff the end product.

On leaving the chapel at dusk, a familiar shape lolloped towards her from the edge of the meadow. The Mance nuzzled her leg by way of reintroduction before bounding off into the dark. She smiled. She had a guardian.

She completed Ambrose I to Ambrose V on the first day, assembling the rubbings in order on the floor and bed of her lodgings. Each figure had for company their dates of birth and death, and a single Latin verb. Most she interpreted without difficulty. Ambrose II, who had completed the chapel, had the accolade *Aedificavi*: I have built. Ambrosia I, who died in 1661, had the less flattering tribute *Peccavi*: I have sinned. Her left hand gestured to the side, while her head twisted in the opposite direction as if too ashamed to look. Ambrose I, who had commenced the works, had the more puzzling *Occului*: I have concealed, with its unsettling similarity to the word *occult*.

She finished the rubbings, including Ambrose VII, who from the dates had to be the Vagrant Vicar, late on the second day. His legend appropriately read *Commemoravi*: I have recalled. His successor, Ambrosia II, had the only negative verb: *Non cantavi*, which Orelia first took to mean I have not sung, only to remember the mysterious instrument which the present Ambrose had given to Oblong. Maybe she had discovered it and resisted the temptation to play?

On the last morning, the eve of the Spring Equinox, she paid her bill and thanked the landlord.

'You're welcome back any time, Sister. There's not been a rough word at the bar all week, which is a record.' He presented her with a bottle of Frackle's by way of thanks.

As on the previous morning, the Mance assumed his post as she arrived. Was he guarding her, or was there some undisclosed enterprise she was expected to undertake? She turned her attention to the remainder of the chapel.

A pair of circular recesses had been set into the altar. Each held a cup fashioned from a hard material, unfamiliar, but not unlike horn. One was blue, the other ember-red – for water and wine, perhaps? The altar turned out to be old polished wood with stipples of paint to imitate marble. Halfway across, the colours changed from red to blue in inverse order to the cups. The cups had wooden handles concealed in their base which opened out. Unconsecrated ground this might be, but it was still holy. She left the cups in place. They had a sacramental feel.

On the back wall of the north transept were two stone fists about five feet apart holding iron rings in their grasp like shackles. Each had tightening cogs, but only one had a lever to work them. Whatever object they had held had vanished, while leaving behind the unpleasant aura of a haunted room. On the floor, Ambrosia I's brass hand was pointing in this very direction. *Peccavi.*

The pillars had the archangels' names inscribed on their base.

The eighth, the inverted angel, aptly declared himself as Lucifer, surely a unique presence for any chapel. The screen, this pillar and the stone fists prompted the thought that Ambrose I had devised a chapel to house the holy *and* the unholy.

Ambrose the Thirteenth kept his promise: a sanguine sunset stained the plain glass of the west window as he entered. In the doorway he dropped a backpack on the floor. 'Any questions?'

'What did Ambrosia I get rid of?'

'The Tree of Knowledge had angel wood and witch wood entwined, hence Good and Evil, or so the legend goes. Ambrose III found a staff of the latter stuff in the other place.'

'Or so the legend goes.'

'He secured it here, only for Ambrosia to sell it. She lived the high life. We don't know who bought it.'

'And the coloured cups?'

'Equally no idea. They're another contribution from Ambrose III. Maybe they mirror the rood screen – blue for the cloudless sky of Paradise and red for the fire of hell.' Ambrose sounded serious, as if the answer might matter in the here and now. 'St Jude rewards those who strive to find a way. That's likely to be true tonight of all nights.' He did not elaborate but walked back to the doorway. 'Find a way, Miss Roc, for all our sakes.'

With that request, Ambrose left the chapel and locked the door behind him.

Orelia stood stock-still in disbelief. Friend and foe seemed bent on immuring her in sealed chambers. Here at least she had the statue to inspire.

And perhaps the bag? She unpacked it methodically. He had provided generously in terms of food and water. Side pockets held a slow candle with a protective glass and a strange key with spikes at all angles.

'All right, good St Jude, I'm trying. Now you help me. *Please.*'

'*The meadow turned red-orange . . .*'

2

Pre-emptive Bids

Dead of night, three days before the Vernal Equinox. Gabriel sat by the peat stove, the carving across his knees: an apple with its leaves. It was not quite perfect; the lighter grain on the cheek needed more work to convey the blush of ripeness.

Panjan did not flutter at the window, his habitual way of knocking for admission, but burst in through the chimney and flapped against the outer door: Panjan-speak for *Get out NOW!*

Apple in hand, Gabriel rushed outside, not pausing for coat or boots. High in the night sky, bearing down from the north and closing fast, danced tongues of flame like Pentecostal fire.

Gabriel cursed. The enemy must have a craft to rival the Hoverfly – and well protected too, or the fearless Panjan would have attacked. Seconds played like minutes; minutes like an hour. Should he risk himself to save his work, or run? His wooden roof-tiles would ignite like pitch. Once landed, they could easily chase him down.

Panjan skimmed towards the alders along the river, his flight path deciding the issue: *Live to fight another day, play the longer game.*

Gabriel followed, sprinting between the tree trunks and turning only when the first volley struck the building and the meadow turned red-orange. His home and workshop blazed. Funnelled globe-lights crisscrossed the meadow.

Panjan had rescued him, but his tools and belongings, and worse, the fruits of centuries of creativity, his own and his ancestors', were being fast reduced to ash.

He could see no alternative but to await events in the other place. Panjan appeared to agree, for he had risen and was soaring towards the white tile.

In the dead of night, two days before the Vernal Equinox, dancer's feet once again descended the main stairs of the Manor, guided by childhood memory.

Nona found the gnarl with equal ease, propped in a corner of the Great Hall.

She stroked the shaft, teasing the wood into growth, and snapped off the single shoot. It was no larger than a small twig, but enough. She bent the ends together. They entwined of their own accord, contracting tighter and tighter into a ball no bigger than a generous pebble.

She left for Rotherweird Westwood in mid-afternoon and waited for dusk. In the distance the charred shell of Gabriel's home and workshop was still puffing like a pipe. Above her, men were patrolling the gateway to the Witan Hall. She smiled. They would soon be otherwise engaged.

She pulled a catapult from one pocket, lodged the ball of wood in the leather pouch and fired it over the sentries' heads into the outer gate. It made no sound, nor did it ricochet, but clung there, filaments spreading from the small dark heart across the oak like tiny cracks in a golden glaze. By the time the sentries noticed the discolouration, the doorjamb was already sealed. Frantic action with billhooks and knives only stimulated further growth, veins branching out and engulfing the door like a rampant leafless ivy.

Nona smiled. She had secured the countrysiders' children for later use and immobilised Ferensen; all in all, a successful day's work. *Time to go home.*

To those inside the Witan Hall, the assault by the gnarl's shoot brought the yawing groan of a boat in distress. They were trapped.

'So it has begun,' said Ferensen to Megan Ferdy.

3

The Reluctant Skipper

'I don't understand, Jones.' Rhombus Smith, the long-suffering Headmaster of Rotherweird School, sounded both hurt and surprised. 'You're the mainstay of the School's athletic endeavours – you're our star and chosen skipper.'

'But I've never actually finished, sir.'

'That, as we all know, is down to your highly tuned sense of Old-World courtesy,' replied the Headmaster. 'Such self-sacrifice is – alas – unsuited to this new team game. Any stricken damsel will have her own to rescue her.'

Jones had not considered this, although it still sounded ungallant. But in any case ... 'I have an ancient debt to pay, Mr Smith. I am mighty sorry. I recommend Mr Fanguin in my place.'

Rhombus Smith spluttered, 'Fanguin?'

'He's getting on,' Jones conceded, 'but he's a master strategist. He skippered last year's joint-winning coracle – and he's back in political favour. I've checked the new Rules: "staff" includes *former* staff.'

Rhombus Smith blinked. Jones had never shown interest in small print before. He conceded gracefully. 'Fanguin it is, then.'

'Thank you, Headmaster, jolly good of you to understand.'

For once, the *bonhomie* rang false. Rhombus Smith sensed change, as if his protégé had suddenly taken the weight of the world on his broad shoulders. He drew no comfort from Jones' closing words.

'Up the School! I'll be with you in spirit – and I'll say farewell before I go.'

Au revoir or *adieu*? the Headmaster wondered. It felt uncomfortably like the latter.

'I say,' said Fanguin, 'this is a turn-up.'

'You're the biologist. What goes around comes around.'

'Or joins the dodo.'

They stood in the Headmaster's study. Swabs of green and fresh silver flecked the roses and lavender: a new beginning. The invitation to lead the school crews, though welcome, had presented Fanguin with an acute dilemma. Records seen by Orelia in Bolitho's observatory and reported to Fanguin by Oblong suggested a final crisis in Lost Acre at the Spring Equinox. Accompanying Wynter might also allow him to study the fauna of this parallel universe – but Fanguin the Contrarian liked to do the unexpected, even to the point of flouting his own objectives. Other factors weighed too: Rhombus Smith had been a staunch supporter in the dark days following his dismissal by Snorkel and was owed a favour. Nor would his good friend Gregorius Jones go absent without a pressing need. Aggs the expert eavesdropper had confirmed that several important players would be remaining in town, including Persephone Brown, Fennel Finch and Sister Prudence. It threatened to be a fight on two fronts.

He clicked his heels, the gesture designed to indicate both acceptance and a need for military precision. 'You will recall the Fanguin rotator technique?' he asked, adding in response to Smith's blank look, 'based on the movement of the Bolivian water beetle: the most revolutionary development in coracle propulsion in centuries. But it requires balance, stamina and practise. I will need time with the crew.'

'All evening classes have been suspended. I'm told the Guilds are closing early too.'

'Have all hopefuls report to me at five in the gym.'

The Headmaster had one further piece of bad news. 'You won't have your friend Oblong either, I'm afraid. He too has another engagement.'

Boris addressed the Fireworkers, packed into their Hall, coffee mugs in hand, in a different vein. 'We exist to entertain, not to win. I want a firework finalé.'

'Even a firework commentary?' suggested Boris' head boffin, predictably known as Sparks.

'We're working on word rockets.'

A question came from the floor. 'How do we keep them hidden and dry?'

'False bottom for the coracles,' replied Boris, 'and waterproof casings for the fireworks.'

'Working on it,' said Sparks, scribbling notes on his cuff.

A contrary philosophy prevailed in the Tanners' Hall.

'We're in this to win,' the Master announced, 'as well as to advertise our hides and impress our new Mayor.' He introduced a frogman in watery camouflage, brandishing a trident. 'Our friend from the North Tower will explain.'

The late not-so-lamented Strimmer's weaselly colleague did so, explaining his curious attire at the same time. 'I'm wearing our "Poseidon" suit: the eye-pieces filter out bubbles and mud. The breathing tube is disguised as a piece of driftwood. The trident is extendable and will puncture all known hides.'

'Including our own?' queried a crewman nervously.

'Our coracles will have a luminous cow's head painted on the underside.'

'And if he's caught?'

'He'll say he's working for the Bakers,' said the Master, rubbing his hands.

The frogman turned to reveal a bagel emblazoned on his back.

Elsewhere, plans of varying eccentricity and moral colour were debated with like vigour; some sank and some floated. Only in the Town Hall, headquarters of the Municipals, did stasis prevail.

Jeavons, whose stock had risen since taking custody of the prophecy coins, chaired the first meeting. His body, no friend to exercise, housed not a single sporting bone. Banging a gavel to call the meeting to order, he announced, 'I propose we number each seat so everyone knows where they sit. That should confer an immediate advantage in what, judging by past form, will indubitably be chaos.'

'How do we order the numbering?' asked an Assistant Clerk.

'By seniority, obviously,' replied Jeavons.

'Am I senior to a Committee Secretary?' asked the Assistant Clerk.

'No,' said a Committee Secretary, 'we're both Grade 2B.'

'But I'm paid more.'

'And I get a better pension.'

'Really? How disgraceful.'

'Let Gorhambury decide,' suggested another Committee Secretary, but the Head Stationer shook his head.

'He's the Umpire, he's conflicted.'

The meeting adjourned seat numbering for other problematic details.

'I propose a standard pole-length,' suggested a statistician, 'based on the average height of the crew for ease of recovery in the event of collision.'

An avalanche of contentious alternatives followed – should it be an average height for men and another for women? Or the average height of past winners? Or should there be a separate average height for each coracle? – and so on, and so on, *ad nauseam*.

As the day approached, a disturbing new rumour filtered through the town. *Apothecaries* had been seen mapping the Rother's pools and shallows.

Surely not . . .

4

Last Things

On the eve of the Spring Equinox, Geryon Wynter entertained Fennel, Persephone, Sly, Master Thomes and Sister Prudence to dinner in the Great Hall, in part repayment for the feast the Apothecaries had provided on the night of his *surfacing*, as he now liked to call the day of his return to town. Slickstone's best had been set out on Flemish lace-edged linen: ormolu cande-labra, Meissen plates, ivory salt and pepper pots, Bohemian cut glass and gilded crystal decanters and goblets. In the centre of the long table, in pride of place, rested the escharion on a red velvet cushion.

Port and brandy dispensed, Wynter tapped his glass with a spoon.

'Out there,' he said with a flamboyant sweep of the arm, 'they have lost respect for the air they breathe, the water they fish and the land they till and build on. I shall cast them into darkness. We shall start again. I offer a new covenant.'

'New legends too,' added Persephone.

Thomes smelled more than a whiff of madness. He was glad he had made contingency plans with the fetching Persephone, who was clearly humouring the Mayor. 'By "they", I take it you mean the countrysiders?' he asked.

'Oh no, countrysiders are of the valley; they'll be brought to heel and made use of. I refer to the rest of the world.'

Listen, you fools, he means *it*, Persephone thought, but did not say.

'So where are we bound tomorrow?' asked Thomes.

'We're bound for the other place. You've never been there, but it's home to the monsters who have plagued us.'

'Won't the countrysiders interfere with whatever it is we're going to do?'

'They're skittled already. I lent Persephone a weapon.'

Persephone liked the *lent*. If only he knew. She supported him quietly. 'They're walled up in their fastness. The more they try to escape, the tighter the lock becomes.'

'My Guild has invested a lot of time and effort in this project, Mr Wynter, and we have had very little detail in return. I shall not take failure kindly.'

Persephone caught Thomes' eye and made a slight grimace. *Don't overplay it.*

'Best not to question Mr Wynter's judgement. What he predicts happens.' Fennel Finch had acquired a new manner of speaking, laconic and quiet, but also ferocious. 'I for one will be here to welcome him back to our brave new world.'

'Perhaps this is your weapon?' said Thomes, less abrasive now, caressing the escharion's silver skin with his forefinger.

'We will see what we will see,' replied Wynter.

The silent make the best observers. Sister Prudence instantly concluded that neither Wynter nor his henchwomen knew what the instrument did – nobody at that table knew.

'It's the last prophecy coin,' mused Thomes mischievously.

'But what can a fancy pipe do?' asked Sly.

The thought came to Sister Prudence so suddenly that she could not resist voicing it. Her theory fitted Wynter's talk of damnation and renewal.

'Gabriel's horn,' she said. 'He blows it at the last trump to signal the death of the damned and the resurrection of the blessed.' She mouthed a few words from *Paradise Lost* by way of corroboration, *'Perhaps once more to sound at general doom.'*

A surge of excitement seized Wynter. The escharion *did* fit his vision and destiny. They – indeed, *he* – had truly been prophesied.

Persephone pursed her lips. She disliked the idea of a player unknown even to her.

Wynter raised his glass. 'You are our Sybil, Sister Prudence. You interpret and prophesy.'

Sister Prudence did not respond. She sensed the devil abroad.

Thomes, glowering at the compliment to a lesser functionary, reasserted his authority. 'All is ready, Mayor. When should we expect you?'

'By nine o'clock the riverbank will be awash with people. We shall give them a brief but stunning display, then head for the other place. Expect me for breakfast at eight. Mr Sly will accompany me while Persephone and Fennel hold the fort here.'

Wynter relaxed. Persephone had taken her absence without complaint. Since Scry's unexpected death, he had regarded her with a degree of suspicion. Bole, once her friend, had never mentioned her in his nocturnal messages, but he remained unsure as to whether to treat that omission as reassuring or disturbing.

5

The Double Address

'It's no single feature, it's the general cragginess. There's so much to work with.' Ember Vine tipped Finch's chin slightly to the left. 'Shadow *and* light.'

Finch lay swathed in blankets on a sofa in Vine's front room. He ignored the remark not out of rudeness but inexperience. He had not received a physical compliment in years. 'Miss Vine . . .'

'Ember, please – the name fits me these days. I used to have fire like my daughter; now it's just afterglow.'

'I have to get back to Escutcheon Place.'

'You're not going anywhere, at least not unaccompanied.'

The antivenom had checked the poison just in time, but the wound, still septic, inhibited Finch's mobility. His skin had the pallor of parchment.

'You're not allowed in Escutcheon Place,' he responded.

'The words *not allowed*, Mr Finch, are a red rag to a Vine. Anyway, you're not allowed in either: there are guards front and back.'

Finch reflected on his dilemma. In his present condition he could barely lift the vast volumes he needed to consult, let alone dispose of a guard – and yet the law was the law. Unless . . . Hadn't Gorhambury said something about exceptions *in extremis*? 'I'll need light in the dark,' he said, 'and a diverting diversion.'

Finch's mannered speech had to be a form of defensiveness, Ember decided, part of the shell of a lonely man: another wound for her to mend, but deeper, in its way.

'Ah, so we're to enter the tunnels! Excellent. Now how are we going to get you on the move?' Ember's eyes lit up, a mix of amusement and satisfaction. 'I have it! You're going to master Amber's scooter, Mr Finch.'

The guard at the basement steps was youthful, male and pleasant-looking; characteristics which inspired a *bravura* performance from Amber Vine. At the mouth of the adjoining lane, she yelped and fell forward, spilling assorted vegetables across the cobbles.

'Heels and cobbles don't go together,' she squeaked, waving the fractured shoe.

Examine the heel. Sigh. Pick up the vegetables slowly, examine for damage. Encourage small talk. Clamber to your feet – mixing evident discomfort with grace. Feign a twisted ankle.

Vine and Finch on his scooter had ample time to reach the steps and descend. A hacksaw quickly disposed of the padlock. They slipped into the former site of *The Journeyman's Gist Underground*.

'If you could get me a bandage, I'd be *so* grateful,' Amber cooed. 'I'll guard your door for you.'

As the chivalrous guard scuttled off to the nearest chemist on Aether's Way, Amber replaced the broken padlock with her own.

Mission accomplished.

'So, this is where Wynter lived,' said Ember as Finch led the way in the gloom, the scooter now replaced by a stick.

'Poppycock and boloney! Only I ever came here – which is how I know the route like a bee to his cell.'

That explains a lot, thought Ember.

When they entered the *archivoire* together, Finch did not dwell on the enormity of the moment – a *non*-Herald in the inner sanctum breached Rotherweird's most fundamental laws. *In extremis*, needs must. He lit the slow candle.

Ember could only admire. Little else in town, save perhaps the interior of the Apothecaries' Hall, could match the quality and ambition of the carving. As for the books, she dared not imagine what forbidden history lay behind those ancient spines. She suspected a resemblance to Finch's mind, even his character: banks of arcane and unused knowledge accessible only to him; affections channelled to care of his books; a lack of warmth, company and sunlight.

'That shelf,' he said, pointing. He had visited this bay before to identify the properties acquired by Bole in his various guises over the centuries, but this time he had a different quarry.

Finch commanded, delved and examined while Ember retrieved. She said nothing beyond the occasional whispered request for clarification; to her, it felt like being in a church.

As details cohered, Finch interspersed his requests with a running commentary on progress to date. 'Ah yes, Madge Brown is indeed the key ... she buys Myrmidon Coil twelve years ago, when she arrives in Rotherweird ... she buys it fully furnished ... she takes it over from someone called Nona. She ...'

After working through a second pile of books, he paused. 'This is really odd. We must go back to the beginning.' He gestured at a low shelf. Without complaint Ember carried more tomes to Finch's desk.

'Hm ... yes. I see: Nona then, Nona now. No new owner has been registered since the building's erection in 1693. How rum is that?'

Ember rested her arm on his shoulder. 'How is the wound?'

'It liked the scooter better.'

Ember translated: *Bloody agony after the long and twisting walk.*

'I need to think. Just give me five minutes. Why not have a wander? A *quiet* wander.'

Finch was caught up in his documents: the claws of duty and bureaucratic toil. On a table in the bay near the *archivoire*'s only visible exit lay a messy pile of post. Instinctively, she leafed through, until one letter caught her eye, as much for its elaborate script as the tell-tale red skull stamp declaring a particular feature of the Delayed Action Service: *To be delivered on the sender's death.*

'This is not the handwriting they teach nowadays,' commented Finch before reading the letter aloud.

Dear Mr Finch,

I choose you as a man who may understand the joins between old and new. Know that I loved Mr Wynter. He showed us untold mysteries; he kept us exceptional; he defied convention and aimed for the stars.

But know too that we Eleusians are not all we appear to be. In the new Mr Wynter lurks another who would destroy you all. Beware Calx Bole; beware Nona; beware the hedge-priest. Nona will have everything to herself.

I fear for my safety, and the town's. There is talk of the Spring Equinox.

Should you receive this letter, light a candle for my tormented soul.

Yours in Rotherweird,

Estella Scry

He reread the letter to himself, not without sympathy for Scry. Wynter had polluted her being and had kept her alive for centuries, only to treat her – and her devotion – as disposable.

He focused on certain words: *loved* (not *love*), the *new* Wynter, the *lurking* character within: layers on layers.

'Who are these people?' asked Ember, who only had her conversation with Oblong in *The Journeyman's Gist* to work with.

Finch gave a potted summary, culminating in Orelia's account of Wynter's resurrection in the presence of Madge Brown as relayed to him by Oblong. He ran a finger over Scry's warning about a hedge-priest. 'The tunnels and waypoints were here long before Wynter and Bole,' he said. 'If there's a survivor from way back then, God knows what his agenda might be, or what he might do with the mixing-point. At least with this Nona we know we're on the right track: she's one of Wynter's Eleusians and she must be in the here and now to threaten Scry . . .'

'Nona and Madge Brown are the same person, surely?' prompted Ember.

Finch rapped the table with his fist. 'And Persephone Brown too! Why else would Madge Brown leave now if she's who we think she is?' Finch rubbed his forehead. '*They talk of the Spring Equinox* – that's March 20 – and in the myth, that's when Persephone begins her rule.'

'And it's also the day after tomorrow, the day of the Great Equinox Race,' added Ember.

Finch returned to the older volume. 'Listen to this: "Today there was a naming of streets." And they list who chose which name. Benedict Roc, the Master Carver, chose Myrmidon Coil.'

Ember had been paying attention. 'Didn't you say he was Bole?'

'He was himself when he carved this room, but he was Bole when he carved the Apothecaries' Hall. That means he was Bole when he named the street, and also Bole when Nona chose to live there.'

Ember looked puzzled. 'I have to ask: who – or what – is a myrmidon?'

'A warrior who does whatever he's asked, or at least that's the modern meaning.' Finch grimaced; the myth troubled him more. 'Zeus fashioned the Myrmidons from a colony of ants – hence their blind obedience to a cause. They fought for Achilles in the siege of Troy.' He drummed the table. 'The Eleusians rework legends for their own purposes: that's how they see the world. I really don't like this. Persephone returned from the Underworld to rule on the first day of Spring. The Myrmidons helped capture Troy. What the hell's going on?'

'An endgame,' Ember replied as the shadows lengthened.

'Pawns against a Queen,' muttered Finch to himself.

'And what of the King?' added Ember.

Down into the Dark

Orelia reconsidered the backpack. The straps had been set for her. The supplies would provide at least two meals. A sleeping bag had been included and a light, despite the plethora of candles in the chapel. *Find a way*, Ambrose had said. Find a way *out*, he must have meant, *and then travel*. A second circuit of the chapel revealed none of the hackneyed triggers for secret doors, no moving sconces or stones.

The problem drove her back to more basic questions: why build a chapel *here*? It could hardly be more remote. A concealed exit suggested some thing or some place to which access should be confined to a select few. She opened the bottle of Frackle's cider and consumed half the sandwiches. *Deconsecrated recently*, Ambrose had said – but why? Lack of a priest to serve? Or . . . *You can dance*, he had also said. So she did what nobody would do in a conse-crated church: she slipped off her boots and danced barefoot on the altar. The soles of her feet prickled, as Valourhand's had done on the floor of Rotherweird Library – and now she understood: a tile lurked somewhere beneath the chapel.

She lay on the stone floor like an effigy and dozed. A shadow-play flickered in her head: Ambrosia the First negotiating her price and loosening the shackle in the stone fist. She woke with a start. Only one fist had a lever, but *both* had cogs. She went to the leverless fist: the spiked key fitted perfectly. She turned, and turned, and slowly the altar's contrasting sides, the red and the blue, parted in the middle to reveal steep steps leading down into the dark.

She started to rush down, only to stop and rebuke herself for being so impulsive. She returned to the chapel, repacked the backpack, adding the red and blue cups from the altar, wound the isolarion round her neck and lit Ambrose's travelling candle.

The narrow tunnel accommodated her easily enough at a slight stoop. She walked for more than an hour before reaching a vaulted chamber, where the tile, in colour a mix of blue and red, had been embedded in the centre of the floor. Set around it, a mosaic of black chips read: *Awake, arise or be for ever fallen.*

She decided against entering Lost Acre at night on the grounds of self-preservation. She laid out the sleeping bag and, not without hesitation, extinguished her light.

Orelia slept fitfully. Ghosts and their captive moments laced her dreams: Hayman Salt selling the stones to her aunt, Mrs Banter's charred body in Grove Gardens, Everthorne's skates carving ice patterns in the frozen Rother. Imagined reconstructions came too: Elizabethan children peering through a primitive telescope in the observatory above Strimmer's study; the same pupils, now young men and women, around the Manor's dining table, in thrall to Wynter's candlelit El Greco face.

She awoke soon after dawn with a renewed sense of mission: *Awake, arise or be for ever fallen!* She resolved to pursue neither justice nor vengeance, for both looked backwards. She wanted only renewal, for herself and Rotherweird: a future worth living.

She finished the food and water and left the sleeping bag rolled up against the wall with the backpack. She would face the enemy in style, not like a hitchhiker.

With a cup in each hand, she stepped onto the tile.

7

A Loss Found

Self-cast as a lone wolf, Valourhand still found ignorance of others' plans deeply frustrating. Jones would not explain his absence from the school crews, Orelia had left on an undisclosed mission and Boris would not divulge the location of his flying machine.

'You'd nick it in minutes,' he had said.

Worst of all, by absenting herself from the Unrecognisable Party, she had missed Tyke, the Mance and Finch, all of whom had since vanished. Only a chastened Fanguin had provided useful intelligence: Wynter was leading an expedition to Westwood on the day of the Vernal Equinox.

That left her one port of call. She arrived just before eight.

When Oblong answered the door, hair still wet, a single epithet described his visitor's demeanour: *bristling*.

'Sorry,' he said cheerily, 'just out of the bath.'

'Why apologise for having a bath?'

'I'm not.'

'You just did. Any info, like where on earth is Orelia?'

'No idea.'

'Finch?'

'Not a clue.'

'Who is Boris' chosen pilot?'

Oblong swayed, an admission by gesture, and Valourhand ground her teeth.

'Have a drink. I'm going to change.'

'Good idea,' she said, and meant it. The dressing gown hovered just above Oblong's knees, an unflattering height for a man of his build.

Fuming at Boris' selection of Oblong for a role requiring derring-do, coordination and a head for heights, she drowned her irritation in a glass of Aggs' *Ginger Grenade*. Her wits sharpened. The last prophecy coin, the escharion, had to be the ace in the pack, and it must be hers to play.

Oblong emerged from his bedroom, mercifully fully dressed.

'I think we should re-examine the escharion. Just a look – physicist's honour.' She awarded Oblong her best Cecily Sheridan smile; it had worked before – and it worked now.

'Face the wall then. The fewer who know, the more secure it is.'

'Prat,' she mumbled, but obeyed. *Reel him in slowly.*

She heard a sound of wood on wood, a gasp, an expletive.

Valourhand turned around.

'This can't be! It really can't—' he spluttered.

The rug had been half rolled up and a floorboard lifted. Oblong was on his knees fumbling vainly in the empty cavity below.

Valourhand, primed for rage, slipped into uncontrollable mirth. Hands on knees she convulsed with laughter. 'The old loose floor-board under the rug trick? Brilliant, quite brilliant! It's like playing sardines and hiding in the nearest cupboard – who would *ever* have thought? You're a phenomenon, Oblong, bloody unique. You're floored by snowballs; your drinks get spiked; you fall off steeples; you ignite gas; you dance in armour! What's next on the menu? An aerial prang?'

'But ... but ... nobody *ever* comes here.' Misery seized him as Valourhand dried her eyes. 'It's a family heirloom – it's a priceless object.' Oblong paused. 'It's not insured.'

Valourhand suppressed a second bout of mirth and poured Oblong a drink. 'Fuck the insurance. It's for the best.'

'Sorry?'

'You'd drop it or leave it on a tree stump or run it over. This way it'll get there when it matters.'

'But Ambrose gave it to *me* to look after—'

'I wonder why?'

'You don't seriously think that – do you?'

Valourhand put her hands on her hips and said nothing. She returned to the kitchen and poured him another drink and mustered a smidgen of kindness. 'I've made a discovery. The useless *can* be useful. *You* found the escharion. *You* discovered the murals in the church tower. *You* . . .' She had run out of positives.

'What will you do now?' asked a muted Oblong.

'Charge the lion's den, of course.'

'The white tile will be guarded.'

'It will. But I do like a gamble.'

8

A Gathering of Forces

Once in Lost Acre, Gabriel ran straight to the great tree by the mixing-point. When inspecting it with Oblong a few days earlier, the buds had shown damage, but no more than the work of a heavy frost. Now, tapping the bark with his knuckle raised a hollow rattle. The whole tree had sickened. Maybe the travails of Midsummer and the turbulence of the Winter Solstice had weakened the roots and admitted disease?

He surveyed the forest below. Lost Acre felt like a place in waiting. The dank mist still prevailed. Chrysalides hung on the limp grass. Bird calls were short and infrequent. Animals large and small had sought refuge in the forest. He found no spoor, but no fresh corpses either. The dark star had vanished. Even the mere worms had retreated underground. He sensed an urgent need for a new vitality.

In these relatively benign conditions, he risked further exploration. Balls of spiky vegetation disfigured another tree that was undeniably dead, its bark scarred by insects and drilled by birds. Nearby, a discoloured patch of grass held traces of sawdust around the edges. Gabriel deduced that the octagon had been constructed here beside the tree which now stood in Rotherweird Town, swathed in virulent mistletoe. Neither Bole nor Wynter were naturalists; other minds had been at work.

He wandered on towards a deep pothole which his father had shown him at the forest edge on a rare visit, only to discover a curious circle of old laid stones in its place.

If only he had Ambrose Claud to consult. His family knew the countryside, but the Clauds knew the history. The answers to these puzzles demanded knowledge of both, and the Equinox was but two nights away.

He set up camp in the spiderwoman's lair. Exploring the passages, he found the mosaic of Ferensen as a young man and Morval's remarkable paintings. Familiar faces from the present stared back from settings centuries old, caught like flies in amber. He located her store of dried food, matches and a candle. With foraged roots and nuts, he made a passable supper, then slept in the kitchen beside a small fire. He hoped that one day Morval might return and complete the cycle of paintings as a warning to posterity, not forgetting the incineration of his house and work.

The next day passed without mishap. He kept close to his new home and studied the timber. Some trees bled like veins when cut; others struck at him with their branches. In Lost Acre one made no assumptions.

At midnight on the eve of the Spring Equinox, he woke with a start. A shadowy figure stood in the doorway. He shook his head to focus on the strong, lean profile which was as comforting as the bottle in his visitor's right hand.

'Gregorius—'

'Gabriel—'

They embraced like reunited explorers. Gabriel built up the fire while Jones plucked the cork from the bottle.

'I've been saving it,' he explained. 'The last surviving bottle of St Elmo's in the world.' Jones paused. He had abandoned his habitual tracksuit for more traditional walking gear and looked and sounded a different person. A new gravitas overlaid the familiar jauntiness. 'I'm so sorry, Gabriel. I loved your house, and everything in it. But that's what happens in war.'

'No matter.'

'I've seen people burn clutching their household gods. Survival is a matter of priorities.'

Gabriel had never heard Jones speak like this before. 'How would you know?'

Jones took a mouthful of Bolitho's finest. 'I was lead scout for the *Valeria Victrix* – a Roman legion, the best. *First in, last out* – that was me.'

'You were . . .' Gabriel did not pursue the enquiry. The enigma which was Jones had been resolved.

'I was the Green Man too, the millennium before Salt. I found the Midsummer flower and walked to the Midsummer Fair, just as he did.' The wrinkles in Jones' face deepened and multiplied in the half-light. 'I was captured and recruited by a hedge-priest – so was Ferox, my tribune.' Jones bowed his head as if in memory of a fallen comrade. 'We Romans thought ourselves invincible.'

Gabriel cut more meat as the fire revived.

Jones raised his glass. 'Before a decisive battle,' he added, 'ask only for the company of friends.'

They talked on, Gabriel questioning, Jones answering with extraordinary candour. He described the Roman assault on Rotherweird, his return to Britannia from the other place and Rome's abandonment of their furthest province as witnessed from the great chalk cliffs which once had welcomed them.

'This is true history,' he said. 'Wynter is but a footnote.'

'I wouldn't be too sure about that,' a female voice broke in.

The two men spun round to see Valourhand standing in the passage doorway. She had a bolus in one hand, daggers hanging at the waist and a bag slung over the shoulder.

'Who are you?' asked Gabriel, for once sounding clumsy.

'Vixen Valourhand – ally and friend,' said Jones, 'and this is Gabriel.'

'How did you get here?' Gabriel asked her.

'I gambled on the black tile. As you can see, it's active again, which means turbulence is coming.'

Jones reverted to his old self. 'Talking of turbulence ...' He handed her a glass of St Elmo's.

Valourhand was not fooled. 'Happily, if you tell me who you really are.'

Jones repeated his narrative and Valourhand could only parrot back, '*You* were the Green Man a thousand years ago?'

Jones grinned. 'I'm in the *Anglo-Saxon Chronicle*. Few can equal that.'

Valourhand felt uneasy. Why the sudden confessional now? Also, if this was true, Jones must know far more. 'What's the escharion for?' she asked.

'On the day of the Midsummer Fair, the one in the *Chronicle*, a hedge-priest offered it to me as a gift. I refused. Nobody gives away an object like that, and I'd already been exploited once.'

'It's been taken from Oblong, the blithering idiot.'

Jones showed little concern. 'Why offer it to me if it matters who blows it? I suspect what matters is *when*.'

Valourhand had said much the same herself to Oblong, although more as cold comfort. She mulled the probabilities. 'Is that why you added the last prophecy coin?'

Jones stoked the fire instead of answering and Valourhand did not press the point. The question had been rhetorical; she did not need an answer. They talked on, rich in theory but bereft of firm conclusions, until Jones called a halt.

'Sleep before battle is an art. Too little and you tire; too much and you're slow when everyone else is fresh.'

9

Oblong Oblivious

Oblong left the town shortly before dusk, crossed to the Island Field and began his long trek along the riverbank towards Westwood. He had never felt so surplus to requirements, or so humiliated. He had spent most of the day in bed to build up his reserves, but it had made little difference. By the time he had passed the Pool of Mixed Intentions, where the Rother plunged underground to pick up the Winterbourne stream, he felt cold, hungry, tired and stiff in the joints. He had resolved to cadge breakfast off Gabriel, only to discover that the house had been reduced to a charred shell. The sight induced caution, luckily, as it turned out, for armed Apothecaries were loitering near the approach to the white tile.

He had one consolation: Boris' craft remained where he had landed it, tucked into a bend in the stream, still invisible and apparently undiscovered by the enemy.

He found a flat, firm section of riverbank out of view and slept.

Nona alias Persephone knew the black tile had been activated. She had followed the tunnels from beneath the Manor every night for the last week to monitor progress.

Bole had mentioned that others knew of its existence and might seek access via the library basement, but she was not concerned; ordinary mortals always rushed. Anyone else in the spiderwoman's lair would be up early on the morning of the Equinox and off to the mixing-point. She felt confident of a clear run and looked forward to arriving like a true royal at curtain-up. Also, she had an ultimatum to deliver before leaving, and the Manor's Great Hall, scene of so much else, was the right place to do it. Wynter, Sly and Sister Prudence would be assembling at the Hall of the Apothecaries, giving her free rein. Every piece fitted.

ENDGAME

A Sight to Behold

Wynter's postponement of the Great Equinox Race to mid-morning yielded the hoped-for dividends: by 9.30 most of the town had emptied as coracles, crew and onlookers clogged the towpath heading for the start.

The Mayor stood beside the craft with his fellow aeronauts, Thomes, Sly, an escort of twelve hardened Apothecaries, and Morval Seer. Her artist's paraphernalia had been crammed into a large satchel, which threatened to overwhelm her slight frame. Since her entrapment, paralysis of speech had returned, but to Wynter's relief, the draughtsmanship remained unimpaired.

Bandoliers draped around the escorts' waists and shoulders held dozens of syringes with capped needles. Racks on the sides of the craft housed crossbows of North Tower design. Nothing had been left to chance. Ropes showed the way to the invisible seats. Poles supported a canvas impregnated with invisibility paint which, when lowered, masked everyone from view. Only Thomes' elevated seat, equal in prominence to his own, leavened Wynter's euphoria.

As they clambered aboard, Morval felt a familiar humiliation: she must yet again draw for Wynter to spare her brother.

'Ascend,' commanded Thomes.

The gnarl juddered faintly in Wynter's grasp.

'When I say,' growled Wynter.

'When *he* says,' echoed Sly.

'Now,' cried Wynter. Thomes had predictably not risked the

test flight himself. Terror seized him as the craft surged upwards, reducing the town to so many dolls' houses. Wynter stood. 'One sweep of the river,' he shouted, 'to let them see their rulers.'

The craft banked hard to the north and west. The Apothecaries furled back the canopy.

Below, poles and coracles rolled across the ground. The hubbub of pre-Race joshing subsided as one hand pointed, then ten, then the entire populace. The Master Tanner, never one to miss an opportunity for ingratiation, bellowed, 'Elijah! Elijah!'

The word took hold, from a lone voice to a chant to a roaring chorus. Wynter awarded his public one magisterial wave before directing the craft towards Rotherweird Westwood.

With the gnarl he traced the contours of the Rotherweird escarpment. 'Behold the frontiers of our new world – to doom and renewal!'

Recent successes had refuelled Wynter's self-belief. The countrysiders had been immured, Morval retaken and Scry and the mysterious Gabriel liquidated, and Calx Bole and Nona had rediscovered deference.

He was again his own master.

Morval's pencil danced. On the pad on her knees Wynter's ecstatic face took shape. She rediscovered her voice, muttering into her lap, '*Methinks I am a prophet, new inspired . . .*'

An Ultimatum

Gorhambury abandoned the Umpire's chair, taking with him the *Great Equinox Race (Guild) Amendment Regulations* from the lectern in front of him. The chaos induced by the spring bore had in the past delivered a random fairness. A flat-water start would mean more jockeying for position, more liberties taken. To be closer to the action, Gorhambury had commissioned from the Polks a coil-driven coracle with a prominent pennant emblazoned UMPIRE – GIVE WAY. All the teams had been informed.

He handed over the Chair to Rhombus Smith and boarded his vessel.

The surprise entry by the Apothecaries had given the Race an additional edge. They looked like well-drilled magpies, here to win. The Mixers eyed them with unconcealed loathing.

Trouble is rarely an only child. An urgent message had diverted Gorhambury to the Manor, where Persephone Brown awaited him in the Great Hall. An Apothecary from Thomes' bodyguard stood beside her.

She spoke in a deadpan voice, but her eyes blazed. 'When I return, surrender the keys of the town to me.'

Gorhambury could not believe his ears. The keys, emblematic of the town itself, rested in the Mayor's sole custody. 'I will do no such thing. You know the law as well as I do.'

'Then I will have to take them.'

'You are not the Mayor.'

'The Age of the Herald passed long ago. Now the Age of the Mayor will pass. We enter the last Age. We stand at the gates of Spring.'

'And I have a race to umpire,' Gorhambury had replied curtly.

'Run along then. But don't say you haven't been warned.'

As Gorhambury surveyed the skirmishing mass of coracles, he shook his head in despair. The Lord of Misrule had been unleashed.

3
A Mixing of Opposites

The tile beneath the Claud chapel unexpectedly delivered Orelia to the curious causeway dividing the two contrasting lakes, which glimmered in a dense mist, red and blue respectively. The stone bench, its natural colour darkened by damp, looked less inviting than on her previous visit. She discovered an inscription on its underside, previously missed, which read:

> *Go find where the wind blows,*
> *Go find its lung of stone,*
> *Learn what only it knows*
> *All else is blood and bone.*

Obscure but lyrical, it had a pagan ring. Did the author mean that all was perishable but the force of Nature? Or was it an exhortation to get to the heart of the matter?

She tramped the causeway in search of inspiration.

The cups: she had overlooked the cups. She gambled correctly that the red cup would take molten liquid and the blue cup the ice-fire.

Thank you, St Jude. Now what?

Kneeling, with her body arched well back, she poured out the contents, each into their opposing lake. From the point of contact, a scarlet line veined across the ice and a blue line went zigzagging through the lava.

Terror seized her: she had triggered a tipping point. The two lakes began to thrash and roil. Waves lapped the causeway from violent cross-currents as the surfaces heaved and steam thickened into smoke.

In near darkness, Orelia ran without looking back.

A deafening roar rent the air as the tile duly swallowed her up.

4

The Poisoning

Wynter entered the white tile first. He would have preferred clear weather for his return. Instead, a clinging mist shrouded the scene of his former triumphs. But the gnarl, quivering in anticipation in his right hand, relegated the disappointment to a minor detail. He waited for the others. He would lead them to the mixing-point as in the old days.

Thomes, for all his limitations, could distinguish fake from real. The journey from the tile and the pyramidal seed heads in the grass convinced him that Wynter had indeed found the monsters' breeding ground. A leathery-winged bird skimming overhead closed the case.

He nodded approvingly.

The Apothecaries arrived, then Morval, then Sly.

Wynter watched Morval like a snake. She looked satisfyingly diminished, so close to the scene of her transformation. He smiled at her. *Feel your punishment for killing my Carcasey Jack*, said the smile.

Morval stared back at him and whispered, 'The abuse of greatness is when it disjoins remorse from power.'

Wynter laughed and turned his back on her. 'Follow me,' he said.

Through the grass they tramped, Thomes, Sly and the Apothecaries all cowed by the strangeness of the place and Wynter's insouciance.

Thomes hastily revised his master plan: work with Wynter, discard Persephone Brown.

Morval alone, attuned to Nature even here, registered a moment of crisis: Life or Death; all in the balance.

Sly complimented himself on disposing of Snorkel. Soon, under his new master, he would have two worlds to administer. He dreamed of mining for jewels and precious metals in this virgin land.

Gabriel had believed before; now he was convinced. Jones *had* been a lead scout. He read the lie of the land like a map, knowing not only what you could see from where, but also from where you could be seen. He had lined their faces with mud. Even Valourhand, a student of stealth, was impressed.

'Move your head up to see; slow, slow, slow. The temptation is to rush when you get close to the eyes. It's movement which draws attention.' Jones sniffed. 'Wind direction could hardly be better. We should hear them, but not vice versa.'

He raised his own head, inch by inch. 'First mistake,' he whispered. 'He's left no guard on the tile.'

Jones slid down the contour and across, ever closer to the mixing-point. They followed, apprentices behind their master.

'This is the place, Master Thomes,' cried Wynter. High in the branches of the huge tree hung a rope. Grass half covered a wrecked rusty cage. 'Up there – that's where the monsters are made.'

Wynter's new acolytes followed his gaze and peered into the mist, where a patch of air shimmered and danced.

'It's a creative energy which rearranges cellular structures,' Wynter said, his tone offhand, 'but it's secondary to our present undertaking. Get your men up and put the needles everywhere, trunk and branches. But no injecting yet.'

The extendable ladders lifted men high; slings and harnesses further aided their ascent. All over the tree, stiletto points bit into the bark.

'It's bleeding,' cried one, as sap trickled along the wood, then fell in viscous threads.

'Of course it's bleeding,' cried Wynter. 'It's a living thing.'

Gabriel, lover of trees, gritted his teeth. 'They're killing it.'

'It's dying already,' replied Jones.

Of course it is, thought Gabriel, *but how can Jones know?* Then he remembered: Gregorius had been the Green Man – he would not only *know*, he would *feel*.

'But why hasten the process?' he asked.

Valourhand, taking her turn to look, responded with three words: 'Yggdrasil and Ragnarok.' So many threads had come together.

As they backed down the slope, she explained, 'He's gambling that the sister tree under Rotherweird will take over, wrenching our valley into Lost Acre's dimension, or at least into a different one.'

'How could he possibly know to do that?' asked Gabriel.

'Bole is scientifically minded.'

'I'll say,' replied Gabriel incredulously.

Valourhand, thinking aloud, continued, 'Why did Bole choose Flask? That may shed some light – but what matters now is that severance would sunder Rotherweird and destroy the rest of the planet. Wynter will then rule everyone and everywhere that's left. With the mixing-point he creates his own legends, monsters and heroes. He can start again.'

'He's playing with forces he doesn't understand,' replied Gabriel grimly. 'I can't stomach this. I'm sorry.'

Jones seized Gabriel by the shoulders and held him down. 'No, we all wait. That's how it must be.'

Gabriel relented. The strange mist and the atmosphere of suspended animation had an expectancy about it. Wynter's objectives might be destructive, but he sensed a chance for renewal too. They were at the gates of Spring, after all. If he could sense it, Jones the Green Man must do so too. But what was Jones waiting for?

Valourhand watched in horror. *That's why Wynter came back.* Only the theory still felt flawed: Wynter could never have had the necessary knowledge in Elizabethan times. Bole must have designed this strategy centuries later, but *all* to the glorification of his master? Wheels within wheels within wheels . . .

Unseen below them, Persephone Brown, in a loose shimmering dress of green, yellow and white, left the spiderwoman's lair and flitted along the bank of the stream.

Wynter held up a gold pocket watch. 'It is time. Humanity has polluted and wrecked his earthly paradise, so now it pays. Go to, go to.'

The Apothecaries, their puritan zeal sharpened by talk of apocalypse, scurried from syringe to syringe, pressing down the plastic plungers one after the other.

Morval faithfully sketched the scene at speed: figures in black and white swarming a giant tree like so many ants.

The branches shivered in agony. Outsize viridian bubbles formed in the wounds, detached and floated away. Then in undamaged areas, more bubbles formed and followed. The great tree was trying to breathe.

The bubbles had a spectacular beauty, an inner life which coiled and smoked. No two were alike. Some travelled fast; some held still despite the breeze – *like different atomic particles*, thought Valourhand. But what did these strange translucent spheres contain?

She raised a hand to one, but it evaded her. The mist began to roil as the earth beneath the tree groaned like the timbers of a ship at sea.

Valourhand eased up the slope again and turned her attention from the Apothecaries to Wynter. The silvery gleam of the escharion nestled in the crook of his arm. His head spun round, but not in her direction, back towards the white tile. He peered, right hand levelled above his eyes.

'He comes,' bellowed Wynter suddenly. 'The fool comes. The beautiful boy would defy us again.'

Tyke wore a simple shirt, sleeves rolled up, breeches and boots, no hat. By some miracle the wounds inflicted by Carcasey Jack had vanished. He carried in his right hand a tall green staff.

Sly seized a pike, but Wynter restrained him. 'He's mine. You can have the pleasure of witnessing due punishment.'

He placed the escharion in the grass and strode forward to meet Tyke.

The Apothecaries in the tree froze, silhouetted like rotten fruit, as Tyke and Wynter closed. Tyke gestured down the slope towards Jones, Gabriel and Valourhand. *Not your fight*, said the sweep of the arm.

The gnarl flicked out thorny tentacles which lacerated Tyke. Blood stained his arms and face. Valourhand cried out as Wynter waved the gnarl from side to side like a scourge. On striking the stems detached – only for more to form.

To Wynter's fury, Tyke did not resist. Only feet away from Wynter, his own staff finally responded, but with nothing more than the thinnest stems of green, which loosely clung to Wynter as a benevolent climber might to a tree, too loose even to hinder him.

'God,' cried Gabriel, '*look*.'

Orelia, walking from the direction of the white tile to the tree, halted on seeing Wynter – only it was no longer Wynter. His form was changing, as if unwoven by the green staff's tendrils. Then his face altered too.

Everthorne! 'No! Please! Stop!' she screamed.

But Everthorne was not truly Everthorne; the lookalike maintained the savage assault on Tyke, who stumbled, fighting to stay upright, as another set of flaying branches ripped at his thighs and legs. Yet still the green staff worked its gentle counter-offensive.

Orelia sank to her knees as her lover lost definition and in his place appeared a diminutive red-haired dwarf – unmistakably Vibes. Tyke staggered on downhill, the shapeshifter and the gnarl relentlessly pursuing him.

Jones read Tyke's intentions. 'He's leading him on,' he whispered to Valourhand and Gabriel. 'Let him, however hard. As you would for me.'

Valourhand in her distress barely caught the oddness of the remark, but Gabriel did.

The diminutive Vibes yielded to Ferox, Jones' old comrade-in-arms, who proved even more vicious than his predecessors. The gnarl's thorned growth had ceased to detach and now encased Tyke, squeezing torso and neck. This time the green staff responded, ripping away the gnarl's grip.

'That's Flask,' shouted Valourhand.

Orelia, sole witness to the original transformation, alone fully appreciated the dark brilliance of Bole's original self-sacrifice. He had let Wynter take his body, confident of engineering a confrontation with Tyke and the green staff in due time, knowing that would restore him – at Wynter's expense. But Bole did not appear next; instead, it was a young man with a kindly face. In a brief lull, Bole's influence diminished and the gnarl's attack slackened: Benedict Roc, the Master Carver and Bole's first victim, had found the will to fight.

But Bole owned him, and Bole duly won.

For the first time, one of the protagonists spoke. The corpulent Bole, now fully in view and his face lit by triumph, cried out, 'Nona, it's done! All is done.'

Only then did they see Persephone Brown, in a dress of shimmering green, yellow and white, with a circlet around her forehead.

'Finish it,' she said, and Orelia's eyes narrowed. The way she spoke jarred.

The gnarl redoubled its attack as Tyke crawled on his hands and knees onto the circle of laid stones at the bottom of the meadow, and at the same moment the green staff abandoned Tyke's defence. Its trails of green fell away, leaving only a single shoot, which dived deep into the ground. A line appeared as it followed the edge of the stones. Orelia ran down to help, only for a shoot from the gnarl to whip her feet away.

As she clambered to her feet, she understood. These weren't stones from ancient times – they were Rotherweird cobbles. Bole had built the tower under Rotherweird's streets, which required a deep cavern. Somehow Wynter's sphere, which had been entrusted to Pomeny Tighe, had replaced the open pothole in Lost Acre with the paved Rotherweird surface. She recalled the last jotting on the list in Bolitho's observatory: *cobbled together*. He must have shared his discovery with Tyke.

Bole was revelling in his victory. 'How would you like it, Tyke? Carotid artery, punctured lungs, a twig in the brain?' He waved the gnarl once more. 'You might have bettered the mixing-point, but *nobody* betters me.'

He raised the gnarl for the *coup de grâce* but as he did, the green shoot completed its circle and with a deep rumble, the ground opened up – and Bole disappeared with the gnarl into the deeps.

Now Valourhand did run, and Gabriel too, for only a single shoot from the green staff was holding Tyke on the chasm's brink. As gently as they could, they hauled his barely conscious body to safety.

Steam rose from far below, yellowish, with more than a hint of sulphur.

'Tyke, *Tyke!*' Valourhand shouted, 'fight! *Fight!* Get me water – *quick*,' she demanded, and Orelia hurried to the stream to fill her water bottle.

Persephone Brown ran uphill past her, apparently unaffected by Bole's fate. Thomes and his Apothecaries rushed to join her at the white tile. One by one, they disappeared as the bubbles from the dying tree drifted about their heads. Only Morval remained by the tree, forgotten and superfluous in Wynter's absence.

Gabriel squeezed Orelia's arm, a gesture of comfort, as Valourhand ministered to Tyke with an uncharacteristic gentleness.

'How did you get past the guards?' Gabriel asked Orelia.

'I didn't come from there. There's a chapel on the escarpment.'

'The Claud family chapel.' He reflected. 'I always wondered why it was there.' He gave her another squeeze. 'Well done. I bet it wasn't obvious. Tiles never are.'

Blood seeped from the wounds crisscrossing Tyke's face and body, but his eyes remained themselves. From the grass, tiny spiders appeared, as they had done before, and wove the skin together.

Morval Seer did not move from the tree, but she spoke in Tyke's direction. '*To me, fair friend, you never can be old,*' she said.

Tyke spoke at last. 'Look to the world, don't look to me.' Around him the bubbles began to burst in tiny flashes of energy like blown fuses. The great tree was shedding a lifetime's memories. Different minds caught different images.

Gabriel saw a barren landscape, rock and dust intersected with mazy lines of ice and fire, with one sign of life: a slim sapling on a shallow prominence, encased in thick protective bark, already boasting a splash of green in fields of ochre brown.

For Orelia, a brilliant bird with azure-gold feathers and leathery booted legs tugged at a seed-case high in the canopy. Beneath, a climbing rose spread from a single cane, its deep carmine blossom rich in something more than mere fragrance. Beside it a flower-less climber, bare and twisted, coiled around the trunk. A second bubble presented a winged monster, dragging itself along a stream, scarred and exhausted.

The tree shared with Valourhand the dying star, its core diminishing with every streamer like a Catherine Wheel. She instantly grasped the physics: Lost Acre was losing the sustaining force of its creator and needed a fresh dynamic to renew. A second scene followed. A press of men and women dressed in leather and fur, cheeks and bare legs striped with woad, surrounded a makeshift hoist. A robed figure in black placed in a wooden cage a large oval stone and a cup, puffing with blue steam, and then fixed four coloured stones to receptacles forged in the bars. He raised a hand

and the counterweight dipped, lifting the cage to the mixing-point. Counterintuitively, there was silence, the faces gaping and visibly fearful of this undertaking. In the distance, women carried a second near-identical stone and another cup, this time red with fire.

Valourhand realised that she had just witnessed the making of the dragons. Nobody could create such perfect beasts from a living monster. The oval stones were *eggs*. They entered the mixing-point with the liquid ice or fire to emerge with it infused in the embryo. She shuddered to think what experiments had bestowed this expertise. Never patronise the past as ignorant.

Gregorius Jones witnessed his own transformation a millennium ago: the green bud of the Midsummer flower wound around his arm like a torc, staggering beneath the tree as the mixing-point flooded towards him.

Time is relative. Though the work of seconds only, these moments of shared experience seared their consciousness. They felt privileged. This sharing between tree and man was a plea for understanding from one to the other, not a deathbed ramble.

A crack of dried timber, sharp and violent, broke their reverie: the tree's trunk split; branches cracked and fell. Only the patch of slippery sky remained unchanged.

Gregorius picked up the escharion, lying in the grass where Wynter had abandoned it. He stared down the slope at his friends. He loved this place no less than the Rotherweird Valley. He flicked through his own memories – parents, siblings, a favourite toy, sea journeys, Ferox, the legion, and the chance encounters which had formed his subsequent life: the hedge-priests and Rhombus Smith, Form VIB, his friends now and those he had cared for down the centuries, all in a matter of moments, if you go by watches.

Failed emperors and generals fall on their sword. He had only half-chosen that fate, or so he hoped. *To die to live.* As to *how*, he had nothing but instinct to go on, but at least they were the sharpened instinct of the Green Man. Ever since their departure from the spiderwoman's lair, he had gripped the seed of the Midsummer flower, his bequest from Hayman Salts, protectively in his fist. Now he laid it flat in his palm, brought it to his mouth and swallowed it whole.

Nothing happened – no surprise; people ingest seeds daily. He cradled the escharion, the two pipes ending in one mouthpiece. He suspected, even hoped, to sound his own doom.

Gregorius Jones prayed to his gods and blew, long and hard.

The plangent note, neither brass nor woodwind, had carry and depth, with the best qualities of both. The moment he heard it echo on, Gregorius felt vindicated. It sounded like a hunting call but promised the opposite: a summoning of allies.

Morval apprehensively backed away from the tree into the meadow.

The ground quivered. The wrenching had begun. Roots were dying beneath their feet even as roots from elsewhere strove to hold Lost Acre in place. Gabriel, Orelia and Valourhand lost their footing as the sky overhead crackled. To the west, long plumes of blue smoke burst through the mist, sprinkling shards of ice on the ground; in the east, flame belched and sizzled.

In death is life, in death is life, Gregorius mouthed to himself as he braced his back against the ruined tree.

The fire-dragon and the ice-dragon, monsters from another time, burst through the cloud, glided over the meadow and hovered above Jones' diminutive figure. Gregorius did not look away: a good legionary faces his end. He raised his arms as if for an embrace.

Claud's poem tripped into Orelia's head:

> '*At the gaytes of Spring,*
> *When trees are hoar white strewn,*
> *Escharion must heat the seed of winter*
> *Lest all men die in bitternesse.*'

'Jones!' she screamed. 'Run!'

The dragons, lungs stoked for maximum effect, exhaled, obscuring Jones in a brilliant ball of fire and ice.

Morval's face glowed silver and scarlet. Impervious to the risk, she drew the line and memorised the colours until, their work done, the dragons veered back the way they had come.

Jones suffered more a drastic diversion of his life-force than mere pain: his physical being combusted into frozen ash as the seed absorbed him and exploded into life. New roots surged through the ground, the green fuse entering the wreck of the old tree. Slender new branches broke through the split casing of dead wood and tiny leaves appeared, drinking in the mist and clearing it in minutes.

In sudden brilliant sunshine, Lost Acre reacquired her colours.

Valourhand, Orelia and Gabriel stumbled up the slope towards the white tile, too stunned to talk, but Tyke tottered painfully towards the tree.

Valourhand let him go: Tyke exuded an autonomy which she respected. Once there, Tyke motioned to Morval to leave for the tile. Her pen ceased its dance and she obeyed. Stooping, his bloody fingers rested the tip of the staff on the trunk and the base on the ground among the roots.

Standing by the white tile, wiping the tears away, Orelia asked, 'Could we have done anything? Somehow?'

Gabriel replied, 'He's alive as could be: the Green Man now and forever. The human plot is for us to sort out.'

He's right, thought Orelia, *and it's horribly tangled.*

'Something is askew,' she said. 'If Persephone Brown is Nona and loyal to Wynter and Bole, why didn't she intervene? Why didn't she look distressed?'

Valourhand, not by nature sensitive to the presence or absence of distress (including, in fairness, in herself), instantly analysed. After a moment, she said, 'The plot was for Bole to appear to sacrifice himself for Wynter, only to retrieve his control, his body and his mind by arranging the use of the green staff against Wynter. He and Nona had worked out the staff's ability to unpick the work of the mixing-point – and she must have guessed Tyke's staff would both engineer Tyke's escape and fight the gnarl.'

'Nona acquired the gnarl centuries ago,' Orelia added, 'from a family in Hoy.'

'She'll be back for it,' said Valourhand, pointing at the cavernous rent in the earth.

Gabriel interrupted with an unexpected change of subject. 'I'm sorry,' he said, 'but there's one thing I have to do for Gregorius. I'm not having his roots cluttered with spent syringes. It's a desecration.'

Orelia rested her hand on his arm. 'You're right,' she said, realising that against Everthorne's maverick charm, Gabriel offered inner strength and kindness. She realised too that both had the artistic talent she liked in a man – Everthorne had been an extrovert but disturbed painter, Gabriel a focused, introvert carver. She had loved the one and now found herself slipping into love for the other.

Valourhand tutted at what she considered an unnecessary bout of housekeeping, but picked up Orelia's concerns about Persephone Brown. 'We all know the legend, and that legend drove Wynter and his followers – and according to Oblong, the ancient Eleusians worshipped Persephone. She rules the earthly world in spring and summer and the underworld in autumn and winter.' She paused. 'So today she takes Rotherweird.'

'How?' asked Orelia before answering her own question. 'The Apothecaries?'

Valourhand filled a gap. 'It's fairly bizarre, but I'd say this is the arrangement: Thomes rules Rotherweird when she's away, presumably here in Lost Acre, during autumn and winter. But she returns to rule Rotherweird in spring and summer. Thomes will think she's mad and easily disposed of; she'll know that and it'll be Thomes who won't last. But that's tomorrow's game.'

Gabriel returned, one arm clutching his coat, the other supporting Tyke. Avian life forms broke cover, the forest crackling with disturbed undergrowth. At their feet a chrysalis released a large crimson insect with a horned back.

'It's wake-up time,' said Orelia.

'Meal time,' added Valourhand as she helped Tyke onto the tile. He disappeared instantly with no flicker of an image left behind: all had been restored to working order.

'Thank you, Gregorius,' whispered Gabriel.

Tyke emerged in his beloved valley wracked with pain and barely able to walk, a mirror to mankind's cruelty and kindness, reflecting back whatever he received. Events dictated to him; he never to them. He could not be sure whether this passivity was a mystical gift or a character fault, but his immunity to the mixing-point had marked him out as unique.

Very occasionally, like a fish from below, conventional feelings broke through. He felt grief for the loss of so many friends, Gregorius but the latest. He registered the interest shown by the fiercely independent young physicist in his welfare, but with it, the irony of what attracted her: his incurable restlessness. She loved the unattainable and his time here was drawing to a close.

Morval Seer, following Tyke through the tile, was perplexed by his peculiar gesture. He had signalled to her *not* to record. How could this be? Didn't everyone crave the telling image to be preserved in the artist's amber? He had laid his staff against the tree, where it had transformed into a climbing rose: a miracle-worker who did not want his miracles remembered? Despite the richness of the scene, she had obeyed. *But why?*

A realisation dawned: this had been Tyke's moment of private grief, so not a gesture for public consumption. He had known Jones as long as anyone alive. Memories of tiny acts of kindness by others surfaced too – from Jones and Finch to the gangly historian – and a prompt formed in the chaos. She must do more than indulge her peculiar talent. She must wear the loss of Fortemain as those around her wore the loss of Gregorius. Pen and paint must be servants, not masters. She must uncoil, unfreeze and open her face to the sun.

His stomach half sunk in the sandy mud of the riverbank, Oblong maintained his vigil. When the Apothecaries' craft landed, he had agonised over whether to attempt attack or sabotage, but the armed Apothecaries on guard had deterred him. He had been appalled to see Morval, but what could he do?

The return of the main party left him the more outnumbered. They walked briskly across the meadow, the twelve Apothecaries, with Sly, Thomes and Persephone Brown. *But where's Wynter? And where is Morval?*

One mystery yielded to another: Persephone boarded first and took Wynter's elevated throne. *Why give her such prominence?* Oblong could only think of an old legend replayed the first day of spring, Persephone returned from the land of the dead to rule the living . . .

The Apothecaries' craft, altogether more substantial than Boris' gimcrack contraption, accelerated skywards and disappeared. Oblong opted against pursuit; he could not fly the machine and fight, not alone. He rose from his hiding place, numb with worry for Morval, and walked to the wreck of Gabriel's house. He poked around in the ash, but nothing had survived. Even the steel wood-working tools had twisted in the heat.

He cursed out loud. He, the only historian, had missed another climactic event. Yet again, he would have to harvest hearsay.

Pull yourself together, barked an inner voice. *Call yourself a historian? Go to Lost Acre – go to the battlefield*, investigate.

Halfway up the woodland path, he met a bedraggled company coming down.

'God, I forgot about him,' said Valourhand, the first to appear, supporting Tyke on the descent. 'We've got transport.'

Orelia was more welcoming. 'Oblong – thank heavens you're here. Wynter is dead, Bole with him, but Gregorius . . .'

'*The tender leaves of hope tomorrow blossom . . .*' said a voice further back.

Oblong beamed; Morval smiled back, stumbled down and hugged him.

Oblong blushed as Gabriel arrived.

'You need to defend the town,' he said to Oblong as the historian clumsily disengaged from Morval. 'Persephone Brown and Thomes are the new enemy.'

'You're coming too,' Orelia said fiercely to Gabriel, but, hand in pocket, he declined.

'I've a mission of my own,' he said. 'It's easy enough, but it has to be done. You save the town; I save the country.' He turned to Tyke. 'You have an extraordinary constitution. I'll be back with herbs and hot water as soon as I can.'

He hurried across the meadow, past the wreck of his house and on, that one hand still in his pocket.

The rest of them were given no time to reflect. Panjan cut through the breeze and landed beside Oblong, who unclipped the canister tied to his leg.

'Finch's writing,' said Valourhand as Oblong unfurled the single roll of paper.

To Morval, the two words, *Cave Myrmidon*, summoned an image of a monster from underground.

Oblong translated. 'He means *Cave* Myrmidon – beware the Myrmidon, whatever it is.'

'That's where Persephone lives – Myrmidon Coil. We need to get back – and quick,' said Valourhand. Reluctantly she added, 'Tyke isn't fit to travel. He stays.'

'Fashioned by nature'

5

Escape by Water

Outside the Witan Hall the fragment of gnarl maintained its ten-tacular grip. Inside, adults fretted, while the children relished the crisis. Would they be here for ever? Would they turn yellow? Would they have to eat each other to survive?

But Ferensen knew the reason for their imprisonment: Wynter needed young cells for the mixing-point, and in this age he could not acquire them from the wider world.

'What feeds the cistern?' he asked Megan Ferdy, who alone had remained calm.

'Aquifers from the Hoy plateau,' she said. 'They drain down to the Winterbourne and on to the Rother. We take only what we need.'

'Can I see?'

She gave him a hard look. Ferensen had a troubled relationship with water. Bill had seen him emerging naked from the river, his skin shiny and black. She had an inkling of where this might lead – but Ferensen was their spiritual leader. He acted for the common good.

The Hall's deepest chamber had been fashioned by Nature. Waterflow had gouged a huge rockpool down one side of the mossy cavern. Ferns gripped the ceiling and in the depths, iso-lated pebbles glowed like jewels. Every drip tinkled and the air left a brackish taste on the tongue. It was an aqueous place to every sense. Interlocking pipes and pumps kept the water on the move and fresh. Piled in one corner, sharp-sided rocks riddled with holes served as counterweights for the buckets which fed the internal plumbing.

Ferensen weighed a rock in his hand. 'There must be an overflow.'

Megan nodded.

'We need several lengths of string.' He paused, then said softly, 'I'm sorry. It's an unpleasant task, but hopefully you won't be needed.'

She looked hard at Ferensen. In recent days his default expression of calm had turned anxious. She had a premonition. 'Let me guess. You weight your ankles, and I mustn't let you come up for air,' she said, more statement than question.

'Something like that,' he replied.

She fetched a ball of sturdy twine, cut several lengths, fed them through the holes in the rocks and fastened them to his ankles. He handed a second, longer connecting line to Megan to enable retrieval and climbed to the rim, cradling the stones in his arms.

She followed and he hugged her. 'Love to Bill and the children,' he said before turning and descending the steep shelf. He allowed the rocks to fall as the water reached his shoulders.

Bubbles rose; the surface threshed briefly. Ferensen had vanished.

6

The Finishing Line

Carnage. Mayhem. Chaos.

The stream of directions, rebukes, rule reminders and penalties from Gorhambury's megaphone passed unheeded as his voice contrived to grow both hoarser and shriller. Paddles flailed; poles jabbed; this was more naval battle than boat race. Guild Bands struck up on the river bank with wildly conflicting choices: 'Jolly Boating Weather' competed with 'Also sprach Zarathustra'.

Every crew member in the Municipals carried waterproof copies of the omnibus edition of the *Great Equinox Race (Guild) Amendment Regulations* (amended). Gorhambury's treatment so outraged them that they abandoned competition for higher ground and appointed themselves Water Marshalls, so outraging everyone else – including Gorhambury, for no such office was sanctioned by the *Regulations*.

Rhombus Smith's pronouncements from the towpath fared little better, although unlike Gorhambury, he did not mind. His headmasterly ear heard more laughter than spite: a case of childhood regained, with one or two exceptions . . .

The enmity between Mixers and Apothecaries ran deep, as did the Master Tanner's ambition to win at all costs. Luck of the draw had sent Sister Prudence and her Apothecaries east and the Mixers and Tanners west of Rotherweird Island. When neck and neck with the Mixers, the Master Tanner launched his frogman with a distracting cry of, 'Man overboard!'

In quick succession, the Mixers' three vessels suffered terminal leaks, but the frogman, an excitable type, lost control in the underwater turmoil and speared the Umpire's coracle too. Gorhambury, his hand to his ear as if saluting the river god, swam only when the water reached his chin.

Meanwhile, the Scholastics, propelled by the Heads of Languages and the Sixth Form swivelling their hips in imitation of the Bolivian water beetle, were closing the gap on the Apothecaries. Fanguin, beside himself with excitement at the revival of his rotator technique, bellowed encouragement: 'Pelvis front, pelvis back—'

Thank God, he had a proper crew this time. Nice young man, Oblong, *but* . . .

From a betting perspective, the race assumed its final shape as the two stations converged. All would surely turn on the imminent showdown between the Tanners and the Apothecaries, although odds on the Scholastics were shortening. Sleeves rubbed and chalk scribbled on the bookies' mobile blackboards at bewildering speed.

Expecting the Mixers, Sister Prudence found her crew confronted by the Tanners' fleet in the home straight. She suspected foul play. The Master Tanner had that kind of face. On the neighbouring riverbank the Water Marshalls arrested the frogman who, true to script, cried, 'It's the Bakers what hired me!'

A floating Mixer confirmed Sister Prudence's diagnosis with a spluttered request for vengeance. For her young Apothecaries, the Race had been a voyage of self-discovery. Physical competition, the open air, slapstick, camaraderie and adrenalin: her crew had re-engaged with their youth. A few Apothecaries among the spectators felt similarly stirred, but their sense of duty suppressed any outward show of excitement. Other layers, however, remained intact: they inhabited a black and white universe where they alone upheld Virtue.

Sister Prudence appealed to this atavistic urge by raising her paddle to the heavens and pointing at the Tanners. 'Sinners!' she yelled. 'Get 'em.'

'Easy, boys, easy,' whispered Fanguin to his crew. 'We're the tortoise, they're the hare.'

7

Myrmidon

Finch, peering down from the roof of Escutcheon Place, observed groups of Apothecaries on manoeuvre. One section was clearing the northern tip of the Island Field; another had lined up at the approach to the South Bridge, whose gates had been inexplicably closed; a third was marching along the towpath as if to block any relief from that direction. A section of the RDF had crossed the North Bridge to form square in front of the gate, pikes levelled forward.

Finch hobbled down to Market Square and launched his scooter along the Golden Mean. 'Why's the gate locked?" he asked the guard.

'Orders, Mr Finch. We can open it to the Mayor, but nobody else. Mr Gorhambury fears an attack of some kind while the town is all but empty.'

I bet he does, thought Finch. Early that morning he had passed on his suspicions about Persephone Brown and the Myrmidon to Boris Polk, convinced that the revised Race had been designed by Wynter to ensure everyone would witness his triumphant return, but that others were planning a different outcome. Wynter had no need to besiege his own realm.

'Next time you won't be so lucky,' whispered a familiar voice in Finch's ear. He turned to see his estranged wife, Fennel Finch.

She had changed for the better – and for the worse. Her default expression of disappointment with her lot had been replaced by an alarmingly ferocious intensity. The mantoleon's claw still hung from her neck.

She rushed past him, followed by their unsatisfactory son, Percy, and took up a position in a corner tower.

Another time, Finch chided himself; *distraction is the general's greatest danger.* He continued his analysis of the troop movements below. The Apothecaries and the RDF were planning a strike for the town over the bridge and through the South Gate. Persephone Brown and Thomes, the old guard and the new, must be in cahoots. *Necessity must mother invention*, he decided.

He sent a runner to *The Journeyman's Gist* to fetch Bill Ferdy and his assistant barmen, while he toured the school for academic types with no interest in the Great Equinox Race, including members of Form VIB in mourning for the absence of Gregorius Jones. Shopkeepers and adolescent idlers, mostly gathered by Amber Vine, also joined.

Finch issued a stream of orders. 'Remember the tables from Bolitho's wake? Get them to the South Gate, quickly now. You three: dismantle the children's seesaw in Grove Gardens and get that there too – just the long section with the seats. Find your catapults, any of you who have them – and I know some of you do – and find more people – anyone, anywhere. Those under seventeen: you will man the battlements.'

Finch spoke with the *brio* of a man who had stumbled on his true vocation, although this flurry of activity masked one serious anxiety. Thomes and Brown were no fools. *How did they intend to break down the gate?*

There was less certainty below than Finch imagined. The Apothecaries on the Island Field glanced up and behind with increasing frequency and unease. Where was their Master? A prophecy jangled in their heads. *Levamus: the Apothecaries will rise.* Or will they?

In their contrasting but equally distinctive uniform, the RDF eyed the Apothecaries with suspicion. The Guild's weapons had a superior, professional look and their movements displayed the precision of the parade ground. Yet it was the RDF's armbands, not the

Guild's magpie dress, which represented the true power of the state. Their powers of search and arrest had made them who they were and conferred a sense of entitlement. In recent days Persephone Brown had been more assiduous even than Wynter in promoting their interests. She had warned against Gorhambury, a pernickety liberal who would disarm them if he could. She understood their priorities and their core value of control.

Together, they waited, the RDF and the Apothecaries, two forces bereft of their generals.

Holes cut in the canopy accommodated telescopes which allowed Thomes and Persephone to observe progress without revealing their presence.

'They're in place,' said Persephone.

'Of course they're in place, they're Apothecaries,' replied Thomes huffily.

'We'll wait until the coracles enter the home straight,' she added.

Thomes bit his lower lip. To be ordered about by a woman, and a young woman at that, in front of your own men! But a waiting game with Wynter had paid dividends. *Levamus*: one Guild to rule them all. He would be the visionary to throw off the reclusive policies of his predecessors.

Persephone Brown watched the surviving coracles enter the confluence below the town. 'Prepare the megaphone,' she commanded.

Ferensen the eelman relished the chill of water and the caress of weed, but his human mind was racing. An alien presence upstream had infected the river. Tiny fish darted past, eyes swollen by panic. Well before the Island Field he registered an unnatural division in the stream ahead and the presence of a powerful construct like himself. He gathered his wits. Now, at the very end, he had been granted a chance to atone.

*

With immaculate timing Persephone flung back the canopy, exposing their return to view. The craft hovered above the finishing line, everyone's focal point, whether still in the Race or not. A large funnel had been fixed in the rigging to serve as an oversize loudhailer. Through it Sly delivered a wholly unexpected message.

'Citizens, I have wondrous news. The Mayor is dead!'

Heads, whether on the shore, bobbing in the river or in coracles, twisted to engage with other heads for reassurance. *Wondrous?*

'Yes, citizens, Wynter was an *impostor*. He fashioned the monsters. He minted the prophecy coins. He *never* spent his childhood here. Lies, lies and more lies. With his dying breath he recanted and appointed Master Thomes and Persephone Brown to rule in his stead – a divided rule: spring and summer for Persephone Brown and autumn and winter for Master Thomes. They offer variety and diversity. Mr Gorhambury will now surrender the keys to the town.'

A woman's scream from high on a battlement rent the air, so primal that everyone heard it: Fennel Finch, ravaged by the news of Wynter's death and defeat. She seized her son's hand and headed to the street below.

Meanwhile, Gorhambury, head striped with pond weed and ears full of water, jettisoned the *Great Equinox Race (Guild) Amendment Regulations* (amended) for graver constitutional provisions. Wynter, an emergency appointment, had no power himself to appoint. That way led to emperors and the death of democracy. As for Persephone Brown, she and Sly must be of unsound mind.

Obligingly, Sister Prudence hauled Gorhambury, his Umpire's megaphone still in hand, from the water into the Apothecaries' coracle.

'This is unconstitutional,' he whispered to his rescuer who, to his surprise, replied, 'I'm inclined to agree.'

A truth dawned on Gorhambury: Apothecaries directed their lives by a meticulous loyalty to the letter of the law, which this putsch unashamedly offended. Encouraged, Gorhambury stumbled to his feet. A gurgling noise like a goldfish in conversation emerged.

Sister Prudence handed him her coaching loudhailer.

This time Gorhambury's voice rang across the water, loud and clear. 'The *Regulations* do not permit Mr Wynter to appoint anyone, and you yourselves condemn him as an impostor. Further, the Masters of any Guild are expressly barred from Mayoral office, as Master Thomes well knows. Miss Brown returned here a few weeks ago to take over her sister's secretarial duties. Her head has surely been turned.'

Sister Prudence found the reedy defiance in Gorhambury's voice disconcertingly attractive, likewise his high forehead and spindly legs.

The figures in mid-air shuffled. Persephone Brown descended from her throne and went to the speaking funnel. 'Understand this, Mr Gorhambury: Mayors have had their day. Your *Regulations* are spent. I do not require appointment. I rule by divine right, as will Master Thomes when the Autumn Equinox comes. Defying the gods is a cue for unnecessary suffering, as you'll discover if you persist.'

A jumble of boats, the lost overboard and the shore-bound listened to this exchange with incredulity as Master Thomes, a connoisseur of the art of self-advancement, added an unconvincing postscript: 'We shall rule for all.'

Faced with revolution, Gorhambury turned to the practicalities. The South Gate remained closed, as ordered by him in response to Persephone's first demand for the keys. On the downside, Apothecaries and members of the RDF had taken up a variety of strategic positions by the South Bridge, on the towpath and on the shore of the Island Field close to the finishing line. They had also surreptitiously acquired spears and shields. Nor did he like the glistening silver levers and bolts of the crossbows in the laps of the air-bound Apothecaries.

In contrast, Gorhambury's scattered forces had only numbers in their favour, with mere paddles and poles for weapons.

'Can you call off your men?' he asked Sister Prudence.

'They're conditioned to obey their Master,' she replied through gritted teeth.

Behind the South Gate, Finch's motley force had assembled two abreast, holding school tables to protect their flanks and heads. In the centre, Ferdy and his assistant held the dismantled swing, which was poking out like a battering ram. Finch had spent much of his childhood buried in books on classical military strategy. He had prepared a *testudo*, a formation well known to Gregorius Jones.

'Land me on the river bank,' Persephone instructed the pilot, 'by the finish.'

'That's madness,' intervened Thomes. 'We can pick them off from here like fish in a barrel.'

'Do it,' hissed Persephone with a look so fierce that the pilot obliged. She pointed at the crossbowmen. 'Six with him and six with me,' she said, as if marking out the rule in months of their respective reigns. This time Thomes did not demur. There had been too many surprises to write off Persephone Brown quite yet. However, as security, he retained his best marksman.

Sly reluctantly joined Persephone Brown on the northeastern tip of the Island Field. An invisible aircraft offered the better chance of survival and, if needed, escape.

Persephone stood stock-still on a rock in the shallows. She extended her hand and with a twist of her wrist, transformed the scene. Yards away, in the middle of the river, the water began to seethe. From the depths rose a monster of legend: twelve feet tall, bullet-headed and green-skinned, encrusted with shells and stones, with fins hanging loose from arms and legs and a powerful tail between them. The Myrmidon had come.

Thomes' shock turned to elation. He had played his hand to perfection. He had backed the right horse.

The creature bent low and scooped up a huge rock as if it were a pebble.

Finch, called back to the battlements, read its intentions just in time.

'Back from the gate,' he yelled to his makeshift detachment, who retreated just in time. The rock, thrown with astonishing velocity and accuracy, smashed the great double doors open. A second quickly followed, tearing them from their hinges.

Outrage seized Rotherweird's citizens. The Gate represented the town's right to admit whomsoever they chose. Crews surged forward; those on the towpath charged too, using grounded coracles as shields.

Sister Prudence glanced at her own crew. They disliked Thomes' hardcore supporters, and the monstrosity confronting them did not resemble an agent of the one true God. They joined forces with their neighbours.

Above them, Thomes watched Sister Prudence's defection in enraged disbelief. Time to nip this fledgling revolution in the bud. 'Get her,' he said to the marksman. 'Get Sister Prudence – now!'

In that split moment, Fortune and maybe St Jude intervened. Sister Prudence, seeing a crossbowman on the ground taking aim at Gorhambury, seized the town clerk and plunged to the left, overturning the coracle, but saving them both.

Misconstruing the capsize as a double strike, Thomes embraced further political opportunities. 'Get the Guild Masters,' he bellowed.

A bolt in the head disposed of the nearest, the Master Tanner, as he wrestled with the quandary of which side to choose.

It threatened to be the shortest of engagements. The Myrmidon swung its arms in the water, like a child in a bath, building waves which drove the flotilla back. The one craft which came within range was crushed and the unfortunate occupants seized and speedily dismembered. The Rother foamed crimson. A third rock halted the charge down the towpath.

At Boris' command, the Fireworkers' coracle launched a fusillade of rockets, but the monster proved impervious to pyrotechnics.

Above, the Apothecaries marched onto the bridge.

In the mouth of the open gateway, Finch, one foot on his silver scooter, muttered, 'Fuggedyfuck!' and hastily reassembled his *testudo*.

'You can't go out like that,' said Amber.

'Leaders lead,' replied Finch grandly.

As he marshalled the tabletops into a smooth shield wall, she bent down and adroitly loosened a few screws in the scooter. Her mother's happiness mattered.

'But this is no place for you two,' Finch added firmly.

'If you think that, you don't know me and you don't know Amber,' replied Ember, cheeks flushed.

'Fuggedyfuck!' he repeated.

Ready at last, Finch's irregulars emerged through the mangled gate. Their entrance gained *cachet* from the Herald perched on the scooter like a chariot in the vanguard. A supporting bombardment of darts and catapulted stones, despite their ill direction, briefly halted the Apothecaries.

Persephone watched the emergence of Finch's volunteers with disdain. They had no idea.

'Wait, my lovelies, wait,' whispered Finch. A volley of bolts from nowhere swept into his *testudo*. The tables took most of the impact, but two men fell and Finch cursed. He lacked that much-fingered trump card, air superiority.

As if in answer to the Herald's unspoken prayer, Oblong's craft arrived. Though itself invisible, the crew, lacking the Apothecaries' protective canopy, were not. Bolts thudded into the superstructure from land and sky, but Boris' eccentric carpentry miraculously held.

Valourhand leaned out. 'There's a kraken-like creature holding the river, but we have to get Thomes first.'

'How?' yelled Orelia. 'We can't see him and we've no weapons.'

Oblong heaved at the controls, banking the Hoverfly left as another bolt passed perilously close.

Valourhand emptied the contents of Gabriel's coat onto the floor: a pile of syringes.

'Darts,' she said, 'as good as.'

Morval upended her bag of artist's materials. Little pots of paint rolled around the invisible deck.

'*To gild refined gold, to paint the lily,*

'*To throw a perfume on the violet . . .*' she said.

Her words hardly matched the situation, but Valourhand translated by removing the lids and distributing Morval's pots. 'One pass, Oblong, one pass; and for God's sake, *concentrate.*'

Orelia exploded. 'Of course, he's bloody concentrating! And he's actually done bloody well for a man afflicted by vertigo.'

The compliment enthused Oblong. His senses sharpened and he drew inspiration from the memory of his elderly cleaner. He just needed a bead on Thomes' stealth vessel.

Far below, Finch read the drama like a map. He whispered to Ember Vine, 'They can't see the bastards. We need to draw another volley.'

He gave Ember a hug and realigned his scooter to face the centre of the advancing enemy. Bill Ferdy and his assistant barman held the seesaw under their armpits like a jousting lance.

'The *testudo* is an exemplary tactic in open ground, but also has uses in a confined space . . .' bellowed General Finch by way of encouragement.

Finch, Ferdy and the *testudo* charged. The steering column on Finch's scooter came away in his hands, propelling him off the bridge and into the Rother, but his erratic gallantry inspired those behind. The seesaw, flailing left and right, tipped Apothecary after Apothecary into the river as their spears bounced off the carapace of tabletops.

Above, hatred of anyone who was not an Apothecary had enthused Master Thomes with the spirit of battle. His eyes turned to the fight on the bridge and beyond. Down the slope towards the towpath ran an extraordinary figure in full samurai armour, waving a sword and accompanied by a huge dog.

'Crossbowmen,' he cried, 'wipe out that rabble and that *thing*.'

One fired at the Mance, missing comfortably – and now Oblong had his bead. He manoeuvred the craft over the point of fire. Valourhand, Orelia and Morval hurled pots of paint. Morval's, guided by an artist's eye for movement and trajectory, hit the target full-on. A large splash of vermilion appeared in mid-air.

Thomes overreacted, ripping away the stained canopy and exposing his crew to full view – and an old-fashioned dogfight. The larger craft had superior speed and heavier conventional weaponry, but Oblong's pursuing contraption was nimbler, its controls more sensitive.

Valourhand seized the syringe with the most juice left and distributed the others. 'Keep your hands away from the needles,' she warned as she twined the mooring rope round her leg. 'I'm dropping in. Distract them.'

'Shoot the bitch!' yelled Thomes.

Oblong yawed left, then right. Valourhand swung on the rope like a trapeze artist. The marksman waited and waited, judging the swing. Morval, transformed by the need for physical action, judged the dynamics with precision. Her syringe lodged in the marksman's shoulder. He dropped his weapon and screamed as a drop of liquid mistletoe burned into his flesh. Seconds later, Valourhand landed. Thomes lunged at her with a spear from the rack, slicing her thigh.

'For Gregorius, for Tyke,' she cried, as the crossbowmen fumbled to reload. 'And a thigh for a thigh,' she added, stabbing Thomes and pressing the plunger, before she and the rope swung away. Thomes danced like St Vitus before crashing into his invisible pilot. The craft rose and dived like a swallow before plummeting into the Island Field, throwing out Apothecaries like rag dolls from a pram.

Oblong landed the Hoverfly near the South Bridge. Valourhand and – to his surprise – Morval seized discarded weapons from the ground and supported Finch's force by attacking the Apothecaries from the rear. The mysterious samurai knight and his huge dog fought beside them with panache and ferocity. The tide was turning in the fight for the bridge, even though General Finch and his scooter were in the river.

Orelia had been watching Persephone. The Myrmidon had put her and her archers in full control of the riverside battle, but Persephone looked distracted. Events since her aunt's death had taught Orelia to focus on the oddest facts and reason from there. Persephone had been Madge, who had been Nona. Scry had recognised neither, which suggested that Nona had changed appearance at least twice. She thought of Bole's mind, and how his personality had been lurking in Wynter's – and then she remembered a most peculiar incident at the Unrecognisable Party.

She strode over to a huddle of musicians, sent to the Island Field in the hope of serenading the Scholastics to victory. They were lying prone behind a stand of bulrushes. The Precentor looked terrified. Persephone and the Myrmidon were no more than fifty yards away.

'This is terrible,' he stammered.

'Which is why you're going to do something about it.' She whispered in his ear.

'What—?'

'Do it.' She ushered the school band to their feet.

The Precentor raised a shaking baton and Debussy's *L'après-midi d'un faune*, initially shaky but quickly gaining in confidence, echoed across the water. The music's easy decadence could not have sounded more incongruous, but it transformed Persephone.

She danced along the riverbank, beautifully – and as she did so, the Myrmidon went berserk, waving arms and bellowing in rage.

Behind the Myrmidon, the eelman eyed the huge legs and the powerful tail snaking back downstream. How could he, little more than a water snake, possibly bring down this monster? His love of Nature and his essential pacifism brought the answer: seduce rather than fight.

He coiled up the creature's right leg, caressing the amphibian's skin while at the same breaking through into the creature's subconscious with messages of escape and freedom. They were kindred spirits from the mixing-point, after all.

As he soothed the Myrmidon, it ceased to flail and let out a strange keening sound, paradoxically suggestive of both pain and release. Slowly, and not without grace, it subsided to its knees and disappeared beneath the water.

His last duty done, Ferensen unwound himself and barrelled along against the current, soon no more than a shadow heading north. The Myrmidon followed. At the underwater tile where he had surfaced after his fight with the spider, Ferensen paused. The Myrmidon, as beautiful in water as it was ugly on land, circled the tile and disappeared for home.

Ferensen swam on, passing shallows where he had waded as a boy. Yet he did not linger. A deeper will propelled him towards an inland sea festooned in weed, the great Sargasso. It was time.

The Myrmidon's departure signalled the end. The Apothecaries and the Rotherweird Defence Force laid down their arms. Nobody cheered: this was a victory without euphoria. The rusty tang of blood infected the air. The wounded cried for help. Aftershock at the brutality of hand-to-hand combat induced silence, soothed only by the Scholastics' band, who played to the finish.

Persephone, flushed from her dance, approached Orelia. 'I have

Nona under control,' she said. 'My name is Varia. I've bided my time. She's not so evil, seen in the round; as much a victim as a perpetrator.' She paused.

'I'm listening,' said Orelia quietly.

'You'll find the four stones in Wynter's study, set around a jade obelisk – and you'd best have this.' She removed a silver ring from her finger and gave it to Orelia. An unusual setting held four chips of coloured stone rising on tiny silver tendrils from the centre. Orelia did not ask what the ring did; she knew. It had controlled the Myrmidon, hence the monster's confusion when Varia had started to dance.

'How did she create you?'

Varia shrugged. 'That she hides from me, but the mixing-point rebuilds cells as well as merges them. I'm her and she's me, you might say. But she underestimated me. Many have. Dancers require a peculiar sense of purpose. In time, I think she'll forgive me.'

'If they were to let you go, what would you do?' Orelia asked.

'I'd teach your people to dance,' she said. 'What else? Wood carving apart, I've never seen a community with so much intelligence and so little art.'

Denzil Prim arrived with the sub-gaoler. 'Nice moves, Miss Brown, but you'd best come with me, for your own good.'

'Call her Varia,' said Orelia. 'That's the name she prefers.'

'I know the way, Mr Prim,' said Varia, leading the two men off.

'You remind me of the Scarlet Witch.'

'Thank you,' said Valourhand with less aggression than she would normally greet such a sexist and patronising remark. The samurai knight had fought with gusto, and under the helmet lurked a bewildering mix of white hair and a face of boyish simplicity. He had skilfully disabled rather than killed. She liked his taste in armour too.

'Marvel Comics,' he explained. 'She has the ability to change reality.'

'You're taking the piss.'

'Samurai never take the piss.' He paused. 'Was mistletoe involved?' he asked.

'Who the hell are you?'

'Ambrose the Thirteenth for my sins.' He stooped to bind the Mance's wounded foreleg. 'We Clauds are of both good and evil effect,' he said.

'Valourhands likewise,' she sighed.

Far below Orelia watched the conversation and, in particular, Valourhand's animation. *At last*, she thought, *at last*.

'You saved my life,' Gorhambury said, helping Sister Prudence ashore.

'Actually, you also saved mine, so we're quits.'

'I thought Apothecaries couldn't swim.'

'As a teenager I had charge of the bees. At dawn, with nobody about, I taught myself.'

Gorhambury turned pink. Did *nobody about* imply she swam *naked*? The thought prompted a statement unuttered by him in his lifetime. 'This calls for a drink.'

Sister Prudence, on equally novel ground, accepted, just as Fanguin appeared, waterlogged and anxious.

'Where's Bill?'

'Fanguin, it's over.'

'No, it's not. You must call a meeting in the Island Field at two. Everyone comes, even the wounded. But I have to find Bill, and we need the charabanc.'

'What's so urgent? There are dead to bury and—'

'Don't you see?'

Gorhambury plainly didn't.

'What do we do about *history*? Apothecaries have been to the other place – everyone's seen the monster. Who is Persephone Brown? Do they investigate or forget? It's like the Green Man. Get it? But we can't trick them this time.'

Fanguin had once explained to Gorhambury the miraculous effects of Bill Ferdy's Hammer, the brew which wiped the memory clean of at least a day's events. Although Gorhambury's own memory of Midsummer's Day had been inexplicably vague, he had dismissed the idea as preposterous.

Boris arrived, laden with smashed coracles.

'We need the brew, Boris,' said Fanguin.

Boris grasped the point immediately. 'Consider it done.'

Behind him, Miss Trimble was tending to the wounded. He gave her a wave, dropped the coracles and ran off towards the bridge to find Bill Ferdy and the charabanc.

8

The Tree of Good and Evil

Despondent would understate the expressions of the three country-siders standing guard by the Witan Hall door, and Gabriel's arrival did not alleviate their despair.

'So sorry,' one said. 'All that work up in smoke.'

It took a moment to register that the remark referred to him, such was Gabriel's sense of mission.

'Still, a great place to rebuild,' said a second in a strained attempt at good cheer.

'True enough,' said Gabriel, looking around at the billhooks, charred wood and empty jars of acid littering the verandah. The hand in his pocket itched as he walked closer to the sealed door.

'Nothing works,' said the first man, laconic as countrysiders tended to be.

'Worse than that,' said the second, 'the harder we try, the stronger it gets. Thank God, they've plenty of food in there.'

'They're in perpetual night on the first day of spring,' said the lugubrious third.

'Watch!' replied Gabriel as the green shoot wrapped around his little finger pulled Gabriel's hand from his pocket, or so it felt.

They laughed. It resembled the stem of a young sweet pea.

'You're a one, Mr Gabriel,' said the first.

Laughter swiftly yielded to wonder as the fragile thread of green unwound of its own accord and attacked the tentacular growth, boring, encircling and prising. The live-dead wood of the gnarl responded. At Gabriel's command, everyone took cover, so as not to be torn apart by the flailing stems.

It ended in an explosion of splinters, shreds of vibrant green and a shattered door.

Gabriel helped usher the children through the wreckage, blinking, into the sunlight. Megan Ferdy came last, the captain of a once stricken ship.

9

Two Journeys:
Over Ground and Underground

The battle decided, Ambrose Claud ran up the road to his bicycle and, with adroit use of the gears and short intervals on foot, he made the escarpment rim in record time. The rolling landscape basked in spring sunshine. The spire of Hoy's church stood proud. The tiny valley of Rotherweird had saved the world: no Ragnarok, no Doomsday.

At breakneck speed, he returned the way he had come.

The boy stumbled for the umpteenth time.

'Watch your feet,' chided Fennel.

'I don't wanna leave. I want my inheritance,' he whined.

'*Want* doesn't *get* without work.'

'But . . .'

'No buts, Percy. We Croyles don't whine, we *fight*.'

Percy scowled in the subterranean gloom. His mother's maiden name had achieved increasing currency in recent weeks: *we Croyles* this, *we Croyles* that.

Fennel held the lantern to the map she had acquired at the Unrecognisable Party and with one finger marked their way towards the only exit on the far side of the river.

Reassured, she marched on and resumed her pep talk. 'Aeneas

left Troy in defeat and founded Rome. You're better off. You've an existing title to claim.'

Percy's step lengthened, driven by a burning sense of entitlement.

'That's better,' added Fennel as the path descended and the walls grew damp.

10

Is Ignorance Bliss?

Gorhambury called the meeting for two o'clock in the afternoon. As at the election, the town emptied onto the Island Field: the able-bodied and the wounded, adults, children and babies-in-arms.

As at the Midsummer Fair, the Ferdys set up trestle tables behind Gorhambury's makeshift rostrum. Fanguin, Aggs and the Polks stood poised to fill the rows of thimble-size glasses from the ancient barrel embossed with H for Hammer, should the vote go that way.

Gorhambury put the motion fair and square. 'Today you witnessed the past's power to infect the present. A few of you have visited the place where the monsters who plagued us are made.'

Many glared at the Apothecaries, but Gorhambury ignored them.

'The way in has long been hidden, but Mr Wynter knew it from the distant past, for this other place can extend life too. So, is it "forewarned is fore-armed" or will it be "ignorance is bliss"? You have the choice, because Bill Ferdy has a miraculous brew which can erase today from your memory.'

His audience paid close attention. Through these months of toil and crisis, Gorhambury had gained authority, even fluency.

'So, this is the motion: Remember, or Forget. To help us decide, Mr Oblong, our resident historian, will speak for releasing our past. Mr Finch, our Herald and Keeper of Records, will speak for maintaining our more secretive *status quo*.'

Oblong had been given little notice. His thoughts, cobbled together on a scrap of paper, ran only to headings. Although an outsider, his aerobatics had won him kudos. *With the Hammer*, he thought wistfully, *they'll forget all that.*

As he climbed the rostrum, Morval resisted the urge to record the moment, preferring instead to weigh the mettle of the gangly historian. Would Fortemain have approved of him? Would Hieronymus?

A system of amplifiers developed by the South Tower stood ready to project his voice across the Island Field. Oblong, recalling an advocate's tip, started with a detail before panning out to the wider view.

'When I look down from 3 Artery Lane, I see a tangle of street names – but you and I cannot know who built them, who named them, or when. What stories lurk behind these names? What lessons could be learned? How proud might you be to know your ancestor carved that particular lion or placed the weather vane on that particular tower? Mr Finch knows the answers – but we may not.'

A low blow, thought Finch, nodding gracefully as Oblong played an even more obvious card.

'I'm ashamed to say that outsiders inflicted this law on you. Why? Only history can tell you. How did Mr Wynter fool us? Why did we believe in his prophecy coins? Because he knew the past and we did not.'

A half-truth, boy, thought Finch.

Ember Vine felt discomforted. The historian's arguments sounded unassailable, and she hated the thought of Finch stepping up to play the atrophied conservative. He was better than that, much better.

Oblong felt the wind in his sails. He recounted his ignominious ascent up the church tower a year ago to the day. He described the murals, how an escape by coracle two millennia ago had laid the foundations for the Great Equinox Race. He glanced at Morval and turned poetic.

'The blackbird and the worm know nothing of their ancestors. A sense of history is Man's special gift. Vote to know yourselves. Vote for enquiry and research. Vote for knowledge. Vote *"Remember"*!'

He descended to applause, a notch short of deafening, but general and generous, more a breaking wave than a ripple.

Finch ascended the stairs to the rostrum like Luther to a pulpit, eyebrows bristling and eyes ablaze. He supported himself on his finch-headed staff. His unorthodox use of the *testudo* and his mounted charge on Amber's scooter had raised morale at a crucial time in the battle. He too had the ear of the crowd.

Finch, however, preferred a different orator's trick: use a good prop and start where they least expect it. He flung back the cloak billowing over his shoulders to reveal a large glass jar, three-quarters filled with round white sweets.

'The latest confection from *Sugar & Spice*,' Finch said casually to his mystified audience, '*Historical Factos!*' He dropped one in his mouth, sucked it for a moment, then announced, 'Blandly pleasant – but being of the gobstopper family, they change taste and colour as you go deeper.' Finch's cheeks bulged. To prove the point, he retrieved the facto from his mouth and held it up. It had turned bright yellow. 'And, of course, we can't resist sucking and seeing, layer after layer in search of new hues and different tastes. One facto leads to another.'

Finch's sweet jar, still held aloft in his right hand, had acquired a mesmerising quality. Oblong grinned into his hands. Finch's metaphor only confirmed the joys of historical research. Where was he going?

'Most are harmless to the core, *but* . . .' Finch bellowed the *but* and rattled the jar. '*But* . . . one or two factos have mysterious dark centres – all sorts of creepy crawlies – old enmities, crimes long past – and the darkest heart of all, how to find the doorway to this other place. There you can play God, evade time's arrow, make your own monsters. You can be a second Mr Wynter.'

Finch surveyed the sea of faces. Despite the 'not me' expressions, he could see the prospect of instant divinity appealed to more than a few. He returned to his quieter opening mode.

'Of course, outsiders like *Historical Factos* too – so much so they design *False Historical Factos* for extra impact. But when they hear we've a dark mystery filling all our own, they'll come a-tasting – and it only needs one. What then? Goodbye, independence. Goodbye to our green and pleasant land. Welcome, concrete research buildings and landgrabbers. Prepare to be colonised.'

Finch played his final card. 'A few Apothecaries already know this secret and of course they'll tell their own kind – who wouldn't? But where will that lead?'

Jaws dropped. Rule by a coterie of immortal Apothecaries was an even more repulsive prospect than rule by outsiders.

'Let be, my children. Live with what you know and see. Who cares a fig about dates? Dig in your window-boxes, but not in the past. Vote "*Forget*"!'

Finch swayed. Wounds from battle and the mantoleon claw had taken their toll. Ember stepped forward and helped him down the steps as Gorhambury called for a show of hands.

A few Apothecaries abstained, but nobody voted for the hell on earth conjured up by Finch's oratory.

Oblong generously shook Finch's hand. 'Isn't light the best disinfectant?' he asked the Herald.

'In Utopia, yes, but not here,' Finch responded.

Backstage, Valourhand and Bill Ferdy accosted each other.

'Nobody's wiping my bleeding memory,' she said, hands on hips.

'Which is why I'm giving you this,' replied Ferdy, presenting her with a small corked phial filled with a golden liquid. 'Ferensen's antidote to the Hammer: it inoculates for life.'

A label in Ferensen's hand displayed the simplest of instructions:

FAO Miss Vixen Valourhand – Drink me.

'Ferensen thought of me? That far ahead?'

'People do sometimes,' replied Ferdy. 'He knew you were in Lost Acre on Midsummer Day. He takes – took – care of his own.'

If Ferensen could do it, so could she. Valourhand hurried away.

Ferdy twisted in his hand one last phial labelled *FAO Whomsoever Bill Ferdy may choose – Drink me*. He turned to his daughter.

'Gwen, take this to Ember Vine. Tell her the names of the townsfolk who've visited our house and ask her to join us.' He added in her ear, 'Metaphorically speaking.'

Ember did not hesitate, once Gwen had disclosed that Finch and Oblong had been among their guests in recent weeks.

Valourhand found Ambrose prostrate on a grassy bank near the oaks in whose shade the Midsummer flower had fruited. 'You might want to a sip of this,' she said.

He smiled, fishing from his pocket an identical phial, labelled *FAO Ambrose Claud the Thirteenth – Drink me*.

Minutes later, masked by the most alluring flavours, the Hammer released its peculiar chemistry. The Myrmidon, the battle, the tile's existence and location and Persephone's dance all passed into oblivion, save for the chosen few.

As everyone else lolled on the Island Field late into the afternoon, the company gathered the bodies of the dead and wheeled them to the catacombs. Valourhand and Claud collected the weapons, Boris and Bert the wrecked coracles.

When reality returned at dusk, the party line from the company was that an earthquake had struck, releasing dangerous vapours from underground which had intoxicated all survivors.

11

A Phœnix Rises

On the following Monday, Gorhambury was unanimously elected Mayor. His army of paperclips and Post-its moved with lightning alacrity: the bereaved were supported from public funds and the dead mourned in a single open-air service on the Island Field.

In April, he unveiled a revolutionary programme. The *History Regulations* were loosened to allow the painting of portraits for posterity. The North and South Towers merged, with a remit to deal only in harmless – if ingenious – entertainments and defensive technologies. Vixen Valourhand, the acknowledged expert in the latter field, was invited to head the Two Towers.

Gorhambury repealed Wynter's house-appropriation law. Country-siders were awarded their own Guild, with a Hall in Rotherweird and representation on committees which affected their interests. The Apothecaries reached out under Sister Prudence's benign direction, while still avoiding undue flippancy.

The town's aesthetic pulse quickened too: the Manor's outer doors acquired three beautifully painted signs: *The School of Dance* (Principal: Varia Brown); *The School of Art* (Principal: Morval Seer); *The School of Sculpture* (Principal: Ember Vine).

At Orelia's suggestion, a small orphanage was built beside *The Shambles*, its residents-to-be as yet unknown.

The gates and the portcullis were repaired first. A competition for the design of a new church attracted a record entry, with the chosen theme: *Deliverance*.

Two outsiders received the freedom of the town.

Ambrose Claud's citation read: *In gratitude for his early warning of the catastrophe to come.* Thanks to the Hammer, nobody knew the detail.

Oblong's citation, by contrast, was accessible to all: *For contributing to the gaiety of nations.*

Dead Men's Shœs

Oblong's summons from the Headmaster rested against a glass on his desk. It offered no clue as to its purpose beyond the timing, for the summer term beckoned. Beneath it lay a piece of paper, virgin but for the title: *A Secret History of Rotherweird*, and four lines of introductory doggerel donated by Portly Bowes:

> *'The truth is often knotted*
> *And in telling may be lost,*
> *If all the Is are dotted*
> *And every T is crossed.'*

He put on his jacket and set out for the School. A warm wind swirled through the town. Sunlight danced across the new cobbles where the tower had been.

'Oblong,' exclaimed Rhombus Smith, rising from a large oak desk overwhelmed by books. 'Enjoying the lull before the storm, I hope.'

'Yes, indeed,' replied Oblong.

'I always set an essay on *The Seasons* to sort the literary wheat from the chaff. Imagine my surprise when last year a boy wrote of five seasons. He called the fifth season Sprinting: that peculiar day or two when Spring hovers on the knife edge of Summer. Brilliant idea – never be a slave to convention.'

Oblong shuffled. Colourful welcomes from the Headmaster

normally heralded an announcement of moment. 'Today *is* Sprinting, wouldn't you agree?'

'Very much so,' replied Oblong.

'It set me thinking. I'm going to relieve you of the toils of Form IV and restore Mr Fanguin, so you may inherit the former charges of the inimitable Gregorius Jones. He said you'd be best at easing them into the summer of their lives, and I agree.' Rhombus Smith administered a hearty handshake as if to seal the deal. 'Excellent – and it comes with a pay rise. As they say between acts at a French circus, *le spectacle continue.*'

Oblong bounded down the stairs. Morval was coming to supper. He had been promoted. He was an honorary citizen. For the first time in his life he felt he had a place and people he belonged to.

13

Absolution

Age and battle had chipped away at the Hoverfly's outer paint. Half visible, like a *pointilliste* painter's cloud, it settled in the meadow by the cottage. In the rigging sat Panjan.

On the roof, Ambrose the Thirteenth was laying new slates like a man dealing cards. He waved. A column of smoke rose from a makeshift kiln where Valourhand was melting down Carcasey Jack's abandoned traps and implements. Chickens wandered free, ignoring the Mance who equally ignored them.

Orelia hurried across, leaving Boris, Bert and Gabriel on the vessel, which was laden with bricks for the restoration of Gabriel's house.

She took Valourhand aside. 'I see you're busy.'

'We both are,' replied Valourhand. 'It's an exorcism.'

While Valourhand washed her hands in a bowl beside the kiln, Orelia peeped inside. The cottage had acquired a welcoming lived-in look.

Valourhand wiped her sleeve across her face. 'Tyke dropped by to say his goodbyes. He looked about eighteen. He said he was both too young and too old for me. It's awful, but I knew he was right.'

'You've not done so badly,' said Orelia, eyes raised towards Ambrose Claud.

'Time will tell,' replied Valourhand. 'Anything's better than Strimmer,' she added with a chuckle.

'You've not accepted Gorhambury's offer – head of the Two Towers.'

'I can't. It's my penance.'

'That's what I came to say: there's nothing to do penance for. Salt was the Green Man, don't forget – I reckon he knew that without the ice-dragon we would have no chance. But you couldn't know that. That's why, before you left, he sent the seed of the Midsummer flower to Aggs to give to Jones. He saved you, he saved the dragon, he saved the valley and he saved Lost Acre. Don't take that away from him.'

Valourhand felt a knot ease. She respected a reasoned appeal. 'Thank you,' she said, 'I'll sleep on it.'

'There's another thing. Cast your mind back to my aunt's blazing house and Bole's familiar, the cat-boy. Remember what he said to me? "Have you the book?"'

Of course Valourhand remembered. 'It couldn't be the *Recipe Book*, because Bole knew Strimmer or Slickstone already had it,' she replied thoughtfully. 'Indeed, that was the plan.' Valourhand's mind flitted back to Ferensen's *al fresco* dinner. 'You had a theory, didn't you? That Morval kept a book of the failed experiments.'

'I was wrong. She did keep a book, but only of those experiments which used children. I found it in the spiderwoman's lair, perfectly preserved between the warm store and the cold store. And thanks to Varia, we have the stones. So, one day soon, if that's what they want, we'll have a Restoration Day.'

Valourhand remembered the owl-like creature which had helped her escape from the Manor. She watched the Mance and thought of Panjan. Would they? Wouldn't they? 'Count me in,' she said.

Back in the Hoverfly, Gabriel released a flouncy buff-and-white hen and a gaudy cockerel with a brilliant green ruff and scarlet comb.

'They're a present from Finch. He says their names are written in stone: Gregorius and Clemency.'

Valourhand looked puzzled. No other name would do justice to the strutting cockerel, but the other? Clemency? She understood the innuendo but begged to differ. 'You're storing up trouble with Varia-stroke-Persephone stroke Nona,' she said.

'When the sin is deep and there is risk but also hope, that's true clemency.'

'You've learned the art of persuasion,' replied Valourhand.

'You've learned the art of being persuaded,' replied Orelia with a grin. 'Once in a while.'

14

A Final View

An easel stands in the grass on a gentle slope looking south to Rotherweird, a present from Gabriel, his first work since the destruction of his workshop. A climbing rose entwines the supports, its flowers in shadow beneath the crossbar. A palette sits on a stool, the splashes of colour in chromatic order. Worker bees are busy in the warmth of mid-morning. Fresh leaf flutters like a choir turning music. The fruit trees are blossom-bound.

This very day, this very month, the wagon descended this very road, carrying the ten brilliant children. She had run with Hieronymus from the orchard to see Fortemain, the most boyish, blinking in the sun. She wipes an eye. Fortemain, who is now buried deep.

Down that same road Wynter and Bole would canter, hot on the heels of Sir Henry Grassal's death. And Slickstone would return with his catch from London, including Vibes and Tyke, the beautiful boy. Her new friend and maybe lover-to-be, the gangly historian, must have come this way too.

Her fingers twitch. She dips the brush.

You have no right to happiness. Contentment is a dull friend set beside experience. Better to make history than merely learn it.

Within reason.

Acknowledgements

Without my agent, Ed Wilson, Jo Fletcher and her team at Quercus/ JFB this trilogy would not have seen the light of the day or would at least have been a lesser work. Their contributions, as addressed in the Acknowledgments in *Rotherweird* and *Wyntertide*, have continued undiminished and need no repetition.

Milly Reid, my new publicist, deserves special mention for her tireless efforts and for being such cheering company.

Readers are unlikely to miss the change of style in Sasha's illustrations. A good artist is a brave one, and they focus more than their predecessors on the darkness at the heart of Wynter's conspiracy. They are powerful indeed.

Other support, hitherto unacknowledged, has come from a wide variety of booksellers far and wide, real and virtual. I owe them an enormous debt as I do to the patience of loyal readers who have had to wait over a year for this final chapter.

Last but not least my long-suffering family should take a bow. But then I do have a fresh idea . . . in a place and time far removed from Rotherweird.

Andrew Caldecott is a QC specialising in media, defamation and libel law, as well as a novelist and occasional playwright. He represented the BBC in the Hutton Inquiry (into the death of biological warfare expert and UN weapons inspector David Kelly), the *Guardian* in the Leveson Inquiry (into the British press following the phone hacking scandal), and supermodel Naomi Campbell in her landmark privacy case, amongst many others.

His first produced play, *Higher than Babel*, was described as 'Assured and ambitious . . . deeply impressive debut' by Nick Curtis in the *Evening Standard* and 'Vivid and absorbing and grapples with big ideas without being dry, difficult or patronising' by Sarah Hemming, in the *Financial Times*, but informed by his love of history, which he studied at New College, Oxford, he was seized by the notion of a city-state hiding a cataclysmic secret: the result, his first book *Rotherweird*.

Sasha Laika studied figurative art in Moscow, followed by a degree in Graphic Design and Illustration in the UK. A London-based artist for the last ten years, Sasha creates highly intricate works that draw on imagery from mythology, folklore and religious iconography. Her works are inhabited by mystical creatures that morph between human and animal, and exist in transition somewhere between the worlds of fantasy and reality.